THE
MAYAN
GLYPH

THE
MAYAN
GLYPH

LARRY BAXTER

ATLANTIC COAST
MEDIA
Gloucester, MA

Published by Atlantic Coast Media
P.O. Box 8008-187
Gloucester, MA 01931

Publisher's Cataloging-in-Publication Data
Baxter, Larry.

The Mayan glyph.— Gloucester, MA : Atlantic Coast Media, ©2005.

p. ; cm.
ISBN: 0-9765767-0-8

1. Virus diseases—Fiction. 2. Epidemiology—Fiction. 3. Mayan languages—Writing—Fiction. I.Title.

PS3602.A88 M38 2005
813/.6--dc22   2005-900633

Book production and coordination by Jenkins Group, Inc. • www.bookpublishing.com
Interior design by Linda Powers/Powers Design
Cover design by Chris Rhodes

Printed in the United States of America
09 08 07 06 05 • 6 5 4 3 2

For Carol,
who makes everything possible.

Prologue

The ball field was one of the largest in the Yucatán. It measured twenty by fifty lom and was enclosed by high walls of stone. Over fifteen thousand Maya overflowed the array of stone seats, even watching from the steps of the nearby temple. The continuous noise from the onlookers was modulated by the events on the field and reached a crescendo each time the Uxmal team attempted to score.

The home team was the most potent in seventeen tun, with the Hero Twins, Moon Rabbit Batz and Zib the Jaguar, as strikers and the widely respected Hun the Lizard and Vucab the Snake as blockers. The opposition was a team made up of the best players from Chichén Itzá and Xcocha, with the legendary Xbalanque the off-side striker. Also playing for the opposition was Tzelzil, once King of Yaxuna but for the last two years a captive of Uxmal. Normally a captive king was a serious hindrance to a ball team, but Tzelzil was one of the best ball players of his time. His skills had not deteriorated in confinement. As an added incentive, he was playing for his life.

The game had been going on for seven kin. Upon the game's outcome depended not only the life of Tzelzil but also the lives of the losing team and the future of the city.

Chortal the Parrot, Supreme Ruler of Uxmal, had consulted his astrologers to determine the proper starting day for the game and the appropriate actions to follow in the event of a win or a loss. The astrologers had recommended sacrifices from Chortal's own family in the event of a loss—a concept not totally repugnant to Chortal the Parrot—and the astrologers also saw that a victory would be a sign that Chortal and his warriors would surely win their long battle with Chichén Itzá.

The game was played four to a side with a heavy rubber ball, which was propelled with the feet, the thighs, and the head. The goal was a vertical stone disk, one lom in diameter and three lom high on the wall, with a hole in the center barely the size of the ball. The winner would be the team to first put the ball through the hole. Uxmal had possession with only a little while to play on this day, only until the shadow of the Cemetery just touched the steps to the Palace.

Moon Rabbit Batz took the ball in the forecourt to the mutters of the crowd. He had not played well; he did not seem to be trying hard. But Moon Rabbit was an experienced player, and he knew the chance of a winning kick with a fresh defense was near zero, as the shot was difficult and the ball was easily blocked. He had played the game at only three-quarter speed all day to keep himself fresh for the time when the defense would have no strength left in their legs. This was the time.

Moon Rabbit kicked the ball back for a better angle as Tzelzil closed to blocking position. Then Moon Rabbit faked a pass to Zib the Jaguar to draw off Tzelzil and then faked a shot as Xbalanque came up quickly from his position to cover the threat. Xbalanque dove to smother the shot, but Moon Rabbit had purposely missed the ball, and now drew his right foot back and cradled the ball on his instep. Clear field for a moment and Moon Rabbit let the screams of the crowd give him the strength he needed as he aimed the kick carefully at the disk. He saw the ball arch gracefully in slow motion against the blue sky, its trajectory perfect, immutable, inevitable. It fell through the hole without even grazing the stone. The crowd exploded in sound and streamed onto the field to help deliver the losers to the sacrificial table.

The day was almost perfect, thought Supreme Ruler Chortal the Parrot. Almost perfect. He rapped his serpent staff on the dais in approval as his priests beheaded the King and his losing team and impaled their heads on the spikes of the Tzompantli. Time and the *small birds would turn them into ceremonial skulls. He would surely become the conqueror of Chichén Itzá.*

The only disturbing aspect to the day was the recent and unexplained deaths of five citizens, strangled on their own black tongues. His own tongue felt strangely thick, certainly just in sympathy. The medicine priests placed the responsibility on the Lords of the Dead, and said that Chortal must find a way to placate the gods else many more would surely die. Perhaps the fire was now inhabited by the Lords of the Dead, he would need to have all the fire put out and send out new fire. Then he would send a message to Tulum, to the laboratory of the savant Peloc. Clever Peloc, Peloc the Magician, somehow in allegiance with the Lords of the Dead. Peloc would know what to do about these strange deaths.

Tomorrow, at first light, he would send a runner. And he would fortify the runner with a goblet of the blood of the Jaguar for speed, and a goblet of the blood of a recent victim so that Peloc would have a test case to study. He smiled at his own cleverness, even knowing that Peloc was ten times his intellect, but the smile hurt inside his mouth.

• • •

Chapter 1

Uxmal, July 25, present day

R ay Soto's wide brown back vibrated momentarily as he slowly straightened with the big carved stone in his arms. He set the stone down on the edge of the excavation and grinned up at Professor Barker, his face shiny with effort in the hundred-degree temperature.

"Nice to have a portable hydraulic lift on site," said Barker, brushing loose sandy soil from the engraved symbols.

"Hey, that's why I'm here, prof. Put in a good word with the weight coach when we get back?"

Soto was the biggest player on the University of Texas' football team, a cinch for early first round selection in the pro draft, and the unofficial leader of the U.T. summer archaeology expedition to the Yucatán peninsula in Mexico.

A mile from the ancient Maya city of Uxmal, the site was a recently discovered rectangular mesa five hundred by three hundred feet with an elevation of only twenty feet over the jungle floor. The vegetation had been stripped and the mesa crisscrossed with trenches and grid markers and monitored by video cameras and time-lapse video recorders. The mesa's limestone and coral composite, a sandy yellow color, reflected the equatorial sun and crumbled into a gritty powder that coated the sweaty bodies of the students.

"Whatcha got, prof?" said Soto, white teeth sparking beneath the wide black moustache, as he vaulted from the trench.

"The date is here," said Barker, pointing out an inscription to the gathering undergraduates. "Anybody want to give it a try?"

"Long count date, fifteen baktuns, nine katuns...823 AD," said Sheila Monson after a few seconds.

"Exactly right," said Barker. He soaked a rag in water and wiped the surface of the stone to bring the glyphs into sharp relief. "And the rest of the inscription?"

"Isn't that the parrot glyph?" asked Sheila.

Barker smiled. "Yes, and that's the key to this whole site. We've had no evidence of the purpose of this mesa until this inscription. Now we can see that it's a huge pyramid."

The class looked at him curiously. "Well, it would have been a huge pyramid if it had been finished. As you know, the Maya generally did not build pyramids as tombs, although of course there were notable exceptions, as in Palenqué. This mesa is the first level in what would have been one of the largest pyramids in the Yucatán if it had been completed. Who was the big boss in Uxmal in 823?"

"Hey, right," said Soto. "Chortal, the Parrot. Is this his tomb?"

"Looks like. This stone says he has descended to the Underworld and will be sustained on his journey by the slaves and provisions buried with him. It also says his tongue is black, I don't understand the meaning."

"Probably eating blackberries. Hey, I don't see any slaves and provisions," said Soto.

"Not yet, you don't. Start digging out grid twenty-seven C."

• • •

The exhaust note from the five-kilowatt generator deepened as Prof. Barker flipped on the light switch. The illumination changed color from the red of the fading sunset to the bluer hue of half a dozen quartz halogen floods. The sarcophagus was now fully exposed, an enormous rectangular block capped with an inscribed stone eight inches thick.

"It's show time!" said Barker. "Roll the cameras! Cue Geraldo! Remove the lid!"

The dozen students began a chant, "So-to! So-to!"

Ray Soto appeared on cue, dragging a steel cable from the Land Rover's winch, posed for a moment with deltoids flexed like the front cover of a muscle magazine, then he looped the cable around the capstone.

The Rover creaked and bucked against the wheel chocks as the motor strained in low gear and the stone moved, screaming in protest, a few inches a minute. When a two-foot opening was clear Barker gestured, the Rover fell silent, and the group gathered to peer inside the vault.

Barker leaned in, holding a flood lamp. The smell was intense and strange, not the faint moldy earth aroma he'd expected but a strong repellent putrefaction. He stepped quickly back with the after-image of the mummified Maya emperor burned into his retina: jade stone wedged into his grotesquely open mouth, white shell crown adorned by quetzal bird, royalty reduced to a wrinkled brown bag stretched over a grinning skull.

• • •

When their flight entered the landing pattern at Meacham International Airport in Austin a week and a half later, most of the U.T. group was suffering from some upper respiratory disorder, like a common cold but accompanied by tightness in the throat. Ray Soto was the worst affected. He was stripped to the waist despite the air conditioning, sprawling across three seats, making a noise like a chainsaw cutting sheet metal and grunting with every exhalation. His convulsions had broken a seat arm, which now hung in the aisle swinging from electrical wires. His tongue, dark in color, lolled out of his mouth. His eyes were like a panicky horse's, looking for an escape from a burning barn.

Professor Barker swallowed uncomfortably and signaled a flight attendant, "Can you have an ambulance waiting at the airport? It's probably just a virus, but he's working so hard to breathe—"

"All done," she nodded. "I called it in ten minutes ago. Three ambulances, paramedics, and a police escort to Conover Mercy. Big, healthy-looking man like that, and the rest of you look sort of greenish through your sunburns—"

Chapter 2

T*he long, narrow, windowless room was brightly lit with more than a hundred oil lamps, improving visibility for this delicate work. The lamps added a sulfurous smell to the air and a dark cloud of black soot that stained every horizontal surface. Peloc was gazing into a microscope. His tiny frame was perched on an extra-tall stool, his head tilted so that his enormous nose would clear the globe of the instrument as he gazed down looking for a pattern. He removed the top brass plate, cleaned the crystal deposit, warmed it a few degrees in the oven, and bathed it in the solution until a new crystal deposit slowly formed. Then, carefully, he lowered the top plate on the specimen, rubbed a cloth on the silver globe, separated the plates and brushed on the powder with the expertise of many repetitions.*

There, perfect, the pattern appeared. With a glance he memorized its shape, then selected a sharp chisel and moved to the wall and recorded it in his tiny, precise hand. Boring, repetitious work, but Peloc felt the satisfaction of knowing that this careful record of the properties of these materials would be useful for many centuries of Maya.

An assistant bearing a small codex interrupted him. "Sir, this was brought in by a runner from Uxmal, just now."

"Wait," Peloc snapped, unhappy with the imposition. He scanned

the codex, absorbing the glyphs in a glance. His face darkened and his head flicked around like a bird's, turning almost backwards. He shot a torrent of words at the assistant with his rapid delivery, like the rattle of the woodpecker. "It's from Chortal. Uxmal has a serious problem. Many Maya are dead. Their tongues are black. A disease. We are to find a cure. We can use this runner as a test. Is the runner sick?"

"No, sir, but he did complain that his tongue felt thick."

"He is sick. Move him. Quickly. To the west of town. Take him to a vacant hut. Near no other. Don't touch him. Move ten captives in with him. We will need many test subjects. Bring back a tzlbt of his blood. Go quickly."

Chapter 3

One of the wards in the isolation wing was set up as a pathology lab. Extra lights hung from the ceiling, illuminating the huge corpse, supine on an aluminum gurney in the center of the room.

As the hospital had not isolated the disease and did not know how it was transmitted, maximum precautions were in effect. Airborne, droplet and contact transmission of the unknown pathogen were interdicted. The entire wing had been depressurized with a jury-rigged ventilation fan exhausting into an activated charcoal filter so that no aerosol-borne pathogens could escape. The staff observed gown, glove and respirator protocols, laundry was handled in the isolated wing with special high-temperature machines, and all disposables were being autoclaved, double bagged and stored.

The nurse's station had been converted into a crude double airlock and disinfection chamber. A tall, slender gray-haired man in green scrubs with a nameplate announcing "Dr. Gary Spender" entered through the outer door and donned the prescribed gloves, gown and mask in the outer chamber. He slipped through the polyethylene vapor barrier, stood briefly in the ultraviolet chamber, and pulled the inner door open against the air pressure.

"Evening, Gary, you can give me a hand here if you like. I'm about to get started." The pathologist held a microphone in one hand and a scalpel in the other.

"Thanks anyway," said Spender, "But I can hardly stand up, I've been out straight for two days. I'll watch. Or maybe just listen." He sank into an upholstered chair and tilted his head back against the wall. He closed his eyes, but the strain on his face was not relieved. From his study of epidemiology he had learned intellectually the increasing risk the human race was facing as emerging diseases evolved into drug-resistant killers. But the reality of the crisis exploding in his city was beyond his comprehension. In days, young healthy men and women were twisted into frightened husks, unable to speak but pleading with their eyes. All he could do for them was ease their last moments with morphine. He had never felt so helpless in his life.

The pathologist fixed the microphone, cleared his throat, and adjusted the controls on the tape recorder while intoning "One, two, three, four..." His voice was tinny through the respirator, "Pathologist Dr. Albert Ericson. Deceased Raymond Sota, Hispanic male, approximately six feet three inches tall, two hundred eighty-five pounds. Cause of death given as acute respiratory failure. No recent skin lesions, no purpura, no evidence of insect bites, well-healed ten cm scar left bicep, new unhealed incision on throat consistent with recent tracheotomy." He paused the recorder for a second and turned to Spender. "The tracheotomy help any?"

Spender's eyes opened. "Gave him a few more hours, is all."

The pathologist shook his head slowly, punched the recorder, and droned on, "Facial aspect normal except for perhaps five-day growth of beard and pronounced distension in throat and neck. Mouth is open revealing grossly malformed tongue, abnormally dark in color."

Ericcson picked up a number one scalpel and made the Y incision with two rapid slashes. "Initial incision at sternum. Thin fatty tissue layer at abdomen, well developed musculature. Heart enlarged but normal, all consistent with well-conditioned athlete. Lungs edematous, infiltrated with blood, blotchy coloration. Some hemorrhagic pleural effusion. Lungs rubbery to palpation with significant hypertrophy, heavy, perhaps twice expected mass."

Spender interrupted his monologue, "Does this look like it could be a hantavirus?"

"That was my first guess, Gary. The blood work supports it, raised white blood cell count, left shift. Some atypical lymphocytes. We've also got bandemia and thrombocytopenia and marked pulmonary edema. But the swelling of the tongue is, of course, not seen in any hantavirus I'm aware of. And I understand that the infection took place in an area without much small animal life, so it's probably not zoonotic in origin. What's his treatment history?"

"We intubated and put him on mechanical ventilation at once. Pulse was up to a hundred twenty, core temperature to a hundred three, BP eighty-five over fifty. We controlled BP with dopamine, wide open, and IV fluids, and shot him with Ceftriaxone in case there were bacterial problems. Arterial blood gases showed respiratory acidosis, we added sodium biocarb to the IV. He went septic within half an hour and we lost him fifteen minutes later. Do you see any indication of degeneration of other tissue, or just the tongue?"

"Let's take a closer look. Incising throat, exposing tongue, trachea, larynx. Airway was completely occluded by distension of tongue above tracheotomy. Preparing sample of lung tissue, specimen jar number one. Sample of tongue, number two. Tongue tissue is hard, blotchy, apparently infiltrated with blood, but the blood seems to have undergone some structural change. It's as black as ink."

"Any ideas?" said Spender, almost inaudible through the respirator. His eyes remained closed.

"Two simultaneous infections? One local, inflammatory, bacteriological, one hantavirus?"

"That would be a long shot," said Spender. "We've got twenty-seven patients with identical symptoms and two more deceased."

"Yes. This is going to be a war. Are the Centers for Disease Control sending in the reserves?"

"Full court press." Spender ran his hand through his hair and opened his eyes. "We're expecting two epidemiologists from CDC, one from the Division of Vector-Borne Infectious Diseases in Fort Collins, two diagnosticians, three techs and a trailer full of equipment. There's also some Washington hotshot named Theslie to coordinate all the agencies."

"It sounds like we have their attention."

"We will have lots of help. I have a bad feeling, though. It's too fast, too slippery, too fatal. Get back to that poor boy, Albert, I'll get out of your hair. Full report tomorrow?"

"First thing in the morning."

Spender pulled himself out of the chair and headed back to his office. He was intercepted by the Chief of Medical Staff, Dr. Tim Maxson.

"Good, we need to talk," said Maxson, following Spender into his office. "This outbreak. Anything new?"

"Just that it's faster and scarier than anything I've ever heard of."

Maxson nodded. "We need a manager for the project. You've been specializing in infectious diseases for us, but didn't you help with epidemiology at Houston?"

"Yes, but the work I've been doing here on infectious diseases is more challenging."

"Does managing this outbreak sound like enough challenge?"

"More than enough. Too much. Won't the CDC have their own people?"

"Probably. But there's a lot to be said for local knowledge. You'll be the man until the CDC says otherwise. Let me know what you need, we'll talk tomorrow. Good luck."

Spender nodded, called his wife to say he wouldn't be home, and walked slowly down to the waiting room off the lobby where he could get a few hours sleep on the narrow sofa.

Chapter 4

A municipal police officer wearing a white respirator ran to move an orange cone, then gestured the Apex One-Day Exterminator van to a parking spot near the main entrance. Dr. Gary Spender hurried through the cold wind-blown rain. He handed respirators to the three men emerging from the van.

The scene was chaotic. White-coated and masked attendants wheeled patients on plastic-tented hospital gurneys down the concrete walks, and sirens sounded in the distance as police evacuated a cordon of nearby buildings.

Conover Mercy Hospital was a collection of half a dozen two- and three-story buildings on a rise of land in the northeast quadrant of Austin. Its normal 3:00 A.M. quiet was being blasted into oblivion. Portable spotlights and the intermittent flash of red and blue emergency vehicle strobes lighted the scene, and the sense of unreality was heightened by the early hour and the reflection of the colored lights on the wet asphalt.

A voice, distorted by a bullhorn, shouted instructions. "Clark building third floor, Room 37, gurney and oxygen, don't disconnect the IV drip. Charlie, get to the Tollens street entrance. Russell, don't forget to log the names in with the driver. You in the news truck, you can't park there, back it up."

A small helicopter clattered into view at five hundred feet altitude and probed the roof of the center building with a spotlight. Then it descended down the beam to hover just out of sight for a few minutes before flying away.

Dr. Spender instructed the van crew, "Put these on, tie them tight. They're activated charcoal, new type. Don't remove them." Spender ran his hands through his thinning hair and tried to dry them unsuccessfully on his already-soaked white lab coat. Activated charcoal. Right. We have no idea how this damned bug gets around, so we're really just pissing into the wind. Activated plutonium, it could be, or activated nitric acid—and still nothing seems to work.

The driver asked, "Doc, what the hell is going on? They said you had a big building that needed extermination. This is more than roaches."

"We've had some kind of disease outbreak."

The van crew stepped back half a pace, fastening their respirators tighter. "Don't worry, we're pretty sure it's contained in the center building there. But we need to take all possible precautions. We just weren't ready for this kind of thing and we've had to improvise."

"What kind of thing?"

"We're not sure," said Spender. "Virus, bacteria, maybe an insect. Maybe even roaches. Maybe something new."

"How do you know the respirators will work?"

"Well, to be truthful, we don't. But they work on ninety-five percent of infectious diseases, so it's a pretty good bet."

"Gotcha. What do you want from us?"

"Extermination," said Spender. "You normally use sulfurol fluoride gas, right?"

"Vikane? That's for cockroaches. We brought Vikane II, works for bacteria and viruses too. Damn near take your paint off."

"Good. The center building there, the Clark building, is the one. We've just sealed the roof vents, and the windows are all closed and locked. Can you gas it right now?"

"Not if we stick to EPA regulations."

"How about if you don't stick to EPA regulations?"

"I lose my license."

"How about if you're helping to control a virus outbreak that could kill half the residents of Austin?"

He shrugged. "Then the license wouldn't be so important. We've got plenty of gas. It's heavier than air, so we'll need to get a hose into the third floor."

Spender keyed a handheld radio. "Spender. We need a ladder truck in front of Clark. How soon?"

He listened to the reply and said, "Good. We'll clear a path. You'll need to extend the ladder to the third floor, but wait for a passenger."

He turned back to the van crew. "Got a long hose?"

The man counted floors. "Should reach."

"You normally tent a building to prevent gas leakage, right? We'll have at least this block cleared by the time you start gas flow. Any problem, working this one without a tent?"

"That should be plenty safe," said the van driver. "This stuff isn't particularly lethal to people in dilute form, anyway. Makes 'em sick. Kills bugs."

"And airborne bacteria and viruses," said Spender. "I hope."

A hook and ladder truck sirened up. Spender raised his own bullhorn. "Fire truck, right here, center building. You won't need water, you have a passenger with a gas hose. Take him up to the third floor window there."

One of the van crew walked to the ladder, unreeling hose, and climbed into the bucket with a firefighter. The ladder extended into the night sky, swaying and groaning with the unexpected load.

A dark blue Ford Taurus stopped near Spender, flashing a blue light, siren winding down. Spender turned to read the letters on the door: "CDC, Centers for Disease Control and Prevention, 37662." A short man in a dark blue suit squeezed his large midsection past the steering wheel and walked up to Spender.

"You Spender? I'm George Hapwell Theslie. CDC Atlanta, Washington. Troubleshooter. Field coordinator. Epidemiologist." He didn't offer a hand, but he took the respirator Spender offered. "Good, respirators, can't be too careful. Call me Hap. What've we got for status, here?"

"Twenty fatalities, all third floor, same ward, same symptoms. The first thirteen were a college archaeology team just returned from Mexico. They died between eight and ten days ago. The entire team, wiped out. The first to die was a football player, a huge man, very popular, I guess. The entire campus is in mourning."

"OK. Sorry, I'm not briefed, they just flew me back from Somalia. Any cases in Mexico?"

"None. They were in the Yucatán, Uxmal. Far from population centers. Local medical people have sealed the site."

"Helluva thing," said Theslie. "What are the symptoms?"

"Flu symptoms at first, then pronounced darkening of the tongue, enlarged lymph nodes, inflamed spleen, difficulty breathing, bleeding from tongue and throat, and finally internal organ failure. We had the whole team isolated after we saw the symptoms, of course, and the staff used antibacterials according to procedure."

"And then?" asked Theslie.

"A week ago we got seven more infections, including two staff. We contacted you people. We sealed the ward, set up an airlock, fitted out six staff with fully sealed Racal suits and started looking for the propagation vector. Post mortems were done in the same sealed ward to avoid contamination."

"Very good, Spender," said Theslie. "Nothing wrong with your procedures. What happened?"

"Damned if I know. It got past the isolation barrier. We have no idea how. We still don't know how the disease is vectored."

Theslie tightened his respirator. "Great job so far, but let's see how safe we can play it from here on in. Anything else you need, call this number." He handed Spender a card. "My phone's on my belt all the time. Almost all the time. I've got National Guard moving in, we'll set up a perimeter ten blocks back. Are you all done here?"

"Just as soon as those people on the ladder dump a hundred thousand cubic feet of ethylene paraldehyde gas in the center building, there. Then we may want to burn it, your call. Everybody's out. We have a quarantine set up for anybody at risk, in the basement of the two-story brick building there."

"Great, Spender, you finish up here. We'll move the quarantine back ten blocks and burn it."

"The hospital?"

"Yeah, and about five blocks."

"You explain it to the mayor."

"That's why I'm here. Remember the Hong Kong thing, the zoonotic virus that jumped from birds?"

"Of course. They killed all the avian life on the island in two days."

"I was the one that explained it to the mayor. We'll move fast, here. I have authority for anything sub-nuclear, but I know who to talk to if we need to go nuclear."

Spender looked at him to see if he was smiling. He wasn't. "Good lord, Theslie, I hope you're joking."

"Me too. I'll get back and coordinate the Guard. We'll beat this thing. The CDC can handle it. Spender, you get good grades for running the ground operation. Can you continue with it for a while?"

"There's going to be an air operation?"

"Probably."

"I'll stick with it until you find somebody more qualified."

"Great. I'll be coordinating with CDC and the military. All hell's gonna break loose here if this thing isn't stopped in forty-eight hours. But we'll get it. We always get it."

"I hope so, Mr. Theslie," said Spender, shaking his head slowly from side to side. "I sure as hell hope so." As he walked back to the exterminator's van, a cold gust of wind threatened to blow his thin body into the gutter.

Chapter 5

Boston, October 7, present day

D r. Robert Asher pushed aside dusty curtains and gazed from the oversize windows on the Commonwealth Avenue traffic four stories below. A few yellow leaves dropped by the scraggly maple trees were blown up to his level by the strong east wind. A little fresh air would be good, he thought, if only the windows hadn't been painted shut. Probably around the turn of the last century.

Boston University was sited on the level plain created in the 1800's when Boston had annexed the mud flats and quintupled its land area. Its light brown buildings, lined up between the Charles River and the Avenue, reached only to the eight or ten stories possible on the unstable fill.

Robert turned back to the room. A low wooden table presented a selection of stale croissants and Danish pastries left over from some morning function. Presiding from his wheelchair was Dr. Edward Teppin, Chairman of the Department of Biology at Boston University, and in attendance were a few staff members and half a dozen professors reporting on their research projects.

A fellow researcher, Art Baker, wandered over, nibbling on a Danish and shedding crumbs on the dark red carpet. "Hey, Robert, how's the new proposal? You ready for your presentation?"

"I'm ready for bed. I thought I'd just finish up the math before I started my slides. Fell asleep at 6:00 A.M. You any good at elliptic Bessel functions?"

"Pass."

"Rats. I thought I could handle it, no go. Now I have no math, no presentation, no sleep and no breakfast. But it doesn't matter, I don't think this one is going to work, anyway. I'll tell Teppin, maybe he's got something else for me."

"Have a week-old pastry. Good luck."

Robert crunched on a croissant as he watched a biological chemist talk about a recently synthesized chemical. Something about E. coli breakouts and sewage outflows.

A beeper sounded. Most of the staffers checked their pagers and cell phones by reflex, but the sound stopped only when Teppin picked up the wireless phone from his wheelchair. He turned the chair away and spoke quietly for a minute, then turned back to the group.

"Sorry for the interruption, but I've been called away. Tracy, if you would, please lead the meeting and continue the review."

He turned to Robert, "Robert, please join me in my office."

Robert, a little groggy from lack of sleep, picked up his tweed jacket and walked beside Teppin. They took the elevator to Teppin's third floor office.

The office was spacious and high ceilinged and cluttered with memorabilia. The windows presented a panoramic view of the Charles River. Books and journals were stacked on several bookcases and various dusty pieces of medical instrumentation shared a large side table. Framed certificates and enlarged photographs of small groups of smiling people covered a wall; Robert picked out Henry Kissinger and James Watson.

Teppin picked up the phone again.

"Dr. Spender? I'm back. Meet Robert Asher, he's my blue-sky thinker. He may have a couple of possibilities in his back pocket. Robert, Gary Spender is at Conover Mercy hospital in Austin. He is fighting a virus outbreak."

"Hello, Dr. Asher, I think I met you briefly a while back at Houston General, you were picking up your daughter and your ex-wife, I think. Her name is Asher, also, isn't it?"

"It was at the time. She's remarried."

Teppin broke in, "Dr. Spender, do you have video there?"

"Yes, of course, I'm in my office. I'll turn it on."

Teppin touched the keyboard mounted on his chair and a nearby monitor blossomed with video from Texas, showing a gray and slender lab-coated man behind a desk piled high with magazines and paper.

"Now, how can we help?"

"The virus. It looks like it is indeed new, or maybe just old and dormant for a long time. It may be a primitive predecessor of Ebola. It's going to be trouble. A whole lot of trouble. I'm looking for help from as many good people as I can find. I read your group's paper on the use of IR spectroscopy in vivo for prion detection in J. Experimental Virology. There's damn little pathogen research that brings in new concepts like that. I was wondering if the device had been further developed."

A woman appeared in the picture, carrying a medical bag. She glanced at the camera. "Sorry to interrupt. We have a couple of problems, when you can get free." Spender nodded and she strode quickly out of the office, yelling to somebody off-camera.

Teppin spoke. "Our group is working on several different projects, but there's nothing I can think of right now that would help. We're no longer working on IR spectroscopy. I'm sorry."

"I thought the IR device was being studied for possible use in designing virus antidotes," said Spender.

"Yes, it was," said Robert. "Antidotes, drug treatment, vaccination. The spectroscope proved out in prion detection, but the tests on viruses and bacterial pathogens were not successful."

"We're working on commercializing a silicon chip from Purdue," said Teppin, "It can classify pathogens. But you need a vaccine or a drug treatment, not classification, right?"

"That's right. Thanks for your time. Sorry to bother you."

Robert held up a hand. "Wait. There's one possibility. Dr. Teppin, remember the charge microscope I was playing with last year?"

"Of course. I should have thought of that. Dr. Spender, maybe that's our one long shot. It could be years away, but maybe we can find a way to put it back on the active list and speed up the schedule."

"What's a charge microscope?" asked Spender.

"It images a molecule with electrostatic charge instead of with light, like an ordinary microscope."

"How does it work?"

"The implementation is pretty simple," Robert said. "It's a matter of preparing the sample in a high-purity crystalline matrix and finding a flat smooth material with a matching crystal matrix to act as sort of a moiré effect magnifying plate. Then you bring the plates into tight contact, put a high voltage on the magnifying plate, and pull the plates apart. This leaves a charge pattern like on a Xerox copier. You have to make sure the humidity is low, and dust the plate with almost any fine powder, and the charge pattern of the molecule appears, magnified maybe ten thousand times. Theoretically."

"How does that help you design an antitoxin?"

"It gives you a way to look at complex hydrocarbon structures in the same way that a virus molecule does, as a three-dimensional array of charges. A virus molecule is inactive without a receptor site, and this microscope maps molecules as if they were receptor sites. Possibly it would allow designer antivirals, molecules that are mirror images of the virus' receptor charge pattern."

"That sounds like a spectacular tool. Why was it dropped?"

"Not dropped," said Teppin. "Just moved to the back burner while we found funding. Cash shortage, we needed to prioritize short-term payoff over long-term research projects. And the charge microscope would have to be considered a very long-term, low-probability project. But we'll see if we can get it back on the front burner."

On the monitor the same woman ran into the office, this time without the medical bag, talking on a cell phone and gesturing to Spender.

"Thanks," said Spender. "I have a fire to put out. Stay in touch if you make any progress. Or if you think about any other possibilities. We need all the help we can get."

Teppin touched his keypad again. "Let's take a look at this one. I was looking at this outbreak yesterday, but it seemed as if it was under control."

On the monitor, Spender's face was replaced by the ProMED website. Robert and Teppin leaned close, reading the new postings on the virus' progress.

"Texas is a pretty strange place for a virus outbreak," said Robert. "Don't they usually come from Africa or some rain forest?

Why Texas?"

"The first people infected were University of Texas undergraduates from Austin."

"Any common factor in the first infections?" asked Robert.

"Yes. A party of a dozen undergrads and a professor had just made some important discoveries in a Maya site in the Yucatan. They landed in Austin with the first symptoms. They are all dead now."

"All dead? Jesus. How long ago was this?"

"They got back in early August with the symptoms of a severe flu, and they all died within a week. The hospital was caught by surprise and the virus was not contained. There is a picture here of the first one to die, apparently a football player." He pushed keys and the picture appeared.

Robert looked at the close-up of the agonized face against the white linen, black hair, dark complexion, brown eyes open and staring, and a hugely distorted black tongue protruding from the mouth like a swollen serpent. A ripple of emotion washed through him and his fist clenched the paper, his fingernails ripping through the material and into his palm. He closed his eyes for a moment. Finally he asked, "What's the fatality rate?"

"One hundred percent, so far, twenty-five fatalities."

"Jesus," said Robert, "How does it spread? Do they know the vector?"

"They are not sure yet. About all they know is that it does not go through walls. Isolation seems to work."

"My ex and my daughter live in Houston. You don't think they're in any danger?"

"How far is Houston from Austin?"

"About a hundred miles."

"They are either safe or they will have lots of warning. Unless the virus is ten times more dangerous than Ebola, it will never get out of Austin. But, it has not been identified yet. Can you see how your microscope could be used to help the effort?"

"Of course. If it can be made to work, it will give us a very accurate view of the binding of virus molecules. It seems as if it could be a year out, though. Should I drop my work for Merck and get back on the charge microscope?"

"How is the Merck project coming?"

"Poorly. It's not working either."

Teppin nodded and thought for a minute. "Robert, you are, as you probably have figured out for yourself, an eclectic sort of person, a Renaissance man, a dreamer, a pretzel bender. I would accuse you of being rather decent at everything you try without excelling in any one thing, except perhaps for swimming. Olympic trials, wasn't it?"

"Well, yes, but not good enough to make the team. The competition was all on split workouts, five hours a day. I couldn't get that excited about winning at any price." Robert stood and paced back and forth as he spoke.

"You had other interests, also. Rock climbing. High-energy particle physics, cosmology, things like that. Are you perhaps spreading yourself a little thin?"

Robert thought of his father, a committed, responsible member of the community, concentrating on his banking and doing an excellent single-minded job at it. His father would grip his arms painfully, push his face so close that Robert would choke on English Leather aftershave, and bellow, "Focus! Focus! Focus! Choose a path through life and do not waver!"

This was his fifth job in the twelve years since he had graduated from college and his third profession. But he liked biology and genetics, and Dr. Teppin was great to work for— intelligent, interested, and supportive. And a legend in academia, his advice and counsel were in great demand. He had made his handicap into an asset, turning his wheelchair into a mobile communications center that kept him continuously in touch with his variety of interests.

Teppin touched a control and the wheelchair moved him more directly in front of Robert. "Robert? Join me? Spreading yourself too thin?"

"Probably. What do you think?"

"Hmmm, well, it is a good way to become a generalist. Most of the important advances in nearly every field have been made by generalists. They can see forests, not trees. You're set up in perfect position, like a hawk, with the ten thousand foot high view. Now all you need to do is make an important advance." Teppin smiled. "The charge microscope would be good."

Robert grinned, starting to relax a little. "By next Thursday OK?"

"Oh, any time before the end of the month would be fine."

"Back when we killed the charge microscope project it seemed like a pretty unpopular concept. And we couldn't get funding for it."

"Yes," said Teppin. "I think your microscope comes across as pseudoscience. Extraterrestrials, crystals, auras, extrasensory perception.... I am not sure, but it sets people's teeth on edge somehow. But your current project is dead in the water, and Spender needs help."

So what now? Robert wondered. This was obviously a fork in the road. Then again, he'd already shot himself in the foot so often that his shoes looked like Swiss cheese, so why not? "OK, I'll give it a try. But where does the funding come from?"

"I will get the funding from somewhere. If the school will not do it, I will use personal funds. But if you cannot show us some results in a month, we will need to find you something else."

"Is there a culture I can take a look at?"

"I believe so," said Teppin, punching keys again. "Yes, here, they grew cultures this morning. I will call Dr. Spender and see if he can get a few grams. What else will you need?"

"Maybe some help in producing a crystal form of the virus, that could be the tricky part. But let me see if the microscope works first."

"Yes. You have not completed the mathematical analysis, as I understand."

"The hell with the analysis, I'll just build the thing. I think I understand the basic concepts well enough. It's worth a shot, anyway."

"Very unprofessional, but go ahead. Any new tool for antiviral research could save many lives. If you can prove the principle, we will get you the virus cultures. You will have to move to at least a Biohazard Level Two facility, of course. Randall's lab probably can handle it. You can follow the progress in Austin on the ProMED site, that will link you to the CDC effort and to local video."

Robert, newly energized, walked quickly to his closet-sized office, took off his outer clothes and hung them in his glovebox-sized closet. He changed into T-shirt and cutoff gray sweatpants for the run home—three and a half miles away in Brighton, down the southern shore of the Charles River—and laced up his Reeboks. He dug the tape machine out of the desk, slipped on the headphones, and tuned to WGBH for some Mozart.

He ran down the Esplanade on the wide asphalt path that bordered the river, sharing the path with several hundred other alternative commuters on bicycles, rollerblades, and on foot. For the first mile, his body felt like a motor without oil as it always did when he was running a lot, then the endorphins and the lubrication of the exercise took over and the near-hypnotic trance set in, breathe out two steps, breathe in two steps.

A purple sunset hung over the Charles River, and a faint scent of illegal leaf burning could be detected. The weather was cold enough for the women in the street to retreat behind winter coats, but on the Esplanade everyone was in T-shirts and shorts, except a few cop-outs in designer sweats. Robert checked the women to see if any of them were eyeing him appraisingly. None of them seemed to be, but maybe they were just sneaky enough so he couldn't catch them at it.

On the other side of the river Harvard University came into view, with its ivy-covered three story brick and stone buildings. Harvard's eighteenth-century boathouse was near the far end of Eliot Bridge, one of the several graceful arched bridges. The boathouse contents, four- and eight-oared racing shells, were now being rowed briskly down the center of the river, staffed with muscular undergraduates and marking their passage with neat parallel columns of swirls in the calm water.

The track took a sharp corner at Soldier's Field Road. Robert kicked the final six blocks, lengthening his stride, getting more air, and feeling his leg muscles at maximum stretch.

In front of the skating club he stopped and stretched out his ham-strings until his breathing slowed. Then he bent forward, planted his palms flat on the asphalt, and levered his body back through his arms and slowly up into a handstand. He held it until his triceps started trembling and he saw, upside down, two college girls jogging towards him, chatting amiably. He tilted over onto one foot and back upright, checking the girls out of the corner of his eye. Still chatting amiably. They ran on by, neither one of them throwing him a room key. Just as well, he had no time for anything except microscopes right now.

Robert let himself into his small third-floor apartment and kicked the laundry bag out of the way. Tomorrow for sure. Why was there never enough time? He washed out his last pair of underwear and socks as he showered. Then he shoved two Healthy Choice instant dinners into the microwave, picked up the phone and dialed his ex-wife in Houston. He had been married to Joyce for one year just after college. Despite her pregnancy they had divorced when they realized they were completely different people than they had been when they had married. There was no place in her orderly, upwardly mobile life for a disorderly, borderline lunatic scientist who walked like a caged tiger and had the table manners of a lemur. She had followed her dream, moving to Houston and remarrying Jordan Kenally, Houston Memorial Hospital's chief of surgery.

Robert's daughter Katie was now a gangly and charming twelve-year-old, seriously interested in horses and ice hockey. Her new father was certainly able to take care of her better than Robert ever could, and his consulting career took the family overseas several times a year. They always worked in a week of skiing in Zermatt or a little sun in Portofino.

Robert was looking forward to improving his economic situation so he could see Katie more often than their once or twice a year schedule, when the family landed in Boston or New York on their way to Europe or Asia. But for now they talked on the phone. Part of his economic problem was the child support, which Kenally had waved aside but Robert had insisted on. It seemed sometimes to be his only link with Katie.

"Hello, Kenally residence, how may we help?"

"Hi, Felicia. Is Joyce there?"

"Of course, hello, Robert. Momentito."

Joyce spoke. "Robert. I hope you are well?"

"Fine, thanks. Listen, Joyce, I'm worried about this virus outbreak in Austin. I think you should consider moving out of its path for a while until it's controlled."

"Jordan and myself were discussing the Austin virus just last night. He is not concerned, therefore I am not concerned."

"You wouldn't have any trips scheduled?"

"Not until mid-October in Budapest; Jordan is speaking at a convention."

Probably in Hungarian. Next to this guy, Robert thought he could give Bart Simpson a lesson in underachievement. "Joyce, please keep an eye on the virus. It could be very dangerous. Is Katie there?"

"Katie is at her French lesson. I will tell her you called. And, Robert—sincerely—thank you very much for your concern. Goodbye."

Great. If they had had any thought of moving, my call probably messed it up. But there should be no problem, a hundred miles was a long way for a virus to travel, and the CDC would be all over it by now.

He opened a Sam Adams and fired up his computer. If he had to demonstrate a working microscope in three weeks, he had only a few days to finish the design.

Chapter 6

Austin, October 12, present day

D r. Gary Spender steered his Subaru up the curving streets in the hilly residential area west of the city. Here, old-growth trees shaded some of Austin's more luxurious living quarters. Spender drove by the English Tudors, framed in exposed dark wood beams, with tiny diamond windows tinted in rose and purple. He passed the low redwood contemporaries with carefully irrigated bright green grass. He thought it remarkable that the ultimate achievement of the landscape art was grass so perfect that it was indistinguishable from Astroturf.

As he approached the top of the hill the homes became more secretive, hiding at the end of twin curving driveways, one driveway guarded by a sturdy gate marked incongruously "Welcome," the other driveway marked "Service" or "Staff." These were the homes of his associates in the medical profession. Any doctor with a few connections and a little business sense could quadruple his $250,000 salary with a private clinic or two and a business arrangement with a few drugstores.

Spender crested the ridge and drove down the western flank, into the glare of the setting sun, to the modest neighborhood where he lived with his wife, Carla, and their youngest girl. When Spender found himself with a little free time, he would rather read the medical literature or attend to a pro bono patient than work on his income.

His home was a white two-bedroom cape fronted by a small scraggly grass plot, at the end of a street of ungated homes with single-car garages and no Service entrance. Carla met him at the door with a smile and a kiss and led him to the dining room.

"Home early this week," she said. "How's the battle? Did you get any sleep at all the last two days?"

"Maybe half an hour. I'm OK, though, I'm used to it. Maybe the body adapts. How's the kid?"

"She's just fine. She must not have heard you come in; she's been asking me to help with her algebra. Would you believe I've forgotten all my high school algebra? Or maybe they didn't teach it when I was in high school. She's probably got the headphones on again. We made sandwiches. I've got one for you."

"Not just yet. Let's just hang out on the couch and talk quietly. Everybody I've been working with has been screaming at each other and running around a lot. This is better."

"Are you making any progress?"

"We did confirm that it is a virus. That's about as far as we've gotten. The virus, on the other hand, is doing very well; I think you could safely say it's totally out of control. I can't get the thought out of my head that I should have been smarter, quicker, sealed it off." He exhaled in a long shuddering sigh.

Her brow creased in concern. "You can rest, now. It's not your fault. I'll put you to bed soon." She reached out to massage his neck. "Did you get anything to eat?"

"Just some junk from the vending machines, but I'm fine, I'm really not hungry."

"You need to eat, you look like a refugee from the death camps."

"That's the way I feel, too. Sometimes it seems like I'm cheating because I'm still alive."

"Don't think like that. You have to take better care of yourself."

"I'll try. We'll probably have to evacuate soon. You should start packing."

"Evacuate! You're kidding!"

"No, sorry. It's not anywhere near official yet, and I'm not the one to make the call, but that's the way it looks to me right now. No hurry, a day or two won't make much difference."

"My God, Gary, I feel like screaming and running around. Evacuate?

Where to? How can that be?"

"We've done a good, careful job at sealing the virus off. We've made no mistakes. But the damn thing escaped, somehow. It's got some tricky mechanism, we don't know how it's vectored, we're not ready for it. I'm sorry to dump this on you, but this one makes me nervous." Spender's eyes closed, and Carla rested her hand lightly on his face.

"I know it's totally unscientific, but remember the dream about the car crash just when your brother died in the accident? I had a dream last night that the world had night all the way around."

"I feel like there's a runaway locomotive heading right at me. Got any ideas?"

"Can you get more help?"

"The CDC guy, Theslie, will be bringing in the army, we don't have to worry about more help."

"What is there that says we can't have an unstoppable epidemic?"

Spender thought for a minute, then shook his head. "Nothing, I guess. We think we have such an awesome medical capability. We're light years ahead of where they were in the dark ages, with the black plague. We're quick, we're ruthless, we're globally organized, and we have an arsenal of weapons. But one lousy little strand of RNA might beat us."

Carla brushed tears away. "Please, Gary, you can't do it all yourself, get help from anybody you can think of."

"I made a call today to Edward Teppin. He's the gray eminence, the most respected man in biotech. His group may have a couple of ideas, we're going to stay in touch."

They were startled by a knock on the door. Spender reached the door in three long strides and opened it to a friend from down the hill, Juanita Mendez. Juanita's expression was like a deer caught in the headlights. Carla joined Spender at the doorway and slipped her arm around his waist.

"Gary," said Juanita, her voice strained. "Please, please, Gary. It's Manolo. I think he has the disease I heard about on the radio, and they said you were the leader. We were going to the clinic, but your car was there, and I thought—I'm sorry, I should not have bothered you, you must be busy—but he can't talk any more—"

"Did you look at his tongue?"

"Yes, it's swollen and dark. He is he going to die, isn't he?"

"Where is he now?"

"In the back seat, right there."

"Anybody else with you?"

"No, just us."

Spender got masks from his bag and tied one on Juanita and Carla and one on himself. He slipped on a pair of rubber gloves, a white cap, and a plastic shield, and he dug out a flashlight.

"Wait here a minute," he said, moving to the car. Manolo's familiar wide cheerful face was in agony, his tongue dark and protruding, eyes frightened and body spasming with the effort to breathe. Spender yelled to Juanita to come to the car.

He dug out an ampoule of morphine and jabbed the syringe into Manolo's arm. He managed to ram a breathing tube into Manolo's throat, behind the swollen tongue, and saw Manolo relax as his breathing eased. Spender found another mask and tied it to Manolo and a minute later saw him close his eyes as the morphine started to work.

"We'll take care of you, old buddy, don't worry," he said.

"Is it the disease?" asked Juanita.

"Yes. I'm very sorry."

"What can we do?"

"We have to get you to quarantine. He'll be with the other confirmed victims. Juanita, the chances are slim. All we can hope for is that one of the hundreds of researchers can find a quick cure. I know that's lousy, but it's all we've got."

Juanita put her face in her hands and sobbed quietly as Carla held her shoulders.

"Juanita, I'm sorry, I have no right to do this now, but maybe we can save some lives if we find out how this happened. Can you help me by answering some questions?"

Carla spoke. "Shouldn't you get to the hospital?"

"It doesn't really matter much now. But if we can trace the virus' path to Manolo, that could help us to control it."

Juanita nodded finally, and opened her eyes. "I'm all right."

"Good. Has he been anywhere near Conover Mercy, especially about six days ago?"

"No."

"He works locally now, right?"

"Yes, the Texaco on Corliss, only two blocks from our home."

"Has he been anywhere else, five to seven days ago?"

"I don't think so. He's been working the day shift as a mechanic and another half shift in the evening pumping gas. We haven't been downtown for a few weeks."

"Thanks, Juanita. If you could, maybe tomorrow you could write down all the names of people that Manolo has come in contact with. I'll drive you to the hospital. Carla, I'll be back in an hour, I promise. I'll take a cab."

She nodded at him, kissed him through the respirator, and went in to the house to pack.

• • •

Spender checked Manolo into the isolation ward and took Juanita to the small chapel. He found two new cases in the ward, which had been admitted in the last hour. He checked the home addresses; they were also from west of the hospital.

There was a large map of the city posted near the lobby, Spender pulled a handful of thumbtacks from a bulletin board and marked the location of the breakout cases.

"Spender! Hey!" Hapwell Theslie shouted from the lobby. "There you are! They said you went home."

"I did. I even got fifteen seconds of sleep. Anything new?"

"Not yet. What are the tacks?"

"Three new cases. The timing looks like infection took place six days ago. I think that was the night the fog came in, sometime mid-evening. Why don't you check on the occupations of these two, see if you can find out where they were six days ago. I'll find out the timing of the fog."

Theslie nodded. "Good thinking, Spender. I see where you're going with this," and then hurried off, keying his cell phone.

Spender called the local television station and got through quickly to the weather forecaster.

"Dr. Spender, I'd be happy to help in any way I can," said the weatherman.

"Exactly six days ago, what was the weather in the city?"

"Hang on a second." Spender heard rustling papers. "Here it is, sixty-eight degrees high, forty-five low. Scattered clouds A.M., thickening P.M. Winds ten to fifteen from the east-southeast. Low pressure area in the Gulf off New Orleans, we picked up some humid air from the Gulf, causing heavy fog between eight and ten P.M. Anything else?"

"What was the relative humidity?"

"About eighty percent midday, increasing to nearly one hundred percent in the fog."

"How often do we get close to a hundred percent relative humidity here?"

"In the rain, often. With no rain, not more than once or twice a year."

"Thanks," said Spender, "That helps a lot."

A few minutes later Hapwell Theslie hurried up with a clipboard. "This Cooper woman was working the cash register at a miniature golf place." He gave the address and Spender moved his thumb-tack a bit. "The Verrazo guy was giving a barbecue party in his back yard."

"In the fog?"

"That's what he said," said Theslie. "Probably alcoholic beverages involved."

"He could talk?"

"No, but he could write pretty good," said Theslie, showing Spender the awkward scrawl. "What's your take on this, Spender?"

"One possibility is that the virus is airborne on a microdroplet, and needs high humidity to survive. An infinitesimal bit of air venting from our isolation ward could have been carried by the prevailing east-southeast winds. You can see the new cases are on a straight line west-northwest of us."

"That's the way I figure it, too. I'll spread the word. You can go home, Spender."

"You spread the word. I'll try to find the leak," said Spender, shoulders sagging wearily. He walked off to the isolation wing.

Chapter 7

Boston, October 21, present day

Robert Asher shared the Biolevel 3 lab with a few other staff members and some students working on their theses, and the large room was often busy well into the night. It was supplied with the usual equipment: optical microscopes, centrifuges, microtomes, a wall of reagents and culture samples, refrigerators, and a high-power electron microscope.

The charge microscope was set up on a lab bench. Its most prominent feature was a black glass plate, almost two feet square, with a movable aluminum plate hinged to make contact with the top of the glass plate. The aluminum plate was wired to an aluminum ball six inches in diameter, supported on a clear plastic column, and provided with a silk cloth to generate electrostatic voltage. That Thursday morning, Robert was demonstrating the microscope to Dr. Teppin and several other staff members.

"Robert," said Teppin, "You beat the deadline."

"It came together pretty quickly. I found a way to get the sample plate and the aluminum plate to come together perfectly without needing to make them exactly flat. Lots of pressure, thin soft aluminum. And the virus sample came in from Austin."

"You have been handling it with great care, of course?"

"I did the virus work in the BL-3 facility, in the Racal suit. I got some good results last night."

"Maybe you can give us some background."

"The theory is based on the moiré effect," said Robert. "You can see it when you look through two window screens from a ways off. The tiny pattern of the screen is magnified by a huge factor and you see giant dark squares which move when you move your head. One of the window screens, at a much smaller dimension, is the sample. The sample is crystallized on this smooth black plate, like frost on your window, by evaporating a liquid solution. Then a charge pattern is formed by contact with a charged crystalline conductor. The conductor is the second window screen, and it needs to have a regular crystal structure with almost the same molecular dimension as the sample's."

"How do you arrange that?"

"Deposit the crystal on the plates at a slightly different temperature. Then equalize the temperature; the different thermal expansion of aluminum and glass causes a slight size change. A tenth of a percent change in size gives you a magnification of a thousand times."

"But isn't it difficult to get a monocrystalline deposit?"

"Yes, impossible, so I simply use the glass plate crystal as a template to seed the growth of a similar crystal on the aluminum. I used aluminum, almost any other metal would work as well. Then you put a high voltage on the conductor to charge the sample plate. I'm using this poor man's Van de Graaf generator to get the high-voltage supply, but I've ordered a fifty-kilovolt lab supply. Field emission pulls charge out where the molecules are closest." He rubbed the silk cloth on the aluminum sphere and moved the large aluminum plate down into contact with the black plate.

"I've set the magnification to ten thousand times here. If the humidity is not over about twenty percent we can make the magnified charge pattern visible with a white powder. I use talcum powder."

He removed the aluminum plate and dusted the surface with an aerosol bottle of powder. A pattern appeared, etched in thin white lines against the black glass.

The onlookers reacted with applause and astonishment. "Sweet Jesus, the goddamn thing works!"

"That pattern shows the electrostatic field of an individual molecule. A single molecule would produce a field far too small to be measured, but when we crystallize billions of molecules and expose them through the moiré plate, the field becomes visible. Since the molecule is probably not symmetric, I will need to repeat this experiment twice more to get the charge pattern at three different possible crystal orientations."

"How do you use the information?" asked Dr. Teppin.

"The charge image of a molecule, once we learn how to use it, may be more useful for some purposes than the normal electron microscope image. It's a more accurate picture of the forces that bind molecules. I can't predict all the uses. We're going to be working on this for years."

He pointed at an electron microscope image on the wall. "This is the Austin virus under ten thousand times magnification from three angles with a conventional electron microscope. You can see that the structure in the first image is similar to the moiré microscope. But the charge image of the moiré microscope will show you how the molecule wants to form bonds with other molecules, so it is a much better predictor of behavior. We can design an anti-molecule with a similar but mirror image charge pattern which will bond to and kill the virus molecule, and ideally not be too harmful to humans by itself."

"Now, this is exciting," another staff member said. "I thought it was just more weird science like Kirlean images."

"Yeah, we got some bad press. There's some parallels. Kirlean images are supposed to show the soul or the aura of a leaf or a rock, but they're really showing the corona discharge pattern. Trust me, we're not looking at the soul of the virus molecule, we're just looking at its charge image."

Teppin spoke. "Congratulations, Robert. This is an incredible achievement. You have officially got all the funding you need as of now. But you also have some work to do. You need to see if you can find some practical demonstration that shows that charge images can do things that standard electron microscopes cannot. The Austin virus is the place to start. Of course, you have a certain advantage in that your microscope probably costs about a hundred times less than an electron microscope. Or a few thousand times less than a cryo-electron microscope."

"Great. I'll get back to work."

"Yes," said Teppin. "You get those other views of the virus and let me know when you can use some help with the antiviral effort. And we'll stay in touch with Spender down in Texas. They're a long way from keeping this outbreak contained. They're going to need all the help they can get."

"It could be many months, or years, before we're ready for a practical application."

"I know, but this virus is a tough one. It may be months or years before anybody figures out a cure. Robert, this may seem unfair, but you should assume that you're the best chance to save a lot of human lives."

"How can that be?" asked Robert. "The CDC is in Austin in force, right? Handling quarantine and isolation? They shouldn't have any trouble with one virus outbreak."

Teppin shook his head. "This one isn't that easy. The virus is a throwback in some ways: it's got a simple structure, like Ebola but with an extra kink that gives it even better propagation and a faster reproductive cycle. And it keeps its host alive longer pumping out aerosol virus particles. Vancomycin doesn't touch it, there's no known cure. And the symptoms don't appear until after the host is infectious."

Robert nodded, face grim.

• • •

The next evening, Robert was at home staring at the three-view projections of the virus on his computer screen, trying to finish the study of the microscope images. But his eyes kept losing focus, slipping past the screen to infinity. The problem was, the concept was too simple. A junior high school kid could build this damn microscope on the kitchen table during lunch hour. Robert realized that he was expecting to fail, expecting that the microscope had been invented already and had some hidden flaw.

OK, then, maybe it was time to find out for sure if anybody had ever built a charge microscope. The concept had unfolded itself slowly in his head more than a year ago—first the longest of long shots—but as he began to refine the idea it had seemed possible, even probable. He had been disappointed when the project had been back-burnered and exhilarated when Spender had needed the microscope's medical capability and moved it back to top priority.

Until now he hadn't seen any hint of any other researcher working on the principle. But now that the microscope was making pictures he could easily make sure that it was unique.

He launched Netscape 12 on the computer. With its new graphical browser capability, it would let him scan through millions of pages of information on the Internet and look for anything that closely matched his image, the charge pattern of the virus.

When Netscape came up, he pasted his three-view image into its browser window and clicked on "Submit." In a few seconds, the computer beeped softly, reported "One match found," and displayed a nearly identical image with an added column of unrelated figures.

Robert was stunned. His incredible new breakthrough was yesterday's news, a rediscovery, a footnote instead of the big story. Nearly a year out of his life, reinventing the wheel. Another dead end, already tested, already failed.

He spun away from the computer. He emptied his beer can in one swig, crushed it, and threw it at the wall. He saw the implication, if this brilliant idea was second hand, there'd be some reason it wouldn't help with the Austin virus. He slammed both hands down on a table with a muffled scream and paced around the room. After a while, the soothing effect of a third Sam Adams restored a measure of calm and he turned back to the computer to get the details of the bad news.

Then his eye caught something strange: the image on the screen was labeled "Stela in Uxmal, Mexico, AD 823."

There must be some mistake. He looked closer; the image on the screen was of a stone carving, not a microscope picture from another researcher. An old stone carving. The accompanying text was, "In the third group, these two columns of three do not resemble any known glyphs. They have not been translated, but from the surrounding glyphs we can guess that they represent some chemical or pharmacological product."

Robert clicked through the complete document. It was the doctoral thesis of a researcher at Harvard who was studying the language of the ancient Maya Indians. The twelve-century-old stone carving that matched the Austin virus had been photographed in 1923. What in hell was going on?

He considered the options. The images were too similar to be coincidental, but how could they not be? And could the second column be a charge image of an antiviral? It looked close enough to be a mirror image, with the differences in structure that would be appropriate for an antiviral. But how could the ancient Maya Indians have built a charge microscope? Or synthesized an antiviral?

He sat for ten minutes, his mind churning over with the possibilities, but nothing made any sense. It was past nine o'clock in the evening, but he would get no sleep unless he got this sorted out, and Dr. Teppin had given him his home phone number.

"This is Teppin."

"Dr. Teppin, this is Robert Asher."

"Please call me Edward after five o'clock. What is it?"

Robert described the situation.

"That is impossible, of course, but you already know that. Can you come over with a printout?"

"Sure, if it won't be a problem this late?"

"You know where I live, right? I will expect you in half an hour."

• • •

Robert had been at a faculty party at Dr. Teppin's suite last Christmas. Dr. Teppin lived alone, in most of the fifteenth floor. His apartment was furnished in a nautical motif: pieces of wrecked wooden boats, a big old brass binnacle from an eighteenth century schooner, marine charts, and an antique brass-and-wood telescope, retrofitted with modern optics and looking out over Boston Harbor to Deer Island and Boston Light. A three-foot illuminated globe in an old oak frame dominated the room.

Robert was buzzed in to the apartment and Teppin in his motorized wheelchair led him to a leather sofa in the library. Robert accepted the offer of a cognac and handed Teppin the computer printouts. Teppin considered the documents for a few minutes as Robert watched the lights of the harbor and a few ships coming back to port.

"Yes. The way it looks to me," said Teppin, finally. "There are three possibilities. One is a coincidence, the second is some complicated kind of hoax, and the third is that the Maya simply got there twelve hundred years before you."

Robert smiled and shrugged his shoulders.

"The possibility of a coincidence can be calculated fairly easily.

The chance of each of the three glyphs matching to one picture element is about ten to the eighteenth power, a billion billion to one. Of course, you have to consider near misses, mirror images, and so forth. If you factor these effects, the odds probably drop to a thousand billion to one. Still, you would have to consider it a rather long shot.

"And then there's the hoax. But the possibility of a hoax is infinitesimal, if you indeed created the three views today and nobody else got a look before you did the net search. Is that what happened?"

"Exactly," said Robert. "I finished the last view at the lab, took the photo with the digital camera, erased the plate, and went home directly. Nobody was in the lab or at home except me."

"Of course, there is another possibility which I must consider: that you are pulling a hoax on me."

Robert was startled. "No way. Sir."

"But you do not have to consider it, of course, just me," he went on. "And it will be easy for us to repeat your experiments with the virus and compare the images with the Maya glyphs. The photos of the glyphs are archived in the Library of Congress, so if you are trying a hoax we will know soon enough. You wouldn't have accomplices in the Library of Congress? I thought not. And you would have figured all of this out yourself, since you are quite intelligent, so I think that we will find that the photos are indeed archived as stated and that you are not trying to hoax me."

"I'm as confused as you are, Dr. Teppin."

"I am not confused. As Sherlock Holmes used to say, once the impossible is ruled out, the remaining answer, no matter how unlikely, must be fact. So we are left with the ancient Maya inventing the microscope twelve hundred years before you reinvented it, hmmm? Is there anything in the construction of your microscope that would have been impossible for a pre-iron-age culture? No fancy electronics, right?"

"No fancy electronics," agreed Robert. "It needs a smooth black dielectric plate."

"They used obsidian, a volcanic glass, for knives and decoration. It was also available in larger pieces, I think they made mirrors of it. Or was that the Aztecs?"

"Obsidian would work. It also needs a flat conducting plate. I use aluminum."

"They didn't have aluminum," said Teppin, "But I think they did have brass and some gold."

"Either would work. And even the Minoans knew about static electricity. I used a simple metal ball and a cloth for my high voltage supply. It works well in the winter with the low humidity, but it would not work at all in a humid jungle climate."

"Yes. So they could move out of the jungle to one of the drier microclimates. We certainly need to talk to an expert, maybe the researcher whose paper you found, but at least at first pass it seems as if they could have built the microscope."

"But the knowledge of how to build it, the theoretical background, what it would do when it was finished, how it would be used," said Robert. "How could they have been that advanced? We're talking about a primitive Indian culture, not a modern university."

"Indian, but not primitive. They did not need to watch television, they did not have far to commute to their jobs, and they did not have to spend Saturday at the shopping mall. They lived in a less complicated universe than we do, but perhaps because it was less complicated they understood it better than we understand ours. I traveled in Mexico and in what was then British Honduras, when I was younger—when I could still walk—and visited several of the Maya sites. Chichén Itzá, Tulum, Cobá. I was astonished at how advanced they were."

"I've never been there."

"In Chichén Itzá, there is a pyramid temple with a stairway on one side, and a feathered serpent head carved in stone at the bottom of the stairs. During just one sunrise every year, at the vernal equinox, the angle of the sun is just right to project an image of the stepped stair rail on the opposite rail, and as the sun rises the projection animates into a serpent of light undulating down the slope to the feathered serpent's head." Teppin moved both hands to illustrate. "It was obviously not built by accident, and it took some excellent mathematicians and architects and builders to make it come out right."

"Fascinating! Did you see it?"

"No, because the knowledge of the event had died and was only rediscovered in the 1970s, but I did see a video a few years ago.

The place was mobbed with visitors at dawn to admire the show. There's also a small observatory, called Caracol if I remember correctly. You can take sight lines from the building's platforms and door jambs to plot the rising and setting location of the sun, the moon, and Venus."

"Not primitive," said Robert.

"Now, about the virus sample itself. Where did it come from? How did they know to look at it with the microscope? How did they precipitate it as a crystal? How far advanced were they in understanding the molecular basis of matter?"

"They wouldn't need to understand molecules. Really, all they would need to figure out is that they crystallized a sample of something and it would make a pattern, and if they wanted to find something else that would be chemically active with their sample they'd look for the mirror-image pattern. They could have had a science based on the charge image of molecules without knowing that they were molecules."

"Yes," said Teppin. "Of course. If your only tool is a hammer, et cetera. And with no transparent glass, they had no chance of building optical microscopes. They may have developed an understanding of chemistry based on their version of a charge microscope. And similarly they would not need to know anything about DNA to do genetic engineering."

"That's still a pretty big leap," said Robert. "There's no record of any of this, is there?"

"Perhaps the record is there, if we had the wit to see it. Part of their environment was the immense chemical factory of the tropical rain forest, and they understood the products of that factory much better than we do today. If they catalogued the charge image of biologically active substances from the rain forest, they could match them with virus or bacterial images. Instant cure. Plenty of test subjects, they had no particular respect for the sanctity of human life. And they had no Food and Drug Administration to slow down deployment."

"But this kind of effort should leave traces."

"The jungle is a hostile environment. The Spanish were quite hostile also, as I recall."

Robert digested this, then asked, "Do you think that the Maya had a *cure* for the virus?"

"Maybe. It does make sense that the virus could have hit the Maya in the ninth century, decimated the population and become the number one research project of the Maya scientists. And it could have been cured at the time and been lying dormant in the Yucatán jungle or the Uxmal excavation until some random native with the antibodies bred out of him, or one of the U.T. group, got bit by the wrong bug, or bird, or animal. There is a group culturing samples from the Uxmal site. That may clear up the mystery."

"So the virus could account for the civilization's collapse. The people that were left would have bailed out of the cities. What do we do next?" asked Robert, finishing off his cognac.

Teppin carefully poured him another half inch. "Precisely. What do we do next?" He thought for a moment. "I will set up an independent group to replicate your experiment. That should take a week. We also need a research team studying the uses of the charge pattern, trying to synthesize an antiviral with the charge pattern data."

"How will you fund it?"

"I will find a way, don't worry. I have some personal reserves if nothing more formal is available. Let me see, what else? Our attorneys will be interested in your notes for the patent applications. And we will need a few adventurous types tracking down the Maya link; if they did discover a rain forest solution, we need it in a hurry. I imagine you would be one of the charge pattern team."

And Katie, down in Houston. One hundred miles away didn't seem as safe anymore. On the other hand, if the ancient Maya had actually used a charge microscope for medical research, they could have easily left some clues that would point to a cure.

"I think I'd be more useful in the Yucatán," said Robert. "The job here is pretty cut and dried. I'll give my writeup and notebooks to an engineer to finish up."

"The Yucatán is incredibly hot. It has snakes. You will contract a particularly annoying form of diarrhea. And it is not called the Mosquito Coast for nothing."

"You know what Brighton in November is like? And I have the feeling that we might be able to get an answer faster." Another fork in the road, Robert mused. The obvious choice is to stay safely in Boston, finishing the industrial design, gearing up for production, discovering the correct process control variables for crystallization. A good job for methodical, patient technicians...lets me out. They'd probably make faster progress without me. Anyway, the chance of a quick fix for any new virus was poor, look at AIDS.

Robert made up his mind. "I'll go to Mexico. But I don't know the territory or the language, and I'll need some help with the Maya translation."

Teppin nodded. "I would think that the student who wrote the thesis you found would be a prime candidate. And, failing that, there is a department at Harvard that has done some good research on the Maya. I know her department manager. I will make a phone call. What was the name of the thesis author?" asked Teppin, punching buttons on his computer.

"Dr. Teresa Welles."

He nodded, looking at the monitor. "That simplifies things; she's a researcher at Harvard." He scribbled a phone number for Robert.

"Sounds good. What next?"

"Next, you and she can try to translate more of the glyphs from photographs. If that does not work, you travel to Mexico with Welles, if she can go. She should know the language. The languages. Do you speak Spanish?"

"Yo hablo Espanol," Robert answered, somewhat truthfully, with three years of study in the language.

"¡Bueno! And you will need a guide, somebody who knows the territory, too, but that should be easier from down there."

• • •

The next day Robert dialed the number at Harvard.

"This is Teresa."

"Dr. Welles?"

"Yes."

"I'm Dr. Robert Asher. I'm a researcher at B.U."

"What can I do for you, Dr. Robert Asher?"

"I'm working with Dr. Teppin on a project in virus research. We need some help with Mesoamerican languages and Maya archaeology. He recommended your department."

"I've heard of Dr. Teppin, of course. But that's an unusual connection. How can I help?"

Her voice was cool and confident, with an undertone of amusement. He momentarily considered trying to give her a summary on the telephone, then realized how confusing it would sound. "Well, it's sort of involved. We are organizing a trip to the Yucatán to track down some mysterious glyphs. Can you give me half an hour to go into the details?"

"Sure, can you come over this afternoon?"

"That'd be great. How about 3:00?"

• • •

At 2:45, Robert took the turn on Massachusetts Avenue at Out Of Town News and was stunned to see an empty parking place, a legal space, with a parking meter. He swung the Toyota quickly into the curb, stepped out and locked the car. Well, he locked the driver's side door; the passenger door lock didn't work. Next week for sure, stop at Goldie's for a new lock. Robert figured that any self-respecting Cambridge car thief would draw the line at sliding across a ripped Toyota seat and climbing over the shift lever.

He walked across the Quadrangle—a tree-lined grassy square surrounded with ivy-covered brick buildings—found the Harkness Laboratory, gave his name to the receptionist and said he had an appointment with Dr. Welles. He was ushered down a long corridor with a chipped dark green linoleum floor and two-tone green walls, through an oak framed door with frosted glass announcing Mesoamerican Studies, Dr. T. Welles, and into a small office.

"Dr. Welles. Hi, I'm Robert Asher."

She looked up from her computer screen. She had dark hair in moderate disarray and a nice smile and extra large glasses enlarging her eyes, and from what he could see her body was attractively arranged. Her skin was the color of antique pine. He looked again at the eyes, somewhere between purple and blue, deep, arresting.

"Hello, Robert Asher." Her voice was a smoky contralto with a surprising depth and power, a performer's voice, not an academic voice.

"Call me Robert."

"Then you may call me Teresa. Let me save this, just in case," she said, punching keys. "Sit down, please. You said you could use some help on the Maya. I'm probably not the ranking expert in town, or even the ranking expert at Harvard, but I could be the cheapest. What exactly do you need?"

"Do you speak Maya?"

"Maya, Yucatec, Spanish, all that stuff." She smiled and turned back to him. "My mom was Maya. I lived in Mexico until I was six years old. I got one name from her, one name from my dad the archaeologist."

"I do molecular biology," he said, "and I invented a new kind of microscope. Or maybe I just re-invented it, I'm not sure. It makes a picture of the charge patterns of the component molecules of a sample, a charge image instead of an optical image. It gives you a better picture of how the sample will interact with other chemicals. Dr. Teppin thought I should take a charge microscope picture of the Austin virus that's causing all the trouble in Texas."

"I've been following that one. Not nice."

"Not nice at all. I got a virus culture and ran it through the microscope. It made a pretty distinctive charge pattern picture. Here it is." He dropped a computer printout of the Austin virus image on her desk. "Then I discovered almost by accident that the same image was carved into a rock 1200 years ago in Mexico. You used a picture of the carving to illustrate your doctoral thesis. Here's that picture."

She compared the pictures. "Huh?" she asked. "Are you saying the ancient Maya built one of these microscopes? And looked at the same virus with it?"

"Exactly. If you do the math, there's no way this could happen by chance. Simply no way. But nobody can come up with any other explanation, so we think the Maya were much farther advanced in science and biology than anybody thought possible."

She spun her chair halfway around and stared at the wall for a minute, then swung back to face him. Her expression was of someone who had just bitten into a jalapeno pepper. "Naaaah," she said.

"Feel free to suggest an alternate explanation."

She thought for a minute, brow furrowing and then smoothing as if she had come to some conclusion. "Can't handle it. I hate to say impossible, but I'll make an exception in this case."

This wasn't going well. I need another approach. I need this woman to translate. Plus she is incredibly nice looking, and probably smarter than I am. Try again. "Definitely impossible," he said. "But there is also a chance that working out this puzzle will give us some clues to a treatment for the Austin virus. Those other symbols on the rock look to me as if they could be some kind of antiviral.

Dr. Teppin said he thought that the glyphs were words, and that you could translate them."

"Well, yes, mostly. There are hundreds of glyphs that we have translated. They're not words but mostly syllables, or phonemes, speech sounds. Some are like Chinese characters, pictographs, representing an object. We can translate about ninety percent of them."

"Can you translate these particular glyphs?"

"No, sorry. I worked on them for a bit when I was doing the thesis, no luck. Then later I worked on them again for this." She gestured at a manuscript open on her desk, titled *Similarities Between Maya Glyphs and Asian Religious Symbols, Dr. Teresa Welles.*

"Perfect, that's the sort of analysis we'll need. Has that been published?"

"Not yet, but *J. Historical Archeology* has it in peer review. And *Scientific American* is looking at it, too, that's this week's exciting news."

"Congratulations."

"It's neat stuff. There are lots of common symbols you can find in early Mexican and Asian cultures, like this one of an eye in a hand, or this one, face of god with rivers for a nose. There's good evidence that there was commerce across the Pacific a few millennia BC."

"That's the kind of thing I'll be looking for in Uxmal."

She nodded and thought for a moment. "When you were looking for matches to your microscope pictures, did you find any other images?"

"No, none. But help me with this; the Maya civilization is all brand new to me. I didn't know that there was so much civilization in the Americas that early. Do you know Uxmal?"

"I grew up in Mexico, but I've only been back once. A bunch of us visited Uxmal and Chichén Itzá during my doctoral studies. Here," she pointed to a large map on the wall. "This is a map of the Yucatán Peninsula in about the time the stones were inscribed. On the right, the Caribbean Sea. On the left, Mexico. To the south, what later became Belize, and to the southwest, what later became Guatemala. You can see, here, the concentration of Maya cities. The Maya population was about fourteen million at that time."

"How old are the cities? Our Indians didn't build cities."

"The North American Indians were migratory, following the game, but here the forest provided crops year round. The population changed from nomadic hunter-gatherers in twenty thousand BC to farmers who lived in villages, and later built these beautiful cities."

"Why the change? And how can you be sure about the dates?" asked Robert.

"A woolly mammoth skeleton was found with a spear point in the ribs, and there were flint knives nearby. The date is about ten thousand BC from soil strata. Then the climate changed. Things got dry starting around seventy-five hundred BC, we can tell from soil cores. Then it looks as if—due to the dry climate—the big, easy-hunting animals died out and the poor Mexicans had to eat snakes and beetles and stuff. So they started doing some farming, and over the next few millennia they got pretty good at corn, and then squash and beans."

"How did we figure that out?"

"Discoveries of agricultural tools, and millstones for grinding corn to make tamales. Things got organized in Mexico a couple of millennia later than the progress of civilization in Europe and Asia."

"What was the timing in Europe and Asia?" asked Robert.

"In Egypt there was a frenzy of monument building, about twenty-five hundred BC; they took over the world championship of math and science and pyramids and then disappeared. The early Mexicans may have learned from them with the contact with Asian civilization across the Pacific back then. I'll give you a copy of my manuscript. Then from one thousand BC to AD nine hundred, the Mexicans created the most advanced civilization of that age, with great art, major advances in science, and dramatic city architecture. In the last stages of the Maya civilization, a dozen or so kings built themselves these incredible temples." She gestured to photographs on the rear wall showing several steep-sided pyramids.

"Edifice rex?" asked Robert.

She smiled. "If you like edifices, you'll love our new virtual reality trip. We're getting it ready for the Peabody; instant Maya culture. Would you like to check it out?"

"Sure."

She popped a disk into her computer and handed him something that looked like a small submarine, but inside out.

"Put this helmet on; you'll see an artist's reconstruction of Palenqué in about seven hundred fifty. You will be able to fly around with the joystick."

Robert slipped on the heavy headset and grabbed the joystick handle. He was transported to the broad main avenue of Palenqué. The buildings were a bright ochre color in the midday sun. He seemed even to feel the heat of the sun, but then he realized that the heat of the electronics in the helmet was largely responsible. He turned his head left and right and the scene followed his movement. Maya Indians moved along the avenue, and in the distance a group of Maya decorated with colorful feathers mounted the steps of the largest pyramid.

With the realism of the scene and the huge crowds of people moving purposefully through the beautiful city, it was easy to think the Maya would be capable of developing a microscope and a drug therapy for the virus.

Chapter 8

Atlanta, Georgia, October 23, present day
Centers for Disease Control and Prevention

The "War Room" at Atlanta's Centers for Disease Control measured forty by seventy feet. Along one of the long walls were arrayed four large flat display screens. With a deep red carpet, a high ceiling, indirect lighting, and liberal use of dark wood paneling, the room had more the ambience of a plush hotel lobby than the venue for a hastily-assembled meeting of industry, academic, and government experts. The long walnut conference table stretched nearly the length of the room, and in a corner two technicians wearing headsets sat before computer screens.

The room buzzed with the conversations of the nearly one hundred invited experts, clad in a variety of dress ranging from dark blue pinstripe business suits to T-shirts. One woman wore green hospital scrubs as if she'd been interrupted in the middle of a surgical procedure. Each invitee wore a hand-lettered identification tag.

A thin man dressed informally in slacks and a wool sweater hurried in late, brushing his gray hair off his face and showing a three-day growth of beard below deep-set dark eyes. He fastened an identification tag to his sweater: "Dr. Gary Spender, Conover Mercy Hospital, Austin, TX, USA." Then he found a chair, sat down, closed his eyes, and rested his head in his hands.

Spender felt like some kind of V.I.P.; CDC had arranged a military jet to fly him to Atlanta for the conference. But he hadn't had time to fully complete quarantine before takeoff, so he made the flight in a very uncomfortable hazmat Racal suit and tested himself for the virus on arrival. Still negative; thank God for small favors.

Just outside in the corridor, several security guards were struggling to close the doors on a dozen camera operators, reporters, and sound technicians carrying video cameras and battery-powered lights.

The leftmost screen displayed an image of Edward Teppin with a superimposed graphic that announced, "Dr. Teppin, Boston, MA." Spender saw the name with satisfaction. Edward Teppin was the one person who could maintain his perspective in a crisis. How was that new microscope coming along, he wondered. Probably should call Teppin right after he got airborne for the return trip.

The next screen showed a video feed from the familiar oval office and a graphic, "President of the United States," but the long desk was manned by the Chief of Staff. The other screens displayed a man sitting at an ornate desk, labeled "Giscard Corot, WHO," and a matronly woman labeled "Phyllis Eisenberg, NIH."

A big heavy-set black man wearing a rumpled white shirt and a loose tie strode energetically to one end of the table, adjusted his tie fractionally, picked up a cordless microphone and tapped it to quiet the room. "Take your seats, please. Forgive me if we neglect the usual formalities, but we are in a war. If there's anyone here that doesn't know me, I'm Robbins, CDC director. We are pleased to have, from B.U., Dr. Edward Teppin. The World Health Organization, and the National Institutes of Health are also linked by video. The President is being represented by his chief of staff.

"We also have representatives from USAMRIID, the United States Army Medical Research Institute of Infectious Diseases; our own Special Pathogens Branch; CBIAC, the Chemical and Biological Defense Information Analysis Center from the President's Executive Office; PHS/OEP; the World Health Organization; the Office of Emergency Preparedness from Health and Human Services; INCLEN, the International Clinical Epidemiology Network; and a few others I can't translate. And we have new rules. I know the normal Washington procedure is to cover your assets and compartmentalize your knowledge. That won't work. Before we leave here today, we must have formal but open lines of command and communication, unconditional cooperation, and clear lines of responsibility.

"Some of you are concerned that we have been attacked by biological terrorists. We have new evidence that suggests that terrorism is not the source, but the capabilities of organizations like USAMRIID that are designed to combat biological terrorism will also help us combat a natural virus outbreak. So we will work together.

"We'll begin by taking you through what we know about the Austin virus and then enlist your help in planning, management, and resource allocation. Interrupt with pertinent questions only, please. We have Dr. Gary Spender here today. Gary was at the epicenter of the event, and he has been leading the field teams in Austin. Dr. Spender?"

A screen lit up with the message "Differential Diagnosis," and Dr. Spender stood to lecture the group. "We haven't found anything that can stop the virus, but we do have a few things that slow it down. Accurate diagnosis does not seem to be a critical element, but we do have a staining procedure that works well. Patients with the prodrome symptoms may be assumed to have the Austin virus and must be quickly isolated. Patients merely exposed to known carriers should also be isolated.

"Early symptoms are difficulty breathing and occasionally a violent coughing attack. Black tongue can be seen within forty-eight hours to confirm the diagnosis. Chest radiographs show bilateral interstitial infiltrates consistent with frank pulmonary edema." His words were punctuated with bulleted text appearing on the screen.

A second screen lit up with the title, "Pathology." Spender continued, "The pathology is distinctive. Dense, rubbery lungs, tongue shows vascular changes with pronounced swelling, generalized capillary dilation and edema." The screen showed pictures of the autopsied organs. "Any questions?"

The woman dressed in green scrubs stood, "Dr. Spender, do you have any clues about the antecedents of the pathogen? It sounds similar to the symptoms of mustard gas."

"We'll have more on that later. We have been talking to experts on biological warfare substances. The black tongue is, of course, unknown as a viral disease symptom."

"Treatment" scrolled across the screen.

"Not so much treatment as containment," said Spender. "We have no successful treatment at this time, we have a fatality rate of over ninety-nine percent. Only one survivor, a fourteen-year old Native American girl of Maya ancestry. We're checking on this, there could be some genetic immunity here. We estimate a minimum of a year to develop any kind of treatment with full resources deployed, but this is, of course, wildly conjectural.

"The field teams in Austin are using strict isolation techniques in depressurized rooms, full face mask respirators, enteric precautions, and body fluid and blood precautions.

"What treatment we have can prolong life by several days. We have tried mechanical ventilation, radical tracheotomy, oxygen, heat, cold, and naturally the full spectrum of drugs. That concludes my report, unless there are further questions."

The representative from INCLEN stood. "We'll need international coordination, of course. INCLEN will be able to handle this responsibility, but we will need additional funding. Is there—"

The director interrupted, "Later, please. We've pulled several people off the front line in Austin and from research labs to help us understand the virus and the epidemic. The first part of this meeting will be hearing from them so we can all understand the problem. Then we will send them back to work and descend into our usual bickering about organizational responsibilities and funding. Next slide, please."

"Epidemiology," barked the director, as the word scrolled into the display. "We have a new and virulent, almost one hundred percent fatal, multi-drug-resistant microorganism. The transmission vector is not completely understood at this time but field work suggests airborne droplets. Initial infection may have occurred in Mexico, in the Yucatán peninsula, where an archaeological team from the University of Texas was excavating in the jungle on an ancient Maya site.

"This team returned on a Texas Air flight to Austin. The team members are all now deceased, along with the two flight attendants, twelve other passengers on the flight, fourteen hospital patients with unrelated admission symptoms, seven hospital staff and twenty other Austin residents who were not connected to the hospital.

"The detailed planning on how we should proceed is, of course, the subject of this meeting, but in conversation with many of you the rough outlines are clear." He nodded to a technician and a map of North America appeared on the screen. "The Pan American Health Organization is back-checking the Yucatán. Although there are no confirmed incidents there, it seems likely that the infectious agent persists. Also, there is a possibility that indigenous Maya populations may be affected but tribal doctors may be handling the sickness and not reporting to health authorities."

A doctor raised a hand. "The Maya girl that survived. What were her symptoms?"

"Good question. Doctor Spender?"

"Flu symptoms, darkened tongue, the virus' signature, but not as severe. She needed hospitalization, flu treatment, fluids and rest. Blood work was negative for the virus, maybe just because of concentration. She was discharged in a week."

The director nodded and continued, "In any case, the archaeological site has been shut down. It has been washed with antibacterials and antivirals, closed and sealed, and is under heavy guard." A picture of the site, surrounded with barbed wire and yellow tape, appeared on the screen.

The director nodded at a technician and a city map of Austin appeared. "Here's the Austin hospital and its outbreak cluster. The red zone, about a ten-block area, has been evacuated and disinfected or burned. We have surrounded the red area with a ten block yellow area, with quarantine procedures strictly enforced and round-the-clock sentries. But over here," he pointed to red dots a mile to the west, "well outside the quarantine boundary, is what really scares us. These people have no known connection to the hospital."

Several people spoke at once, and the director gestured to one. "Dr. Robbins, do you have any theory about how the virus could have jumped the isolation barriers?"

"One possibility is that the pathogen can survive indefinitely in an airborne droplet and infects on inspiration or skin contact. Gary, can you help?"

Spender stood slowly, nodding. "That's correct. And the violent cough seems designed to propel a large volume of small-particle aerosol pathogen. We now mask all patients as well as staff. We also found a correlation between relative humidity and propagation. The outbreak occurred during a rare hour or two of nearly one hundred percent relative humidity, and it was directly downwind."

"What evidence do you have that indicates that the infection is more likely viral than bacterial?"

Spender continued, "Our lab has a quantity of acute-phase blood serum drawn from victims. They have attempted to amplify the pathogen adequately for electron microscopy, and they have some microscope images that show a tiny nail-shaped form, certainly a virus. Primitive, a half strand of DNA, but almost absurdly simple, less than a quarter of the size of Ebola."

Dr. Teppin spoke from his screen, "Is that it, then? An Ebola strain?"

Robbins answered, "Possibly, or a hantavirus-like relative, except it looks like the ancestor of Ebola or Hantavirus instead of an evolutionary successor. But that may be consistent with an etiology in which this virus was active in ancient Maya civilization but was eventually nearly exterminated by its own success as its hosts died. This is unsubstantiated conjecture, of course, but the mummified occupant of the tomb in the Yucatán showed some evidence of a severely swollen tongue."

The room quieted again as the delegates searched for reasonable options. The President's Chief of Staff spoke from his screen, resonant voice echoing, startlingly loud. "Well, what the hell are we going to do? Does the human race have to die out to kill this sucker again? Somebody give me the worst-case scenario."

The director's brow furrowed. "Dr. Teppin?"

"Worst case? You would like worst case," said Teppin, bending his head down and covering his eyes, talking so softly the delegates seemed to stop breathing to absorb his words. "Worst case, this makes the Black Plague look like a head cold. In five weeks, the disease engulfs Austin. We close the airport and barricade the roads, but too late. The media sensationalizes the virus, not that it isn't sensational enough, and panicky Texans slip through the quarantine barriers despite shoot-on-sight orders to the National Guard.

"The government considers a thermonuclear drop but waits too long. By the time approval is received, there are carriers in half of our major cities. But we don't know which cities they are, so we would have to kill most of our population to stop the disease. This, unfortunately, turns out to be politically unacceptable.

"A second outbreak in Mexico evades the Pan American Health Organization's cordon and creates a parallel bloom through Mexico and Central America. We are unable to find an antiviral or a treatment. Russia and China meet together and consider joint thermonuclear strikes, but, even combined, do not have enough warheads for adequate containment.

"Governments quickly collapse and urban violence begins to kill more people than the disease. Then, as you say, we kill the virus as its host dies out, except for tiny residues of pathogen which may survive in the desiccated corpus of victims interred in humid climates, or protected by heavy tombs."

The man on the WHO screen abruptly stood up, knocking several items on his desk to the floor, and moved off-camera.

"Hopefully, several pockets of humanity survive, maybe on isolated islands or near the poles. In a few millennia the survivors repopulate the earth and the cycle begins again."

After a long silence the Chief of Staff said, "I wish I hadn't asked. How come it's more serious this time than the Maya thing?"

"The Maya thing was fairly serious, it destroyed their civilization. We have several complicating factors, particularly our superior mobility. I'm assuming that we will confirm the pathogen as a virus, and the virus droplet-borne, and Dr. Spender's humidity thesis makes sense. Then propagation would be more efficient in areas of high humidity like southeastern U.S., less efficient in the dryer Yucatán, the coastal plains of Texas and the U.S. West. Curious, no? In this model, the virus prefers wet days to propagate but prefers dryness to incubate after killing its hosts.

"In any case, the Yucatán geography could have acted as a natural barrier. The western deserts would act as a similar barrier if our population weren't so confoundedly mobile."

"What would you recommend, Dr. Teppin?" asked the director.

"I'm not an epidemiologist, so you are free to disregard this. Sacrifice Texas and a slice of northern Mexico. Draw a line through the sand. Bring in half of the National Guard and the armed forces to maintain the cordon. Shoot down departing aircraft."

"Good Lord, Teppin," snarled the Chief of Staff. "Condemn ten million people to a horrible lingering death? That is absurd."

"I suppose a thermonuclear drop would be more humane, but the full quarantine at least gives them a chance at life."

Robbins picked up the microphone again. "For obvious reasons, we have not invited the media today. We will release a carefully worded press release this afternoon, presenting a more optimistic scenario. You are all instructed to avoid making any public statements. Doctor Teppin, do you have any less-dramatic suggestions?"

Teppin spun his wheelchair, appearing in profile as he looked out a window. The delegates in Atlanta saw with him the first big slow snowflakes of an early Boston snowstorm. "Discover an antiviral. We'll need to be very good and very lucky. Another long shot would be to discover a previously developed antiviral."

Many delegates shouted at once and the director distilled their questions. "What are you talking about, Teppin?"

Teppin looked back into his camera and one corner of his mouth pulled up a fraction of an inch. "Such a long shot that I do not dare to give you any details now, except to say that it should not be considered as a viable option, just a little entertainment for a nearly-extinct biologist and a promising young scientist. But I would like to ask for a little nominal funding for this project, say a hundred fifty thousand now and twice that within a few weeks."

"With no other explanation? Preposterous," said the Director.

"Give it to him," said the Chief of Staff, gesturing to someone off-camera. "President's discretionary fund. We'll need a reasonably accurate accounting, of course."

"Of course," said Teppin.

Gary Spender watched this interchange with a wry smile. Even after the careful explanation, they didn't get it. They couldn't handle reality, so they retreated back to the comfort of reasonably accurate accounting. He wondered how long money would be a meaningful concept as he grabbed his bag and headed for the airport. Austin's Meacham International was still operating, but George Hapwell Theslie had scheduled its shutdown for noon tomorrow.

Chapter 9

R obert Asher moved the joystick and his viewpoint moved with it. He jockeyed up to a decorated wall covered with symbols and admired the flowing, complex, almost amusing design of the glyphs. Whoever designed this language was more interested in art than in economy of representation. He lifted the joystick handle and soared into space. The breath left his lungs. He regained control and arranged a soft landing on the top of the big pyramid. The view was spectacular. The city's architecture was like the written language, with more attention to aesthetics than to efficiency.

Just below him the priest was laying out a selection of sharp implements and a limp, glassy-eyed young woman was being tied to a marble table. Robert jetted away and flew down to the marketplace, a large open square at the periphery of the city clogged with vendors of fruits and vegetables, jewelers with objects of jade and basalt and obsidian, and women with sacks of provisions over their shoulders. He was astonished with the detail of the scene. It was obviously computer-generated, as the faces when they moved broke up into triangles, blocky three-dimensional representations, and the motion was a little jerky, but it was miles better than any other virtual reality trip he had taken. He removed the helmet and snapped back to actual reality.

"Very impressive," he said, handing her the helmet. "Spectacular graphics. Who did this?"

"Isn't that excellent?" said Teresa. "Some of our people and some computer graphics guys at MIT are working on it."

"Where were we? You were in the middle of their history. Was that a religious ceremony on the pyramid? It looked like it was going to get bloody."

"Yes, well, the priests convinced the hoi polloi that only the priests could keep the gods in control, and they needed high temples to do it because the gods were way up there. The first Mexican culture to make their mark, edifice-wise, was the Olmec. They built massive monuments, they designed a calendar, and they drew hieroglyphics and created some truly beautiful art, elegant jade sculpture. They invented the concept of zero before the fifth-century Hindu and well before twelfth century Europe. The big city was Teotihuacán." She gestured to the wall. "There's an artist's reconstruction. The main street was the Avenue of the Dead, one hundred fifty feet wide, two miles long. The architecture, the use of space, the forms and angles were spectacular, the Romans should have seen it. The Pyramid of the Sun was over two hundred feet high. A quarter of a million people lived in Teotihuacán."

"What happened to them?"

"The Maya took over around AD three hundred. Their big city was Tikal, it has an even larger pyramid. The Maya were expert in math, astronomy, and physics. But they were pretty violent. Human sacrifice was popular as a way to placate the angry gods. Then they became warlike and their civilization started to deteriorate, with each city ruled by warriors and at war with its neighbors. And then the Maya sort of disappeared. About AD nine hundred, they all started abandoning the cities. Nobody knows why, but the consensus is a major war or agricultural failure of some kind. What was left of the Maya civilization was decimated by the Spanish Conquest, and by the new diseases the conquerors brought with them."

"Maybe we have some more clues, now," said Robert. "It looks as if the Austin virus is easily the deadliest killer in history, potentially much worse than the Black Plague. They're trying to keep it confined to Austin, but if it breaks out we all could be in trouble unless a cure is found. If the Austin virus was really in Maya

Mexico in the ninth century, that could have been the reason the Maya died off."

"But I thought they had an antiviral, if you read the glyph correctly."

"After they identified a candidate antiviral charge image, they would need to synthesize the drug. Or maybe they could have found it occurring naturally in the rain forest. But they'd need a high enough quantity to treat millions of people. The timing, or the production schedule, may have been such that the antiviral saved only ten or fifteen percent of the population. Or, from what you tell me about the culture being unfriendly, they may have withheld the cure to teach their enemies a lesson."

"Makes sense."

"Teresa," said Robert. "To change the subject slightly, I need a Maya expert to join an expedition to Mexico, the Yucatán, to track down these glyphs. Do you think you might be interested?"

"Just science? I have a jealous boyfriend."

Robert felt his mood slip down a notch or two. Boyfriend. Damn.

"But he might let me go, if I call him a lot and if it's not just you and me on the expedition. His name is Armand. He'll probably want to meet you. He might want to go with us, except he really hates the heat."

"Well, tell him I'm no threat, I have a girlfriend." Robert grinned at her, trying to sell the lie. "And we'll have at least one more field person, hopefully a local. If it's OK with Armand, what do you think?"

She nibbled on an orange pencil and looked at him with her disturbing blue-purple eyes as if she understood all of his faults. Could she read him this easily? Was this entire concept ridiculous?

"What's your actual position at B.U.?" she said, finally.

"Confusing. My undergrad degree is in physics, my grad studies in molecular biology. Then I got into electronics and instrumentation. They call me a staff scientist, but I think they use me for anything confusing that nobody else wants to do. Our department does industrial consulting, mostly for the biotech firms."

"All the glyphs in Uxmal have been photographed. I have prints. Why go there?"

"Are there enough untranslated glyphs so we could maybe find the medical references we need from the photos?"

She thought a minute. "I don't think so. But what do you expect to find down there?"

"I'm not sure. But the stakes are high, and it's a new angle. Maybe the fact that we're looking for a medical history will give us a different slant on translating the unknown glyphs."

She nodded agreement. "Would we fly down? I haven't flown in a while. I guess driving down would take too long, though?"

"Probably four days instead of four hours. Is flying a problem for you?"

"I hope not. Maybe. Have to get through it. Fear of flying. No, wait, more like fear of crashing. No, fear of the thirty seconds between when the plane stops flying and starts crashing. Behaving in an unfeminine manner. Screaming a lot."

"What about if I promised not to tell anyone?"

"I don't know, I suppose it might be all right. I'd have to check with my boss. I can probably get away right now. Can your project pay for it? We don't have much funding. Can I take some photos for my manuscript? How long would we be gone?"

"I think I can get funded. We'd need to spend a day or two in one of the coastal cities putting a team together and collecting equipment. I guess the Austin virus is scaring the pants off everyone in the medical field and funds are available for any long shot program. I don't know how long we'd be gone, maybe a couple of weeks."

"I hardly ever get offered all-expense-paid trips to Mexico. Sign me up, I think. Provided, of course, Armand is OK with it. And my boss; I'll find out." She glanced out the window. "Another thing. Dark is happening outside. The official quitting hour is happening inside. We could grab some of these books and walk down to the Square for some latté. Or something else trendy. While I fill you in on Maya history."

"Done. Is Sam Adams trendy?"

Teresa stood and pulled a selection of books from the wall and filled a nylon shoulder bag. Robert admired the pleasant curves under the white slacks. Armand, huh? Well, who cares, she seems nervous, unapproachable. Sure knows the Maya, though.

"This should do. We'll continue your education in Ancient History 101."

• • •

The mis-named triangular-shaped Harvard Square was the center of social life for academic Cambridge. Teresa found an establishment with both latté and Sam Adams, not an easy task even in cosmopolitan Cambridge, and they spread out some books on a small table in the corner.

"Here's your homework, Robert Asher," she advised. "Von Daniken. Ancient spacemen invade earth. Did you know that the Roman-era Turks dug underground cities to escape the ancient spacemen? Total wild-eyed fantasy, but there are probably a few glimmers of truth hidden in the corners. And, heck, your whole project is a little fantastic. But interesting. Here's another potboiler, *Mysteries of the Ancient World*. It asks some interesting questions like" —she turned to the first page— "'Who carved the Great Sphinx, five thousand years before the Egyptian Kingdom?' and 'How did the gigantic stones get to Stonehenge?' and, of course 'How did the primitive Easter Islanders move twenty-five-ton statues onto pedestals constructed hundreds of years earlier?' Or the weight award, six hundred ton stones at Baalbek?"

"Tell me."

"Same thesis. Same explanation. Those old guys were smart. Why do we have the arrogance to assume civilization and intelligence and knowledge all follow an upward curve, with us at the pinnacle? We're finding more and more evidence of early civilizations with spectacular achievements, all blown away by earthquakes, tidal waves, meteorites, or diseases. In the more scholarly tradition, we have Coe's *Breaking the Maya Code*. Read all of these, there may be a quiz."

"Those first two don't look particularly scientific."

"You bring me a fantastic story about Maya microscopes, you get science fiction. Besides, we don't have a clear direction, right? We need to keep our options open, throw a big net."

"Tell me about the glyphs."

"We've been working on a translation for a while. The early linguists who were trying to translate Maya glyphs would always start by assuming they were pictographs, picture-writing. Chinese has a few pictographs, like the character *shan*, mountain, which looks like a three-peaked mountain. But try to write, say, 'you can't really mean it' in pictographs. It doesn't work."

"Makes sense. What does work?"

"Well, these linguists thought written languages all evolved from pictographs to ideographs, symbols representing ideas, to the final evolution which was phonetics, symbols representing the sounds of the spoken language. Letters in the written English language more or less represent the sounds of the spoken language. Early linguists made the usual error of assuming that because the old guys were old they weren't smart, and they got stuck trying to decode the Maya language as pictographs. But it turns out that almost all known writing is phonetic, or mostly phonetic.

"When did they start translating Maya? Did somebody find a Rosetta stone, like the Egyptian hieroglyphics?" he asked, trying not to look at her disturbing eyes.

"It wasn't that easy. People have been trying to translate Maya since 1850. Hundreds of people helped, using the stone carvings and a few tree-bark books, codices. For a hundred years they went down blind alleys, but starting in 1970 or so, they started to make some good progress. In comparison, the Egyptian hieroglyphics were translated by one person in about ten years. It's not that the Maya inscriptions were any more difficult, just that the hieroglyphic translator had a better dictionary to work with and he didn't get caught in blind alleys."

"This has all been fairly recent, then."

"The civilization was missing, for a while. When the Maya Empire collapsed in the eleventh century, it returned to jungle. Then a Spanish Dragoon rediscovered Palenqué in the eighteenth century. He sent back a report with engravings of Maya art and writing, and it got more explorers started. They cleared trees, excavated some buildings, and brought back more examples of the writing, including codexes, books written on flattened tree-bark. More people joined the effort to translate. The calendar was translated pretty quickly, and the number system, and the writing was correctly thought to be a chronicling of the history of the Maya. And a lot of the glyphs were pictographs, like the glyph for a king would be a pictograph so even the common people could read it. But not much progress was made on translating the bulk of the glyphs."

"Why not?"

"Tricky. Finally in the 1970s, the researchers started to crack the language. By then, there were more than a hundred people working on the problem."

"Pretty good crowd."

"Then in 1980, some American explorers discovered a huge cave system down near the border with Belize. The ancient Maya thought caves were the entrance to the Underworld, a place to be feared and respected. The caves were the homes of the Xibalban, the lords of death. And they may have been right, one young archaeologist was killed by a lightning bolt on a pyramid in Chichén Itzá just after exploring Maya caves."

"Did the Americans get zapped by the lords of death, too?" Robert asked.

"Well, no, actually. They found that the caverns were covered with glyphs and murals and made some major contributions to the translation. In the decade of the eighties, the percentage of properly translated glyphs went from twenty percent to eighty percent, and since then we've picked up another ten percent or so." She glanced at her watch. "Half past ten already. Time to call it a night."

"Thanks, this has been helpful. I'm starting to think that the Maya could really have developed the charge microscope."

"I continue to think you're seriously sanity-challenged."

"But you'll go, right? You think?"

"I think. I'd like to get some pictures. I'll help with your translation until it hits a dead end. Don't tell anybody what we're doing, the department already thinks I'm missing an oar or two."

Chapter 10

Robert, freshly showered after his morning commute, trotted up three flights of stairs and knocked on Dr. Teppin's office door.

"Good morning, come on in, sit down. Good, we have to do some planning. I guess you hit it off with Dr. Welles, she just called me to see if you were an axe murderer or anything."

"You didn't give me away, did you? She's still coming?"

"Hmmm, do I detect a shade of concern in your voice?"

"Well, she does seem to be perfect for the job. She knows the Maya language."

"She did tell me that she was coming." Robert felt as if the queen of the senior prom had accepted his invitation to the dance.

Teppin unfolded a laptop computer from an arm of his wheelchair. "Did you see my new toy? It has a high-resolution display, GPS navigation and mapping, and high-speed wireless Net access. One excellent thing that happened with this computer revolution, wheelchair life got much more interesting."

"How long have you been in a wheelchair?"

"Since I was twenty. Traffic light on Route Two. The truck that hit our car never even slowed down; the driver was asleep. We went from a family of four to a family of one half in a millisecond. The next year, they made the traffic light into an overpass."

"I can't think what it must have been like, the loss."

Teppin thought for a minute, his eyes far away. "It was a bad year. A bad decade. Better, now. You live in Boston, do you not?"

"Yes, well, third-floor apartment in Brighton."

"You are unmarried, right?"

"Right."

"Engaged?"

"Nope, not even close. I've dedicated my life to science, at least until I meet Mrs. Right."

"That did not happen yesterday, hmmm?"

"She is impressive. But she made a point about having a serious boyfriend. I think I made her nervous."

Teppin gazed out the window in silence for a moment. "I have seen you running on the Esplanade. You are fast. I used to run on the Concord High School track team. Now I run sometimes when I dream."

"I do about twenty miles a week, when everything's working. It's my favorite way to commute."

"Yes. Stick with it. Do a few miles for me. One other thing. Normally, a field trip like this would require communications to home base on about a bi-weekly schedule. But I would like to tie you in more tightly, and use both video and audio communications."

"How would it work?"

"I have a camera, a microphone, and a speaker on my computer. If we give you a portable Net video camera and a microphone and speaker, I can look through your eyes, listen through your ears. Run with you."

"How big would it be?"

"About this big," said Teppin, pulling a black box with shoulder straps, about the size of a dictionary, out from under his chair. "The latest thing from PictureTel. It has a remotely positionable camera, so I can look around, and a steerable microphone. It has lithium ion batteries that last twenty hours between charges."

"How does it connect?"

"There is a 650 MHz radio link to the central station, it has about an eight mile range. You can also take a few of these radio intercom headsets on the same frequency, so if there's a group of you that needs to keep in touch they wear them."

"How does the central station get hooked up? Phone line?"

"Too slow. The central station communicates by satellite. It is about the size of a breadbox. The central station is, I think the satellite is bigger. You kids know how big a breadbox is?"

"About the size of a computer monitor, sir?"

"Right. Just pull out the antenna, plug it in, and set it up with a view of the southern sky. Electronics does the rest. When are you leaving?"

"Day after tomorrow, I think. If Teresa's OK with it."

"Teresa?"

"Dr. Welles."

"Have a nice flight. And have good luck. Very good luck."

Chapter 11

Cancún, October 27, present day

Robert and Teresa were settled in on the tenth floor of the three-hundred-room Hotel de Finca at Cancún. The hotel featured four bars and five pools. It was located on the narrow, hotel-infested strip of sand separating the lagoon from the sea. The airplane had deposited them at the Cancún airport two hours earlier, and they had agreed to go out for dinner at 7:00. Teresa checked out her wardrobe to see if it had survived the trip. She slipped on the white linen dress and inspected the fit critically in the mirror. The new Teva sandals seemed like the appropriate footwear.

She opened the door to Robert's knock. He was wearing a nice smile, a Hawaiian shirt featuring angular green parrotfish over a bright red coral sea, khaki shorts, shaggy dark hair, and sandals. Sort of a nice face, all angles but good looking, with smile lines around his eyes. Pale white feet, but what would you expect in the middle of winter? He'd need number fifteen suntan oil for a few days. She checked her own feet; they looked as if she'd been on the beach for weeks. It was good to have a little ethnicity in your genetic makeup.

Teresa glanced again at his shirt, squinted, dug into her bag, and slipped on a pair of sunglasses.

They strolled down the strip. The sea breeze had turned onshore and carried the exotic smell of burning steer beef and rotting tropical vegetation with perhaps a trace of trash fire. Big hotels competed for the weirdest shape: gigantic wastebaskets with windows, fake Maya pyramids, fifteen-story airplane propellers. They lined up to present their attractions, lots of neon, more like Vegas than she had expected. Air-conditioned taxis and stretch limos eased the rich and famous from the hotels to Planet Hollywood, The Flamingo, and Carlos O'Brian's.

They walked a mile or two in silence, footsteps scrunching the white sand drifting off the beach, passing vacationers in sandals and beach wear and pale or pink skin, watching the sunset redden and darken across the lagoon, and listening to the variety of sounds and music coming from the bars and restaurants.

They chose a quiet Mexican restaurant called Chihuahua, set back from the road, apparently constructed entirely of wicker and partial-ly hidden by the broad gray-green leaves of huge dusky green aloe plants. Teresa was captivated by the warmth of the breeze on her bare skin, the colors, the sounds, and the feeling of relaxation, of freedom.

Inside the restaurant, a dozen wicker tables were almost filled. The wicker motif extended to the walls and ceiling. Teresa discovered the menu, cleverly painted on small wooden canoe paddles, and they ordered the Carta Blanca cerveza, Chiles Rellendos, the enchiladas, and the stuffed Jalapeno peppers to ward off respiratory illnesses.

"This town is pretty cool," she said. "It looks just like the post-cards. We didn't get to see the coast, when I was here before. The turquoise water, I thought that was fake, like the Chamber of Commerce painted it or something. And this restaurant. There's no back wall. They'll be in big trouble if it snows."

"I think the temperature extremes are seventy-nine to eighty-one degrees," he said. "Big savings on snow shovels and heating."

"I think I'll move down here permanently. Time to get back to work. Did you bring the books?" she asked.

"I just unpacked 'em. Read 'em all."

"Quick read, huh? How'd you like the pseudoscience? Forgive my departure from academic tradition by including Von Danikin, but I think pseudoscience is what this project needs."

"Questionable scientific methodology."

"I think his main contribution to science is loosening up people's heads," she said. "Big science is ruled by cautious old guys that don't jump onto new bandwagons. You're not a cautious old guy, are you?"

"Not too cautious, anyway. But go back a few dozen centuries for me," he said. "If we're going to trace this glyph, we need to get into their heads, 1200 years ago. How did the Egyptians manage to build those big pyramids in Egypt? I saw a TV program a few weeks ago that explained how impossible it was. Maybe if we had some sense of how they could throw up a five hundred foot pyramid with two hundred ton stone blocks, we'd get some hints about how the ancient Maya could throw together a charge microscope."

"If we only knew. There are dozens of ideas, but for every idea there's somebody who explains why it couldn't work. One mistake everybody makes is to think that modern civilization must be better because we obviously have more knowledge than the ancients. But that's only because civilization, after the invention of writing and then the invention of the printing press, finally got a way to build up and save knowledge, and the process—the information—fed on itself."

"Those old guys weren't dumb," he said. "I'll get it, sooner or later."

"Well, yes, I was thinking about information rather than intelligence, but that, too. Human beings are getting taller, over millennia, but there's no data that says we're getting any smarter. And, historically, because of the lack of record-keeping tools, things kept getting invented and forgotten. The Sumerians of eight thousand BC knew that the earth was round and knew that the planets orbited the sun. Then, almost ten thousand years later, Galileo reinvented that particular wheel and got clobbered for it because everybody knew we were the center of the universe, not some hick backwater in the galactic boonies."

"That TV show said the Great Pyramid was built around twenty-six-hundred BC, using more than six million tons of stone," said Robert. "Its design needed really advanced geometry, surveying, geology, and physics. They said that the architects knew the Fibonacci series and pi. There are all sorts of astronomical connections in the pyramid: the Diagonal Gallery is at the exact angle of the North Star. The craftsmanship was superb, Herodotus in four-forty BC said that the limestone facing was polished to a mirror surface and the stone was so accurately cut that the joints couldn't be seen from an arm's length away."

"Herodotus was notoriously nearsighted," guessed Teresa.

"They were impressed that the typical modern large building sinks an inch or two a year, but in nearly five thousand years the pyramid has sunk less than half an inch. There are long passages accurate to the thickness of a playing card. A modern contractor would laugh at you if you asked for these specifications for a building, and if you were willing to pay through the nose for that kind of accuracy, he'd use laser surveying tools. Do you suppose they had laser surveying tools?"

"I doubt it," said Teresa. "But I bet they had some ingenious tools that we haven't guessed. That's the key for the Maya to have invented your microscope, right? We have to guess at the ingenious tools they could have invented that got lost when their civilization disintegrated. Not that I believe for a moment that they did, you understand, I'm just trying my willful suspension of disbelief."

She started to wonder if he could actually be correct. No, the Maya could no more have invented a charge microscope, the way Robert described the device, than the Egyptians could have invented the laser rangefinder. Astronomy, agriculture, medicine: she could see the Maya making some unexpected advance in these sciences, but not microscopes. Probably. She sipped her margarita and asked herself again what she was doing down here.

"Robert? Can I ask a personal question?"

"Try me."

"What's your motivation, as they say in actor's class? I don't exactly get it. You build this neat new microscope and then abandon it, let other people finish the development. What are you doing in Mexico instead of back in the lab in the US?"

"The virus, it's moving too fast. We could finish the design, learn how to use the microscope to analyze the virus structure, and lose the war. And there's people working on it that will be better than me. Our best chance to save lives is the research that must have been done twelve hundred years ago."

She nodded slowly in agreement, almost starting to believe him. But how could the ancient Maya have that sort of technology? But if they did, they might well learn something. And a slim chance was worth pursuing. She had been following the unstoppable progress of the virus on television.

As they finished dinner a band started to set up shop around the upright piano in the corner, positioned safely away from any sprinkles of wind-driven rain slanting in from the ocean. Rain was not a hazard tonight, as the clouds had disappeared, leaving a dusting of stars and the low moon reflecting off the ocean like a motel-room painting on black velvet.

Teresa checked out the musicians: piano, Fender bass, drums, and tenor sax. The drummer didn't bring a full trap set, just snare, tom, and hi-hat cymbal. The tenor player set up a vocal microphone feeding Bose 902 compact speakers. Two of the musicians looked like natives, but they weren't playing native instruments. They slid smoothly into a quiet version of a *De Nina A Mujer* with the sax player taking a turn at the vocal. He looked like a displaced New Yorker who didn't want to go back to Wall Street. But he should stick to the sax, she thought, as she hummed along with the familiar lyrics.

"Hey, you can sing, too!" said Robert. "Grab the microphone from that amateur. Where did you learn music? Do you play any instruments?"

"My father plays jazz piano, weekends, with a group like this," she answered. "They play all the old stuff. I used to sing with his band, when I was real young, like high school. But I wasn't really all that good, and I gave it up for science. Ah, the things I do for science."

"Sing for me now?" he asked.

"Maybe after three or four drinks, and if everybody else leaves, and if the wind picks up so nobody can hear me."

The band played a tango, *Milonga,* with a little more spirit. I hope the sax player doesn't sing this one, she thought. I hope they play Julio Iglesias covers all night. I hope the night never ends and I never have to go back to work, maybe it will snow like crazy, no school tomorrow morning.

The waiter asked about the possibility of dessert, and they ordered, instead, the Cuervo Gold tequila on the rocks. It went down smoothly. They probably kept the good stuff for home. What the heck, she thought. I don't get to Cancún that often, who'll know? She sipped on her drink and began to calculate the possibility that anybody from Harvard would walk in if she sang a song or two. C'mon, bigmouth, nobody cares. Her stomach tightened as she realized that she was going to ask the band if she could sing with them. Can I do this? They were finishing up *No vengo no voy*, maybe they *were* going to play Iglesias all night. She knew every song he wrote. Oh, might as well, how bad could it be?

"Excuse me a moment," she said, rising, holding the table to assist her balance, "I have to consult with my new backup band." He grinned up at her, nodding in agreement. She walked up to the sax player, conscious of many eyes tracking her.

"Hi," he said. "Play something for you?"

"Possibly. Do you happen to know *Besame mucho*?"

"Sure. No problem. We wrote it."

"Umm, does the key of F appeal to you?" she asked.

"That's the usual key."

"Ummmmm, can I borrow the microphone for a minute?"

"Aha, Karaoke night at the Chihuahua." He handed her a microphone.

"Sí," she said, "About like this." She took the microphone and tapped a measure, choosing a slow beat.

The piano played a few chords and she felt the knot in her stomach change into butterflies. Her mouth was dry. Could you still sing with a dry mouth? Sure couldn't spit, if she had to. What the hell is a girl like me doing in a place like this, all tippy from tequila? Straying a long way from her plan, for one thing. Marry a Harvard professor, settle down in Cambridge, author razor-sharp enunciations of previously unsuspected correlations, have two point seven kids and a dog. No, just have the kids, *buy* the dog. She really hadn't done any singing in a long time, except in the shower. Would it still work? Would all the words come back? She stayed facing the band, not wanting to look at the room, feeling awkward and vulnerable.

The band finished an eight bar intro and she started singing, tentatively, holding the microphone well away from her mouth, "Besame, besame mucho, como Si fuera esta noche la ultima vez..."

It still worked. She nailed the pitch, something her father's band had always thought remarkable. The sax player smiled with encouragement or maybe relief. After a few phrases she felt comfortable enough singing into the microphone to bend the tempo a little. She heard her own voice for the first time in ten years through the good speaker system, richened with a little electronic reverb, the voice a little huskier, more breathy than before. Jeez, it still worked, actually the voice sounded more mature, it seemed to fit the song better. The words all came back. The butterflies disappeared. She felt the band's response to her singing, felt the bass player fit the bass line in a little tighter, felt the piano player give her the nice comfortable cushion of the old chords, not waiting for her but keeping the tempo himself, the way she liked.

She closed her eyes and turned to the room and thought about the meaning of the words instead of the pitch and the rhythm, "Que tengo miedo a perderte, perderte despues?"

Then she listened with her body quiet and her pulse slowing, eyes still closed and her head bent down, the microphone held loosely in both hands with arms relaxed, extended down, while the sax soloed, playing with the chords himself, repeating her time shifts, mimicking her breathy delivery, and then leading her back to the chorus.

She finished the chorus and sang a four bar tag slowly, and then another tag *a tempo*. The band followed her lead like a good dancer, and as she let the last note linger for an extra few beats the sax played the sixth above, holding it with her.

She hadn't noticed when the room had gotten quiet, but as the note faded she opened her eyes again to see if everyone had left. The first thing she saw was Robert, with his mouth hanging open, a shocked look on his face. Then the applause burst upon her like a bomb. People had stopped eating and were turned towards her. The response frightened her; I can't let this happen, I can't be good at this. I'm a scientist, this isn't what I want. Then she became calmer as she realized that it was under her control, really. She could enjoy singing if she wanted. Other people could enjoy it with her. It would be all right.

"Holy cow, lady," said the sax player.

She turned and smiled, murmuring "Thanks," as she handed him the microphone. He held up both hands, palms forward; he wouldn't take it.

The piano player stood up and said, "Gringo, if you don't do another song, we'll play nothing but the Mexican Hat Dance until you leave. How long are you down here for? Want a job?"

"Well, does everybody know *Un Poco de Amor*? Key of C?" she asked. "No, wait, take it down to B flat, my voice seems to have gotten lower in my old age." A little love. That might not be a bad idea, she thought, looking at Robert, wondering how it would be to feel his hands on her naked flesh, how it would be to wake up in his arms.

But there was so much stuff in the way—why couldn't she just clear away the baggage of the last ten years and start fresh? She should maybe be more like Robert, he didn't seem to need security or any kind of plan for *his* life. He just needed a challenge, the more impossible the better.

The sax player intruded, "You want to do the verse?"

"Please."

She again set a slow tempo, breathing the lyrics into the microphone, "Hoy es un dia de aquellos, en que miro hacia el cielo..."

After one slow chorus the drummer put down the brushes he had been using all evening and picked up a set of sticks, and as the sax soloed he changed the beat to an insistent bolero rhythm which carried them through the final vocal chorus. Teresa, eyes closed again, felt moved by the music, by the tropics, by a feeling of change and growth. She felt unexpected tears on her cheeks as she finished the song.

She sat down as Robert's cell phone beeped. He keyed it to receive and listened for a moment, then said, "Hold on a second, Gary. Dr. Welles is here also, and she'll want to hear this too." He turned on the speaker and told her, "Dr. Gary Spender, from Austin."

"Sorry to call so late, but we've been out straight. I don't know if you heard, but there's definitely a racial bias in the morbidity statistics. If you have Maya ancestry, your chances of dying in the first two weeks go from over ninety-nine percent to eighty-five percent."

After a second's pause, Robert said, "And you said the virus looks like a precursor of Ebola. As if the Maya may have been exposed, maybe at the time they cut that glyph into the stone, and they still carry the antibodies."

"That's right."

"That tells me two things. The chance that we can help just went from zip point nothing to maybe fifty-fifty. And we better get the hell out of this restaurant and get back to work."

"Thanks, Robert. Good luck."

Chapter 12

Cartegena, October 27, present day

Ernesto Raoul Porfirio Diaz caressed the sleek dorsal curve of the torpedo as he had caressed, only an hour earlier, the sleek ventral flanks of Rosa Garcia, his current favorite. Ernesto chuckled in his throat as he made the connection, but he knew that if he needed to choose between Rosa and the torpedo, he would surely choose the torpedo. As a lover it was useless, but as a mechanical business partner it was more than spectacular, saving him from losing twenty-five million US to the D.E.A. in the last three months alone.

Ernesto was the proud holder of a diploma in the best engineering school in Medellin, el Universidad Flotin, and shared that fact freely with anyone who spent more than five consecutive minutes in conversation with him. And he had, in fact, a certain talent for the field.

His torpedo, El Remora, was named after the remora eel that hitchhikes on sharks to feed on the crumbs of the host's meal. It had a capacity of seven-fifty kilos of heroin, six-eighty kilos of cocaine, or three hundred kilos of marijuana. When fully loaded with heroin, a single Remora's contents was worth between sixty and eighty-five million US to the brokers in the States, nearly two hundred million to the mid-level distributors.

El Remora was two feet in diameter and twenty feet in length, and it was curved and tapered to contours chosen after many hours in the university towing tank so that it would cut cleanly and noiselessly through the water and place minimum stress on its magnetic attachment sucker. It was designed to mate with a steel-hulled boat, ideally a big tanker or freighter over four hundred feet in length for proper match to the hull curvature.

Ernesto had designed the attachment mechanism himself. It used a powerful neodymium magnet to clamp to the steel, with its pull modulated by an electromagnet. The electromagnet was carefully controlled with a capacitive sensor to provide a soft landing, since a metallic *clang* would alert the ship's crew. El Remora was later released from the hull by momentarily nulling the magnet's field with a current pulse.

In operation, El Remora was filled with cargo near the processing plants in the hills, locked and sealed and booby-trapped, and trucked to the dock area at Cartegena. There, El Remora was attached to a minisub. The freight coordinator would dispatch the minisub to rendezvous with an unsuspecting northbound tanker, match speeds, and latch El Remora to the tanker hull at a point well below the unladen waterline, but not so low as to be in danger of being scraped off if the tanker's captain miscalculated the depth of a reef.

El Remora emitted an ELF, Extra Low Frequency, radio pulse at a frequency of twenty kHz at ten minute intervals. This pulse was tracked by RDF receivers operated by Ernesto's cartel on Andros, Grand Cayman, Elizabeth, New Jersey, and the town of Akumal, just south of Cancún on the Yucatán peninsula. When the tanker passed the destination port for its secret cargo, the RDF would send a powerful ELF coded response and El Remora would detach and sink to the sea bottom. Later, a cartel-operated yacht would be dispatched to the location and send the coded message causing El Remora to inflate an air bladder and ascend to the surface. There it would be tied with a hundred feet of line to the yacht, resubmerged, and towed to shore.

Ernesto was considering the redesign of the nosepiece of El Remora to add a parachute that would allow air drops. Boats were reliable, but slow. And the parachute would permit air pickup from the production facilities in the hills and allow drops to just outside the D.E.A.'s radar surveillance limits. The saving in inventory costs would be ten million US dollars per year.

Ernesto was proud of his design, which worked so well that of the fleet of fifty-five torpedoes only one had been lost, in a violent storm. He was prouder still of the English language lettering which he had had screen printed on the sides. The words were designed to discourage investigation in case El Remora was found attached to a ship or found waiting on the sea bottom for pickup.

DANGER
DO NOT DISTURB
U.S. Dept. of
Environmental Safety
Contents deadly poison
May be fatal if disturbed
If found, call 1-622-555-8212
$5000 REWARD
DANGER

The telephone number was connected through a series of relays to the Cartegena facility, where an English-speaking cartel employee was instructed to express heartfelt thanks, wire the reward, and get the location of the torpedo. Ernesto thought how really excellent it would be if somebody saved his drug-filled torpedo, thinking they were helping the government of the United States.

With a final loving pat on the torpedo's dorsal area, Ernesto walked through the windowless cinder block building that housed the cartel's transportation and distribution facility. He had risen rapidly to second in command by virtue of his cleverness at problem solving, his knowledge of English, and his skill at arranging unfortunate accidents for his competition. *El Jéfé*, Señor Ajuzar, was not even worth an accident, as he was so old and so afraid of the *Federales* that he was becoming totally ineffective, and all of the important operational decisions fell to Ernesto by default.

Ernesto walked up a flight from the storage basement into the large operations center. Here, on the ground floor, narrow windows looked out on the ocean and on the industrial district of Carteghena. They were the only occupants of the small building. A sign outside announced "Arquiera Industrial Waste Disposal" and in smaller letters "Beware of the Dogs." They were not often bothered with unwanted visitors, and the local police were well paid to keep distractions from law enforcement to a minimum.

Inside on the far wall was an inspirational poster that Ernesto had made:

"Each year, Americans spend thirty-eight billion dollars on cocaine, ten billion on heroin, and seven billion on marijuana. WE WANT IT ALL! Do your share."

A large wall-mount computer monitor showed the Atlantic Ocean, with the radio stations outlined in yellow and the paths of the active Remoras outlined in bright red. All the latest flat-panel computer displays, thought Ernesto. It really pays to have a large equipment budget. Nothing like working for a firm with a ninety-five percent pre-tax gross margin. And they didn't even pay taxes.

Two technicians saw Ernesto enter and straightened slightly at their consoles. "You!" Ernesto jabbed two fingers into the shoulder of one of the technicians. "Anything to report?"

"Nothing out of the ordinary, sir," said the man. "Number fourteen was with *Toshu Maru*, she is a Japanese tanker. Her cargo is Venezuelan heating oil heading for Elizabeth, New Jersey. She changed course unexpectedly for Fort Lauderdale, and we monitored the captain on the ship-to-shore radio. He said that one of the diesels had low oil pressure and as a precaution he was anchoring for repairs."

"Did you detach El Remora?"

"Yes, sir. Your orders are that no Remora gets near any ship repair facility. We detached in twenty fathoms off Miami, and the pickup has already been made by Jorge on *Bluefin*."

Bluefin, Ernesto knew, was a fifty-five-foot sport fishing boat out of Miami that did a lucrative charter business as cover. Jorge was sometimes angry when he was asked to give up a fishing party for company business. Jorge did not seem to have a proper work ethic. Jorge would someday need to be disciplined; perhaps Ernesto would attend to it himself. He needed the practice, it would not do to get rusty. He smiled to himself.

"Is *Bluefin* reattaching her to another host, or taking her north herself?" asked Ernesto.

"We could find no good carrier leaving soon, and the New York sales channels are almost out of product, so *Bluefin* is making the run, up the Intracoastal. She should be off the New Jersey coast in twenty-four hours, so the pickup rendezvous will not need to be altered."

Ernesto thought again that El Remora was almost too good to keep private. He could sell the torpedo to the other cartels, or franchise to the Asians—but the idea was, of course, senseless; more Remoras in use meant a larger chance of discovery by the D.E.A. But even discovery would probably not expose the operation, as the hidden fifteen-pound charge of plastic explosive would vaporize the torpedo, the cargo, and the person unfortunate enough to open the access hatch without using the correct sequence of bolt removal.

"What is the status of the inventory?" Ernesto asked. The technician punched up another computer screen showing the stockpiles of cargo at the warehouses in Cartegena and Tulum in Mexico. One of the advantages of El Remora was its dual use as warehouse storage, hidden on the sea bottom from visual sighting by its dark green color and hidden from magnetometer detection by its fiberglass construction. The Cartegena warehouse, in the basement of the computer building, was serviced by the minisub through an underground water passage. In Tulum an underwater cave was used, part of the thousand miles of unexplored underground aquifers that lay beneath the Yucatán peninsula on the Caribbean coast of Mexico.

Chapter 13

Uxmal, October 29, present day

In the morning, Robert and Teresa rented a battered VW van painted in several layers of different colors, fenders tied on with rusty coat hangers. It featured two extra tires, both inflated, and a dented five-gallon can full of water, and aside from a hissing noise from the motor and a pronounced pull to the left, it seemed to run well.

They packed up the communications gear, the laptop computer, a portable printer, a digital still camera, a camcorder, small-scale maps, drinking water, an assortment of fresh fruit, Imodium AD, and number fifteen sunscreen.

On the road, they checked the map and headed northwest to Uxmal to find the glyph that Robert had seen on his computer screen. Robert looked over at Teresa, her dark-skinned arm carelessly draped out the open window in the full rays of the sun. Her hair was drawn back from her face today. She wore a crisp professional white short-sleeved shirt and white shorts, making a nice contrast with the rich butterscotch tones of her skin. She looked absolutely wonderful.

"So, anyway," said Robert, feeling clumsy next to her control and coolness. "Tell me all about yourself."

"What's to tell? My career as a concert pianist, or all the World Cup skiing championships, or the Fulbright scholarship at eight?"

"No, really. You said you were born in Mexico?"

"Yep, pretty dull story, the visiting Harvard Ph.D. archeologist and the innocent young Spanish girl. No, that's unfair, my parents are neat people. My mother studied at the local equivalent of Harvard. I got my mother's hair and skin and my father's eyes. There was a bit of stress early on, she was Catholic and he was Baptist, but they worked out compromises—my mother named me after her favorite saint and sent me to her church, my father taught me Gospel music. I liked the music best."

"And you did your undergrad and graduate work at Harvard?"

"With those genes, I was a cinch. Then I guess I threw myself into my work—the Mesoamericans—probably trying to please my father, and I've always liked languages. I've been studying them mostly by remote control, though. Even though there's lots of photographs, it's going to be a kick being there again. This is only the second time I've been out of the U.S. since I was six. I've only been on a plane once, that trip to Uxmal."

"Ever been married?"

She gave him a sideways look with a little smile. "You first."

"Nobody ever asked."

"Same here. Armand might, though; I'm working on him. He doesn't talk much. What's your girlfriend like?"

Robert thought for a minute.

"Hard to describe?" she said.

"Well," he said. "Um. Actually, I don't have a girlfriend. But I didn't want you to worry about coming down here."

"You're not all that scary, Dr. Asher. The plane trip, that was scary. No girlfriend, huh? Other than that, what are you really like?"

"Really dull. Poor but honest family. College career featuring lots of part time jobs. Married for just about one year, but we did not meet each other's expectations. We parted friends, though. One daughter, Katie, living in Texas with mom and new dad, really neat kid, twelve years old. Maybe you'll get to meet her. My professional career features a long succession of near misses. I'm probably trying to please my father too, he was into winning, but I think I'd rather just compete. I sure would like to win this one, though."

"Where abouts in Texas? Your daughter?"

"Safe by a hundred miles in Houston. I don't feel really good about not being there, though."

Teresa thought about that for a minute, then said, "Maybe you can help her more here. How do you feel about this trip? Is it an academic boondoggle or does it have a chance of helping?"

"When I think of the Maya building microscopes and finding virus medicines and also leaving some record of the whole thing—a record that nobody's been able to find—I think it's a flagrant misuse of funding. When I talk to Dr. Spender, I get a sense that he believes in us. And then I think we're going to find the answer against all the odds."

She nodded.

• • •

About noon they stopped at a tiny store in the tiny town of Peto to restock their soft drink supply. As they were leaving, Robert tried to shift into first gear and produced instead a scream of protest from the transmission. He pumped the clutch and tried again more gently, to no better effect.

"Forget how to use a manual?" asked Teresa.

"It's the clutch. I thought it was getting a little low in the pedal."

"Major oops? Do you have AAA?"

"Better than that, I spent my entire youth in junk cars. Not to mention my old age." He turned off the engine, shifted into first, and started the engine in gear. The VW lurched forward. The synchro seemed to be in pretty good shape, he thought, as he matched revs to upshift, and there weren't a whole lot of traffic lights to worry about.

• • •

Six hours later, Robert pulled the VW into the dusty parking lot marked "Uxmal, Parking, No Buses." They joined a few dozen cars in the lot, and he patted the VW's dashboard affectionately. "Yeah," said Teresa. "Got us here. Good car."

"And we have a gallon or two of water left over."

"And you thought it was for the radiator. It was for us. Now we can wash the windshield or something."

"Not that it needs it."

"Maybe we should leave it buggy and take the windshield home with us. Any stateside entomologist would kill for these samples."

They unstuck their shirts from the vinyl upholstery and got out. Robert set the satellite communications module up on the roof rack of the van, clamping it to the rails to discourage any local satellite communications module thieves. He flipped the power switch on the portable unit.

Robert's portable conference unit sent an encoded radio message to the van's satellite transponder which bounced a radio signal off a low-orbit communication satellite to the dish on the roof of Teppin's building. It then traveled through the lab's Ethernet communications lines to the small transceiver in Teppin's office. The RF message was bounced to the receiver on Teppin's wheelchair, cueing the video camera to turn on and relay Teppin's voice and image through the reverse path to Robert's tiny television monitor. The loop was traversed with a one-second delay, and Dr. Teppin's image popped up on the small display screen.

"Robert. Good, I was wondering where you were. And you have Teresa with you, I see. Excellent." Robert heard the tiny whine as the little camera scanned around. "Does that sign say Uxmal, by any chance? You are early."

"The call of duty pulled us away from the beach. We are in the Uxmal parking lot, we just drove from Cancún. Would you like to walk around with us?"

"That would be excellent. I could use a little virtual warm weather and sunshine, it is quite cold and gray here."

Robert put his arms through the shoulder straps of the portable unit. "How's that, up there?"

"Perfect. I can see fine."

He grabbed a water bottle and they walked up the dusty path to the old city. The heat, without the wind of the van's passage, was like being clubbed in the back of the neck. The ocean breeze had no effect here and the temperature was ten degrees higher. Ugly rough-skinned iguanas sunned themselves on the rocks, how do they stand the heat? "Dr. T," he said, "Just so you get the full picture, the temperature here is about a hundred degrees, there's no wind, and the drinking water tastes like gasoline."

"Sometimes I rather prefer being handicapped," said the small voice from the speaker. "Step carefully, there. Don't drop me."

At the park entrance, just past the Kodak and Fuji Film sign competition and the soft drink vendors, a half dozen guides waited for business. Teresa consulted a spiral-bound notebook.

"One of the Harvard guys recommended a guide called Artoz. He's supposed to be a pretty serious student of the Maya."

"Anybody here know Artoz?" called Robert.

All six guides ran over, explaining the details of their intimate knowledge of Artoz. Most claimed that Artoz would in general prefer it if they were selected instead of he, as they were more humorous, more knowledgeable, more fluent in the English. One squat, dark-skinned man arrived a little late and spoke more quietly, but his story was more persuasive: he was Artoz.

Robert dismissed the others with some difficulty and asked Artoz if he was available, perhaps for an extended period of time. Artoz answered that he could indeed be had for an extended period, especially if the fee were commensurately extended. They shook hands and introduced themselves.

"Ah, scientists. I should give you a discount. Later I will ask my accountant if that is possible. Meanwhile, you are certainly in the best hands. Pleased to meet you. It is not often I can talk to somebody who cares about the Maya. And you are from Harvard, Teresa Welles? There is quite a good archaeology department at Harvard, I have read their papers many times. You are with that group? You could probably teach me about Uxmal. Are you to be called Dr. Welles?"

"I haven't done much work on Uxmal," she said, "Except look at the glyphs. I'm sure you can help us a lot. Call me Teresa."

"Artoz," said Robert, "You should also meet my boss, Dr. Edward Teppin. He's on my shoulder. Sort of." He indicated the three-inch screen showing Dr. Teppin's image.

"Good afternoon, Artoz," said Teppin.

"Caramba! Never before have I seen this."

"Saves airline tickets," said Teresa.

"OK, I take three people for the price of two. Special deal only today. My heart is soft, I think."

They walked up a narrow dirt path. The first building they came to was a huge gray rectangular structure. "The Nunnery," Artoz announced. "Although the Maya had no nuns. The early Spanish Conquistadores thought it looked like a nunnery and the name remains. Notice the carving: Chac the rain god, with a serpent. And here you will see a *stela*, the large stone that the Maya used to inscribe their complicated writing. Oh, but excuse me, you know this."

"Teresa," said Robert. "In the computer virtual reality pictures, these buildings were brightly colored, bright red and white."

"Yes," she said. "The original colors can be deduced from small chips of paint left in sheltered corners, here and there. But the paint is mostly gone, and the stone has weathered to this gray color."

"What do we have here? Training to be a Uxmal guide? Stealing all my secrets? Much prettier than I am, no fair?" asked Artoz.

"Artoz, we need your help with something a little unusual," said Robert. "Ah, sí?"

"We're looking for a particular group of glyphs." Robert showed Artoz the N.Y.U. pictures. "We are trying to translate these particular three and we need to look at nearby glyphs to help in the translation. The glyphs were photographed in 1920 here in Uxmal."

"Uxmal does not have much writing, in fact it is actually quite poor at writing, with not many stele and not in good condition. But what is here I can find, and also I have some secret places with more writing that you may be interested in. No extra charge, all is covered on my low hourly rate."

"Can you find these glyphs in the photographs?"

"But certainly. Come with me. They are just here, near the Palace of the Governors."

· · ·

The Austin virus glyphs were engraved on a stela—a large stone slab like a big gravestone—still readable but showing some deterioration since the date of the photograph. Teresa explained their problem to Artoz, that the glyphs were not translatable because they described a chemical, not a word, and they needed to try to find clues to the way the chemical was created.

They looked at the nearby text for help with the problem and found none. The Austin virus glyphs were embedded in a description of a harvest ceremony. Artoz showed them around the site, pointing out more glyphs, but again they got no answers.

Finally Artoz said, "There is one more place, but it is not yet official."

"What do you mean?" asked Robert.

"Do you know about the ceremonial cave?"

"I've read about it," said Teresa. "A couple of miles to the north, a natural cave with some cave paintings but no glyphs. Discovered just last year. It was supposed to have been the reason that the city was sited here."

"A few months ago another guide and me, we found a side tunnel leading to another big room. This room has glyphs painted on the walls and paintings of jaguars and warriors. Nice, bright colors. I take you first thing tomorrow."

"Sounds good to me," said Robert. "But how about tonight? We can grab flashlights from the van."

"Overtime for sure," said Artoz, "All at the same low hourly rate. I am indeed a prince."

"Dr. Teppin," asked Robert, "are you still there?"

Teppin said, from Robert's shoulder, "Right here. I'd go with you, but the system has no penetration through rock or soil, maybe a few inches. Why don't you drop me back in the van."

Armed with flashlights and a digital camera, they walked north down a well-defined path for half an hour, carefully following Artoz' instructions to watch their feet so they did not step on a poisonous snake. Ducking under a low overhang, they walked into the cave. Badly faded images of ancient Maya celebrities decorated the walls. Artoz pointed out the Principal Bird Deity, Vucab Caquix, and Lady Blood, the young Underworld princess.

In the center of the room was a low round altar of some sort. The ceiling was blackened above the altar as if fire had been a part of the ceremony performed there. The cavern was natural limestone, evidenced by a small collection of stalactites and stalagmites. To one side, water dripped off a stalactite into a carved ceremonial bowl.

Artoz led them to the rear of the cave. On one side, under a low ceiling, was a pile of rubble. He went to his hands and knees and scraped it away, revealing a small aperture through which he disappeared. They followed him through a winding passage several hundred yards long, sometimes returning to hands and knees to scrape through a low spot, once wading through a cool stream of water. The temperature fell several degrees, actually getting into a comfortable zone. They emerged into a second larger limestone cave, painted with well-preserved bright figures of feathered warriors in some epic battle. The floor was an irregular assortment of tiny stalagmites and terraces of white and pink limestone deposits. On one side was an area of painted glyphs, about four feet wide and curving up to the peak of the ceiling ten feet off the floor as if rendered by some Maya Michelangelo. The paint, dark blue against the white limestone, was chipped and mottled with age, but readable, and the Austin virus glyph was again represented.

As Robert snapped photos, Teresa and Artoz discussed the translation, but made no progress and decided to wait for morning to look at all the pictures together and try to find some linkage. They worked their way back through the caves and walked back through Uxmal to the parking lot under a sky full of stars, with the surrealistic scene backlit by the rising full moon.

"Teresa?"

"Yes, O great white hunter?"

"Would you sing Stela by Starlight for us?"

"No sir, not without my backup band."

"Wait here, I'll call Cancún."

• • •

Robert closed his notebook. The heat of the sun at mid-morning seemed to slow his brain as well as make every movement difficult. He stood on the yellowed grass of one of the courtyards of the big Maya city. The ceremonial cenote, the fresh-water well, was behind him. It had been carved by the city architects as a perfect twenty-foot cylinder from the limestone ledge. To his right stood a fifteen-foot *stela*. To the left stood the main temple, a steeply stepped pyramid almost two hundred feet high. Near the top of the pyramid, a wide platform accommodated a large stone chacmool—the sacrificial table—a reclining figure holding a basin for the heart of the sacrifice. Dr. Teppin had opted for education today, so the weight of the satellite communications gear was not on Robert's back.

The tourists had arrived in force; platoons of them dressed in flip-flops and shorts and colorfully lettered white cotton T-shirts. One family group was looking noisily for a lost child, teenage boys climbed up and down the steeply sloped pyramids, senior citizens with parasols against the relentless sun held color lithographed guide books in three languages. Robert wandered over to the shade of the broad-leafed Baobab tree where Teresa and Artoz were sitting comfortably on a cool stone slab near the cenote, working on last night's photos and sipping bottled water.

"Hi, chief, pull up a monolith and sit down," said Teresa. "We may be on to something here."

"I think you will like this," said Artoz. "We have always thought that the travel between the old Maya cities was not too hard, and the sacbé, the sacred white roads, were well used. That would mean that the cities could specialize, some cities could do maybe pottery, and some cities could concentrate on the astronomical studies.

"Here is *stela* twenty-seven, with your special glyphs. We thought the *stela* was a description of the harvest ceremony. But here you see" —he gestured at a computer printout— "a triad of three unknown glyphs. And here from the cave is the same triad, near your Austin virus glyph and near the glyph for the city of Tulum repeated several times. The meaning seems to be quite clear."

Robert sipped a warm soda. "Not to me."

"The Maya are thanking the harvest god for an unusually good crop with none of the worms that ate most of the corn in some year before. And then they are thanking the city of Tulum for sending a yellow powder to sprinkle on the earth as the crops were growing. The powder helped the harvest god. And there's something here about a great shaman, Peloc, who cures the sick. We see his name also, just here."

"So Tulum is specialized for science?"

"Yes, it looks as if Tulum was the Maya university town."

"But the timing doesn't work, does it?" asked Teresa. "Tulum was supposedly built about 900 and this *stela* was carved in 820."

"Yes, you are correct. Perhaps Tulum was built earlier than that and new buildings were built over the old. That happened for many of the Maya cities. Possibly Tulum started with a cave, many cities started with a cave. Caves with running water. Caves were important because the Lords of the Dead lived there. Maybe Tulum had a cave which was covered by Tulum."

"Does it look as if Tulum sent the Austin antiviral, too?" asked Robert.

"It's not here, exactly, but I'd bet on it," said Teresa.

"Next stop, Tulum. I'm glad we got the free mileage on our vehicle."

"You pack up the stuff," said Teresa. "And I'll run over and get us some more bottled water for the trip."

Chapter 14

Uxmal, Mexico, June 16, 823

T he funeral ceremony for the great King of Uxmal, Chortal the Parrot, brought the Maya from many miles around. They filled the vast quadrangle, they stood in serried array on the stepped sides of the Great Pyramid and the South Temple, and they brought maize and jewelry and carved jade statuettes to help send Chortal on his voyage.

The ceremony brought the people close to the gods, and the people always came in their finest dress, spoke in soft voices, and turned their faces to the sky as if they could glimpse the gods themselves.

But the ceremony was nothing like the extravagant tribute that had accompanied the interment of Chortal's predecessor, Xtabtal the Strong, only three cycles ago. Chortal had died of the disease of the black tongue, as had many others of the city, and the city elders were more interested in discovering the cure for the disease than in properly honoring a king who many thought should have been called Chortal the Stupid. Only five hundred warriors conducted the funeral, but they were impressive with the bone armor and the colored feathers and the shields and spears.

The big fire seemed to please the crowd. But only one sacrifice was made—a shocking departure from protocol—and no ball game was played except by the small children who ran unchecked in large numbers up and down the ball field pretending to be Xbalanque or Moon Rabbit Batz.

One of the elders, a confidante of Chortal and the man who had urged him to enlist the assistance of the great savants of Tulum, sat near the top of the House of the Magician as the ceremony concluded, gazing into the sunset. He stared fixedly at the orange disk, then closed his eyes to find a sign in the green circle that danced in the dark brown sky. But no sign appeared.

The sun was setting almost in line with Pauahtun, the earth god as turtle, and Middleworld, the place where the sun descended to the underworld.. The symbolism was not lost on the elder. He felt the sun setting on Uxmal, on the Maya, the entire city descending to the underworld. The people were screaming in pain and dropping in the streets with the black tongue, who could blame the survivors for running into the jungle? The priests did not offer correct tribute to the Jaguar god, how were they to ensure that the sun would appear the next day? The civilization was disintegrating. They would awaken to darkness.

The elder knew just one fact that offered a ray of hope: Peloc, the mighty Peloc, the greatest savant of all, was said to be close to a cure for the black tongue.

Chapter 15

Austin, Texas, October 29, present day

The huge camouflage-painted tent was set up in a farmer's field, isolated from buildings and trees by half a mile in each direction. A light warm rain was falling. Nearby, hundreds of cars were parked on the dark red mud, flattening the remnants of the corn crop. At eight in the evening the sun had fallen, but the area was illuminated by the harsh yellow light from tripod-mounted sodium vapor lamps powered by a generator trailer behind the tent, and the air was perfumed with last week's still-fresh pig dung fertilizer. The scene had the aspect of a major military center, as several guardsmen stood with rifles slung upside-down against the rain, looking uncomfortable despite their non-regulation cowboy-style broad-brimmed hats and the mild temperature.

A half a mile towards the city, more guardsmen were moving stiffly in isolation gear. Their unprotected but immune dogs were patrolling the red zone boundary, a ten mile circle of concertina wire lit up with the same yellow light. Hydrophone installations in the Colorado River near Panther Hollow and Onion Creek picked up a few SCUBA divers strong enough to swim against the swift water and too impatient to wait out the quarantine. And a series of thirty-foot poles mounted remote-controlled infrared video cameras as a check on the proper behavior of the quarantine population.

Inside the tent, a young population making notes on yellow pads sat on a sea of folding metal chairs. They were listening to a gray-haired man in a white lab coat talking on an overloaded sound system. The speaker, Dr. Gary Spender, was describing the symptoms of the Austin virus to the several hundred hastily assembled medical staffers.

"The virus has a short incubation period. Two days. It then becomes contagious." Spender mopped perspiration from his forehead. "The first symptom is a black tongue, followed by swelling of the tongue and the throat so that the victim has difficulty breathing. Fever and convulsions are seen in about five days, and the patient usually becomes incoherent. Seven to ten days after contact the tongue develops lesions which bleed profusely. Somewhere in this course the victim dies of strangulation, or his life can be spared for another day by radical tracheotomy, surgically opening an airway through the trachea.

"If this is done, the victim dies a day later from massive pulmonary failure as the alveoli become involved, lose structure, and collapse into jelly, making the lungs completely inoperative. If the blood is oxygenated with a heart-lung machine, the victim's life can be unmercifully prolonged for another week or so, after which will come massive organ failure, usually starting with the kidneys, leading quickly to death."

"How is the disease vectored?" a doctor in the first row asked.

"We're still working on that one. Some of you will be helping. Right now we're pretty sure that it is airborne." A slight exhalation of breath from the audience. "And communicated by inhalation. That would naturally be a serious factor, except in this case it seems as if the airborne virus has a short life. One theory is that the virus needs water and can travel indefinitely airborne if it is immersed in a microscopic water droplet, as from a cough, but in a low humidity environment the life of this drop would be only seconds."

"How about a day like today, how long?"

"The humidity can approach a hundred percent in fog and rain. That would give the droplet an indefinitely long lifetime. But in practice, the droplet will probably be absorbed in a raindrop and fall to the earth."

"Any other carriers besides human?"

"Almost certainly," said Spender. "Just about all human viruses can be carried also by animals or birds. In fact, all human viruses originated with animals or birds. But we have a good test for the virus in blood, a microscope stain preparation, it works in minutes and appears reliable, and we have not found any animal or insect carriers nor have we been able to infect any lab animals to date. But tests are incomplete. So we will for now attempt to prevent animals from crossing the buffer zone.

"But I'm getting a little ahead of myself. Let's get to the tactics. We have encircled the city, with a red zone radius of two to ten miles and a narrow quarantine buffer zone. Anything coming out of the red zone will be delayed for the incubation period, two days, plus a half-day margin. Medical personnel inside the buffer will wear full BL-4 isolation suits and work on four hour shifts."

A doctor in the second row whispered to his neighbor, "Beats internship by a mile. Four hours."

His neighbor replied with a smile, "I guess you've never been in a Racal suit. It will seem like four days by the time you're done. The usual shift in those things is two hours. Less, in hot weather."

Spender droned on, "The inner buffer zone will be surrounded with a ten- to twenty-mile yellow, or outer zone, with more relaxed precautions and more comfortable living conditions. Anyone moving out of the yellow zone is delayed for another three days to guard against an infection contracted inside the yellow zone. The buffer zones are in place and enforced but are not yet fully staffed. That's your job."

A listener in a white lab coat interrupted, "What will we have for laboratory facilities?"

"We have a six hundred square foot lab, just completed, two miles north in an old industrial space. It is built to BL-4, Biosafety Level Four, and it is available now for your use. It's got optical and X-ray fluorescence microscopes, incubators, Beckman Optima ultracentrifuges, inverted and light microscopes, Gravity sterilizer, walk-in incubator, spectrophotometer, Mettler balances and a cytocentrifuge. Plus, lots of other equipment."

"That should do it," said the listener.

"If there's any other equipment you need, just ask," said Spender. "We have an unlimited budget. Inside the city, the population is of course at extreme risk. We can't do much for anyone with the disease except make them as physically and mentally comfortable as possible. Right now, all we have is morphine and religion, but we keep running out of morphine. We have a full garrison of guardsmen inside in Racal suits, and we're moving the healthy population out as fast as possible within the time constraints of the quarantine.

"How many of you have not been checked out in Racal suits?" Five hands went up. "See me tomorrow morning, we'll set you up. They're the new version, double layers of soft vinyl, drinking water, fully sealed, autonomous air supply. Nothing gets through unless you rip it. Don't rip it."

Spender walked over to a wall-size topographical map with a pointer. "Transportation. The major highways all lead to quarantine parking areas like this one just outside the inner buffer zone. CDC is working on tightening the barrier now to make sure infiltration is zero or near zero.

"We have no facilities to handle the expected number of patients in isolation, so we're having people stay in their cars as crude isolation chambers. They're parked on a fifty-yard grid, so they're reasonably well protected against airborne infection. The only good thing about this damned virus is the incubation period is so short we don't need much isolation time to find out who's healthy and who isn't."

A voice from the rear of the hall interrupted, "How many people are expected in isolation? How do we feed them?"

"We may get a peak of thirty thousand. We have patrols of guardsmen in biosuits to keep everyone where they belong, and we brought in every catering truck and airport food service truck in Texas to shuttle food to the cars."

"My God," whispered a listener. "Two days of airplane meals. I'd rather get the virus."

Dr. Spender went on. "The next few weeks will make your internship seem like summer camp. We're undermanned, underfed, exhausted. But we're in a major war. This thing has the potential to get away from us and put the entire population of the world in jeopardy. With the mortality rate of ninety-nine percent we won't lose everyone, but we'll come damn close."

A woman near the front stood up. "Dr. Spender, what about the survivors? What is their condition? Is there any common factor?"

"Youth helps a lot," answered the doctor. "Most are under the age of five, none are over thirty. Apparently a strong immune system can counterattack and repel the disease before irreversible damage. Maya ancestry helps. The survivors have completely recovered within two weeks."

The woman remained standing. "What is Washington's involvement? Is there national commitment to this effort, or are we on our own here?"

"I was about to get into that. Washington is fully engaged; they're getting reports twice a day. Unfortunately, the reports are now simply mortality counts. Our liaison with Washington is the senior executive field epidemiologist from the Centers for Disease Control, Mr. George Hapwell Theslie. Mr. Theslie would like to say a few words." Spender sat down in a metal chair.

A large, ruddy-faced man with a wrinkled sweat-stained light-weight beige suit and a black-on-yellow tie stood up and took the microphone. "Hi, everybody. I'm George Hapwell Theslie. I'm the senior federal epidemiologist for CDC, and I'll be your official liaison with Washington. I'm here to make sure you get everything you need. Whatever you want, just let me know.

"Here's the story. The organization here will be military style. The discipline also has to be military style. Dr. Spender is the commander, you do what he says. I'll be working with CDC to handle the big picture. Since most of you are not military personnel, we can't court-martial you. If you can't take it, you can desert.

"But if you do bail out, if we lose too many troops to hold this thing, you will not be safe anywhere in the world. Think of it. There's our team, and nearly a hundred other teams worldwide, but this is the front line. We've got to hold the line right here, everybody is counting on us. We must not underestimate the task, it's not going to be easy. It's going to be the toughest thing any of you will ever have to do. What you all have to remember, it could go either way. Either way. And we have to make it go our way."

"Got it," said a listener.

Theslie continued. "OK, let's go over the rules of engagement. The key is isolation and quarantine. We're setting up three zones of isolation and we have armed guards patrolling the borders. You people will handle quarantine, and administer painkillers.

Volunteers in biosuits will work behind the lines helping the folks that do not yet have the disease to move into quarantine. I will be monitoring your activities so we can estimate our probability of success. If we slip under 90%, we will be pulling back and reconsidering our options. We don't want to have to reconsider our options."

He droned on for a few minutes before handing Spender the microphone. "Thank you, Mr. Theslie, for that clarification. People, we'll be breaking up into groups of ten; your instructions are on the printed sheet that you're holding. Breakfast tomorrow is at seven A.M. Get some sleep, you'll need it. Thanks, and good night."

The words replayed in his mind: "Zero or near zero infiltration." Near zero. Christ. He wondered if the Maya, with their genetic resistance, would be the only race to survive the epidemic.

Spender walked to the recreational vehicle where he lived in close quarters with Carla and his daughter. Carla had moved most of their household goods to a basement room and purchased the old Winnebago.

She took the lab coat off his shoulders and looked at his midsection critically. "You missed lunch again. And dinner. You probably weigh ten pounds less than I do. I'll make you a tuna sandwich and some soup."

"Thanks, love. That sounds good."

"How's the battle today?" she asked from the tiny kitchen.

"We got a new batch of cannon fodder today. I feel like a general with a battalion of rookies. I think we will have many casualties."

"You take care of yourself, Gary. Don't be a hero. Be really careful."

He nodded. "Stick around tomorrow. And the kid. I think we'll be moving again." He closed his eyes.

Chapter 16

Tulum, Mexico, November 1, present day

The trip from Uxmal, on the northwest corner of the Yucatán, to Tulum, on the southeast coast, was almost five hour's difficult driving. They bumped along at forty miles an hour, avoiding a deep pothole every thirty seconds. Every half hour or so they passed a small settlement, with palm-thatched huts, walls made from close-spaced saplings, and occasionally a satellite TV antenna dish. The clutchless VW held up well despite its age and afflictions, even though Robert could have used a little air conditioning.

They had asked Artoz if he knew anything about Tulum, and he had told them that he taught in the university at Mérida, Maya studies and archaeology, except for summer vacation and sometimes when he had no classes. He of course had studied Tulum. And he had spent much time there as a guide. They brought him along, shoehorned into the small rear seat.

They checked a guidebook for accommodations and selected Akumal, a little north of Tulum, as it appeared as though Tulum was a park area without hotels. Akumal was perfect, with inexpensive low-rise tourist hotels on the water and a couple of small restaurants serving Mexican food. They checked in at one of the hotels, in separate rooms.

In the morning Robert awoke to his wristwatch alarm at 6:30. He dressed in shorts and running shoes and ran for an hour on the beach, in the band of dark sand left by the receding waves where the soft sand was firmed by the water. He cooled off with a quick dip in the ocean.

As he walked up the beach to the hotel, a piercing whistle stopped him. Teresa, reclining in a beach chair, smiled prettily, set a large hardback book down in her lap, and looked up at him through dark glasses.

"Wow, nice body! Do you pump iron or something? Come here often? What's your sign?"

"Ha, the Schwartzenegger pills are working. Nice, huh?" He flexed his triceps. "You putting moves on me? Armand dump you?"

"Naaah, I was just hoping you'd buy breakfast."

They breakfasted with Artoz on *huevos rancheros* in the hotel restaurant, packed their cameras and their bottled water, and rattled thirty miles down the coast road to Tulum. At Tulum they parked the VW, tightened up the fenders a little, and checked in with Dr. Teppin. He said he would like to visit Tulum with them and Robert put the camera backpack on.

Tulum was a small town compared to Uxmal, set on a beautiful piece of coastline, on a headwall fifty feet high that sloped steeply down a coral-limestone rock face to a curved white sand beach. The town was inhabited only by tourists and it was surrounded by shops selling film, serapes, carved chess sets, pottery, and 'Life's a beach' T-shirts.

The entrance was guarded by the usual collection of guides eager to educate the uninformed. They greeted Artoz, "Hola, Artoz, you maybe wish to learn about Tulum?" and laughed.

In the city, Robert asked Artoz where the virus glyphs might be found. "Well, let's walk around town," he said. "I don't think I have seen these, but I may be mistaken. And it's a small city, it won't take too much time to look at all the glyphs here; half a day, I think."

They entered the gate and stood on a flat treeless rectangular area where the entire city was visible, less than half a mile in its longest direction and surrounded by a low wall. There were no massive pyramids, the largest structures were rectangular stone buildings just two stories tall. They began looking at glyphs carved into the buildings, with Robert taking pictures, more out of reflex than in the hope anything was worth recording.

"Dr. Teppin?" he asked. "Are you still there?"

"Off and on. On, right now. Gary Spender is conferenced in, for some reason he thinks your approach is his best hope. We've been chatting, I filled him in on progress or the lack thereof."

"Hi, Gary."

"Hello, Robert. Please, be lucky."

"Anything positive to report from Austin?"

"Austin is off the map. We now refer to our location as 'the Austin area'. Next week, we may refer to our location as 'the Texas area'.

"I'm sorry. You must be stretched thin."

"Actually, no, we're getting all the help we need. The CDC and the Feds are throwing all the Armed Forces medics at us and strong-arming a lot of civilians. But we sure are getting frazzled."

"We're praying for you. Dr. Teppin, are you recording the video we're sending up?"

"Yes, I've got it all."

"OK, I won't bother taking pictures. It's pretty uninteresting, so far." He signed off and looked around for Teresa without finding her. "Artoz, have you seen what happened to Teresa?"

"Not for an hour or so. She cannot be too far."

They quartered the area and found her snapping close-up pictures inside a small round building. "Teresa," said Robert. "Find something?"

"Well, sort of. This looks like the hand-in-the-eye icon you can find in ancient Chinese sites. It's just the kind of thing I need for my paper."

Robert was quiet for a moment. "A lot of people could be depending on us. Could we track down the Austin virus glyph first?"

"That looks like kind of wishful thinking right now, and I need these pictures."

"Teresa, please, we need to play this out all the way. No diversions. No side issues. The stakes are too big for a half-ass effort."

"Oh, poo, slave driver. Tell me when you give up and I'll get the rest of my pictures."

"Deal," he said, and stuck out a hand for a high five.

• • •

During the lunch break, Teresa asked, "Artoz, in the books Tulum is described as a fortress and a port town. But it isn't much of a fortress, the walls are only fifteen feet high, and there's no particular structure that looks like a port. No warehouses, no docks, no place to tie up a boat."

"Yes, you are right. Many guides here think the town was more of a vacation place, people would come here to swim or enjoy the beach, and the sea breeze here keeps it cooler than inland."

"But it's so small, maybe a thousand people. With fourteen million Maya, it couldn't hold many vacationers."

"*¿Quién sábe?*" asked Artoz, squeezing a lime into his beer.

They were lunching on enchiladas and Dos Equis from one of the snack bars near the town's entrance, sitting on a block of stone on the outside of the city wall. Robert noticed faint carving on the nearby city wall, brought into relief at just this time by the grazing angle of the sun. He peered closer.

"Hey, that rock has a glyph on it."

Teresa turned and looked and walked over to the wall. Artoz joined her, and they had soon brushed dirt and grass away from the base of the wall and from several stones, which appeared to have fallen from the city wall.

"Shoot this, Robert," she said. He got the camera out again and took pictures.

"What is it?"

"It looks like a geographical reference, a place," she said. "It shows a cenote, or maybe an underground cave."

"Quite close, to the south," said Artoz.

"How close?" asked Robert.

Artoz studied the inscription. "A man can walk this distance twenty times in a day."

"There's the diving god, again." Said Teresa. "Artoz, the diving god symbol is found in just about all Maya cities, but nowhere with anything like the frequency it appears in Tulum, right?"

"*Sí.* One man said the diving god was a sign that the alien invaders came down right here in Tulum."

"Maybe not alien invaders, maybe the Maya used to dive. This section certainly seems to describe a sacred underwater something-or-other, and how would they get there without diving?"

"They didn't have SCUBA gear, did they, those old Maya?" asked Robert.

"I wouldn't put it past them," said Teresa.

"It would be like Uxmal, the interesting stuff is underground. Did you ever do any diving?"

"WHAT? You mean *underwater?*"

"No, huh?"

"I did try snorkeling, actually. That went pretty good. Heck, I'll go diving with you if you want."

Robert felt a chill of premonition. He was a good SCUBA diver with some cave experience, and he knew he should not take a novice anywhere near an underwater cave. Diving was dangerous enough, and caves were right up at the top of the dangerous scale even for experienced cave divers. But this business had changed quickly, from a long-shot research project to a long-shot archaeology trip to maybe the best chance to save the lives of many thousands of people. They had to take chances. He'd play it by ear, see if she seemed to be comfortable in the water. But there was a prickling in the back of his neck, a little warning tickle.

Chapter 17

Robert fought the wheel as the VW bucked over the dirt road, over waves of packed earth like a congealed ocean storm. Main street in Playa del Carmen, ten miles north on the coast, bisected this regional center of commerce and industry. Low clapboard and adobe buildings lined the street, which was shared by vehicular traffic, dogs sleeping in the gullys, goats, bicyclists, and pedestrians.

He glanced at Teresa, cool and pretty, her hair swept up into a red bandanna, looking more like a female pirate than a scientist. She was so casual, so alive, so unlike any other woman he had met. He felt a flash of concern, should they be doing this, cave diving? But what else? The virus was still uncontrolled. There could be clues he would not understand.

Then he thought of the tenuous chain of logic that had led them this far—Maya microscopes, mysterious glyphs, diving gods—and the whole thing seemed beyond sanity. He should get back to Houston, grab his kid, and head for Greenland. But he drove on.

He located a small dive shop on the ocean. The dive shop proprietor, a dark young man who said he once lived in Montreal before getting it together, told her that SCUBA was just like snorkeling except you didn't get water in your snorkel. She looked apprehensive but let him outfit her with a full set of equipment.

"Hey, how much more of this do I get?" she complained. "This weighs about two hundred pounds. I'll sink like a rock, if I make it to the water."

"That's about it, except if you do any deep diving you might want a wet suit to keep warm."

"Do the natives wear 'em?"

"They do, in the winter."

"Is this the winter? I guess it is. Gimmee one."

She emerged from the changing room and checked the fit of the green skin-tight wet suit, along with Robert and the proprietor. "Where will you be diving?" he asked.

"Just past Tulum," said Robert. "We're doing a little archaeology."

"Watch yourselves. That's not a healthy place to dive."

"Sharks?" asked Teresa.

"Sharks won't bother you," said the proprietor. "Unless maybe you cut yourself and thrash around a lot. But there have been a few people that were diving near there that got their anchor lines cut, or got a mysterious hole in their boat. Nobody's ever seen anything, though. Supposed to be haunted by a shipwrecked sailor from a hundred years ago."

A block down the street, Robert found an electronics store where he bought an old fashioned analog ohmmeter. Then at a hardware store he bought copper sheet, silicone glue, and plastic bags. He connected the meter to the copper through holes in the bag, sealed the holes with glue, and sealed the bag around the meter.

"OK, Mr. Science, I'll bite," said Teresa. "What is that supposed to be?"

"Here's the way I figure it," he said. "We'll be diving in the salt water looking for an underwater cave entrance, right?"

"Right."

"And ten to one the underwater cave has a fresh water underground river, since as you pointed out earlier, they don't do surface rivers in the Yucatán peninsula, right?"

"Right again. Ten to one."

"So we could either swim around for years checking out each little hole or we could use the Little Dandy Underwater Salinity Detector, here." He grabbed both electrodes and watched the meter swing to the right.

"Say no more, Mr. Science. I think I get it. When we swim through a fresh water flow the resistance goes up."

"Yep. Not only that, I also got extra plastic bags we can use for lunch."

"Underwater? Wait a minute, I draw the line..."

"No, ma'am, not underwater, too salty. Lunch on the beach. You'll love it."

• • •

Driving south to Tulum they checked in with Dr. Teppin, but they had to tell him again they'd be out of range, as the high frequency radio would not penetrate the salt water. He told them the latest fatalities in Austin, seven hundred fifty dead. The medical community had no confidence that the virus could be checked, and successively larger circles of state and federal government were trying to figure out how to help.

"Dr. Teppin," said Robert. "I'm worried about my daughter."

"She is in Houston, right?"

"Yes, Houston. I've talked to my ex, but they won't move."

"If you give me their address, I can have a CDC representative track the situation. If it even begins to look dangerous, we'll talk to Spender. We will encourage local police to enforce an evacuation."

"Excellent, thanks a lot. That should do it."

• • •

In Tulum, they parked in the same lot and walked south past high dunes to the beach. After some instruction Teresa looked comfortable underwater and they crisscrossed back and forth at different distances from shore watching the salinity meter. At two hundred yards out, they drifted near the reef, surrounded by brightly colored reef fishes and rocked gently back and forth by the low waves. On the ocean side a sea turtle five feet across paddled slowly south. Teresa grabbed Robert's arm and pointed up.

At the surface, she said, "Wow! Did you see that big mother turtle? And those fish? The colors are incredible. The blue flat one, it looked like it's lit from inside. That bunch of little silver guys, they looked like somebody just polished 'em. It's like swimming in an aquarium. I wouldn't have believed it. My God. What was that big gray job that smiled at us?"

"Barracuda."

"Will he bite?"

"No, he thinks you're probably dangerous because you're so much bigger than him. If the fish ever find out we're helpless we'll all be fish bait. Smile back at him. Show him your teeth. Pretend you're going to eat him if he gets in range."

"Right. Smile. Teeth. What's the little bright blue one eating rocks? He crunches on 'em. You can actually hear him crunch."

"Parrotfish. Eating the coral, actually. The outside layers are still alive. It's probably pretty tasty, try some."

"No thanks. Gotta get back to work."

They swam over a few dozen black fissures in the coral with no indication from the meter, and then got a strong response from a fairly large hole. Robert marked the spot by tying a ribbon on an elkhorn coral and they swam further, locating another hole. Robert pointed down, checked their remaining air, handed Teresa an underwater light, fired up one of his remaining three lights, and tied off one end of his thin safety line. They entered the hole, unreeling the line to mark their exit route.

The passage led them straight down for a dozen feet, then bent inland. They worked their way against heavy current in a featureless smooth-walled stone fissure—four feet high and thirty or forty feet wide—sometimes finding a tiny crevice in the limestone to hold on to and rest. After about a hundred yards the passage started narrowing and they found themselves swimming hard to even hold position. After a minute Robert pointed back and they let the current float them back to the reef.

After a brief conference on the surface, they swam back to the ribbon and tried the first opening, but the passage turned out to be nearly identical in shape and they had to give up again due to the heavy current. They returned to the beach.

Back on the beach, they stripped off the SCUBA gear, located their picnic basket, and ate a lunch of warm Italian sub sandwiches and Dos Equis.

"Mmmm, nice change from enchiladas," said Teresa. "Prosciutto. Where'd you get Italian?"

"Bribed the hotel chef. His name's Luigi."

"Good job." She yawned and stretched her arms over her head, flexed her body, and settled back into the sand. "This is when I get my nap." She looked straight at Robert with the disturbing eyes and a bit of a smile. Robert felt a warm thrill, did she know the effect she had on him?

"You get your nap, too," she told him. She was fully relaxed like a jungle cat, her eyes now closed.

Robert sat back in the sand but did not nap. He preferred watching Teresa as she dropped off to sleep in maybe ten seconds and began snoring lightly. Their strange errand churned his mind. Maya microscope? They'd find something completely different, some other explanation. Or they'd find nothing at all. It probably didn't matter, CDC would trap the outbreak and nothing would matter anymore. He should take this desirable woman in his arms and forget the science stuff. Except she still seemed to have her "look, but do not touch" sign up. At least the sign seemed to be a little smaller now.

He looked out at the turquoise ocean, its color deepened by the dark coral heads and the passing shadows of the clouds. One or two clouds on the horizon were sheeting rain showers. A hermit crab scurried by on some errand wearing another crab's shell, pausing a moment to stare at Robert with one of his eyes swiveled around on its stalk. Robert stared back. Won that one, the crab broke eye contact and hurried away. Ten or fifteen minutes later, after the wind had completed the job of drying his body and the sun's warmth was making him drowsy, he struggled to his feet.

He put a hand on Teresa's warm shoulder and she shuddered, then awoke and squinted at her wristwatch.

"Rats, back to work. What's your next move, chief?"

He wondered briefly if that was an invitation, then discarded the idea. "I don't know if you noticed, but the entrance to that second underwater hole had been marked up a lot."

"Huh? By what?"

"I'm not sure. In the first hole, the rock was smoothed by ten or twenty thousand years of running water. It was hard to find a place for your fingers. But the second hole, especially near the opening, had sharp-edged longitudinal scratches that looked fresh."

"Analysis, Spock?"

"Beats me. Like something hard or metallic came zipping down the passage, banging into walls. Maybe floating rocks, if rocks floated."

"Not anything that'll eat us?"

"I wouldn't think so," said Robert. "Of course, I've been wrong before. That passage was quite straight, I bet it goes right under us where we're sitting. If we follow a straight path inland we may locate the cenote."

"The one in the glyph on the wall."

"Yes. Artoz didn't know of a cenote here, so it may be buried, or caved in, since the inscription."

They left the heavy gear on the beach, put on their shoes, and walked straight inland through thick, grabby scrub brush. Progress was slow and Robert was about to call it off and get a machete when he stepped into a hole, one leg disappearing up to his pelvis.

"Quit kidding around," said Teresa. "What did you do with your leg?"

"Actually, I used it to locate this hole. Give me a hand, here."

They levered him out and pulled bushes away from the hole, enlarging it to about two feet in diameter. Robert dropped a pebble that hit water almost instantly.

"Only a few feet down. I bet this is it. Let's get the equipment and check it out."

They returned to the beach to gather the SCUBA gear and walked back to the VW van for the submersible flashlights, rope, shovels, and the reel of safety line. As they closed the hatch, a beat-up Lincoln limousine drove up, siren screaming, blue light flashing. A big Mexican federal police officer with a comic handlebar moustache and a less well-dressed policeman emerged and walked towards them.

Moustache leaned against the VW and chewed on a toothpick. He had mirrored aviator's glasses, an ammunition belt, two chrome pistols and an imposing hat decorated with gold braid. His short-sleeved uniform shirt revealed big biceps and a tattoo, "Mi casa es su casa," in a frame of iron bars. The other man, with a nameplate identifying him as Lt. Antonio Martinez, followed a pace behind.

"May I help you?" said Robert. "Here's my driver's license, if that's what you need."

The policeman looked at him, his expression unreadable. Finally he snorted and said, "We don't need your focking driver's license. Ha. I am Colonel Muñoz. I am the commander of the police force for this area. You are the archaeologist?"

"Well, sort of, myself and my associate Dr. Welles. I'm Dr. Robert Asher. We are from Boston, U.S.A."

"Thank you for the lesson in geography. Boston is in U.S.A. I will try to remember. What is your business in Tulum?"

"We're trying to find a Maya inscription which will help us to cure a dangerous virus outbreak."

"And how, exactly, does a Maya inscription fix a virus?"

"It's sort of confusing, but we think the Maya may have known about this virus in the time of Tulum, twelve hundred years ago. We're looking for inscriptions—glyphs—which will tell us more."

"You think I am a simple man? Focking fairy tale? You think I am maybe a complete fool?" said Muñoz more loudly.

"Not at all," said Robert.

"Show me your permit for archaeology." He held out his hand.

"I'm sorry, I didn't think we needed permission, we are not even in the city of Tulum here."

"Get back into your vehicle. Drive away. You need permission for archaeology. You must get the form." The other officer nodded agreement.

"Officer, I can prove this to you, the thing with the virus. We can work through your government, through the United Nations if you wish, but we need to move quickly. This is an important expedition. Many lives may be at stake. We do not want to waste time."

"Waste time? Waste time, is it? So our little stupid regulations are not convenient for the big city archaeologist and his girlfriend. So you can come down here with your dollars and turn them into so many pesos you are rich gringos overnight. So you can buy off the little pain-in-the-ass local policia with your big government." Muñoz' face was getting red. "So the big city archaeologist from Boston, U.S.A. and his whore and the United Nations and the focking President of the focking United States and the goddam Marines think they can walk up and down on the poor little Mexicanos?"

"I must be missing something," said Robert. "What is going on, here?"

"I will tell you what is going to go off. You are going to go off." Muñoz was bellowing at Robert, six inches away, blowing spittle into his face. "If I see you within three miles of Tulum I put you both in jail for six months for trespassing. You will not like my little jail. But some of my other prisoners will be happy."

"Suppose we get a permit for archaeology?" said Robert.

"That is signed by me. I see already that you are not qualified. Do not waste my time. Do not try your Marines or your United Nations or we will have a little war here. Get into the vehicle. Go back to the Alamo and board up the windows. Now. Move. Before I squash you. *Rápido.*"

Robert felt a flash of anger and stepped closer to Muñoz, weight forward, arms slightly spread, looking at his eyes. Muñoz moved back to his car, gesturing with the back of his hand as if to an annoying bug. "*Rápido. Rápido.*"

Robert and Teresa got back into the VW and drove back to Akumal.

"Jesus, I thought you were going to hit him for a second. I'm glad you didn't hit him. What in the name of God was all that?" said Teresa.

"Beats the hell out of me. Do you suppose we should have gotten an archaeology permit?"

"I suppose, but I thought they were only if you were digging in a proscribed area, like Tulum City inside the walls. And the penalty is a fine, not a jail term, Muñoz must know that. And we can probably get one, with Dr. Teppin's help, in a few days."

"There's more than that going on," said Robert. "Colonel Muñoz must have some other action going. Maybe he was looking for a bribe."

"Well, he didn't even give us a chance to offer one. But he did say that thing about the dollars and the pesos, maybe he does want money."

"It's pretty clear that we don't know what's going on. I think we could use a local expert."

"In what? Permits?"

"No, in bribing cops," said Robert. "Suppose Dr. Teppin knows anybody that bribes cops in the Yucatán? He knows a lot of people."

• • •

Back at the hotel they turned on the videophone, called Teppin, and filled him in on the day's events.

"Don't go back there until we figure this out," he said. "More than eight hundred people have died from the Austin virus. The death rate is increasing. We could certainly get you out of jail but it would take a few days at a minimum. We have to find a faster way."

"Any advice?" asked Robert.

"I think you are correct, you need a local expert. Somebody that could handle a bribe, somebody who would know what the police are doing."

"Dr. Teppin, do you possibly have any contacts in the Information Technology department of a large company?"

"Certainly. Tom Huang at Pennex Drugs, for instance."

"I bet his database privileges are spectacular. I bet he could look up about any fact online anywhere."

"If Tom does not have access, he can hack into any computer in a few hours, maximum. Where are you heading with this line of inquiry, Robert?"

"If we could find somebody that was running a business here, or at least handling some financial transactions in the Yucatán, and also was a proven lawbreaker and also had plenty of capital, we probably would have our local expert."

"Good thought. Hang on, I will call Huang on the ISDN line."

A minute later, another small face appeared on the screen. "I'm Tom Huang, Robert. Dr. Teppin filled me in. How can I help?"

"Can you patch me into the IRS database?"

"Sure, I've got that bookmarked. It's a biggie, don't be surprised if it seems sluggish. And don't chat with anybody while you're in there, we're not supposed to have access. You'll be read-only, they're pretty careful about write privileges. Your password is, let me see, FLUID RANGER. Ready now?"

"Any time."

In a few seconds, Robert's computer screen changed to the IRS home page. He selected the search engine and keyed in "tax evasion" "fugitive" and "Yucatán." After a minute of thinking, the computer presented the records of a man named Phillip Schwartz, a fugitive from IRS and SEC prosecution, estimated net worth six hundred seventy-five million dollars, last known location Yucatán Peninsula, extradition denied by the Mexican government.

"Score!" said Robert.

Teresa was looking over his shoulder. "That's enough capital for me. I'll see if he has a telephone number." She picked up the telephone.

"So will I," said Robert, punching keys.

"No listing," said Teresa.

"I got it," said Robert. "Dr. Teppin, Tom, thanks," said Robert. "We'll check out this guy. He looks perfect."

"I'll be in my office all afternoon, if you need some more names," said Huang.

Chapter 18

Cartegena, November 4, present day

Ernesto sat in a straight chair tilted at a steep angle against the wall, with his feet resting on a long table where he had arranged his monthly paperwork. It was not an easy job, controlling an enterprise of nearly five thousand people, especially since the quality of his help was so bad.

Production rates, processing rates, purchasing kerosene and gasoline and amyl sulphate, making sure the aging fleet of trucks and planes and boats was at least half-assed working. Recruiting, enforcement, motivation, and the constant circling dance with the various law enforcement organizations: who to bribe, how much to bribe, when to move the processing plants, setting up blind cut-outs and disinformation, enforcing the rigid compartmentalization and military need-to-know control.

He could use a break. He rammed a clip into the silenced Glock nine mm and squeezed off a few rounds into the pistol target hung on the warehouse's wall. This practice kept his shooting accurate and kept the flunkies from barging in unannounced. The cinder block walls kept the rounds from escaping to downtown Cartegena, although a few thin spots were developing.

His private phone rang. "Yeah, what?"

"Scramble," said the voice. Sounded like Muñoz.

"OK, scramble code four," said Ernesto and flipped the switch.

"Something kind of interesting in Tulum," said Muñoz, his voice choppy from the scrambling.

"You gonna make me guess?"

"I ran into a couple kids, like maybe college kids, said they were archaeologists, poking around near the dry entrance to your cave. They were talking like they knew about the cave and needed to get into it, something about looking for a cure for some disease, some big underground Maya cave or something. Sounded like garbage to me, but they were pretty excited about the whole thing."

"They find the entrance?" said Ernesto.

"Don't think so, they weren't wet or anything, and I called Lopez, he's seen nothing."

Ernesto slammed a fresh clip into the Glock and emptied it at the wall, into the thin spot. Maybe he could punch one through. "Well, fuck. Exactly what I need. I don't suppose you can handle this yourself?"

"No problem. They need a permit for archaeology on government land. They won't get it. And I'll make sure they can't get anywhere near the place."

Ernesto thought for a minute, jacking the slide of his automatic back and forth. What were they after? Only one way to find out. Let 'em in. Find out what they want. "No, give 'em the permit." He smiled to himself. "We'll crank up the security a notch, maybe staff up a little, and welcome them to our humble warehouse, if that's where they wanna go." He hung up the phone and called Lopez.

That evening he found a reference to a virus outbreak in the newspaper. Something in Texas, big news in the U.S., not too much of a problem for him, but the article said the origin might be in the Yucatan. Was that a coincidence? But why the hell does an old limestone cave have anything to do with a virus? He thought about it carefully for a while. Stupid enough to be true. Maybe there's more in that cave than we know about. Something they want. Something we should have.

If they really could get a cure for the Texas virus from his cave, it's *his* cure. After all, his guys discovered the cave. So, let 'em in, watch 'em, see if they find some secret formula or something, scoop 'em up, bring 'em down here and set up production. We got plenty of production capability. Sell it in the U.S. for prices that'll make their noses bleed. Christ, that might be worth, what, two hundred million U.S.? Maybe more, especially if the thing spread. And even fairly legal, if nobody missed the archaeologists. Make it look like an accident.

He picked up the phone and talked to one of his science guys.

Chapter 19

Playa del Carmen, November 4, present day

Teresa rang the number.

"*Sí?*"

"I'm looking for Mr. Phillip Schwartz."

"Mr. Schwartz is hardly ever at home. May I ask who is calling?"

"My name is Dr. Teresa Welles, and this is a medical emergency."

Robert waggled his eyebrows at her, she gestured back with the OK sign. Ah, yes, he thought, major medical emergency back home.

After a minute a rough-edged voice came over the phone, "Schwartz here. You've got fifteen seconds."

"I hope you've been following the news from Austin. The virus. We're researchers from Boston. There's some evidence that the ancient Maya may have found a cure; we're tracing a connection between an old glyph that looks exactly like a modern representation of the charge pattern of the virus molecule. If we find a connection, we may get a clue to a cure. Now we've got a problem with the local law. We hoped you could help."

"That's the all-time stupidest thing I ever heard."

"You won't even listen to us?"

"I didn't say that. I said that's the all-time stupidest thing I ever heard. Come on over, nobody would make up anything that stupid.

And I like talking American. Even Boston American. How much money do you want, did you say?"

"We don't want money. We need to investigate an archeological site for clues. The cops won't let us near the site, and we need someone who knows the protocol for dealing with the *Federales*."

"Aha! And you think, for some reason, that would be *moi*? What *chutzpah*! What *je ne sais quoi*! How did you get my name?"

"We, um, tapped into the IRS database, Mr. Schwartz."

"You can do that? Suddenly I find you interesting. Call me Phil. Would you mind erasing my records?"

"Sorry, read privileges only," said Teresa.

"Where are you now, exactly?"

"We're in Akumal."

"Perfect. I'm just past Xél-Ha, just a few miles up the street. Join me for lunch, here at my luxurious *pied-a-terre*. How many are you, did you say?"

"Just the two of us."

"Too bad, cook loves a challenge. High noon."

Phil gave them directions, and they drove up the coast. They found the driveway bracketed with big stone pillars and guarded by an iron gate that swung open to an invisible command as they approached. They drove east up a curving asphalt driveway, slightly wider than the main road. Robert estimated it at close to a mile long. In Boston you'd pay at least two hundred bucks a whack to get this thing plowed, another advantage of living near the equator. The last asphalt curve revealed a colossal Italianate home in grey granite and adobe, with a luxurious green lawn featuring a *bocce* court and a putting green, a terra cotta tile roof and an enormous entrance. A short, overweight man in his fifties, with a receding hairline and LaCoste swimwear, swung open both of the two big carved wooden doors as they approached. He took Teresa's hand in both of his. "I'm Phil. You're Dr. Teresa Welles, I bet. Who's the guy?"

"Dr. Robert Asher, meet Phil."

He ignored Robert, kept her hand, looked up into her eyes and said, in a stage whisper, "You ever wanna dump this bozo, sweetie, and move up to the big leagues, call my social secretary."

She smiled a little, but her eyes weren't in it. Finally he turned to Robert and grinned, "Just kidding. You can come in, too."

Phil led them through the center hallway, still talking with Teresa with Robert trailing along behind. The guy looks like a fireplug, talks like a fire hose, and he's worth over five hundred million US. Well, one out of three is OK. The wide hall was obsessively formal with high ceilings, marble, oriental rugs, dark wood paneling that looked as if had come from a British castle, and some paintings that looked like Utrillo and Cézanne. "Check it out. As you can see, my decorator was in her neo-Impressionist period. She was fond of the interplay between rococo, baroque, Louis Quinze, and Bauhaus. She went on from this to decorate the Bowl-A-Drome in Hallandale, another successful commission, I don't know if you've seen it, she got more into neon and chrome with that one."

They walked past this magnificence to the less formal pool area. The pool had the negative edge treatment on the ocean side, with the water edge suspended in space. To the right of the pool stood a small palm-thatched bar area with a pretty dark young Mexican woman in a bright orange blouse.

"Conchita!" Phil yelled to her. "Drinks all around! Margaritas!"

They sat at a glass-topped table under a Cinzano umbrella and sipped the cold drinks. "So, you probably want to hear my life story, right?" said Phil. "I'm just a struggling financier, between wives right now, hanging out in this rustic beach house with just my cook, my housekeeper, my security staff, and, ummm, Conchita, here. I used to work in Wall Street until I got busted for a perfectly legal penny-stock leveraged buyout deal. Well, OK, fairly legal. Well, maybe not so legal, but creative. They gave me a choice between five to ten years of minimum-security or taking it on the lam to some country with subvertible extradition agreements with the U.S., and here I am, subverting like crazy. Not that I don't want to pay my debt to society, you understand, but I'd rather drink piña coladas on the beach. I keep busy with this and that down here, odd jobs, you know how it is. I don't visit the States any more unless I wear a disguise, and I take care of the *Federales* so they would rather keep me here than export this valuable resource. Keep the Yucatán green, I'm sort of a one-man environmental movement. I'm on a first name basis with the local fuzz. How can I help you? Want somebody to show you the Maya relics?"

They explained their problem, filling Phil in on the Austin virus and their search for the origin of the old glyph that matched the new microscope image, and giving him the details of yesterday's encounter with the local law.

"Did you get the name of the cop that busted you?"

"Colonel Muñoz."

"Yep, it's his territory, all right. We're like brothers, Luis and me. I call him Luis. He calls me Phil. He likes Conchita. Her name isn't really Conchita, it's Shirley, if you can believe it, long story, but I couldn't call her Shirley. Muñoz is, believe it or not, no worse than your average *Federale* Colonel. Better than some."

"I'd hate to meet a bad one."

"Oh, he blusters a lot, but he's fairly OK."

"How do we handle him? Offer him a bribe? I've heard that the police are basically paid in bribe money."

"HA! They're paid *only* in bribe money. In some districts, the cops pay two hundred bucks a month to keep their jobs. There's a finely tuned system here, bribes are part of the cost of doing business. *Mordida*, that's the local term for it: *mordida*, the bite. Speeding costs twenty US, Leaving the Scene of an Accident is a C, Drunk Driving is two Cs, Vehicular Homicide While Legally Intoxicated will cost you two or three thou, but they'll take credit cards. You're probably up against Police Protection for Drug Smugglers, something like twenty-five thou per event or seventy-five thou per year. It could be pretty expensive to get into a bidding war: it might set you back a hundred thou cash, one time payment, U.S., works much better than pesos. No checks, no credit cards; cutouts, untraceable cash; bagman must be acceptable to bribee."

"One hundred thousand dollars?" said Teresa. "That's not fair, they're criminals. We're trying to stop an epidemic."

"Right, I forgot. Justice. Humanitarianism. OK, we'll try fifty thou, appeal to his sense of fair play and the sanctity of human life. Or maybe some other angle; Muñoz likes cars; maybe I can do something there. He always checks out my car collection when he visits. Or, Conchita?" Schwartz looked at her carefully, "No, I couldn't do that to Muñoz."

"We don't have anything like fifty thousand."

"Don't worry about it. I can handle that without even going to the bank."

"We can't take that kind of money. We may have no way to repay you. Washington may have trouble with a bribe."

"Hey, I got nine figures worth of bank account, twelve or thirteen figures if you do it in old pesos, I don't need your Yankee dollar. This is the thing, though. I'm dying down here; I want to go home. If I get Muñoz off your back and you pull this off, and you guys get your fifteen minutes of fame, ask the Pres to get the IRS off *my* back."

"You mean the President of the United States? I don't think we'll get to talk to him."

"Well, then, don't worry about it. Just if you do, is all. Besides, I've been watching the news from the U.S. If you pull this off, the Queen of England will clean your windows. *You'll* be the next president. And maybe I'll look in on your operation, see if you bring up the buried treasure. Help you polish the gold statues." He grinned at them, exposing a fortune in stateside porcelain.

Conchita arrived with a silver tray, small sandwiches, caviar, smoked salmon, wheat crackers, and two bottles of California Chardonnay in an ice bucket.

Teresa spooned some of the dark gray caviar onto a wheat cracker. "Nice lunch. We don't get caviar at the Akumal hotel."

"I have it flown in from the Caspian. Beluga sturgeon. It only costs pennies more to go first class. Where are you digging?"

"Just a little south of Tulum."

"Makes sense, I've heard some strange things have happened on that piece of coast. Fast boats anchored offshore. Watch yourselves. Make sure your insurance is paid up. Want to check out my car collection? Just got a Hispano-Suiza, you'll love it. The 1929 H6-B"

"Thanks for everything, but no, we should get back to work. Can we call tomorrow to see how you're doing?"

"Sure. Call anytime, it's nice to talk American for a change."

• • •

When Robert phoned Phil in the morning, Conchita answered, recognized his voice, and put Schwartz on the line.

"Hey, Robert, what's happening?"

"Pretty quiet here. Any progress with Muñoz?"

"Not just yet, but we're optimistic. Give Conchita your telephone number and address and sit tight. Events are moving quickly, here."

Robert found Teresa out by the pool, lotioned, reclining, and clad in a black one-piece bathing suit. She was reading a large old-looking book with pictures of Maya glyphs. He sat down and ordered a piña colada to match hers, but before the drink arrived an agitated waiter appeared.

"Señor Asher? Señorita Welles? The *policia* are in front. *Muy importante*. Colonel Muñoz. He ask for you."

For Christ's sake. No, it can't be happening. Muñoz is going to arrest us. He doesn't want a bribe. "Could be trouble," he said, thinking of Mexican jails.

"Or, maybe he's just selling tickets to the *policia's* ball," said Teresa, "Let's go see."

They walked through the open lobby and saw—under the coconut palms that lined the circular driveway—Muñoz, sitting in a huge convertible. He was impeccably attired in crisp new dress uniform. An old leather cap was on his head and he wore leather-framed blue-lensed sunglasses. A white silk scarf was around his neck despite the warmth of the day. The automobile, a beautifully restored Dusenberg, was at least twenty feet long. Wire wheels with white sidewalls were protected with sweeping clamshell fenders. Chromed exhaust pipes curved down from the engine compartment and under the running board. The car was painted cherry red. A deep, resonant engine note at idle hinted at a big engine under the hood with enough torque to pull stumps.

"*Hola*, Asher. *Como 'sta?*" said Muñoz, grinning widely under the moustache and tapping the throttle.

"Colonel, I..."

"*Sí*, I know, you need a ride to Tulum. But you will have to take your own vehicle, I am going to Cancún."

"But..."

"Ah, yes, you are maybe thinking 'when will the good Colonel ever finish the archaeological permit which we discussed yesterday?' Well, place your mind at ease, the *policia* are at your service, hands across the sea, two great countries working as one." He handed a piece of paper to Robert. "*Adíos*."

He drove off with a great roar from the engine. Robert and Teresa looked at each other and at the form, titled "*Permiso Arqueologia*," and at the Colonel's signature at the bottom.

"Schwartz," said Robert. Teresa nodded.

Chapter 20

Tulum, November 5, present day

An hour later they were at the cenote south of Tulum. Robert tied some knots in a half-inch nylon line for easier climbing and tied an end of the knotted line and an end of their light safety line to a rock outcrop. They donned SCUBA gear and worked their way hand over hand down the line. Robert cautioned Teresa to hold on to the line until they got their bearings, as he expected to descend into the fast-moving stream.

The water was only a dozen feet down. They slipped beneath the surface and dove down maybe fifty feet through a ragged passage filled with swirling inch-long silver fish. The visibility, without the fish, would have been hundreds of feet in the clear water. With the fish, Robert could hardly see Teresa five feet away.

The fish population dwindled as they dove, and they reached a horizontal passage, testing the speed of the current carefully. The passage was wider here and the current was slow.

They played out the lifeline from the big reel as they swam easily upstream, emerging into an impressively large cavern, lit by a pencil-thin shaft of sunlight. Teresa rolled on her back and kicked like a dolphin.

The colorful stalactites and stalagmites merged to form vertical columns like the bars of a jail, but they found a path and swam slowly through the formations, finding—finally—the river's entrance tunnel.

Robert signaled Teresa and pointed up to show her a silvery mirror at the top of a wide section. He pulled his regulator from his mouth and swam to the mirror, stuck his head into the air pocket and took a few breaths. Good air. He returned to her and she gave him an OK sign.

After swimming a few hundred yards down the smooth limestone passage, they saw a small aperture in the right-hand wall. Robert pulled out a loop of line and let it show that the water flow, although slow, was into the aperture: it was not a blind alley. Robert debated with himself for a minute. He had seen no scratches in the walls; they may have found the southerly passage. Should he try this side passage? He thought again that he should not have come even this far with an inexperienced diver. But the virus was winning, back home. And Teresa seemed totally relaxed underwater, she used even less air than he did.

OK, into the abyss. Robert unstrapped his tank but left the regulator in his mouth, and Teresa, understanding, unstrapped hers. He thrust his tank through the opening—too small for a diver with tank—and wriggled his body through with some difficulty. She followed more easily, and they strapped the tanks back on.

He saw no scratches here either. Either the wrong passage, or the events were downstream. He turned downstream. More current here. At least if there was trouble, the current would take them back to the reef. Or would the passage constrict so that they'd be stuck like a cork in a bottle? No, the current would need a bigger hole to flow through. Unless it branched...it better damn well not branch, they wouldn't make much progress swimming against it.

After swimming fifty yards or so, a totally unexpected sight surprised him: shiny steel rungs were stapled to the wall. He looked at Teresa, she shrugged. Surely, the Maya did not make stainless steel ladders, and this one appeared new. He pointed a lamp upwards along the ladder and saw a rectangular opening in the tunnel ceiling and the reflecting mirror of the water surface. He looked around, saw no other signs of civilization, and started up the ladder.

The ladder led them up twenty feet, and near the top they came out into fresh air. They were near floor level in a long man-made cavern, trapezoidal in cross section, about a hundred feet long and maybe fifteen feet high and wide, with a pair of narrow-gage conveyer tracks leading down its center. At the far end of the tracks a large steel mechanism articulated with hydraulic cylinders seemed poised to lower its long arm into the river.

Robert spotted a yellow forklift truck parked near the mechanism. Forklift truck? Must be a dry entrance somewhere.

The place smelled of mold and oil, and they could hear the lapping of the water and a muted low humming that may have been a generator. A floodlight was mounted in the wall near them but it was not lit, the only light was from their waterproof flashlights. The floor and walls were limestone, but they seemed to have been smoothly worked with a fine tool of some kind to a flatness that could not be natural.

They stripped off their SCUBA gear and deposited it near the hydraulic mechanism. "Look!" she whispered, pointing at the far wall. "Glyphs!"

They illuminated the far wall with their flashlights, and she quickly read the columns of glyphs. "It looks like this place was some kind of entrance hall to something. Something important, but secular. The ancient Maya dug this place out. I can read most of this. It's not what we're looking for. But it looks like there's more here, more rooms. Let's look around."

Robert felt a sudden chill. He thought of the wet suit he had not needed for the seventy-degree water, but here without the insulation of the air-filled buoyancy vest his body temperature seemed to plummet. He shivered slightly and his stomach tightened. What was this installation? Why the secrecy? Some government project? A mining operation? Whoever the operators were, they didn't want this place on the tourist maps.

"Let's not talk," he whispered to Teresa, turning off his light. "And turn off your flashlight. Just in case. Wait, stick it into your wet suit sleeve so you get only a narrow beam."

"Just in case this cave is crawling with rats?" she whispered back. "You go first."

Robert walked to the hydraulic mechanism in the darkness with Teresa holding his arm, turned on his flashlight briefly and found a crude wooden door blocking a side passage. Robert leaned on it without effect. He looked more closely at the door. Vertical heavy hardwood planks, recent construction, no handle, hinges maybe on the opposite side. Scratches on the stone showed where the latch bolt was located, and a narrow gap in the planks revealed a glint of metal.

Robert removed his diver's knife from its calf holster and pushed its point through the gap, working it back and forth to move the retaining bolt a fraction of a millimeter at a time until the door swung free.

They moved forward a few feet and reached a T junction with a larger tunnel in the limestone, a natural cave with no signs of masonry. Its irregular floor was bisected by a deep crevice carved by a fast-moving stream, and along one wall a row of bare low-wattage bulbs flickered in time with a generator's mumbling.

"Don't have to worry about noise level in here," said Robert over the roaring stream. "Watch your step, though, that looks like the WaterWorld Thrill Ride down there."

A great irregular pile of green trash bags blocked the upstream direction, and beyond there was a rough wall with no apparent passage except the low tunnel carved by the stream.

"Look at that, will you," observed Teresa. "Not ecologically conscious at all. Let's call Greenpeace."

"That lets out any authorized expedition, and it means there are a few of them at least. Be careful."

They walked downstream. Robert noticed black circular marks on the light-colored rock of the walls and imagined the forklift truck wheels making intermittent contact.

Teresa stopped, looking down. "Got something?" Robert asked.

"Trilobite. Fossilized. This stone was under water in the Cambrian."

"Thank you, Doctor Welles. See anything else?"

"No Maya artifacts. Rubber marks on the wall. Poor maintenance, half of these bulbs are out. The stream is much faster than underground rivers in the Yucatán are supposed to be."

"Maybe Bernoulli effect. I think it's time to get out of here. I'm getting nervous. We can come back with reinforcements."

"Oh, come on, just a little farther. Those glyphs at the entrance cave seemed to say this was a big installation, many rooms, and some kind of institution."

After a few minutes they had reached the bend, and the tunnel stretched another hundred feet, revealing four man-made openings cut into the walls on their side of the stream. As they neared the first opening, two men stepped quickly into the tunnel, each with a week's growth of black stubbly beard, each dressed in black sweats with a black bandanna around the head, each holding a machine pistol. The taller of the two flashed a twisted smile and said, "*Buenos días. ¿Cómo estás?*"

"*Muy buen, gracias,*" said Teresa, in a heavy American accent. "Is this Pirates of the Caribbean?"

The men grabbed Robert by each arm and slammed him against the wall. His head rattled off the stone, causing a shower of sparks in his vision. "Your name, *Señor*, quickly, and how you came to be here," said the tall one, still smiling, "or I will be shooting your balls off."

"I am here to help," said Robert. "Trust me." He managed a grin.

Robert felt the man's grip slacken and whipped an arm free, bringing the blade of his stiffened hand down on the wrist in the same motion. The gun bounced on the floor and Robert kicked it with his right foot and sent it spinning across the wet stone. He spun and his other foot caught the shorter man on the kneecap. Robert grabbed the shorter man's pistol arm and brought it up high, then down on his own knee, hearing tendons snap as the second gun went spinning to the stone.

The tall man screamed and dove for the gun. Robert dove with him and knocked the gun over the edge into the stream. The man drove a knee deeply into Robert's stomach and scrambled away, but Robert grabbed an ankle, brought the man crashing down, and quickly twisted the foot and the man attached to it until the man had been rolled to the rim of the stream.

Then he heard a single pistol shot, echoing like a cannon blast in the confined space, and looked up into a third man's greasy face with tiny malevolent brown eyes almost obscured by thick eyebrows. The third man also held a machine pistol. Robert released his hold and braced himself to deliver another kick when he heard a cry from behind him. Teresa was on her back with the short man kneeling on her stomach, a knife pressed into her throat. "She dies," he said.

Robert relaxed in surrender just before a powerful blow to the back of his head smashed him down to the stone. In the remaining few milliseconds of consciousness he experienced a sudden close-up of the cave floor from an inch away and saw a tiny fossilized fish. Trilobite? Cambrian. Pretty sure it was Cambrian. The fossil turned red as the burst capillaries in his retina leaked blood.

Chapter 21

Houston, November 5, present day

Joe Rossi, of the firm of Rossi and Viscuso, Trucking and Rigging, tightened down the last chain clamp. They'd used the two-inch logging chain for the job. He stepped back for a final look. The Caterpillar D13N was a bitch and a half, all right: two hundred tons, thirty foot blade, fourteen hundred horsepower, almost two million U.S. At eighty-five freaking feet long it stuck its ass out over the back of his biggest trailer.

Rossi and Viscuso did a lot of oil field work and they were as good as anybody with the big iron, but this thing was humungous. Even the thirty-six-wheeler looked like it was sagging a foot. If Caterpillar and Komatsu didn't stop the contest to prove theirs was the biggest, nobody was gonna be able to truck their shit to the job.

He walked around one more time and motioned Lee into the driver's seat for the haul to Austin.

Kirtland Air Force Base, Albuquerque
58th Special Operations Wing

The maintenance chief jockeyed the cart under the starboard wing of the F-16 and toggled the lever to start the hydraulic lift. His cargo, an unguided NAPLPS-12A gravity air-to-ground weapon, lifted to the hardpoints and the lift held it there as he scrambled up the ladder to secure the explosive bolts. He'd been trying to figure what the hell was going on, the F-16 now had four of the seven-hundred-fifty-pound napalm bombs fitted. What was the target? The ordnance was Vietnam era, about the oldest stuff in the ammo dump. Kosovo heating up again? Seemed unlikely that they'd load up the planes with napalm and do a long refueling flight instead of picking up the NAPs from some NATO dump. But, jeez, they had over one hundred NAPs hung off F-16s and the birds were getting fuel now: there was enough napalm to fricassee Cincinnati, right here on this runway.

• • •

The first of the five C-130s lumbered down the long runway. Loaded to the maximum, it needed every foot of the strip to get airborne in the searing hundred-and-five-degree heat.

Lieutenant Commander Harry "Horse" Lilleman and the 114th Combat Engineering Battalion's specially trained C Company heavy-equipment operators sat on the nylon mesh seats, stripped down to camo shorts and T shirts. Racked on the far wall were their supplies: square main chute, round reserve chute, helmet, first aid, SPF thirty sunburn oil, bug juice, GPS, rain gear, six canteens of Gatorade, VHF radio, night vision goggles, a selection of K-rations, and some chow put up by the mess. A few of the old hands also smuggled beer and pulled-pork barbeque put up by Smokin' Joe's, but they didn't advertise the fact.

The cargo was four DEUCEs—Deployable Universal Combat Earth-mover—rubber tired dozers with earthmoving blades, capable of thirty-five mph on highway. But each was rigged for airdrop, as the target city's airport was in the red zone. Somebody was in a hell of a hurry.

Their briefing was pretty weird, something about a road building thing, but just the dozer stuff, no asphalt. And fast, round-the-clock operation, three shifts. But no armament, they thought it would be pretty much a tit job. But what the hell were the F-16's up to? That wasn't covered in the briefing. And there were a shitload of 'em: four squadrons, all flown in overnight. Brought their own maintenance, and they were all fueled and ready to boogie.

A wide climbing turn off the end of the runway brought a dramatic sunrise into view as the flight formed up and pointed to Austin, Texas.

Austin

"What's this about another zone?" asked Hapwell Theslie, scanning the flat Texas farmland through gyrostabilized military binoculars. He and Gary Spender were sitting on the roof of a Humvee.

"We're pretty sure the yellow zone has been compromised," said Spender. "We figured on thirty-six hours quarantine to make sure symptoms would appear. But it looks like there's a percent of victims, the people with some Maya ancestry, that carry the virus for up to a week before showing symptoms, and then they show just mild symptoms. They often recover, but it gives us a big problem with quarantine. I was almost happier with everybody dying in a week."

"Did you brief CDC?"

"They knew as soon as we knew...yesterday afternoon. We've divided the yellow zone into two rings and we plan on moving the red zone back another ten miles."

"Shit. Take a look at this." He handed the binoculars to Spender, who adjusted the focus and scanned the activity two miles away. There was a wall of smoke or dust, easily visible to the naked eye, rising in a ribbon. Underneath the cloud Spender spotted a frenzy of activity, led by a bulldozer about the size of a shuttle booster rocket. And about the same power, if the unmuffled roar clearly audible from this distance was any clue. The dozer was grinding westward at a fast walk, toppling mid-size trees like toothpicks.

Behind the giant machine Spender could see at least a dozen smaller rubber-tired dozers, circling around like little black flies, tidying up after the monster.

"You're reinforcing the red zone barrier?"

"It seemed like a good idea at the time," said Theslie. "We got a ring around the city, bulldozed fifty feet wide, hay-baled and staked. Then there's five feet of Mylar, and thirty feet of mist net for the small birds. If you don't think the Audubon Society is pissed, you don't know bird lovers. We didn't tell 'em about the PAHELs."

Spender handed the binoculars back and drank from a plastic water bottle, then splashed some on his head. Another scorcher. At least it wasn't raining.

"You know the equipment operators are going to need quarantine?"

"Oh, yeah. They don't yet, though."

"What's a PAHEL?" Spender wasn't sure he really wanted to know.

"Portable Array-steered High Energy Laser. It's been in our armory since Star Wars days. It fires a ten thousand joule near-infrared laser pulse. Capacitor bank, CO_2 laser. It was supposed to kill incoming MIRV missiles and saw the wings off enemy bombers at forty thousand feet."

Spender closed his eyes briefly. The military complex seemed more interested in practicing with all their latest toys than in actually controlling the outbreak. "And are we expecting enemy bombers?"

"Naaah," said Theslie. "It didn't work that well, anyway. Just scorched the paint. But it does a helluva job on light planes at low altitude, and on birds. And we don't even have to worry too much about bringing down a few commercial flights, we've theoretically got them all diverted. The military flyboys are on their own. Look over there, they've got one of 'em set up. It should be on full automatic by now." He pointed to a distant bright spot and held out the binoculars again. Spender zoomed in on a white-painted trailer with military markings. A forest of small dish antennas on the roof swiveled in unison. As he watched, the scene shimmered as if a big blowtorch had been touched off. He heard a few distant clicks a second later.

"It just fired," said Theslie. "Keep looking, you can see if they got a bird or a plane."

A smoldering black object entered Spender's field of view as it fell to the ground just inside the barrier. "A bird," he announced.

"Other than deploying weapons of mass destruction, and reinforcing a barrier that's already been breached, what are your plans?" asked Spender.

"Oh, the usual. The transition from civilian to military authority has gone pretty well. The mayor and the city council gave us some flak, so we declared 'em exposed and moved 'em into quarantine. They didn't like it, but there's not much they can do, right? Security on quarantine is really, really tight. What else? Lemme see. We have some volunteers inside in full Racal suits looking for pockets of infected people and animals and lighting 'em up."

"Lighting them up?"

"With lasers. So the Air Force birds can target them."

"Birds?" asked Spender. He was pretty sure he knew what Theslie meant, but he hoped he was wrong.

"Flyboys. Look over to the east."

Spender didn't need the binoculars to see dozens of slender fast-moving military airplanes with bombs hanging off the wings. Three broke formation and dove steeply at some target just out of sight across a low line of trees, and he caught the release of the bombs, tumbling through the air and flaming furiously on impact.

How many people had just died in flames? He thought about the Hippocratic oath. Was this evil, insanity, or essential? Cruel, ruthless, or just effective epidemic control? How many lives should be sacrificed for the concept of the greatest good for the greatest number? He didn't know for sure whether Theslie's methods were right or wrong, but he thanked God that he didn't need to make those decisions.

Chapter 22

Teresa awoke and looked around at some kind of storeroom illuminated with a single flickering incandescent bulb. Her head throbbed. She heard some kind of motor sputtering in the corner. Her hands were locked behind her somehow. Robert was slumped next to her—a bloody wound over his ear, a bruise on his forehead—not moving. She felt a flash of fear—he was still alive, wasn't he? She could just reach him with her foot and kicked him gently on his side. He grunted. His eyes were still closed, though. No blood, but his face looked bruised.

They were alone in the room. A dozen slender dark green pointed tubes, about twenty feet long, were stacked on nearby wooden cradles. Near the far wall a set of metal shelves held disorganized supplies, tools, cardboard boxes, tarpaulins. The room also was apparently cut from the bedrock limestone and the room's cross section was corbelled, trapezoidal, suggesting Maya origin again, but no glyphs appeared here. The rough chisel marks in the stone suggested a utilitarian use, not ceremonial. But the temperature was cool. Underground, she thought, but not ceremonial—unusual for the Maya, maybe a late construction. A big double metal door and a smaller metal door, obviously recent additions, were set in opposite ends of the room.

Maybe she could figure a way out herself, it was a little cold and clammy down here. She looked at Robert's hands, strapped to a three-inch iron pipe. She moved her hands, she was securely tied also. Hmmmm. She tried to move the pipe. Nothing. All right, maybe she would need a little help. She prodded him again. This time he didn't even grunt.

"Hey, sleeping beauty!" she said, maybe a little too loud.

She realized her error as two men entered the room a minute later with guns drawn. They looked Hispanic, young, dark but unhealthy-looking skin—maybe it was the sunless environment. They had black eyes, thick black eyebrows and stringy shoulder-length black hair, and they chattered in rapid Spanish. The short one smoked on a big cigar, the tall one had arms like a mountain gorilla. They spoke with a South American accent, maybe Venezuela or Colombia, debating how she and Robert had got into the caves. A moment later a third man appeared in the doorway with a rifle.

The tall man spoke to her in accented English, "You! What are you doing here? What are you looking for?"

She thought of what she should say, and how it probably would be smart to speak in English so she could continue to eavesdrop on the Spanish, then she thought she should pretend to be paralyzed with fear and shut up. Actually, she *was* just about paralyzed with fear. She did not reply.

The man with the cigar slapped her face and grabbed the zipper on her wet suit, pulling it to her waist, revealing an orange halter. He yanked the halter down roughly, leaving painful scratches from his fingernails. Cigar smoke filled her nostrils, triggering a wave of nausea. "First tell me what you do here, then I may do you a big favor." He squeezed her breast in an oil-stained hand, sending a wave of revulsion through her. Anger pushed away her fear.

The big man, José from the Spanish conversation, kicked at Robert. Robert grunted again, and this time his eyes opened, or at least one eye sort of opened. She could feel her fear washing away. He was awake. Time he used those big muscles for something constructive, like beating up on these guys. Could he break loose of these flimsy-looking wire ties, or what? But his eye, what was wrong? She looked closer. Jesus, bright red, he could be really hurt.

Robert shook his head sideways a few times and moaned again, then he looked up at her with both eyes more or less open, but they didn't seem to be pointing in the same direction. She could see him struggle to focus, staring at her. Migod! She looked down at the direction of his gaze; her breast was hanging out like a cow's, greasy fingerprints and all. She twisted away as far as she could. At least he didn't seem to be able to see too well yet.

The big man slapped Robert across his face with a pistol, drawing blood. Robert's head tilted down again, and Teresa felt a burst of concern. He could be badly hurt. "Stop that!" she screamed. "He didn't do anything!"

The man casually hit Robert again and spoke, "You! Idiot! What are you looking for?"

Robert coughed, cleared his throat, shook his head and tried again, "Relax. We're just archaeologists. We're looking for ancient Maya relics." He coughed again and spat blood onto the dark floor. "We don't care about whatever you're doing here."

What the heck were they doing here, Teresa asked herself. Secret military installation? No uniforms. Not neat enough for the military. Grave robbers? Too many of them. Terrorists? In Tulum, for Christ's sake? Drugs? Maybe, but why underground?

The big man jerked Teresa around to face Robert, and this time she saw his eyes focus clearly, saw his face darken in anger as the man grabbed her breast and twisted it, bringing tears to her eyes. "We keep her. If you don't tell truth, we kill her, after a while. What you looking for?"

"We're archaeologists, dammit! Dirt archaeologists! Diggers! Looking for Maya ruins! Don't hurt her!"

José hit him again and he slumped. Then José turned and walked to a table, unclipped a radiophone, pushed some buttons, and spoke in Spanish, "Lopez? José. You will not believe this, but two college gringo diggers showed up in the warehouse...Yes, one man, one woman...No, English only, they don't speak much Spanish. They had SCUBA gear, that's how. But how do they get past the net...OK, we'll keep them here all year, if you want...No, no alarms at all, they didn't open the underwater grate or use the dry entrance. OK, we'll wait, but Carlito wants to bang the woman, he's like a dog in heat...OK, sure, three hours, we'll be here, where we gonna go?"

José spoke to the other man, "Carlito, Lopez says no banging the broad. Until he gets here." He walked back to zip up Teresa's wet suit.

"How does he find out, if you do not tell him?"

"From the smile on her face, idiot. Maybe when Lopez talks to them, he wants to make sure they're not D.E.A. or something. Maybe he wants the woman for himself first. After that, it will be our turn, if they are still alive."

Carlito patted Teresa's thigh, revealed his missing teeth in a smile and spoke in English, "Later, *querido*. Wait for me. You are much happy here, I promise." They walked out.

Chapter 23

Peloc moved quickly to the machine at the far end of the cave with his short, precise steps. Every minute was important now, if he was to unravel this tangle which had so quickly and so unexpectedly ensnarled his Maya. The eternal, the magnificent Maya, his Maya, chosen of the Jaguar God, favorite of Chac, builders of the tallest pyramids, the largest cities: the Maya were humbled, panicked, running to the forests, no longer able to live in the cities with the horror.

Peloc called for his main assistant, Bird Eater Xcatca. He sighted down his impressive nose at Xcatca like a crossbow being brought to bear and asked for the body of the next victim, already cold with the temperature of the cave, already stiff in death. With the obsidian knife he scraped the tongue and collected the thick effluvium in a dish, then added berztl liquid and mixed the solution.

He carefully decanted the solution onto the stationary plate. Perhaps ten minutes would be needed to precipitate the crystals that he needed. He asked Xcatca to replenish the supply of Zbltbl powder and sat back to wait, rubbing his eyes. He had been driven for many days and nights, excited that the solution lay nearly within his grasp, but unable to close his fingers on the slippery core of the thing that he needed.

The cave was his masterpiece, carved from the limestone by two dozen of the city's finest stonemasons, faced with obsidian tiles which had been polished to a mirror finish, and kept dry with the accurate construction of the tiles which allowed no air infiltration and by the exposed trays of fire treated Shotjtl. The walls were already half filled with the records, the testimony to the pinnacle of excellence that his university had achieved. Another few years would fill the walls with glyphs; he would need to start another cave soon to have space. But perhaps if the killer black tongue could not be stopped, there would be no need for another cave.

The far wall was arrayed with the equipment that would make the chemical—waiting for him—if he could just dissect the secrets of the disease. But his attempts to crystallize the enemy had not succeeded. He checked the plate in the dim light from the oil lamps: at last. The breath escaped from his lungs in a long shuddering gasp. Good crystals, lovely rainbows of peacock iridescence. He lowered the brass counterplate with his hand shaking and rubbed the shiny cloth on the globe. He raised the counterelectrode and dusted the white Zbltbl powder.

He was instantly filled with a quiet peace, an easing of the tension that had gripped his body for months. It was there, sketched in white—so simple, so serene, so lovely. He easily visualized the structure of the antidote: the molecule which would mate passionately with the disease molecule, draw it tightly in, neuter it with affection. He saw too that the antidote would not even need his waiting equipment, if he remembered correctly. He looked on his wall for the record—yes, the Ctlactan flower had exactly the pattern he needed.

"Xcatca!" he called. There was much work to do. And he had not slept in a week. He would not get to sleep again tonight.

Chapter 24

Tulum, November 5, present day

Teresa shifted her weight so the ties on her wrists didn't cut into her skin. How about Robert's wrists? He was hanging awkwardly from his hands, head slumped, mouth hanging open. But he was still alive, he had groaned a little. His hands looked OK; good circulation.

What to do? She had never felt so helpless. Robert. He came at you from a strange direction, that man. He didn't seem to think like normal people did. He walked like he was on springs, like he had infinite reserves of strength. She felt that he could make this nightmare go away as soon as he woke up, even though her logical mind did not agree.

She yanked at her bindings in frustration, banging the pipes together. No one came. She turned back to Robert and watched his inert face with concern. He groaned again, spat blood on the floor and opened his eyes. He looked terrible. She could see the consciousness returning, the eyes focusing as he scanned the room. He pulled strongly on the pipe for a minute and stopped.

"Robert, are you OK?" she asked in a low voice.

"Nhhhh," he answered, waggled his head back and forth and seemed to be listening for something. Then, "Jeez. Well. Maybe."

"Do something before they come back."

Robert pulled hard on his ties, and sagged back. Then he turned his head to study the pipes and she saw a shift in his expression, something like amused happiness, unless she misread it completely. He looked over at her and smiled. "What?" she asked.

He didn't answer for a minute, concentrating still on the pipes. Then he said, speaking slowly and quietly, "I took sixth grade in the Calvin Coolidge Elementary School in Newton Upper Falls. Mr. Finney handed out puzzles with loops and bent nails and wire rings. The last one, the tough one, had two rings on a bent wire and nobody could get it apart."

That's it, thought Teresa. He's reliving his childhood. Christ.

"I kept fiddling with it, though, until it came apart. Mr. Finney said I was the first person to figure it out. Funny how that sort of thing sticks in your head, isn't it? I can still remember the shape of that puzzle."

She whispered. "So, how does that become relevant to our current dilemma? I don't like it here."

"I've been figuring it out. Imagine these pipes are bent wires and we're rings."

Robert grabbed the pipe in both hands and levered his body up to a horizontal position, swung through one of the curves of the pipe and dropped to his feet behind her in the loop of her arms.

"This might be a little close for a second, but I think it'll work out," he said. "OK now, straighten up," he grunted, as he lifted her over his body.

"Free at last!" he announced quietly, passing his still-cuffed hands under his feet and in front of him and then holding his hands in the air like a victorious prizefighter, free of the pipe.

"Lord God Almighty! How the hell did you do that? And how about me?"

"Mr. Finney. Wait here a second."

Robert rummaged around the junk pile, emerged with a pair of cutting pliers, and worked behind Teresa for a minute.

"Any luck?" she asked.

"Nope, that's pretty tough wire. But that looks like an oxyacetylene rig over there."

Robert detoured to look at the big green-colored tubes. One was open, and he pulled out a clear plastic bag containing a white powder and caught Teresa's eye with a frown.

She heard a noise from the corridor and hissed at Robert. He jumped over his manacled hands so they were behind him, and he was back against the pipes in two fast strides with his bloody head lolling sideways and his eyes half closed. Quite convincing, even his breathing seemed slow and painful. But the cutting pliers were visible on the floor, out of her reach.

"Pliers!" she whispered, looking at them. He caught the direction of her gaze and tucked the pliers into his waistband as José walked in, talking on the radio.

José moved behind her and grabbed her hands, then dropped them and reached around Robert to yank a college ring from his finger. "Sí, nothing for the girl, the man had one. Sí, it says Boston University with some little animal or something. U.S.? Sí, I think so." He walked out, still talking, tossing the ring in the air. The double door slammed closed and a latch was drawn.

"He didn't see you were untied," she said.

"I certainly wasn't going to tell him."

"Robert? No, don't look at me, I'm a little undressed. I just wanted to say you're awfully good at a lot of things. Possibly you might not be quite as crazy as I thought."

He grinned up at her with his eyes shut tight. The cheery lopsided smile contrasted with the wreckage of his face. He listened carefully for a minute before he pulled his hands back to the front and moved to the oxyacetylene machine.

Then he rolled the welding rig over to Teresa, opened the acetylene valve and sparked it to a yellow flame with the ignition tool. He fiddled with the valves till he had a tiny hot flame, then handed her the handle and quickly melted through his ties. Then he moved behind her. She felt a pinch and was free.

"Good one." She adjusted her suit and licked a burned spot on her wrist where a spark had landed. "Now what? There's at least five of those guys, all armed."

Robert opened the metal door and they looked into a small closet with oilcans on the floor. Open electrical wiring was stapled to the walls. "Do you suppose that guy with the cigar smokes all the time?"

he asked, "Or, actually, that cigar was just freshly lit when he came in here, right?"

"Yes. Why?"

"There's enough oxygen in the welding rig to do the old exploding cigar trick, I think. It's worth a shot, anyway." He opened the valve on the oxygen tank fully. Then he grabbed the welding helmet and pushed Teresa into the closet.

She watched, fascinated, trying to understand the concept as he dug the cutting pliers out of his pocket, traced the wiring, and cut one strand of the white wire. The lights went out. A second later they came back on as he stripped the wire and bent the wire ends loosely together.

"Here's the plan," he said. He put on the helmet and flipped the dark glass window down. "I'll get my eyes dark-adapted with the helmet. You scream and the bad guys show up, all excited. The oxygen atmosphere blows up the cigar. You move this white wire and the lights go out. I run into the room and clobber them. Then you turn the lights back on."

"You'll get shot."

"I hope they won't be able to see me. But there may be shooting, stay behind the wall in here. Don't worry if you get a little light-headed, it's just an oxygen high."

"This is crazy."

"Got any better ideas?"

She thought it over, feeling a little light-headed. "I guess not. Should I scream now?"

"Not yet, let's get all the oxygen we can." After a few minutes the hissing from the oxygen tank quieted and Teresa noticed her breathing had slowed almost to a stop in the oxygen-rich atmosphere.

"I think the scream now, please."

She thought her scream was nice, very theatrical. Robert, in the helmet, looked through the crack in the door as two men ran in. Carlito's cigar exploded like a grenade in a shower of sparks. He fell to the floor. The tall man frantically beat out multiple fires burning fiercely in his pants, then gave up the effort and yanked his pants down around his ankles.

"Lights!" said Robert, and Teresa pulled on the wire and watched by the flickering illumination of the burning pants as he ran into the room in the near darkness, but the tall man moved quickly, shaking his feet loose and bringing up the pistol.

Teresa held her breath as Robert dove, tucked and somersaulted with the helmet crashing on the hard floor. She heard the sound of the gunfire but he somersaulted again, planted his feet and drove his helmet into the tall man.

"Lights!" he said, pulling off the helmet, and Teresa worked the improvised switch. The tall man was on his side, holding his crotch and groaning through clenched teeth. The pistol was nowhere to be seen. The other man had moved to his hands and knees and was shaking his head back and forth.

Robert kicked the tall man in the head, grabbed a length of electrical wire and tied him to the same pipes they had been handcuffed to. Teresa moved into the room and they started to tie up the cigar smoker, with his eyes still tightly closed and his face blackened. They were interrupted by the sound of footsteps running down the corridor.

Robert dragged her through the big door and into a dimly lit corridor and they ran towards the darker end. A voice screamed behind them, and then another voice and a door slammed.

In a moment they came to a dimly lit, wide platform with a lift truck and stacked burlap bags. Beyond that the walkway ended abruptly. Teresa looked back. She saw no motion, but she could hear a group of men, sure of their quarry, getting closer but still out of sight. They were finally out of options.

She heard a motor cough to life behind her and spun around to see Robert fiddling with the controls of the forklift. It moved forward and the tines rammed into a stack of bags. Something like beach sand spilled out as he raised the pile and turned the machine towards the attackers.

"Get on, behind me," he said as the machine crept back up the corridor. She squeezed in, holding him between her thighs as the vehicle accelerated. Gunshots. Bullets thudded into the bags and ricocheted screaming off the walls, whipping past her ears like angry wasps.

Then something heavier thudded into the bags and a face appeared over the top, followed by a gun. She screamed. Robert slammed on the brakes and the gunman fell backwards, buried under a pile of sandbags. Robert jumped sideways as automatic weapons chattered, dragging her with him into the darkness of the stream.

Teresa heard slugs slap into Robert, behind her, and she was gripped again by fear. She fell into blackness as she heard him yell out in pain and she tumbled into cold running water.

Teresa struggled to the surface and gasped for air. She spun around in the current, looking back at the rapidly diminishing patch of light and the flashes from the rifles; no Robert, and he had definitely been hit at least twice. She twisted around until she could see the shape of the tunnel in the rapidly diminishing light. The rough ceiling sprouted stalactites, lowering down to the water level in places. She crashed into a little forest of stalactites and was pinned there by the current.

She caught her breath and tried to push off the rock but the water was too fast, she was trapped there, one leg caught painfully, her mouth barely above water. Blood dripped down her nose and into her mouth.

Think. Don't panic, think. This passage must be new, the stalactites must have been created when the sea level was much lower, but the rapid flow should have eroded the channel smooth like the others. Unless the flow here was new, diverted by the new construction in the caves. That might explain the high flow rate, also, if several old channels had been blocked. So, good, now do something.

A body crashed into her back. Better be Robert. He better be all right. She shouted over the current, but she got no response. She was unable to move against the pressure to see if he was unconscious or dead. God damn, this wasn't what her mother had in mind for her, nice little Catholic girl. They'd find two skeletons right here on this stupid limestone spear, all tangled up, maybe a hundred years from now. She felt her heart hammering at some impossible rate and saw tiny bright flashes of light in her peripheral vision, in sync with each heartbeat.

She thought she saw a dark swirl in the water and she smelled the coppery sweetness of fresh blood. Is that mine or his? Dammit, dammit, dammit. She squeezed her eyes tight together. Make it go away. Please.

It was weirdly pleasant, though, in some twisted way, nice fresh cool water to sip if you were thirsty, Robert's warmth protecting her from hypothermia. At least he was still warm. She felt her mind drifting downstream without her body. He seemed to shift against her and she felt an unexpected pleasurable response, felt her hips arch back against him. Where did that come from? Holy Christ, get it under control, think of something besides sex, we're about to die here. Unprofessional. Stay under control, you sex-crazed fool.

Anyway, he's probably dead, just sloshing around in the current. Then he moved again, more strongly this time, and after a minute two hands came around her abdomen. She felt a wave of relief, he was definitely conscious. This was not a good place for romance, though. We really should be figuring out how to get out of this before the Colombians find a sub or something. Robert coughed, his mouth just behind her ear, and grunted with effort and she was levered slowly back off the rock like an abalone peeled off its coral reef by a diver's pry bar. They fought through the tangle of stalactites and were again spinning downstream.

Then it was complete blackness, twisting, tumbling, no way to breathe. She felt for what she thought was up, but there was no air, just smooth stone. She was about to give up the hopeless fight and inhale the dark water when his strong hands held her up and she felt her face burst through into an air pocket and she breathed miraculous fresh cool air and got swept away again, and then everything seemed to speed up, the walls of the passage slammed into her, one side then the other, and the breath she thought would be her last was knocked from her lungs. She knew from the burning and the fierce clutching of her plexus that she had reached the end. But again the hands, weaker now, held her up and there was briefly air and she inhaled a huge shuddering breath and a stronger current spun her down and a gigantic blow struck her head and she seemed to spiral softly down as blackness rose and enveloped her.

Chapter 25

"*No, no no,*" *said Peloc, jumping up and down with frustration.* "*Ktalban! It is the ktalban flower, look, look, is it not obvious?*" *He gestured towards the swirling images on the obsidian plates.* "*Never mind, follow me, we have little time.*"

He led three assistants, four students, and a clerk out of the darkness of the cave into the bright sunlight where he stood helpless for a minute with his eyes shut. He had been in the cave for three weeks straight— sleeping for an hour or two on a reed bed, testing, evaluating, synthesizing. Now finally the answer was clear. He managed to open his eyes finally. The sun was directly overhead and the day was completely windless, the sky clear of clouds, and the temperature so hot that the ground seemed to be hissing like the jaguar.

The colorful buildings of Tulum were arrayed to the north, and west of the rise of land where the cave entrance was hidden, the huts of the people were scattered to the horizon. Thin streams of smoke drifted into the blue sky, and the villagers were bringing in the crops, harvesting the shoblt and tsa-tsa as if the Maya in the West were not falling like the shoblt stalks before the blade.

The people saw Peloc had come back to life again, risen from the Lords of the Dead, and they ran to the hill where they knelt and touched their foreheads to the stony ground.

"Arise!" said Peloc. "Runners! We need one hundred runners who will carry the honor of Tulum and the trust of Chac! Runners whose names will be carved into the largest stela! Runners who will live forever with the gods!"

All the young men stepped eagerly forward, at least a hundred.

"People! We have our runners. Bring them food and water for six days. Bring them containers, jars. Hurry."

Peloc motioned for Bird Eater Xcatca and sketched the plan. The ktalban flower would be found after a three day run. Bird Eater would run with the group, half of the runners carrying all the supplies. Then when the bearers dropped from exhaustion, fresh runners would carry the supplies. The ktalban flower would be found in the tall tree, harvested, crushed to a liquid that would cure the disease. The runners were to fan out with the liquid to Chichén Itzá, Cobá, Uxmal—all of the cities—and mix the liquid with water. Then all of the people were to drink, starting with the sickest.

Bird Eater Xcatca knelt for the blessing of Peloc and ran with the runners to the sacbé, spurred on by the cheers of the villagers. Peloc walked slowly to his room in the city, feeling every one of his sixty-five years.

Chapter 26

Cartegena, November 5, present day

Ernesto's voice was quiet and menacing, "Let me see if I understand this. The two college kids I told you about got in the cave. OK so far. The four of you were somehow able to overpower them, even though they were unarmed. This, too, is OK. Then you handcuffed them to a pipe and called Lopez."

"*Sí.*"

"Didn't call me."

"Lopez, he was closer."

"Uh, huh. They say anything under your relentless questioning?"

"They said they were archaeologists, doctors, looking for a cure for a disease. Bullshit, probably."

Ernesto squeezed off a few more rounds into the target, now shredded to ribbons. "No, true, probably. And we would have owned that cure if you hadn't let them escape and then killed them. Two little blunders, right in a row." He slammed a fresh clip into his automatic and punctuated each word with a shot: "Two. Little. Two. Hundred. Million. Dollar. Blunders."

"I cannot understand how they could have gotten away."

"I cannot understand how you could not have listened to my careful instructions. Let them in, I said. Keep out of their way, I said. Keep an eye on them, I said. I should have told you under no circumstances are you to kill them."

"We didn't mean to kill them, but they were getting away."

Ernesto unscrewed the silencer and emptied the clip into the wall. As the echoes died away he raised his head to the heavens and spread his arms wide. "Lord, please, carve this on their tombstones, 'We didn't mean to kill them, but they were getting away.'"

Chapter 27

Tulum, November 5, present day

The small blue fishing boat, its motor throttled down to a slow trolling speed, coasted down the long coral reef that curls from Belize to Cozumel. The fertile reef was warmed and nourished by the Gulf Stream running near the coast at this latitude, bathing the reef with nutrients from the South Atlantic.

It had been a long day and a good day, the boat was heavy with the catch: red snapper, grouper, even today one nice mahi mahi. The sun was setting in a clear sky over the Yucatán. At the stern, Miguel tended two rods with surface lures, nudging the motor from time to time to keep his course just to the ocean side of the reef. His teenage son Pépé watched from the bow, looking for the big ones lifting to inhale the first of the evening's black flies.

"Papa! Look!" He pointed to port at a floating object.

Miguel thought it looked like trash floating in the water, but he steered to port.

"Papa! It's people!"

The current rolled the object over to reveal human faces. Not dead faces, marinated in the salt to the greenish pallor, almost alive-looking faces, but quiet, still, not breathing. A man and a woman. Young. Miguel asked Pépé to go far towards the bow and hauled the bodies over the stern so he wouldn't swamp the boat, already low in the water. The woman made a small noise and as he pounded her on the back she coughed up seawater. She was wearing a wet suit, but two of her fingers stuck out at an odd angle and her head was covered in blood.

The man was dead—wearing only a ripped swimsuit—his side bleeding from three or four wounds, his head, too, bruised and bleeding. He lay unmoving in the bilge water in the bottom of the boat with the fish, with the dirty water running in and out of his open mouth as the boat rocked. As Miguel tried to make a splint for the woman's broken hand she saw the man and she screamed, "Robert!" and she slapped at his face and put her head to his chest. "Pulse!" she screamed. "Breathe, you bastard!" She rolled him over with help from Miguel, and they pressed on his back together until a large quantity of water came from his mouth, then they rolled him back and she held his nostrils and breathed into his lungs. "Check his pulse!" she looked at Miguel.

He reached for the man's wrist and found a thin, too slow pulse beneath the cold skin, skin like a plucked chicken. Every three or four seconds, he had never felt a pulse like that one. "Slow," he reported.

She nodded and looked at him with strange colored eyes and he kept his hand on the man's wrist. She breathed into the man's lungs and he could see the man's chest inflating, but when she stopped the chest would go down and not move. "Goddam you!" she said, slapped his chest with her injured hand and screamed in pain, and breathed into his lungs again.

Miguel looked at this woman, angry now, yelling at the man. She had regained color and even though her hair was matted and wet and bloody and her fingers stuck out at a funny angle she had much beauty, a look of purpose and strength. He kept a hand on the man's wrist and when she looked at him, he nodded yes. But the pulse was slower, if anything. He shrugged.

He steered the boat towards the coast where his friend Ricardo had the car; the woman needed a doctor and the long trip to Playa del Carmen would need almost an hour. The man—Robert, she had called him—he didn't know what the man needed. Help from God.

The woman kept breathing the man's lungs full of air. She watched as the man's chest sank and then just before they reached shore his chest slowly rose again, by itself, and again, and again, and she fell beside the man into the bottom of the boat. She made small noises like quiet screams and curled closely behind him to warm him with her body.

On land, Miguel headed up the coast in Ricardo's old Toyota sedan. The woman was riding in the front seat with a temporary splint, fashioned from a cardboard box, supporting her hand. Her bleeding had stopped. The man in the back with Pépé—his side bandaged as well as they could—was still breathing but still was not conscious.

"Where are you taking us?" she asked.

"Playa del Carmen, little hospital."

"My name is Teresa. That's Robert, in the back seat. He saved my life. I was dead. He saved my life."

"You saved his life, too. I am Miguel, that is my son Pépé. We are happy to help." Fairly happy, that robber Ricardo had demanded the mahi mahi in return for lending the car and getting his fish to market for him.

"Can you take us to the hospital in Cancún, instead?" she asked.

"*Sí*, better hospital there."

"Not only that, but the people who shot us will be looking to make sure we're dead. If they find us alive, we'll be dead. Does that make sense? I'm a little groggy. Talk to me, Miguel. I have to stay awake. You speak good English. Were you born around here?"

"*Sí*, I worked many years in the hotels and I learn the English good. It is not so easy a life...but it is better than most to have at least the job. Cancún, there they have the fancy hotels and the *turista* think that Mexico, it is a beautiful country, but there in Cancún City two miles away it is the place where the staff lives, with big rats in the trash all night and sometimes the bad diseases. But I learn to tend the bar and make the drinks—Piña Colada, Margarita—smile a lot, make good tips. And I learn not to like the *turista*, but secretly, for the *turista* must feel you like him if he is to give the tips."

"Uh-huh," said the woman, softly.

"Then I move with Rosa and little Pépé to Playa del Carmen and I am more of a free man, and in the town lives the staff and the *turista* both and you cannot tell which of them is which, and nobody cares if the streets are made of dirt and the dogs lie in the sidewalk, and the *turista* see that Mexico is not always so beautiful and yet they love it as I do, and the sea is there with the soft friendly blue water, and the reef and the fish and the long sunsets. And they do not so much need to be the big boss and need me to be the servant person, and I find *turista* are like Mexicans, some good, some bad, most regular people."

The woman said "Ummmmm," and rested her head on the windowsill. "And then I move to Puerto Aventuras where the big boats with the *gringo* fishermen tie up and where the sidewalks are cleaned every hour and the bar is full with big shots, and the staff is in a junkhole town across the big road where they burn the trash and the rats live with us and the *turista* are never, never supposed to go. But I do not care, as the tips are big and I think I can buy finally a boat and a motor, too. Now I have it, the boat, sixteen feet long, with the stainless steel Yamaha motor and the sail I use when the wind is good to save the gas, and Pépé is grown big and plenty strong and we take the boat to the reef and fish for yellowtail and snappers and eels and we sell them to the chefs at the fancy hotels and we don't make the tips but it is a good life. And I teach Pépé the English, so he speaks now three languages, he is smart boy, he speaks Yucatec, Spanish, and English. Better even then me, the English, hey, Pépé?"

"Father, you are much better than I at speaking English."

He looked at the woman to see if she understood, but she was asleep.

Chapter 28

Cancún, November 7, present day

The hospital was a two-story cinder block building on the edge of Cancún City. It had four small rooms on the second floor, each with two beds. The walls were two-tone green, decorated with last year's calendar and a poster of cliff divers at Acapulco. Glass brick windows admitted light from the morning sun but kept out the views of the unlovely city.

The place smelled strongly of disinfectant. An elderly Mexican lay in one white-painted metal bed, snoring loudly. A needle in his arm connected to tubes ran from a plastic bag half full of liquid. Opposite, Robert Asher lay quiet and unmoving in a corner bed, also connected to tubes from a glucose drip. His eyes were closed and his head bandaged.

Teresa Welles sat beside the bed—dressed in street clothes but with a plaster cast on her left hand—holding Robert's hand. "The man said his name was Miguel, he rescued us both. We will meet him again after you recover, you'll like him, he's nice. He and his son were in the boat. He told me all about what it's like living down here, for the locals. Such a different life from Cambridge, it's hard to realize."

A nurse entered with a bouquet of flowers and handed them to Teresa. "These just arrived. There is a card. I put them in a bottle, we have no vase."

"Thanks, they're lovely. Who sent them?" She looked at the card. "They're from Dr. Teppin, Robert. He says you should get better. No, actually, he said he insists that you recover."

"More than a day, now, and he has not moved, he cannot hear you," said the nurse. "It could be weeks, months, who knows. I know it is difficult, but you may have to leave here soon."

"No, he knows I'm here, he needs me. He saved my life. He held me up to the air, I didn't even know it was there. I will stay here."

"For a while, if you wish," said the nurse. "I will pray for him."

"For who?" said Robert. His eyes fluttered open.

"¡Caramba! Gracias a Dios!" The nurse ran out.

"Well, hi, sleepyhead," said Teresa, a sudden strong ache in the back of her throat. She turned her head so he could not see her tears.

"Hi, Teresa," he spoke slowly and quietly, "Where is this? What happened?"

"This is a hospital in Cancún. Do you remember the SCUBA trip to the cave?"

"Sure. And getting untied, and getting shot at." He thought a minute. "Nothing after that. Did I get hit?"

"Well, yes, a few times. One went right through, two ricochets got stuck in you but they got the slugs out cleanly and nothing important got dinged. You were hit in your side. And your right hip. You saved my life. You lost a lot of blood, and you got a concussion. How do you feel?"

Robert was quiet for a while. "Not bad, I guess, considering. My backside feels as if somebody's doing acupuncture with railroad spikes. Probably something to do with the slugs?"

"Yep. Anything else?"

"Well, lemmee see. My mouth feels like it's full of crushed gravel and there's a violin playing my right ear, one long high note. When I move my head there's a funny sloshing sound, maybe there's still water in my ears. But, all in all, not too bad."

He closed his eyes slowly and was silent for a minute, then seemed to awaken again. "Are you all right?" he asked. "What happened to your hand?" Robert placed his hand on top of her good hand.

"We fell into the underground river and got washed out to sea. You saved my life. Then I got smashed into a rock and it broke two fingers, but they say it'll heal quickly." Was she letting her hand linger a little too long for a professional relationship? Probably.

"How did they get your hand into a cast so soon? How long have I been out?"

"Two days."

"Wow. Have you been here all that time?" She moved her hand away.

"I just stopped in to see if you were going to get back to work."

"Not too soon, I think," said the doctor from the door. "His wounds are still healing, and we need to keep him here for at least another day in case the concussion has more bad effects." The doctor turned to Robert. "Your pulse is low, forty or forty-one. Is that normal, or an effect of the concussion?"

"That's normal, I get a lot of exercise."

"Fine. You are lucky you are in excellent condition, you came close to death." He wiped a film of perspiration from Robert's forehead. "Is the pain bad? I would think the wounds would be quite uncomfortable."

"I have some pain. I can live with it."

"I'll get codeine pills."

"Maybe later. I need to think clearly right now."

"As you wish. Also, the police would like to talk to you."

"And I would like to talk the police," said Robert. "Can you contact Colonel Muñoz?"

• • •

Teresa was still sitting near Robert a few hours later when Colonel Muñoz walked into the hospital room. He carried a black swagger stick that he banged on the metal bed frame. "So, Asher, you are awake. You are more than just an archaeologist, I think. Do you have any professional contacts you would like to tell me about? CIA? DEA? KGB?"

"Hello, Colonel. I am a medical researcher and Dr. Welles and myself were tracking down a reference to an antiviral medication. We need to find this medication, the virus is very dangerous and many people will die. We can work through our governments if we need to, but it will take too much time."

"You will forgive me if this sounds unusual," said Muñoz. "Medical research is done in laboratories in the city. And, as your colleague has told me, you were in a cenote in the Yucatán."

"Yes, it's unusual, but we have done nothing wrong. We did not expect the cenote to be occupied. And the crime is not ours; it was committed by the people we encountered in the cave with guns. I believe I would like to swear out a complaint for attempted murder."

"That would be unwise. You have no proof. I have done all I can to help you, but you must now give up and go home before you are killed and we all have a big problem. The hospital removed two thirty-caliber high velocity slugs from your body, slugs that would come from an AK-47 assault rifle. Another slug went right through you. They said it was a miracle that no organs were hit. Leave this to us, we are the professionals."

"We must find the clues to the antiviral medication. We must. We need to go back to Tulum, but we may be able to avoid that same cave."

"Then you take your chances. Make sure you pay your insurance first. If you get in the way of the *policia* you will be jailed. If you get in the way of the people with the AK-47s you will probably be killed." He turned and left the room.

He looked at Teresa. "Is this a little bizarre? What's going on here? Does this man go hot and cold in a heartbeat or what?"

"We could ask Phil."

"Good idea. Except I bet I know what he'd say, Muñoz is working both sides of the street."

"That makes sense. If that's what's happening, we won't get any help getting those guys out of the cave."

"We have three choices," said Robert. "We find another way in that bypasses their installation. We talk to them or their bosses and do a deal. We get help with heavy artillery."

She thought about the options. She didn't like any of them. Why wasn't get out of town on the list? "What do you think?"

"You saw those long green rocket things? They're full of white powder in plastic bags. I'm no drug expert, but if that's heroin or cocaine we were looking at millions of dollars worth. They probably figure us for dead, it's a miracle we got out alive. If we try to bypass their caves and look for an underground laboratory, they'll hear us digging and we'd need the heavy artillery anyway. If we talk about a deal, they'll know we're alive and that we know about the drugs. That would give us about ten minutes to live."

"Um. Good point. What do you think they do with the rockets?"

"There were fragments of sea grass on the one I looked at," said Robert. "It grows underwater after a month or two. Those rockets look like underwater cargo carriers. Ingenious. Almost risk-free. If they know we know, they'll be strongly motivated to make sure we keep the secret. Maybe we'd be down to five minutes to live."

"Uh-huh. What's your next plan?"

"Got the videoconference system? We can ask Dr. Teppin if he has any contacts with heavy artillery."

She went down to the van to get the videophone, then set it up in the room and made the connection. Teppin's face appeared on the small display screen. "Well, Robert, rejoin the ranks of the living. Good to see you with your eyes open. We were all pretty worried. How do you feel?"

"Oh, not too bad," said Robert. "A little lighter without the lead slugs, and the violin music has almost stopped."

"How is he, Teresa?"

"A few hours ago he was still in the coma. He awoke like somebody turned on a light. He seems good now, I guess the bullet wounds are not too serious, but the doctor is worried about concussion and wants to keep him here for at least another day."

"That is excellent news," said Teppin. "In normal circumstances, I would encourage you both to spend a few weeks sipping piña coladas on the beach, but the curve of virus deaths vs. time continues to accelerate. We will send help, but we need you back quickly, as soon as the doctor releases you."

"How's my daughter?" said Robert.

"We are tracking that situation carefully for you. The family is at home, but CDC says there is no danger."

"Any progress in treating the disease?"

"Lots of activity, no progress," said Teppin. "I have also commissioned a half dozen teams to work with the charge microscope on the virus, and we are starting to work on commercial production. But that production is probably going to take more time than we have. Anyway, tell me how you were hurt."

They described the events in the cave and their conclusion that the unfriendly cave residents were drug smugglers.

"Dr. Teppin," said Robert. "We think that the local police are compromised, bought off by the druggies. We talked to Colonel Muñoz here a few minutes ago, he said he wouldn't help. And he warned us that if we persisted we would be killed. We thought we'd bought him off, but the other side must have talked to him. But we need to get back into that cave. Do you know anyone in the neighborhood with heavy artillery? Marines? Anybody?"

"We can start an operation with the Marines," said Teppin, "But it would take at least a day on this end and a few days with the Mexican government. And that is if everything works, the Mexicans do not like our soldiers in their country. I will make some calls. Maybe somebody more local, like Mexican armed forces. Wait a moment." Two minutes passed. "Got it. There is a capable, well-armed crew on a boat called *Bolero*. They are somewhere in the Cayman Islands, I should be able to get a call through. They will love this one, they are all borderline insane."

"What are they?" asked Teresa. "Marines? French Foreign Legion? Republican Guards?"

"The captain is named Gabor. He is a treasure hunter, an adventurer. He made a bundle in Mediterranean shipping before he cashed out. We used him and his boat for a phytomedicine project in the Amazon, a while back. His crew includes a man called Kiraly who is the most dangerous man you will ever meet."

"What is Gabor doing on a treasure boat?"

"He retired. But I think he would still accept this commission. Wait a second, my call is going through now." A minute later, he returned. "It is all set up, he will be in Puerto Aventuras in about eight hours if the seas stay calm. Teresa, maybe you can meet him there and fill him in. Look for a yacht called *Bolero*. It is about 85 feet long, if I remember correctly."

Chapter 29

The Caribbean Sea, November 8, present day

The yacht was styled with the expensive rakish cut of an Italian sports car. It was 85 feet long, and it looked as if it could run at fifty knots all day. Its aluminum hull was white, its trim was dark green, and its windows were heavily tinted against the strong equatorial sun. It was anchored about fifteen miles north of Cayman Brac, in turquoise water unruffled by wind and warm in the unusual midday calm. With the flat calm, the nearly transparent sea, and the sun almost directly overhead, the ship looked as if it were suspended a hundred feet in midair over the sandy sea bottom.

The ship's aft deck held not the expected collection of sport fishing equipment but a large and efficient-looking crane. The transom was cut away sharply in the center to allow easy movement of cargo onto the deck. A large radar arch carried a Furuno dish antenna and a long magnetic anomaly detector, and the cabin roof was shingled with photoelectric cells for power generation.

The foredeck held an impressive array of nautical playthings. Two Kawasaki jet skis, demure in flame-striped iridescent emerald paint, were tucked in behind the anchor winch. A float-equipped ultralight aircraft with high-aspect-ratio cantilevered carbon fiber wings was positioned amidships, wings folded for storage. Two windsurfers were tied down to port of the ultralight, four one-person minisubs were arrayed near the windsurfers, and a black and yellow Zodiac inflatable was suspended vertically on starboard-side davits.

The ship's anchor chain dropped directly down into the ocean, and near the chain the smooth surface of the sea was disturbed by bubbles released from a diver on the sea bottom. The outlines of a wrecked ship could just be discerned, lying on her side, encrusted with barnacles, obscured by seaweed, and drifted over in places with sand.

Below decks in the yacht, marble and teak alternated with industrial-strength computers, satellite communications gear, and a workshop with both electronics and machine tools. Work and play functions alternated here, as on deck. A big Jacuzzi hot tub dominated one room and in the next a side-looking sonar system and a sensitive magnetometer array fed a bank of video monitors.

In the communications room, Todd Goldstein handled the audio and video link to the diver. He was an expert in the latest technology of treasure hunting, and he was also a pioneer in the new science of synchronizing the assortment of data that contributed to a successful hunt. The most dependable data was from towed video cameras, working both the visible and infrared bands. But the sensor inputs included the latest proton magnetometers and side-looking sonar arrays. The magnetometer arrays showed any concentration of material that altered the earth's magnetic field, and the side-looking ultrasonics revealed undersea contours even in murky water.

Goldstein also synchronized a variety of written records like old commercial and shipping manifests and historic weather data. Carbon dating was used to make sure that a wreck was from the right era. Goldstein superimposed the data on a high-resolution computer monitor, with color-coded three-dimensional overlays of all the data types, and he added the position of the diver, determined from the ELF radio transponders he wore.

Goldstein also handled communications with the diver, feeding Grateful Dead audio to the young man below, interrupting sometimes with voice commands to reposition any wandering. He handled local audio from a different player, selecting classical music

CDs for the ship's sound system. The skipper hated rock 'n' roll. And Goldstein used the ship's radar to check on the position of Bartok, the skipper's number two son, on the second ultralight aircraft. Bartok was now about twenty miles due east and flying at an altitude of two thousand feet.

On the aft deck of the yacht a crewmember named Kiraly sat in a comfortable deck chair. Kiraly, compact, well muscled, deeply tanned, and completely bald, worked with brushes and solvents to clean off several pieces of bronze statuary recovered from the three-hundred-year-old wreck below. From time to time, he would sift through the screen tray that was receiving the airlifted detritus from below, but it all seemed to be pebbles and sand now.

Kiraly had been hanging around boats since his youth, except for a five-year hiatus as a mercenary. He had joined the Hungarian skipper, Gabor, to hunt for treasure. He had thought that modern treasure hunting was sort of like ice fishing, an excuse for the men to go off and drink and swear a lot, but Gabor and Bolero had brought a new high-tech approach to the exercise. They actually nearly broke even while donating the most interesting finds to museums.

Nearby, feet propped up on the port rail and sipping a rum and pineapple juice, Gabor paged through a copy of the shipping log for the port of Havana for the year 1822. He was generous of midriff, with a craggy, lightly bearded face lined from spending most of its life in the sun. He wore a bright red "Bolero" T-shirt and a straw hat.

Gabor had run away from home in his teens, ended up in Athens and invested wisely in a small fishing boat. By his twenties, his fleet had expanded to include several larger cargo ships, and when he reached fifty he ran one of the largest fleets of mixed-use ships in the Mediterranean. His wife had borne him two sons, Bela, now a hundred feet below, and Bartok in the ultralight. Now in his sixties, his wife dead eight years, Gabor was retired from business and kept himself amused with his new boat and his new crew, diving on sunken ships and making trouble in seaside ports.

"Ha! Kiraly!" asked Gabor with a voice like a train wreck.

"Ya?"

"Gotta bail out here. Nothing's happening. What you think about Costa Rica next? Here's this nice little square-rigged brigantine,

Eudora: cargo ship, two-master, a hundred forty feet at the waterline, loaded up with wax, sisal, and a ton and a half of silver. Headed out of Havana, March 18, 1822, bound for London. Never arrived."

"Costa Rica's a little out of the way, skipper."

"Hey, I'm thinking Costa Rica west coast, way the goddamn hell out of the way."

Kiraly got out the toothbrush for the final cleaning, turning the little statue this way and that so the sun could catch the bronze. He glanced up at Gabor.

"Maybe a little weak, maybe I look a little more into it." Gabor slipped the reading glasses back into place and turned back to the old shipping log.

In Bolero's galley, a third crewmember, Sarah, assembled club sandwiches for the crew and added pickles and olives for plate decor. She chose a California Chardonnay from the wine locker. Fastening the thick sandwiches with colored toothpicks, she sang, "The stars desert the skies and rush to nestle in your eyes, it's lunchtime."

Distributing plates to the crew, she continued, "How else can I explain the rainbows when there is no rain, it's lunchtime."

"Goddamn betcha," said Gabor. "Hey, cutie, sit over here near the old man." He pulled a deck chair close. "I'll teach you how to sing."

"I'll teach you how to drink," she answered, filling his wine glass. "Put down that rum thing. Check out this grape. We have today a crisp young Chardonnay and this awesome roast turkey sandwich with the Béarnaise sauce. Pay attention. Get your hand off there."

A hundred feet below, Bela, wearing a two-tank aqualung, manhandled an airlift pump nozzle. Bela, Gabor's number one son at twenty-one years old, was the more mature and focused of the two boys; but then, everyone was more mature and focused than the nineteen-year-old Bartok. Bela was an experienced diver, as each summer his father had taken him and Bartok on a cruise around the Mediterranean, diving on ancient Roman and Egyptian underwater relics in Greece and Turkey.

They had just about picked the old schooner clean. There was not much loot. It appeared that someone else had been through the old relic some time before, not surprisingly as the wreck was visible to the naked eye in calm seas.

Above, on the aft deck of Bolero, Gabor was eating his sandwich with one hand and talking on a radio handset in the other, a wide smile on his face. He put down the handset and turned to Kiraly.

"Ho ho! It is Edward Teppin! In trouble again! He says one of his college boys, he got beat up pretty good in Mexico. We go pull his nuts out of the fire, hey? Goldstein, get that bum off the bottom, pull the anchor, get Bartok, get the steam up, we're heading for Puerto Aventuras! Bolero, to the rescue!"

Goldstein broke into the Grateful Dead selection with the news for the diver and hauled up the air hose with Kiraly. He changed the ship's music selection from Mozart to Wagner.

Under way, Gabor at the helm steered for the position of Bartok and the ultralight aircraft. Bartok had given up on high school after two years and instead had opted for a career as a world-class goof-off. His father had offered him a position as chief goof-off for Bolero and sweetened the deal with an assortment of aquatoys, figuring that it was the only way to keep his problem child under a semblance of control.

Bartok was cruising at forty mph in the second K-Craft airplane, practicing loops and listening to music tapes. The K-Craft had a wingspan of thirty-five feet, a weight of three hundred twenty pounds, and a forty-five-hp engine. The engine, unlike the standard K-Craft 30 and unbeknownst to the regulatory authorities, had been tuned slightly with a high compression cylinder head, and that plus the plane's clean aerodynamics and unguyed cantilevered wings made the craft loopable. But you had to start with a steep dive and really snap it around. Bartok wondered if the wings would break off. So far, they seemed to be fine.

Below, Bolero was matching speeds with the aircraft and waving to the flier to land. Remembering the time he had landed on deck, they gave him a few hundred yards margin this time. Everyone watched on the starboard rail, as Bartok's reputation for over-the-edge behavior was well known. And Bartok did not disappoint them; at an altitude of about a hundred feet he throttled down to thirty m.p.h., near stall speed, unfastened his seat belt, cut the motor, and climbed down until he was hanging from the open seat by one hand, the other hand held out to the yacht as if requesting applause or conferring a benediction.

On the boat, Gabor muttered loudly, "Oh. Sure. Do something young and foolish. Why grow up?"

Sarah guessed first, "Omigod, he's going to jump. Pretend not to watch."

Bartok swung his feet forward, then back, and dropped in a perfect pike position before making a reasonably clean entry into the water.

In the silence at the rail, Bela said, in a bored voice, "five point eight, maybe five point seven. A little too much splash."

The boat crew circled to pick up Bartok the Younger as they watched the ultralight settle gracefully down on its floats. They hauled him in over the transom and he explained, "Wow, what a rush. Sunovagun. I've been meaning to try that all summer. Gotta have a flat calm day so the plane can land itself. What do you think? Wicked cool, huh? Anybody film it? Do I have to do it again?"

Nobody commented. Sarah brought him a towel, a sandwich, and a beer as they stowed the ultralight and resumed cruise speed.

Chapter 30

Puerto Aventuras, November 9, present day

Robert and Teresa pulled the rental van into the access road for Puerto Aventuras, slowed for the security gate, bumped over the junior-size speed bumps, and admired the architecture in the flattering red rays of the setting sun. To the left was the eighteen-hole golf course, on the right a low beachfront hotel. Curving around with the access road, they passed a row of small stores and found themselves surrounded by condos and timeshare units, and a large hotel with a huge sign announcing its name, Oasis. The hotel seemed to mark the northern end of the resort.

They retraced their path and found a canal with maybe a hundred boats tied up, parked the VW, and walked towards the water. Robert, still weak, leaned on Teresa, away from the splinted hand. The violin was still playing in his right ear, and when he moved his head or heard any loud noise, there was a strange sloshing sound. He moved carefully.

The vessel of choice in the marina seemed to be a sport fishing boat, mostly anywhere between forty and seventy-five feet long, with tuna tower and at least half a dozen tuna rods. They walked past Carlos 'n' Charlie's and The Neon Margarita with the colored lights. A green parrot sputtered in a cage near a group of tourists getting happily drunk. They located Bolero tied up at the end of the pier.

"Holy cow, is this what an eighty-five-foot boat looks like? It's gigantic," said Teresa.

"Leave it to Dr. Teppin," said Robert. "He's got more contacts than the Republican National Campaign Committee. Let's see what's for dinner."

Gabor emerged from the aft cabin and welcomed them aboard. "Ha! Ha! Nice! Pretty young people! Just what we need! Come in here and meet everybody!"

They were surrounded by Gabor and conducted inside. Kiraly produced an extension to the monkeywood dining table, more chairs materialized, they all sat down, and Gabor introduced the crew.

Robert had been on many boats, but not with this kind of *grande luxe*. The trim and furnishings seemed to have been selected with little regard for weight or price, with solid-looking marble and granite pillars and dark tropical wood everywhere. The harsh edges of ambient sounds were smoothed by the heavy dark-brown curtains on the walls and windows and by the multiple layers of oriental rugs on the floor.

The sound system surreptitiously emitted a classical piece. Ravel's Bolero, wasn't it? Cute. The stereo had the untroubled confidence of a kilowatt of audio amplifier power. Gabor sat them down at a large table and introduced the crew: the teenagers Bela and Bartok, the dangerous and efficient-looking Kiraly, technologist Todd Goldstein, and chef Sarah.

Robert looked again at Sarah—pretty, young, blonde hair, with a warm curve of neck and cheek. He looked over at Teresa: she had done something effective with makeup tonight. And the glasses? Oh, yes, they weren't there. Perhaps she wore contacts, or perhaps she used glasses for reading only. She had nice smile lines at the corners of her eyes. The eyes were compelling, with the exotic color almost glowing in the subdued incandescent lighting. Wonder what those eyes looked like from maybe three inches away?

"So!" bellowed Gabor, jarring him back to reality. "Teppin says we have to pull your nuts from the fire. What is happening here, exactly? Somebody beat on your head? Nice bandage."

"Kind of a long story," said Robert, refocusing on his problem. Gabor's vocal volume triggered the noises in his ear, but Gabor didn't seem like the kind of person who could quiet down successfully.

"We got provisions for two months, liquor for six," said Gabor. "We have enough guns to fight off the Mongol hordes. We have the eternal patience of the serious treasure hunter. We should be able to handle one helluva long story." He leaned forward, his face crinkled into an eager smile.

"OK, you asked for it," said Robert, his voice unconsciously rising in volume.

"Sarah!" screamed Gabor. "Can you handle dinner for eight?"

Sarah replied, "Oh, I'm sure I can find something. Hot dogs work for you?" She retired to the adjacent galley, where she could continue to audit the conversation. Actually, thought Robert, she could probably continue to audit the conversation in Cleveland.

"Two months ago," said Robert, "I used a new kind of microscope—call it a charge microscope—to make a picture of a virus, the Austin virus, the one that's killed two thousand people in Austin, Texas. The microscope shows the charge pattern of the molecules rather than the physical structure, so it predicts how the molecules will behave rather than what they look like. It made a distinct and unusual pattern, take a look at this computer printout." He pulled a piece of paper from his pocket and unfolded it on the table.

"While I was checking to see if any other researcher had come up with the same thing, I found a picture of a Maya inscription on a stela in Uxmal, engraved about 1,200 years ago. Here it is. You can also see a column of glyphs that may represent the structure of an antiviral. There's not enough there for us to synthesize an antiviral, but it looks as if the Maya may have built the same kind of microscope and used it to help find cures for disease. We're looking for more records the Maya may have left, with pointers to an antiviral."

"Not possible," said Gabor, loudly, "I think."

"Well, we found photographs of the stela made eighty years ago that showed the identical glyph. And carbon dating of some of the pigment puts the inscription in the eighth century or earlier."

"What does the stela say? We can pretty much read Maya now, hey?"

"Most of the glyphs are known," said Teresa. "We have a translation, as good as we can come up with for now." She handed him a paper from her case. "We poked around in Uxmal for a few days. It looks as if the Maya cities were more specialized than we had thought. Uxmal was the accounting and administrative center; it handled the exact requirements of the various gods, making sure that the sun god, for example, was adequately rewarded for producing the sun every morning."

"Good, that's an important job."

"Tulum was quite small but powerful, as the academics were concentrated there. It was the university town of the Maya empire. The stela in question seems to have been a thank-you note from Uxmal to Tulum for a powder of some kind that helped the crops. And look down here; this group with the matching glyph describes what may have been a plant derivative that cured a sickness. And here, clearly, is the glyph for Tulum."

"You believe this?" Bela whispered to Bartok. Bartok whistled a few notes in a minor key.

Robert took over. "Apparently the research center of the Maya empire was in Tulum, in an undiscovered laboratory. And they may have built a charge microscope, back in the year 822 or so, and used it to analyze the Austin virus. They may have been facing destruction by the virus, in fact that may have been the reason that the Maya abandoned the cities and were decimated in population in the next few decades. But they may also have found a cure. They didn't completely die out. They knew a lot more than we do about plant cures, natural cures, and they lived in the rain forest—the best pharmacology lab in the world. This is all incredibly speculative, of course, but nobody is anywhere near a way to control the virus with conventional medicine."

Sarah leaned into the room. "Two white! Two red!" she barked.

Bela said, "Got it," opened a cabinet door and grabbed two bottles of Gewürztraminer from a refrigerated compartment and a bottle of Bordeaux and a California Cabernet from another compartment.

"The Alsatian Gewürz is OK with everyone?" he asked. "Much more interesting than the sweet California version. And we can see if Mondavi's solid Opus One is a match for the '61 Mouton."

Bartok looked at the guests for their reaction. "Gracious living in the tropics," he explained.

Bela located a carafe of ice water, wine glasses and water glasses, extracted a cork and poured Bartok a taste of the Gewürztraminer with an accomplished flourish. He held the bottle so he could read the label.

"Unexpectedly flinty for the vintage," announced Bartok. "But we think that you will find it aggressively contoured, with the typical varietal spicy overtones. The house would recommend waiting for the appetizer course before tasting it; you will find that it is more of a team player than an individual contributor."

"I was hoping for steely, not flinty," complained Bela.

"Don't kid me. You want Rolling Rock, not wine," said Bartok. "No tannic aftertaste, no tricky corks to remove."

Gabor poured the white wine for everyone. "So, then, off to Tulum?" he asked, ignoring his children.

"Off to Tulum," agreed Robert. "We spent two days wandering around the ancient city along with ten thousand tourists, fifty guides, and two hundred serape vendors. There was nothing we could learn above ground, so we checked underground."

"Underground radar?" asked Goldstein.

"Not at twenty-five thousand a pop," said Robert. "We're not that well financed. They're working on a bigger government subsidy, back home, but it'll be a few more days. We found a few glyphs that pointed us underground. We looked for fresh-water outflow off the nearby beach and found a large underground river half a mile south. It comes up out of several big holes, about five hundred feet offshore, hidden by a coral reef.

"Where did it go? How much current?" yelled Gabor.

"Maybe eight knots, peak," said Robert. "More than we could handle; we got turned back. The main passage was maybe eight feet by twenty feet at the narrowest spot, and it seemed to run almost horizontal at a depth of fifty feet or so.

"After we, um, resolved a discussion with the local police, we headed inland up the headwall and found a small cenote that looked like it connected with the main flow where the passage was wider. We dived in and worked our way up the river, figuring we were boldly going where no man had boldly gone before. But we spotted shiny new stainless steel rungs leading upwards. So we headed on up. And then these scruffy-looking Hispanic types with guns found us, tied us up, and beat on us. They put us in a storeroom with a dozen torpedo shaped things, maybe twenty feet long. One of the torpedoes was open at the top and full of white powder wrapped in clear plastic."

"Robert untied himself like a gigantic rope trick," said Teresa. "It was maybe the most amazing thing I have ever seen in my life."

Robert smiled inside and looked again, Teresa seemed to be lit from within tonight. Or maybe it was the wine.

"They called somebody named Lopez on the phone, in another room full of guns and communications equipment.

"Druggies." said Bela.

"Seemed to be," said Robert. "They had all the earmarks."

"Hey, guns and everything," said Bartok. "So, what did you do? Beat 'em up?"

"Not exactly," said Robert. "We beat up a couple of them, then we found out we were pretty well outnumbered, so we tried to sneak out. But they saw us and started shooting. I got hit, we fell into an underground stream and got carried out to sea."

"Wow, way cool," said Bela. "Same way you came in?"

"I wish," said Teresa. "We took the high speed express lane out. It was another underground river, quite a bit smaller and faster and twisty, and we had no aqualungs. Luckily, I got Robert to batter through the rocks with his head. We both were pretty well busted up and concussed. We must have surfaced well out to sea, near the reef, and we got picked up by a fisherman and his son just before we got picked up by the sharks."

"So!" screamed Gabor. "Very bad guys! Did you try the *Federales*?"

"The *Federales* were a little slippery. I think that they know all about it, but they will do nothing. *Baksheesh*. They're getting paid off."

"The drug trade is a pretty important component of the economy here," said Kiraly in a quiet voice, almost a whisper. "The cargo is black tar heroin, opium resin, cocaine, and marijuana. The normal path is from the fields in Columbia up the coast to Mexico, then it fans out to border crossings for the western U.S. markets and hops to Florida for the east coast markets."

"Can you trust any of the Mexican agencies?" asked Robert.

"The SDN, the National Defense Secretariat, and PGR, the Federal Attorney General's office, mostly. Although even here you will probably see a little shrinkage in any confiscated cash. The local police are usually not as reliable."

"Yes," said Robert.

Sarah whistled from the galley, "Wait staff! Front and center!"

Bela and Bartok jumped up and ran to the galley, returning with a huge pile of grilled foccacia with tomato and rosemary and mesclun salad with warm goat cheese, fresh basil, and croutons.

They dug in. Gabor asked, rhetorically, if anyone had any idea how difficult it was to find fresh basil in the Caribbean.

During the pasta course, Robert broke the silence, "Gabor, we need your help, but we can't pay you anything, and it will probably be dangerous, unless the heavies we ran into last time have left town."

"We like dangerous. But why bother these guys, hey? Can you just find another way in?"

"Maybe, but we'll be working pretty close to the cave. We may run into them by accident. Or they could spot us aboveground, and then realize we weren't killed in the cave, and then they'd have to try to protect their secret."

"How about the D.E.A.?"

"No help. Dr. Teppin checked through Washington. They're working with the government in Mexico City, but it could take weeks."

"Weeks? With a deadly virus breakout?"

"They're pushing at the highest levels, but the Mexican government is sending a fact finding mission to Texas. And I guess there's an excavation near Uxmal that got sealed off, but it doesn't seem to have any active viruses, that's the priority right now. They hope the situation can be resolved in a few days, but who knows."

"The government in Mexico City may be making too much money from the drug business. How about the local police?"

"We got some help with the local cops. We found a displaced American named Schwartz who lives near Playa del Carmen; he helped bribe the local colonel. He said that the police were probably taking money from the drug smugglers. He said the druggies could put much more pressure on the cops than we could, so we had to take what they gave us. And the police didn't want to hear about our encounter in the caverns."

Gabor nodded, frowning, pulling on his short beard. "Suppose we send them a nice letter? Put a note near the cave? Tell them we are coming at them with the Marines, the *policia*, the D.E.A.? Then do they think they cannot continue in Tulum and move out?"

"Maybe, but if they have the local police bought off and if they know the D.E.A. is unwelcome, maybe they laugh at us. Or sucker us in and clobber us."

Kiraly spoke. "No matter how it goes, say you want a few days alone in the caves. If you sucker punch the druggies, you are going to get clobbered later. They don't like to lose, and they have all the manpower and the firepower they need. They're tough, smart, and well equipped. And they're killers."

Robert finished his wine. "We need one day, maybe two at the most, then we're out of town."

"It will take them two days minimum to get reinforcements, if they're from South America," said Kiraly. "They're not local or they wouldn't need a warehouse on the coast, it would be inland. Probably Medellin or Cali. If you want us to buy you two days, we can go in armed, look to find another way to your cave, and hope to miss 'em. But we can also have a contingency plan in case they show up shooting."

"Sounds good to me," said Gabor happily. "I like contingency plans. I haven't gotten my gun off since Dubrovnick. But, Kiraly, I thought you were getting out of the mercenary business."

"This is different."

Robert shook his head. "We can't ask you to put your lives in danger. It's not your fight."

"Hey," said Gabor. "Life is short. We like to make it interesting. This is by plenty the most interesting thing I've heard of so far this year. And we owe Teppin one, too. So, crew, what do you think?"

"You bet," said Bela.

Bartok nodded agreement, a broad smile on his face.

"You guys aren't going," said Gabor.

"Gotta go," said Bela. "I've never gotten my gun off. Bartok, you ever get yours off? In public?"

"Uh-uh, me either. No discussion. We're going. We have our reputation to consider."

Kiraly slapped a big hand on the table. "Just guns, right? No flame throwers, no grenades?" Robert nodded. Kiraly went on, "If we plan it right it should be OK. Not safe, but only a five or ten percent chance of getting killed."

The others nodded, and Gabor shouted, "OK, that's done, we're in. So, you know the terrain. How do we discourage a nest of angry drug smugglers with automatic weapons?"

Robert said, "We don't necessarily have to fight fair. I bet the military planning types haven't written the book about fighting in caves. Suppose, for instance, you put grease in the right place on the rocks? There's a passage with a narrow, sloping ledge and the river just below. Anybody stepping on the grease would get a free ticket to the Caribbean Sea. Or a little sleeping gas, that should work really well in a cave."

Sarah excused herself and came back in a minute or two with plates of Saga and smoked Gruyere cheese and a bottle of Offley's 1972 Vintage Port. Bela poured himself a generous glass and said, "Oh, good, it's the Offley's."

Bartok said, "Offley, Offley good," and poured a large glass for himself.

Gabor turned to Robert, shrugged, and said, "Disobedience. Lack of discipline. God knows I tried."

Robert drew a rough map of the area:

"Here's the layout. You can see the three fresh water outflows we found in the ocean. We ignored the escape tunnel, because it didn't look as if the tunnel was big enough for us with our tanks. We tried the north passage first, from the ocean, and did fine until we hit that narrow spot. Then we tried the south passage and ran into a similar narrowing, with current we couldn't swim against. We think they must bring the torpedoes through the north passage, using a minisub capable of eight knots. The torpedoes themselves don't have propellers."

"So then you tried that cenote. Does it have an obvious entrance?" asked Kiraly.

"No, it's a natural crevice in the limestone, small, hidden by scrub brush. I doubt that we were the first to find it, but it probably wouldn't be discovered unless you knew what you were looking for. From the cenote, we swam upstream against light current and entered the north passage through that small cut. We drifted downstream, found the ladder, and got our clocks cleaned."

"They may have been protected from downstream, gates or alarms or something, but they couldn't have been expecting visitors from upstream," said Kiraly. "Then that escape tunnel is where you got bruised up as you were leaving."

"Oh, yes, something else. There was a forklift truck in the entrance cave. I can't imagine anybody hauling that in a submersible, so there may be another dry land entrance. But it may be pretty well camouflaged; the locals don't know about it."

"They did say something about nets—in the cave—the drug smugglers," said Teresa.

"Robert, how do you think we should plan our visit?" asked Kiraly.

"I don't think they expected us to survive. They fired a lot of rounds at us, and they probably thought we'd taken serious hits. And even healthy, we were long odds against getting through that tunnel alive."

"Then they may not have even discovered the cenote entrance, and we can catch them by surprise again?" said Kiraly.

"Maybe. What do your think?" asked Robert.

Kiraly studied the sketched map for a minute. "The north entrance has got to be well defended; that's out. We could use the south underwater entrance or the cenote entrance. They were guarding at least five million dollars worth of drugs—wholesale, from your description—so they would probably look around to see if they could backtrack your route. They had three possibilities to look at, upstream, cenote, or south passage. How big is that cut between the north and south passages?"

"Just about big enough for us, we had to take our tanks off to get through the hole."

"Good. Do you think you could see any light from the cenote if you looked back into the hole from the north passage?"

"No. It's too far away, there are too many twists in the passage."

"Excellent. Our best chance is that they missed finding the cut. So it's a crapshoot whether they'll keep an eye out underwater or aboveground. Or both. How well is the south passage entrance concealed?"

"It's hidden under a coral reef. If you didn't have a salinity detector, it's like any of hundreds of dark crevices in the reef."

"That's how I'd go in, then. With personal minisubs; ours can handle eight knots easily. We can take a pass with the robot minisub. Mount the low-light video camera to check for bad guys. And also make sure the current doesn't get too high for us."

"We only have four minisubs. One's only putting out half power, we can't use it for this. Do we go in with three people?" asked Gabor.

"Me, you, Robert?" asked Kiraly.

"No way," said Bela, Bartok and Goldstein simultaneously.

"Todd, you have to stay with the ship to run the comm and the robot. Let's see. We could either try to tow people with the subs or use the rock climbing gear to run a line back."

"Too far," said Gabor, loudly.

"I got it, I got it," said Bela. "We can let two unmanned subs drift back on the current."

"Hey, yeah, neat!" said Bartok.

"Should work," said Robert. "The walls are pretty smooth."

"And those subs can survive a direct hit from a nuclear weapon," said Goldstein.

"Let's do it," said Gabor. "Make a list of what we need. Goldstein, write this down."

Goldstein found a notebook and the group produced a list of equipment:
Available:
Wetsuits and Scuba gear
Crampons
Night vision underwater goggles, with flash protection
Inertial navigation unit, LCD readout
5 Browning 9 mm automatic pistols, 4 extra 13-shot magazines
Kevlar vests, level IIIA
Radio intercom, headsets
Map
Personal minisubs

Needed:
AK-47 assault rifles (3)
30-round magazines (6)
Smoke grenades (10)
Flash-bang grenades (10)
Pitons, caribiners, braided 3/8 in. nylon line

"Kiraly," shouted Gabor. "Can you get hold of those things in a day or two?"

Robert was startled. What was wrong? Gabor's voice sounded strange. What happened? Oh, yeah, no ringing in the ear. No sloshing noise. He moved his head, still nothing. Blessed silence. What a relief.

Kiraly answered, "Shouldn't be too much trouble." He left the room to make a phone call. He came back in a few minutes, "On the way. Arrival scheduled for tomorrow afternoon."

Robert gazed at the list. Small armies could be supplied for a full-scale war with this stuff. Were they getting in over their heads?

Chapter 31

Puerto Aventuras, November 10, present day

Robert and Teresa took advantage of Gabor's offer to move them into Bolero. They packed their luggage and equipment at the Akumal hotel and checked into small but well-equipped staterooms with a view of restaurant row at Puerto Aventuras. Setting up the videoconference system on deck, they contacted Dr. Teppin and filled him in on the recent events.

"Excellent, really excellent," said Teppin. "I thought Gabor would come through for you. So are you going in soon?"

"As soon as we're set up, tomorrow or the day after," said Robert, "We're going to use a robot minisub with a television camera tomorrow to look around."

"I could probably find some more soldiers for you, but I think in a cave you do not want too many people. And Kiraly, I understand, is as good as any two squads of Marines. Anything you need after you neutralize the occupation forces?"

"We may need some survey equipment. We'll be looking for a large, complete Maya laboratory, if our understanding of the glyphs is correct. We didn't see anything even close in our previous trip. How's our budget?"

"I have been in touch with Washington," said Teppin, "and they've given me a blank check. I will set up an account in Mérida with five hundred thousand dollars to start. Let me know when you need more."

"Wow," said Teresa. "The heck with saving the world. Let's grab it and fly to Pago Pago."

"Could you order an underground radar for us?" asked Robert, "We may have to look through some walls."

"Look for it on tomorrow's flight to Cancún. Anything else?"

"Ultrasonic subterranean imaging gear. Excavation equipment. Pneumatic hammer drills. Generator. Compressor. Power chisels. Heavy duty extension cables. Halogen lamps. Hand tools, picks and shovels. Put it on my tab."

"Pumps, in case you need to pump out a flooded cave. Support timbers. A backhoe." added Teppin.

"Maybe hold the backhoe," said Robert.

Tulum, two days later, 2:00 A.M.

Bolero prepared to sail. The power and water lines were disconnected, a check for a week's dockage was left in the marina office to reserve the spot, the motors were started, the radar was turned on and warmed up, the bridge lights were dimmed and the dock lines were cast off, all with as little commotion as possible.

The lights of the marina illuminated the scene well enough to make the outward passage through the tight channel uneventful. Bolero had twin-screw propulsion and a bow thruster, and Gabor was used to snaking clumsy hundred-fifty-foot single-screw freighters through crowded Mediterranean harbor traffic.

The white ship eased into the Caribbean Sea. The ocean was roughened by the usual fifteen-knot wind, with low swells and light chop. Bolero slipped through the well-marked channel in the offshore reef and headed south, navigating with GPS and the light of the moon—nearly full now—to the shoreline off Tulum.

They set the anchor off the reef and deployed a few fishing rods, hoping any interested parties would mark them down as another drunken night fishing expedition. Robert and Kiraly lifted the remote sub over the transom and held it in place until they heard its motor start up. In the computer room, Goldstein took control of the sub through the ultra low frequency radio link and brought the video picture from the sub's camera up on a video monitor. He added the audio channel and the side-looking sonar display.

Steering with a joystick and controlling the throttle with the computer keyboard, he gave Robert and Kiraly a thumb's up and they gathered in the computer room with Teresa, Sarah and Gabor and the boys to watch progress. Goldstein turned on the sub's lights briefly as he passed the coral reef and worked through a forest of large elkhorn coral and then turned off the lights and the motor to look around in the dark. Nothing was visible except phosphorescent fish and the refracted yellow moonlight, and nothing was audible except the splash of waves on the reef and the muffled hum of Bolero's generator.

Goldstein turned the lights back on and steered the craft under Robert's direction until he found the ribbon that marked the channel entrance. The picture changed to show the rock walls as the craft entered the tunnel, and Goldstein's computer screens showed them water speed, absolute speed, and a superimposed bird's-eye-view track on the local map. The sub's inertial navigation system substituted for the GPS navigation system, as the GPS was unable to receive the high-frequency satellite signals underwater.

Goldstein had calculated that the sub's batteries would be adequate if the sub could maintain an average absolute speed of three knots in the tunnel. As its peak speed in still water was a little better than ten knots, he was counting on the river staying under seven or eight knots. But the screen showed that the sub's speed was slowly diminishing, and Robert felt the tension in the room as they all figured out the implication. The display of absolute speed in the corner of the screen fell to two knots, then one, then a half knot.

"This is the narrow part that you could not swim through?" said Gabor in an uncharacteristic raspy whisper. "If the current is over ten knots, we can't get the sub through, hey?"

The speed display fell to zero and motion stopped, except for a slow oscillation as Goldstein fought to keep the submersible centered in the passage.

"Rats," whispered Teresa. "Do something, Robert."

"Try moving the sub up to the ceiling into that narrow crevice," said Robert.

"Don't want to get stuck."

"I know, but if you're careful, the current flow should be a little slower up there. And a little is all we need."

The sub slipped into the crevice, and they heard through the hydrophones the scraping of its hull on the rock walls. But the sub's sensors and robot arms were concentrated on its prow and underside, and it did not get snagged. Slowly the craft inched forward again and the audience let out its breath. The absolute speed display worked its way back up to three knots. Teresa leaned forward and gave Robert a noisy kiss on his forehead.

Robert had added a map note at the spot where he estimated they would find the cut to the north passage, and nearly fifteen minutes later, Goldstein closed on the spot, slowed the sub and panned the camera to make sure they didn't miss the turn.

The cut was located as advertised and Goldstein jockeyed the sub through, with the audio again announcing the scrape of steel against stone at the passage. Turning downstream, he let the sub drift without power, with the automatic ballast tanks keeping the depth at the tunnel center. The sub drifted downstream past the ladder and they saw a steel mesh net, bolted firmly to the walls and apparently controlled by a hydraulic cylinder. An armored conduit, stapled to the wall, led upstream.

Goldstein turned the sub back upstream to the ladder and guided it up to the surface, turned off the light, broke the surface with the camera pod, and looked around the cave where Robert and Teresa had first entered. The cave's light was on, showing no activity except that the hydraulic crane now held one of the green torpedoes. Goldstein held the sub in position.

"So, that's the spot, hey?" asked Gabor.

"That's the spot. The torpedo is new, maybe they're moving the inventory," said Kiraly.

"Or adding to it," said Robert. "See the water puddle underneath the torpedo?"

"Quiet now, though," said Kiraly. "Maybe they do think you bought it."

"Next time," said Goldstein, through their headphones, "I'm adding some legs to this sub so it can crawl out of the water. Evolutionary improvement."

• • •

"You're in command, Kiraly," bellowed Gabor. "Do we go?"

"We go. Pull the sub. Suit up."

Sarah, Teresa, and Goldstein were to wait on Bolero, with Goldstein continuing to monitor the robot sub and handling communications and Teresa keeping an eye on the horizon. The others dressed in Kevlar flak jackets and wet suits, and added SCUBA gear, gas masks, communications headsets, wide rubber belts that carried nine mm pistols, spare ammunition clips, lead weights, crampons, and grenades. Kiraly handed out Sig/Sauer 9mm handguns that included a powerful LED-array lamp and laser aiming spots in different colors, and showed the team how to operate the weapons.

Robert carried nylon line, pitons and caribiners, a gallon of grease, and a variety of miscellaneous gear stowed in the big zipper pockets of the black nylon combat vest. Kiraly carried an AK-47 assault rifle in a plastic bag, smoke grenades, flash-bang grenades, and gas grenades.

Teresa observed them in amazement. "I don't believe it. You can still stand up."

"Absolutely nothing to it," bragged Bartok. "Child's play. A mere bagatelle. Ice cream. Piece of cake." He fell full length on his face with a huge crash on the mercifully deep carpet, still talking in a muffled voice, "Walk in the park. Taking candy from a baby." Bela exploded into laughter.

Kiraly yanked Bartok to his feet, "Good Christ, you idiot, your sense of humor will kill us all one of these days. Those are live grenades."

"And excellent live grenades, I'm sure," said Bartok. "Sorry, Sergeant, I'll be a good little soldier from here on in, I absolutely promise. I don't know what happens to me sometimes, I guess I get a little crazy. It won't happen again, honest, sir." He walked to the transom and appeared to lose his balance, flailing his hands in the air, overbalanced into the water and screamed, "Man overboard!" Kiraly growled deep in his throat.

They launched the minisubs from the rear platform. Kiraly and Robert entered the water more gracefully, checked communications with Goldstein, and unclipped the subs. They grabbed the steering handles and pushed the throttle levers forward, working their way up the channel and coming in view of the robot sub in fifteen minutes. Then Bela and Bartok submerged, and Gabor joined them—after some last minute advice from Sarah—to await the reappearance of the minisubs. The minisubs arrived on schedule, drifting slowly up through the fresh water outflow, and they each grabbed one and motored up the passage and through the cut and then back downstream to the steel ladder, joining Robert and Kiraly.

They tied up their subs to the ladder, removed their weight belts and slung them on the lower rung. Soon the team was assembled in the water at the entrance cave, just under the surface, breathing through snorkels.

Robert poked his head up and saw the cave was as before: narrow gauge rails, forklift truck, hydraulic equipment. The air smelled strongly of oil and motor exhaust. One of the green torpedoes had been added, on a cart near the hydraulics. He pulled up Kiraly. "Your show, commander."

Kiraly nodded, and then he and Robert removed their SCUBA tanks and ran to the other end of the room to check the entrance door. Kiraly signaled all clear and the team followed.

Goldstein spoke through their headsets, "Hey, guys, if you pick me up and carry me with you, I'll watch your back." Kiraly motioned with a nod of his head to Bela and Bartok, and they returned to pick up the hundred-pound robot sub and carried it to the door.

Back on *Bolero*, Sarah, Teresa, and Goldstein watched the scene on the monitor. The team's breathing, a faint hum, and sounds of waves came from the speaker.

"Todd," Teresa said, "Can you show both directions at once? I know they're there in the cave somewhere, they must be."

"Sorry, no, but I can swivel the view around pretty quickly. I'll keep it scanning." The scene bounced as the robot was carried down the corridor.

She stared at the monitor as if she could will the Colombians from appearing.

Robert disengaged the latch on the door as he had the first trip, motioned them through, and produced a wooden wedge and slipped it under the door, kicking it into place, and then looping a nylon line around the door fittings. That would hold for long enough, in case more visitors arrived from the tunnel. He looked down the corridor, remembering details, as Kiraly led the team to the T intersection and peeked around the corner. No activity. The scene was still darkly illuminated with low-power incandescent lamps. But where were the intrusion alarms? Why was it so quiet? Maybe they were alone. No, that torpedo at the entrance cave, if it was full of cocaine, was probably worth more than Biloxi. They wouldn't abandon it. He couldn't believe their luck, they still seemed to be undetected.

Bela and Bartok positioned the robot on the narrow ledge, then the team strapped crampons to their feet and slipped night vision goggles over their eyes.

Kiraly moved down the ledge, staying low, his rifle ready. He disappeared around the bend, returned, and signaled for the team to follow. As they passed the bend, Robert emptied the can of grease and spread it on the floor. He checked his grip with the crampons; they worked well, the steel teeth digging through the grease into the soft limestone.

Kiraly stopped a little way up the corridor and gestured to the lights. Robert spotted the bare Romex stapled to the wall a little too high to reach and pantomimed to Kiraly who crouched, back against the wall. Robert pulled the wire cutters from a belt loop, stepped onto Kiraly's knees, reached up and cut the wire. The bright flash penetrated Robert's closed eyelids. When he opened his eyes the lights were out and he saw the scene through his night vision goggles, illuminated by the infrared lamps in their helmets. Robert then bared the ends of the cable and touched them together to short out the power. A smaller spark was accompanied by a momentary surge in the note of the generator. Robert heard a low hum. A ribbon of smoke curled up from the length of the cable and the wire in his hand got too hot to hold. As he dropped it, the hum stopped and the generator shut down. Robert hoped it was the master breaker that had tripped.

Farther down the corridor, the river dove out of sight under a rock outcropping and the corridor widened, leading to another door. Kiraly spoke quietly, "Goldstein. See anything?"

"The lights went out, is all. I'm on infrared. Nothing's moving."

"That was us, we killed the lights. Keep me informed."

He opened the door slowly and all hell broke loose. A klaxon siren sounded and room lights went on brightly. They glimpsed a workroom, with a large wall-mounted display screen, a computer console, and communications gear. Seconds later, two men looked around an open door and drew back out of sight, shouting in Spanish. Kiraly unclipped a gas grenade and rolled it into the room. The whoosh of escaping gas was heard, followed by more screaming in Spanish. Kiraly gestured the team back around the corner as a head appeared in the door, wearing a gas mask and night vision glasses and raising a rifle. A chatter of shots echoed through the cave, several of them impacting on Kiraly's chest—on the Kevlar vest—some ricocheting down the corridor. He retreated around the corner.

Kiraly emitted a blood-curdling scream, then fired a burst of three shots and the gunfire stopped. He unclipped a smoke grenade and a flash-bang grenade, yelled "Flash-bang" to his team, and threw the grenades simultaneously through the open door, shielding his eyes. The incredible noise of the explosion echoed back and forth and finally died out. Goldstein's voice, a little awed, came through their headsets, "I hope that was us?"

"That was us," confirmed Kiraly. He looked at his team. "Everybody OK?"

They nodded. Bartok's eyes were wide, looking at the bullet holes in Kiraly's chest showing the frayed Kevlar fabric. "Jeez, that scream, I thought you were killed."

"Always a good idea to let the opposition think you're hurt," said Kiraly in a whisper, "Unless, of course, you are actually hurt. Go back to the entrance cave. They'll counterattack, we can check their strength, and we can try out the grease trick."

They moved quickly back to the entrance cave. The door that Robert had blocked was still closed and quiet, he unblocked it and they slipped through. A minute or two later, they heard the opposition working down the corridor. Kiraly ran back to the bend far enough to let himself be seen, drawing a salvo, and ran back to the entrance cave. Robert thought the scraping of the crampons would give the game away, but three men ran after him, rifles raised, looking for a shot. At the bend, all three kept going straight—their legs moving in the air like cartoon characters—and fell into the river. They shouted back something Robert didn't catch as they disappeared under the outcropping.

Goldstein's voice again, "Was that us? That screaming?"

"That was them. Did you catch it on the monitor?"

Teresa spoke. "It's a little hard to follow. What happened?"

"Three down," said Kiraly, quietly. "All them. Unknown number remaining. Goldstein, get Sarah to handle communications. Launch the Zodiac and take it north from your position, about, what, five hundred yards?" He looked at Robert.

"Closer to three hundred."

"Three hundred yards north. Take a lamp and some quarter inch line. Look for three dead bodies, or three live ones if they can hold their breath good. Tie up the live ones, no slack. Load 'em up. Then bring the Zodiac back and tie it up. Robert, how long for the trip?"

"Something like four or five minutes."

"They'll be getting there before you do. Watch yourself."

"Now what?" asked Gabor, in an uncharacteristic whisper.

Robert spoke. "They're pretty well equipped. Night vision, gas masks."

"Everything but crampons," said Bela.

"Good thing, too," said Bartok. "I was getting a little worried, there, I don't mind saying, yessir."

"Praise the Lord," said Kiraly. He turned to Robert and continued, "If I was them, I'd sit tight, it's always easier to defend a position than to attack one. They don't know our strength or exactly what happened to the other three guys so they'll move slowly. And they could call for reinforcements. I assume there'll be an aboveground installation nearby with a minisub. They'll open the net for them, they could be here in half an hour. Or maybe if there's a dry back door, they'll be here sooner. We could be in a bit of trouble, here."

Teresa spoke through their headsets, "Goldstein's away, Sarah's got the comm, I'll get back topside and see if there's any activity."

"Use the night vision binoculars, and be ready to move ship if you're threatened," said Gabor. "You should be able to outrun anything except a Cigarette. Head towards Cancún."

"All quiet here," said Teresa after a moment.

"Standoff, here," said Kiraly. "They'll have a point man just around the corner." As if to prove his point, a volley of shots launched a dozen small slugs, screaming up the corridor. "Any ideas?"

"Here's one," said Robert. "I jump in the river and float downstream underwater. There's that little midstream island maybe twenty yards past them. They won't be looking that way. I'll take a flash-bang and a smoke. Attack from behind."

"Did you see how fast that current is running? That's suicide."

The lights went back on in the corridor.

"I did a lot of swimming in college," said Robert, "I think if I strip down to lighten the load I can make it."

Kiraly looked at him. "You have no chance to pull yourself out. The stone is slippery. You haven't healed yet."

"I have one chance. If I time it correctly, I can make it. If I don't, hey, I've been down that road before." He touched the bandage involuntarily.

"Right, and damn near died."

"I was weighed down with lead. Any other ideas?"

Kiraly shrugged and looked at Gabor. Gabor shrugged. Bela said, "That's crazy." Bartok nodded. Robert removed all his equipment except the belt and the grenades, filled his lungs with air and slipped into the water, diving to the bottom. He watched the walls go by in the pale green illumination, estimating the distance carefully, and surfaced twenty-five feet before the island. Just enough time, he thought, as he dove as deep as the river permitted and stroked to the surface. He felt a deep ache in the freshly stitched wounds in his back and hoped he had not ruptured anything vital.

He broke the water as silently as an eel and stretched both hands up to the outcrop. But he did not have a good grip on the slimy water-smoothed stone, and he slid back down towards the fast moving river, an inch at a time. Christ. Got to do something. His feet swung in midair, no help. One more inch. Too damned slippery, in rock climbing you got nice dry rocks and chalk. One more inch. Try something, anything, not much time left. He flexed his arms to pull his weight up a few inches, grabbed quickly for a new hand hold, and started slipping slowly down again. Good, you've bought yourself another ten seconds. He repeated the move, this time edging sideways by a foot, and this time his frantically searching left hand found a deep crevice. He wedged his right hand in the same crevice, hung there for a moment, and muscled his body up in a single smooth motion. Yes! Never in doubt.

In seconds he was prone on the cool rock, back throbbing but not dripping blood. Sure enough, there was only one man—barely visible around the curve of the passage—prone in the corridor, holding a short-barreled rifle pointing towards the access cave. But the island Robert was perched on was too far downstream, he was pretty sure he couldn't lob a grenade accurately that distance. With a three second timer, not an impact fuse, it would bounce away before exploding. And he sure didn't want to miss, he had exactly one chance. As he tried to figure it out, the lights came back on. Great. That guy had better not turn around.

How could he get closer, and quickly? The walkway narrowed and disappeared ten feet upstream from him, too far to jump. He looked on the other bank, no help, he could swim across but he'd never be able to climb the slippery walls. Stymied.

Then he saw a possibility from his rock-climbing experience, a narrow oblique crack in the ceiling, leading just about to where he wanted to be. It was about four inches across. He reached up a hand, stuck it into the crack, and made a fist. The stone was dry there, and the size of the crack was perfect. He picked up his feet and hung suspended for a second. OK so far, except it feels like someone is stabbing me in my backside.

Then he swung forward, wedged his other hand in the crack, and released his back hand. Eight more feet. Ow. Goddamn. Please, don't let this crack change size. He repeated the move, gaining about a foot every time, and just as the muscles in his forearm were about to give up the effort, he landed lightly on the walkway.

Robert gauged the toss: too hard or too soft and the grenade would roll into the water. But he had two grenades, double the odds, which first? The flash-bang. He got it ready and pulled the pin.

The man on the corridor floor seemed to sense his presence, turning, looking. José! Sonavabitch! He tossed the grenade, closed his eyes, and ducked as the first shots thudded into the rock where his head had been and then the explosion seemed to lift his body a foot off the ground. He got the smoke grenade ready as he refocused but it would not be needed.

José was out cold or dead, half on and half off the shelf, a large smoldering hole in his shirt revealing a Kevlar jacket that looked a little the worse for wear. Kiraly appeared around the corner; Robert gave him a thumb's-up sign. Bartok looked at him with new respect. Hey, thought Robert, us older guys like to have fun too.

Kiraly tossed a smoke grenade through the open door to the workroom they'd abandoned before, then a flash-bang grenade. They heard shouts in Spanish, only two or three different voices this time, and automatic weapons fire, wildly impacting the rock walls and screaming away in harmless ricochets. Kiraly fired a short burst through the door and they heard a scream of pain.

Finally a voice spoke, in Spanish, "We give up. Don't shoot."

"Throw your guns through the door," said Kiraly, in the same language. "Carefully. Safeties on. I don't want to see anybody's face just yet."

Several rifles slid through the opening.

"Now the pistols."

Half a dozen pistols followed.

"Now the grenades. With the pins in."

A dozen grenades appeared.

"Good. Now lie on your stomachs. I will appear with a grenade in each hand with the pin out. Shoot me and we all die. Nobody moves, nobody gets hurt."

"Nobody moves, nobody gets hurt," said Bartok in a whisper. "Class act."

Kiraly glanced back in irritation and pulled the pins on two flash-bang grenades. He walked through the door. Robert's back itched in sympathetic apprehension.

Kiraly looked around, apparently liked what he saw, and motioned for the team to join him. Robert was next into the room. Four men were on their stomachs and two more on their backs, wounded. The room was the bunkroom, half a dozen cots and a couple of mattresses. Low-class accommodations. Gabor produced the nylon line and started tying people up until Robert remembered the handcuff supply—steel reinforced wire ties—located them in a drawer in the workroom and handcuffed the survivors to the pipes.

"Hey! What's happening?" said Sarah, in their headsets.

"Yeah! Me too!" said Teresa.

Kiraly checked his troops. "Anybody hurt, besides Robert?" he asked. Robert couldn't understand what he was talking about until he followed his glance and found a shallow gash in his good side, dripping blood. In the excitement, it had gone unnoticed.

"ROBERT!" screamed the headset.

"It's just a flesh wound," he said.

"But, what wound isn't?" said Bartok.

"Good one," said Bela.

Gabor ripped a piece of cloth from a bed sheet and bound it up.

"Sarah, see if the local cops are up yet," said Kiraly. "Almost six thirty, somebody should be stirring. Ping 'em on the ship-to-shore.

We need *gendarmes* with SCUBA gear, let us know if you raise anyone. Teresa, any sign of Goldstein?"

"Here he comes, hang on a second. Yes, three bodies. Hang on.
Two are alive, one unconscious, one groggy. They're pretty beat up."

"Leave 'em in the Zodiac. Have Goldstein stand by with a gun. Ask
for a cop boat for those bad boys. Is the sun up yet?"

"We have a pretty sunrise up here."

"Enjoy."

They began a search of the facility and soon turned up a tunnel
leading upwards from the workroom. It looked like a recent addition
with the rough surface of recent excavation, just big enough for the
forklift truck. Climbing the gentle slope, they found a well-hidden
entrance in the scrub brush, concealed from prying eyes with a veg-
etation-covered steel door and big-leafed trees. Kiraly punched up
Sarah on the radio again, "Sarah, did you find cops with SCUBA?"

"I found cops but no SCUBA yet."

"Good enough, they won't need it. Send 'em to the brush about half
a mile south of Tulum, three quarters of a mile inland. We'll station
a man to guide them in. Two should do, with the wagon for the prisoners."

Gabor waited by the entrance to direct traffic. Two hours later, after
a complete inspection of the caves revealed no new secrets, and after
a police boat took custody of the men on Bolero, a police squad
joined them in the caves. Robert asked for Colonel Muñoz and was
told he never started work before 10:00 A. M. They showed the
police the torpedoes, one still open and half-loaded with plastic bags
full of white powder.

An officer found a wrench and started to unbolt the access hatch of
another torpedo when Kiraly spoke. "Officer, I wouldn't do that.
That would be a good place for the booby trap."

The cop dropped the wrench as if it were a coral snake. "Let's look
at the open one." Kiraly and the officer unloaded bags from the open
torpedo and looked inside the hatch opening. A large block of brown
plastic was fastened to the inside surface near the access hatch and
wired to the threaded boltholes.

"That's enough plastique to blow us all into Guatemala," said
Kiraly. "There's probably some sequence of bolt removal, or
some special tool. Better leave this one for the experts." The

policeman nodded agreement energetically, found a roll of cloth tape and a felt tip pen, and fastened a sign, "¡*Muy Peligroso!*" to each torpedo hatch.

The team, starting to slow down after thirty-six hours of activity, climbed up through the tunnel to the surface. They emerged, blinking, into a bright sunny day and picked their way carefully across the sharp coral rocks in their bare feet. The little parking lot was overrun with vehicles, most of them with flashing lights, along with a news truck, some tourists trying to find out what was going on, and little kids selling serapes.

Phil Schwartz was sitting in a huge Cord Phaeton in the parking lot, sipping a tall drink with an orange slice over the rim. As they approached, he pulled out a cooler of beer and tossed them all a can. He grinned. "And when it's time to relax, one beer stands clear, beer after beer..."

"Hi, Phil," said Robert. "What's happening?"

"Hey, you guys are what's happening! The Yucatán hasn't seen so much action since the Spanish Invasion!"

Chapter 32

Cartegena, the same day

"**S**onavabitch!" screamed Ernesto Porfirio Raoul Diaz as he kicked furiously at a wooden desk. A leg broke off and the desk listed to starboard as computer disks and notebooks fell to the floor. He paced back and forth in front of the now-frightened communications technician. Diaz crumpled the printout in his large hand and kicked the books against the wall. "I don't fucking believe this!" he said, and uncrumpled and reread the paper to see if the words had changed.

*Scramble code: *36**
To: Ernesto Diaz, Cartegena
From: A. Lopez, Tulum
Date: 27 Oct. present day
Subj: Invasion

The Tulum facility was invaded early this morning by a well-armed superior force. At least 17 soldiers with smoke and grenades attacked by surprise at approximately 3:00 A.M.

One man was one of the two people we thought we had killed last week.

We fought valiantly but we were outmanned and over-powered. One is confirmed dead, three missing and pre-sumed dead, two are injured. We have no confirmed kills of the opposition but one confirmed injured.

Myself and Carlos are unhurt, we escaped through the back tunnel.

The opposition force and the police now occupy the facility. We are not sure about the status of the equip-ment or the inventory of product.

Myself, Carlos, José and Elisio are now located in the Akumal house. We are communicating this message on the CDMA transceiver at 1090.3 MHz. We will monitor this frequency and await instructions.

"Who the fuck are these bastards?" screamed Ernesto. "Garcia is paid off, the D.E.A. aren't allowed in country, there are no goddam independents operating anywhere near the Yucatán. Tell 'em this. Tell 'em to find out who the fuck it is without blowing cover. Tell 'em not to fucking screw up again."

He rammed a fresh clip into his Glock and put three rounds into the listing desk, sending it to the floor. "Tell 'em to put a man in Tulum to listen for fifteen pounds of plastique blowing." He punc-tuated each word with a round into the cinder block wall. "If those fuckups left a Remora open where the goddam D.E.A. can find it we're gonna lose the sweetest little transport gimmick we ever had. Our only hope is that they open one up and blow the whole fucking cave sky fucking high."

Ernesto got on the phone to the cop he owned in Tulum and got a few more scraps of data. An hour later, he was talking with his secu-rity chief, Antonio Rojas, and a half dozen of Rojas' lieutenants.

"Smartass college medics!" he screamed. "Goddamn smartass col-lege medics! Fucking dirtbag archaeologists!"

"OK, OK," said Rojas. "Calm down. We'll blow little pieces of smartass college kids into the sea. Let's just figure out how to save the inventory, and how to do it without pissing off our remaining friends, if we still have any."

"The cop, Muñoz, is still in our pocket. At least he says he is. Our

inside guy says the D.E.A. is watching but they haven't dealt themselves in. Yet. Looks like these guys are just college types, diggers,
and we were in their way. And they smoked us."

"Don't make sense. Where do college boys get soldiers?"

"There's gotta be somebody heavy backing 'em," said Ernesto.
"D.E.A., Mafia, Asia, Palestinian terrorists, who knows? But whoever it is, they're way the fuck out of their territory."

"But why? Diggers don't get excited like this. It must be something fucking amazing that they're digging for. Maybe something
we could use."

"Shut up a minute," said Ernesto. He balled both hands into fists
and banged them together. "OK, do this. Number one. We can't let
our organization get whacked like this, it's not fucking professional. Two. We want our inventory back. Three. If these guys are
digging for something fucking amazing, we want it. Rojas, you
know about stuff like this, these diggers, they ever dig up, like,
gold or anything?"

"Yeah. All those Indians used to bury piles of gold. That's what the
Spaniards came for."

Ernesto then remembered the gimmick he thought was long gone,
picking up the cure to the virus. The news from Texas was all bad,
anybody with a fix for that sucker could charge whatever they wanted. Maybe it was worth a billion, U.S. And if the medics were in fact
not dead, they were back in the drug business. The street legal drug
business. Mother would be proud. The cartel would be proud.
Cartels, he'd bring in the other guys on this. And bring in
Alejandro—*El Presidente*—cut him in for, say, a hundred million to
get the government on his side.

"So, number four. Here's the beauty part. Maybe we're back in the
medical business. Take a week, find out what they're after. Grab a
college boy, do a little interrogation. Break his fingers, cut off his
balls. Whatever it takes. Find out. The timing's tricky, we gotta wait
until they find the formula but we gotta get 'em before they take off.
Then we move in big."

"How big?"

"Big. I'll head up there now with some muscle, reconnoiter, talk to
Muñoz. You take twenty-five guys. They'd stick out like a whore convention at a flower show, in town, so bring sleeping bags and tarps and

stay in the bush. Make sure at least five guys are the types that can get along in town. Better if they know some English. Go with 'em. Get yourselves in place in thirty-six hours. Make sure you got good paper: passports, visas, credit cards, licenses. Supplies for ten days. Grenades, semi-automatics, explosives, flak jackets, night vision goggles, gas masks, radios, sleeping bags, boy scout crap—the whole fucking deal. I'll set up a float plane so we can scoop the medics and get back here quick. You got thirty-six hours. Questions? OK, move."

Rojas was ready for the assignment. He relocated five men from Mexico City, from their normal task of making sure that the wheels of illegal commerce were appropriately greased. He moved ten men from Tijuana, San Diego, Juarez, and El Paso, from their usual work of supervising the border crossing activities. And he recruited the remainder from the permanent staff in Medellin, checked their papers, briefed them, equipped them and booked them on two separate commercial flights to Mérida.

Rojas then checked out the weapons from one of the Medellin armories, loaded them on a Remora in Cartegena, and, sacrificing stealth for speed, loaded the Remora on the ancient float-equipped Grumman for a quick trip to the sea off Akumal.

Ernesto walked down to the first floor and found Hector Estevez, the best muscle man in Cartegena. If the muscle pool in this organization was a car pool, Hector would be the Rolls Royce, surrounded by a fleet of Ford Fiestas. He was about the height of a Rolls and damn near the width. Hector was not overly talkative, had a twisted sense of humor, was not overburdened by excessive brainpower and smelled like a pig farm, but he was everybody's first choice for muscle.

Ernesto smiled to himself as he remembered the time Hector had found his dented old pickup truck blocked by an Isuzu on the waterfront. He had simply picked up the rear end of the Isuzu, swung it over the low railing, over the Atlantic, balancing the car delicately, and driven off. Ernesto had watched the car sway in the breeze until it finally overbalanced and splashed wheels-up into the ocean twenty feet below.

Ernesto told Hector his new assignment, to accompany him to Cancún for a discussion with the police contact, Muñoz, and an interview with Lopez. Hector grunted.

Ernesto was careful to assign Hector a seat on the Cancún flight about six rows behind him, more for olfactory relief than for deception.

• • •

Ernesto looked out the airplane window at the Cancún peninsula, the narrow strip of sand appearing in danger of capsizing with the weight of the twenty-something-story hotels. The plane wheeled into the landing pattern. Muñoz would need persuasion, he thought, in case the D.E.A. or some other scumbags had bent him. No telling what kind of cash they would come up with, and he didn't need a goddamn bidding war. What he needed, he needed Muñoz in his pocket, nice and quiet and obedient.

Best thing would be to interview him in Ernesto's hotel suite. He'd asked for the top floor of the Princess, big big bucks, lots of marble and gold and Oriental rugs, Muñoz would be way off balance. If he went to Muñoz' pigsty sweatbox of a cop station, Muñoz would be comfortable, and he'd have help, real close.

Ernesto and Hector collected their baggage and called Muñoz from the airport.

"Colonel Muñoz."

"Ernesto Diaz, colonel. I'm at the Cancún Princess, room twenty sixteen. Come to this room in an hour."

"Senor Diaz, always a pleasure. To what do we owe the honor of a personal visit?"

Shut up, sleazemouth bastard. It would be a pleasure to see the fear on his face. "An hour, Muñoz."

"But why? Can you not see me here? I'm in the middle of a difficult interrogation."

"I do not do 'Why.' I pay you five thousand US every month so I do not have to do 'Why.' One hour. Say nothing but *Sí*, unless you wish to put your fat salary and your fat body and your fat family at risk." During the long pause that followed, Ernesto could feel the hate and power that Muñoz had built up in his "interview" dissolve into fear.

Finally, Muñoz said "*Sí*."

Ernesto said, "Room twenty sixteen. One hour," and hung up the phone. That went well, it should put Muñoz in the proper frame of mind to continue his education. He caught a cab for the hotel with Hector, rolled the window down for fresh air, and they drove to the hotel in silence. Once in the suite, he turned up the air conditioning and explained to Hector his responsibility in the upcoming meeting. Hector grunted.

Muñoz was a large man, maybe five feet nine in his sweat-stained khaki uniform but carrying an extra thirty or forty pounds like most of the older Mexican cops. *Mordida* had made their lives too easy. He had a ludicrous handlebar mustache waxed to an oily gloss, and wore a wide belt studded with nine mm cartridges like Pancho Villa. On his belt he wore two matching pearl-handled stainless-steel Glock automatic pistols. He had his confidence back; he swaggered into the room as if he spent all his spare time in two thousand dollar a night penthouse hotel suites.

Ernesto made himself a scotch and water at the minibar, adding a single ice cube to two minibottles of the excellent single malt scotch. He took a long sip.

"I'll have a whisky and water," said Muñoz.

Ernesto watched Muñoz in expressionless unmoving silence. Hector stood at the far wall. Muñoz dismissed him with a glance. Lots of people dismissed Hector with a glance, Ernesto thought, smiling to himself. This would be amusing. He enjoyed this work.

The silence deepened, and Muñoz waited, not speaking, not afraid now. Must be his interview experience, he's not babbling at all.

"Colonel Muñoz, perhaps you would care to explain the recent event, where our Tulum operation under your protection was invaded by a small army?"

"Ah, *sí*, I have heard of that. I knew you would be interested, so I myself personally investigated."

"You yourself? We are indeed fucking honored. I don't suppose you found anything?"

"Unfortunately, not too much, except that probably some college archaeologists from the U.S. were behind this. There is also something about some disease in the U.S., they say the caves show how to cure the disease."

"College archaeologists did not do this thing."

"It seems strange to me, also."

Ernesto turned to Hector. "It seems strange to him, also." Hector smiled and nodded. Ernesto turned back to Muñoz. "Have you ever run a business? No, of course not. You could not possibly run a penny ante poker game without fucking it up. I am trying to keep this thing working. I have schedules, customers, supply problems, labor disputes. I have cash flow problems, inventory management problems, and transportation problems. I have employees who suck up enough product to make them stupid. Top-heavy management, five goddam tiers of distribution. And at least fifteen organizations in seven countries are trying to put us out of business." Ernesto pounded both fists on a table. "And so you know what my biggest fucking problem is, Colonel Asshole?"

Muñoz shook his head no.

"Of course you don't. You don't know jack shit. My biggest fucking problem is employees who fuck with me. Improvements must be made. Lessons must be learned. Discipline must be maintained. Colonel Muñoz, look out the window."

Confused, Muñoz did so.

"Now look straight down."

"The window does not open, Ernesto."

"Señor Diaz."

"Pardon. Señor Diaz."

"Hector, open the window for the Colonel."

"It is fixed in place, Señor Diaz, it does not open, the window," said Muñoz.

Hector slowly detached himself from the wall, picked up an overstuffed Chippendale chair and threw it through the quarter inch glass with a casual flick of his wrist. Muñoz stood staring at the wreckage.

"Hector, help the Colonel to look down. He is still having trouble looking down."

Hector moved with an unexpected swiftness to Muñoz' side, wrapped an arm around his waist, picked him effortlessly off the floor, and propelled him towards the opening. Muñoz emitted a muffled noise and grabbed the windowsill with both hands to check his movement but Hector with a quick motion of one hand slapped his arms up and shoved the upper half of his body through the jagged hole. Muñoz screamed in terror as his center of gravity passed the point of no return, but Hector held on to his legs.

Ernesto said, "Be quiet. Look down. Are you looking down?"

"Yes! Yes! I am looking down!"

"Would you like to try to fly?"

"No! No!"

"Are you working for anyone else but us?"

"No! I swear! No! Nobody!"

"Not the *Federales*, not the D.E.A., not the peons, not the stupid college boys?" He signaled to Hector, who rolled Muñoz back and forth on the broken edges of the window.

"Nobody! *Madre Dios*! I swear on the grave of my mother! *Jesùs*, I am cut in half!"

"I spit on the grave of your mother. Pull him back in."

Hector dragged Muñoz back into the room with blood dripping from a dozen small cuts around his ample stomach.

"Ha!" said Ernesto. "Now you must pay me for the fat removal surgery! I think two thousand a month would be fair. I will adjust your salary. Get out. Do not let those college dirtbags anywhere near Tulum. Move. Now."

Muñoz fled, leaving a trail of blood on the carpet. Hector shadowed him closely to discourage any ideas he might have about drawing his guns. His uniform hat with the gold braid had been knocked off in the struggle; Ernesto tossed it through the broken window. A minute later the telephone rang.

"Front desk. Security reports a broken window in the penthouse. Are you all right?"

"*Sí*," said Ernesto. "But your housekeeping staff is totally incompetent. Such a mess. Get somebody up here to straighten this room, pronto." He heard a strange snuffling noise and looked at Hector, unruffled by his exertions. Hector appeared to be doing something which might be laughing. He had never seen Hector laugh before.

Chapter 33

Tulum, November 12, present day

Robert ran the probe along the west wall of the cave in the bunkroom, watching the color display. The sensor used a combined field of high frequency ultrasonic and electromagnetic radiation, and it had an effective range of between ten and fifty feet, depending on the soil composition. In this irregular limestone, the ultrasonic probe reached a little farther and its magenta image showed a larger visual field than the electromagnetic's green image.

Teresa and the *Bolero* crew watched the display. As they worked, Phil Schwartz arrived carrying a cooler. "Hey, guys, this is where it happened, huh? Anybody thirsty?" He produced a frosted bottle of Corona. Bela grabbed it. Phil produced another. It, too, was claimed and soon the entire crew was sipping Corona or soft drinks.

"Hold it! Hold it!" said Phil. They turned to look, and he handed out foil packages of Macadamia nuts. "Almost forgot the nuts. Conchita sends her love, Robert, I think she really likes you."

Robert moved to the north wall and quickly found a strong return. The display showed a void starting a foot or so beyond the wall. He stopped and scanned the sensor beam laterally. It painted a picture of a long rectangular room. "Here it is," he said, and they all gathered to look.

"Goddamn," said Phil, "That box can see right through rock? I want one."

Robert brought the hammer drill into position and bored a two-inch diameter hole about waist level. It broke through in a foot and a half, and he asked for the fiberscope. Threading it into position, he looked around. Score. Home run. His heart started hammering like the drill and the image danced as his hand shook. "This is it. Big, long room, flat walls, man-made. No glyphs I can see. There's niches in both side walls—shelves—with some kind of statues on them. There's water on the floor, we'll go in at this height."

They quickly enlarged the hole.

The room was not completely flooded, with only two feet of water on the floor. It was about eighty feet long, twenty feet wide, and at least ten feet high. The black walls sloped in at a slight angle. Robert had learned that the Maya did not know about the arch, or did not use it. Instead they supported ceilings with this sort of construction.

As they moved into the room, they got a better look at the walls. The niches in both walls held an incredible collection of small art objects, mostly jade and gold. Colored gems were everywhere, inserted for eyes, studding sword handles, making decorative borders on plates and goblets. At the far end of the room a steep staircase led up to a small opening outlined with engraved green stone tiles.

Robert was caught up by emotion. Twelve hundred years of history—perfectly preserved—sealed in this museum. The smell was strange, ancient, and slightly sweet with an odor of hazelnuts mixing with the musty aroma of an old cellar. The objects in this room surely doubled the world's collection of Maya art. And this must be where the scientists of Tulum had done their work, although it did not look like a laboratory. The connection with the past was strong through the twelve centuries of elapsed time. He felt the people who had carved the statues—who'd chiseled the caves out of the living stone—as if they were still nearby, hacking out another room, setting an amethyst eye into an obsidian jaguar.

"They look as if they were made yesterday," said Teresa, her voice soft and reverent, "I thought anything this old would be inches thick with dust. They're just a little fuzzy."

"No air circulation," said Gabor. "Nice shiny sealed walls."

"Yes," said Robert. "If no dust gets carried in by air currents, they'd stay clean. But then how did they work in here, without air? Wait; maybe they had ventilation shafts and a way to close the vents if they

wanted, say, to lower the humidity. If they did have a charge microscope in operation, they would need a way to keep the humidity
down. And they could easily work for many days without exhausting
the oxygen in this big space."

The rest of the group filed into the room and stared in respect-
ful silence for several minutes at the scene, illuminating it with
the beams of many flashlights. Bela panned a video camera
around the shelves.

Teresa rushed from one to another, brushing tears from her face, "I
can't believe this. Look, look at this one, early Toltec. And look here,
this parrot looks as if he could take off and fly. Feathers carved from
jade. Here's Olmec work, you can see the characteristic rectangular
shapes, but this jaguar looks as if it is ready to jump off the shelf. The
stones, emeralds, sapphires, this must be ruby. Some of these pieces
must have been a thousand years old when this city was built. There
are only a handful of pieces from early Mexico with inset gemstones
in museums, and here they're everywhere you look."

Phil picked up a figurine and weighed it in his hand.

"Not bad, not bad at all," he said, as he looked at the bottom as if
for a label or maybe a price.

"Hands off," said Robert. "These are heading for a museum.
Teresa, I thought the Maya had no gold."

"They weren't supposed to. But most of this is clearly Maya craftsmanship. This room may rewrite a few history books."

"Before we start rewriting history, we better see if we can take
care of the present," said Robert. "We still need to find the glyph.
The rooms have been sealed to prevent humid air infiltration.
There's a charge microscope somewhere." He climbed carefully
up the steep steps. The small opening at the top led to another
room, very long but narrower and completely dry, its floor level
with the bottom of the opening. He moved in, and the room was
soon lit with many flashlights. No charge microscope here, there
was no furniture or shelving.

The walls sloped in, but in this room they were glossy black obsidian with tiny neat glyphs inscribed from floor to ceiling. Teresa moved
to the wall and started reading as Robert tried to estimate the size of
the room, maybe twelve feet wide and high and so long that his flashlight beam did not reach the other end. He clapped his hands and timed

the echo from the far wall. Nearly one second delay, more than four hundred feet long. Amazing. Dead straight, from what he could see.

In a few minutes, Teresa announced, "Astronomy, planetary orbits, a calendar date of a comet. Temple design and construction. Mathematics, here's the Pythagorean theorem. The law of cosines. Fibonacci series."

"Any Bessel functions?" asked Robert.

"Not yet, why?"

"Nothing."

"Maybe we'll find them here somewhere, this'll take weeks. These glyphs are tiny, a tenth the usual size." Her fingers traced the carving. "Agriculture, here's a record of corn harvest compared to planting date. This is truly incredible. This room records the scientific knowledge of the Maya kingdom. It's a giant lab notebook. Better than those tree-bark jobs, this is for the ages."

"Do you see the glyph for the Austin virus?" asked Robert.

"No. I'll keep looking, I bet it's here somewhere. It looks as if the Maya scientists did work here in Tulum, mostly. The observatory is above ground, of course, but I bet we find more labs underground. Hey, information, I bet these science types were selling information. The same thing happened in ancient Greece, like the oracle at Delphi. Same thing happens today on the Internet. You want a good corn harvest? Bring a jade figurine, or maybe food and clothing, you get planting tables and fertilizer suggestions. You building a pyramid? Complete, detailed plans are yours for a gold statue or two."

"Of course! And some of the loot is next door, the room outside is the bank!"

"That would explain the gold. Other cultures, Aztecs, they would have known about the knowledge bank, here, and could have brought gold. We don't have a laboratory yet, though, just the library."

Robert walked down the long room, footsteps echoing as if in a cathedral. About half was inscribed, the rest of the walls were untouched. Blank pages. The cave seemed to have been cut from obsidian, an amazing feat, as obsidian had the characteristics of glass. The hill here must be the residue of an ancient volcanic outflow to deposit that much pure obsidian. On closer inspection he found the secret, almost invisible razor cuts in a foot-square pattern: the entire room had been carefully tiled with obsidian.

At the end of the room, a six-foot disk, a terra cotta bas-relief of a man holding a small pointed tool, was set flush against the wall.

"Goldstein! Could you bring the electromagnetic probe over here?"

Goldstein brought the probe and its display and following Robert's gesture, scanned the wall and moved the probe across the bas-relief. A picture built up slowly of another room behind a foot thick wall. The probe revealed an aperture in the wall behind the bas-relief.

Robert tried to move the bas-relief but it seemed to be cemented permanently to the wall.

"Kiraly!" he called. Kiraly materialized. "Can you help lever this sculpture off the wall?"

"Do you care if we break it?" asked Kiraly.

"No. Forgive me, Maya scholars."

They both pushed on one side, and with a crunching sound the large circular sculpture slowly rotated to one side, happily without breaking. It revealed a small trapezoidal opening, roughly two feet high and set low in the wall. Robert knelt and shone his beam into the aperture. Almost the first thing the beam illuminated was a metal globe, half a foot in diameter. Robert's pulse began to accelerate. He and Kiraly crawled through the hole. The charge microscope! It was set up vertically instead of horizontally, but it was unmistakable. He quickly scanned the wall. It appeared that they had used the polished wall to receive the image and then used a hard stone, maybe sapphire, to inscribe the image for permanence. And near the microscope—possibly the last image it had made—he found an unmounted obsidian tile bearing the Austin virus glyph.

"Teresa!" he yelled.

He heard echoing sounds from the next room. Bad acoustics. He ran back and stuck his head through the small opening.

"Teresa!" he called again.

"There he is!" she said. "Or, there's his head, at least. What did you find?"

"Here's where you earn your paycheck. We found the microscope. And the glyph."

"Goddamn!" she responded.

The rest of the group squeezed through the opening and joined Robert in the smaller room.

"There's the microscope. There's the Austin glyph. Can you translate the text over here?"

Teresa knelt before the glyph as if in prayer, running her hand over it reverently. Then she studied the adjacent text. It seemed supernaturally quiet, as if everyone in the room was holding their breath.

Teresa spoke one soft word, "Wow," and it seemed to become even quieter. "Here's a description of the symptoms. Black tongue, bleeding from the mouth. They understood the connection between the symptoms and the virus molecule. They got five days incubation time. And this glyph—the one you said might be an antiviral image—is connected to these glyphs for some kind of a tree. Or part of a tree. Maybe blossoms, flowers. Then here's a group of glyphs I've never seen, I can't translate these, maybe we'll be able to figure it out from the surrounding text. They seem to be in a hurry, here, you can see the carelessness of the inscription and they're leaving out words."

"How long will you need to finish the translation?" asked Robert.

She stared at the wall for another minute. "Hard to say. Some of these glyphs are like nothing I've ever seen."

Chapter 34

Cancún City, November 12, present day

The barroom was floored with hard packed brown dirt and smelled of beer and urine. The walls, roughly framed in two by fours, were decorated with an assortment of calendars from auto parts companies and breweries. No insulation was needed in this climate, so the galvanized corrugated steel was simply nailed to the framing and the roof rafters. A steel panel had been ripped off by the last hurricane and hung by a corner, swinging and scraping in the breeze and revealing a large slice of dark sky. One side of the room was the bar, a huge refrigerator stocked with beer, and rows of transparent glass bottles racked without labels. Muñoz and Antonio Martinez sat in the exposed corner for privacy as the regulars tended to hang out in the protected end of the room.

Muñoz lifted his shirt and revealed a wide swath of bandages. "See this? Focking Ernesto did it."

"*Caramba*! With a knife?"

"Focking Ernesto thinks I told the college archaeologists what he was doing."

"You did?"

"No." Muñoz popped the lime section into his mouth, chewed it and swallowed half a bottle of Corona. "I did not." He slammed the bottle down. "We had a slick deal, working both sides. I got a nice car out of it. But I have thought this over carefully. I will kill Ernesto, next time he lands here."

"He is said to be tough to kill—"

"You can help." Martinez whitened.

"But there is the very generous payment—"

"There are some problems with the very generous payment. If you follow the news, the college boy was telling the truth. You read the newspaper? There will be so much pressure here the top will blow off. You see the virus in Texas? Everybody in the U.S. is very excited about this. The college boy is working on some kind of cure, he needs to get into the cave."

"So? Ernesto will squash him."

"Maybe, maybe not. There's going to be backup. Mexican army, U.S. Marines, who knows. Ernesto ain't gonna make it. He'll rat us out if he gets a chance. So we switch sides first, so we don't get caught with our hands in the cookie jar." He jerked his head towards the bar and Antonio jumped up for two more Coronas.

Muñoz popped a fresh lime into his mouth and took a generous gulp. "Another problem: Ernesto pissed me off. Here's the plan. Suppose we were to help the college boy? We could get the *Guardia Nacional*, maybe a hundred men, or a SWAT team from Mexico City if there's time. We tell them we're going to capture a few dozen drug smugglers from South America and a ton of coke. We take Ernesto and whoever he brought for muscle, we make sure Ernesto gets killed in the action, and impound the inventory. There'll be a lot of confusion, and if it turns out Ernesto's rocket things weren't all full, who'll know?"

"How do we sell the stuff?"

"I got a contact or two in Tijuana that can take it at half price—all we got—no questions asked. We might clear a couple of million pesos. You get twenty percent. You ever want to live in Jamaica?"

Chapter 35

Akumal, November 13, present day

Robert woke early, dressed quickly in shorts and T-shirt, and powered up the videoconference system to talk to Dr. Teppin. Teppin's image formed in the small display and the speaker emitted the sound of Boston traffic.

"Teppin."

"Good morning, Dr. Teppin. Mexico calling," said Robert.

"So I see. Set the camera up on that railing so I can look at the ocean, would you? Yes—perfect—thank you. Not that you are difficult to look at, you understand, it is just that the ocean there is such a different shade of blue. Something in the algae, I think. Now, what is happening?"

"We scored. We found a cave system under Tulum—perfectly preserved—covered with glyphs and with charge microscope images. We also found a pile of statues, jade, gold, jewels. And we found the charge microscope they must have used, 1,200 years ago."

"That's incredible. Even though we knew it had to be there, it is still a shock. This will revolutionize Mesoamerican studies. The virus, what about the virus? Did you find virus molecule images, too?"

"Yes, sir. The Austin virus molecule was there. An image we thought was the antiviral was there, and from the nearby glyphs, it appears that we guessed right. It looks as if the entire cave was set up to record and preserve the knowledge of Tulum. This is the Mesoamerican version of the Library of Alexandria. I'll show you some video we shot in the caves, if you can tear yourself away from the ocean."

"Please. Wait, let me see if Gary Spender is on line, he'll want to see this too." A minute later he announced that Spender was away from the video terminal, but he was on audio.

Spender's voice came through, sounding far away, "Robert, hello, I hear you're making progress."

"Very exciting, Gary. I'll run the video for you." He keyed the machine on.

"There! I'll pause that, that's the Maya version of the charge microscope. It looks like they had mastered its use and also mastered the technology of using its images to design biological materials. Here, they're showing the method they used to produce the antiviral. It's pretty clearly something that they harvested from the rain forest, but our translators aren't sure exactly what. But Teresa's got a good-sized team on it, I bet a day or two does it."

"Is there any evidence that the antiviral worked for the Maya?"

"Yes, indirectly," said Robert. "The glyphs in Uxmal seemed to say that, and also this entire cave seems to be a how-to book for the Maya, they didn't record failed experiments here."

"Let me fill you in with the news from here," said Teppin. "It can be summarized with this graph."

Teppin sketched a few lines with his mouse.

"First, the deaths from the virus—the solid line—are increasing at a high-order exponential rate. The population of the world would be dead in fourteen months if this curve continued. Second, the deaths from violence—the dotted line—are starting late but threatening to cross over soon. This outbreak is so frightening, the symptoms of the disease so ugly, that some Texans near the isolation zone are shooting strangers who get close. Dr. Spender, have you seen this violence?"

"We've heard reports, and we've heard a lot of shooting in the distance, but we are very well protected by National Guard and regular Army troops. It is like a war, here, though, I've seen napalm drops inside the red zone, and we have maybe ten thousand troops enforcing quarantine. But I think some of the troops are running out on us."

"Is the buffer holding?"

"It's more like the buffer *du jour*. I don't think anything is going to hold this thing. It's like holding light in a bottle."

"How about Houston?" Robert asked.

"Houston is directly downwind," said Spender. "It will be evacuated as a precaution, but many people are leaving. Your daughter and her family are not at home, we think they probably evacuated."

Robert felt his fists clench, his nails digging into his flesh. Goddamn better have evacuated. "Then what we've got here is the best shot? What if we can't get any farther?"

Teppin answered him, "We may all be dead. I do not consider myself a religious man, but I've been doing a lot of praying lately. I know you do not want any more pressure than you have already, but we have nothing else. I am sending down a team, maybe twenty people."

"Twenty people? They'll be bumping into each other."

"You can keep them straightened out. Half of them will be on standby to set up a pilot production line in case you can give them anything to work with. Some will help with administration, the nuts and bolts of keeping everybody fed. Some will help with translation. Some will help with synthesis and analysis. We will set up and staff a field hospital and have medical staff standing by in case they get anything to administer."

"But, why not have this installation in the States?" asked Robert. "It would be much easier to handle the logistics."

"Time. Look at the curve. In a few weeks, saving an hour will mean saving a thousand lives. Now, until you find the cure, time is free. And maybe the antiviral can be found only in Mexico."

"All right, that makes sense, send 'em down. We'll see if we can keep them busy."

"We have been in contact with the Mexican government and they pledge complete support. The *Guardia Nacional* has been mobilized and a battalion will be deployed in the Yucatán to help in whatever way they can. They are preparing for possible virus outbreaks."

"In the Yucatán?"

"Yes. You see, the source of the virus outbreak at Austin seems to be understood now. The archaeological team members that were the first to die visited some of the more remote sites—Copán, Yaxchilán—and excavated extensively in Uxmal. It is probable that a human, bird, animal, or insect vector in the Yucatán is responsible, almost certainly at the Uxmal site."

"That would imply that the Maya themselves may be carriers?"

"Possibly. They may be racially immune after surviving the attack in the ninth century. But it is more probable that the virus just lay dormant in some pocket of vegetation for hundreds of years until it was disturbed. In any case, you can expect to see an outbreak in the interior Yucatán soon, or it may be happening already. You must take every precaution. We will send appropriate isolation gear. One mitigating factor is that the virus may need high humidity to propagate and you are coming into the dry season there."

"And it must be inhaled?"

"Yes, that has been proved."

"Suppose we do dig up a candidate antiviral? How do we test it?

"Good question. I can get you any number of victims, but then we have the hazard of starting a new outbreak if the virus escapes containment. I think that is not a good risk at this time. We will fly the antiviral to Texas. I have asked for military jets to stand by at the Cancún airport, Mexico has provided two F-14's. Contact a Colonel Estancía. No, I will have him contact you. Of course, if there is the outbreak in the Yucatán jungle, you have your test subjects."

"We have a lot to do."

"Be ready for the new people, think carefully how you will set up for them. Your job title is changing from research to management."

Chapter 36

Uxmal, November 13, present day

Ixtac lay on his belly at the edge of the clearing. He was a small man, just a little less than five feet tall, not quite one hundred pounds, a perfect size for this night. He felt the excitement begin to flow in his veins as he looked over the scene.

Ixtac's small size and his dark skin would help him now, would make him invisible to the guards. The moon was overhead now, a big enough sliver so that Ixtac's dark-adapted eyes could make out the bright wide ribbon that stretched around the clearing with its printed warnings, *"muy Peligroso"* and *"prohibidad! Politzia,"* and the three-pointed symbol that Ixtac did not recognize. Perhaps the symbol of the company that had made the ribbon.

Ixtac had visited many of the areas where the *gringos* dug into the earth to find the sacred places of his ancestors, and he knew that the treasures were not for the *gringos* but for him—Ixtac, with the pure Maya blood. In his visits—quiet visits well after dark—he had saved Maya things from the *gringos*. Alvarez, in the town of Playa del Carmen, would buy these things. Alvarez would pay many *pesos* for the statues of the jaguar god or the frog god made from the green stone and the black stone, and Alvarez would take them—he had once said to

Ixtac—to the big museum in Mexico City where the Maya could all see them.

Once Ixtac had seen a frog god made from the green stone hanging around the neck of a fat old *gringo* woman in Playa del Carmen. It looked like the one he had sold Alvarez only a week before and he wondered if perhaps Alvarez was not completely honest, but then he thought that there must be many similar green stone frog gods in the world and it would not be the same one.

Ixtac saw the shiny metal trailer with the same three-pointed symbol and in it two guards, listening to the radio and smoking cigarettes. On both sides of the spot where he was hiding stood the posts with the black glass spots. He knew about the posts, he had crawled between these posts in Palenque when he was a young boy and the posts had screamed like the jungle pig when you put an arrow in it—like a thousand jungle pigs—and all the lights had come on and he had run like a crazy man.

He did not see the dogs but he had brought their dinner—the rabbit his wife had skinned for him the week before—and he himself had slit the rabbit open and poured the bottle of the fluid he got from his cousin who worked at the hospital.

He had carried the rabbit on the bus from Akumal and he knew the dogs would find the rabbit of much interest as the others on the bus did not sit with him in the last row or in the row next to him or even the row in front of that one.

Now he pulled the rabbit from the big bag on his back and slung it thirty feet away. The small noise when it fell or maybe its strong smell brought the dogs quickly—strong-looking dogs—two dogs that moved quietly to the rabbit and quietly ate it, making a low growling only when one seemed to be taking more than a fair part. Then soon the dogs laid down and were quiet.

Ixtac dug with his machete a shallow hole under where the posts looked at each other through the black glass, removed his bag, and pushed it ahead as he crawled through. He could use his flashlight now as the guards were in the brightly lit trailer, and he picked his way over the trenches and under the tight white strings and found the great block of the tomb under a blue tarpaulin in the center of the mesa.

He cut a hole in the tarpaulin on the side away from the guards and looked at the heavy cover with dismay, but he found a crack where he could lever the stone with his machete and then chip out a new resting place for the tip of the blade and lever the stone again.

After an hour and a half, Ixtac had a hole of sufficient size to squeeze through. He dropped into the tomb and sifted through the dust and chips of wood and pieces of stone and fabric and bone, trying not to breathe the stench which was not as strong as the rabbit but which somehow made his stomach clench. When he saw the first lightening of the sky he had found only a few old coins. Alvarez would give him maybe enough *pesos* to pay for the bus. His wife would tell him again to get a job at the hotel, and she would sleep with her face towards the wall for a week.

Ixtac sighed, scrambled back through the tomb, burrowed again under the eyes of the posts with the black glass, and walked back out to the road. He would use his thumb to go home, he was no longer a man rich enough to take the bus.

· · ·

Ixtac found Alvarez drinking tequila *con limon* in the Green Parrot. Alvarez signaled for the waiter and provided Ixtac with tequila also, then shook the coins out on the table and studied the coins for many minutes, then washed them with tequila and studied them some more, and then surprised Ixtac by handing him enough *pesos* to keep him drunk for a month.

· · ·

As the sun came up, Ixtac woke with a mezcal hangover that banged against the inside of his head and made his legs weak. He checked that the remaining pesos were safe in the bag with his tools and left the alley where he had slept to find his way home before his wife became too worried. Now perhaps she would not face the wall and pretend to fall asleep.

Ixtac worked his way home through the jungle near Akumal, taking the diagonal route from where the banana truck had dropped him off, and came upon a strange thing. Many men in dark clothes were there, most carrying big rifles, looking fiercely about as if for something to shoot. Dark men, not *gringos*, but not clean-shaven like the *Federales*.

He would pick up a little bonus. But it was daylight now and he would need to be careful. He picked up a big bo-tan leaf and tucked it into his rope belt, and wriggled his way with the patience of the jaguar into the camp—his slender body no higher than the grass—moving along fissures in the rough rocky ground.

Ixtac found a big rifle and pulled it to him, wishing he knew how it worked, but then he stopped as a strange feeling of tightness in his throat stopped his breath for a moment and he gave a great cough before he could think how to stop it and he closed his eyes almost shut and tried to sink deeply into the ground, his small body braced for the blows of the bullets.

Ixtac's cough launched a fog of aerosol particles into the air at near-supersonic speed. As Ixtac's throat and nasal passages were rich with the virus, each microscopic droplet hosted between a hundred and a thousand molecules of the deadliest virus ever evolved. Each molecule was a single strand of RNA, measuring only one millionth of an inch long, in the shape of a nail, floating inside the drop. The day was not humid and the drops evaporated rapidly, mostly within a few feet. The virus particles died a millisecond later, their hydrocarbon constituent elements oxidizing and rearranging themselves into an amorphous, inert fleck of dust and wafting away.

But one larger drop wafted upwards in a vagrant air current, ventured near the nose of the Columbian sentry, and was inhaled. It successfully dodged a thicket of nose hair and landed on the man's nasal passage where it slowly evaporated, but not before several molecules of the RNA virus found a home. Their new home was warm, moist, and rich with amino acids and proteins, and they settled in comfortably, contemplating mitosis. In five minutes, they had divided into six molecules. In ten minutes, twelve molecules. In an hour, twenty-five million.

"Esteban!" shouted a voice, moving closer. "That you?"

It was Esteban that coughed, thought Ixtac. Not me. Esteban.

Finally the owner of the voice came walking straight at Ixtac, and Ixtac thought the beating of his heart would give him away, but the man stepped over him as if he was a weed or a rock and walked down the little hill, calling still for the missing Esteban. Ixtac dropped the rifle and crawled quickly—low like a snake—away from the camp.

His wife was asleep still—lazy thing—and he climbed into the bed without undressing to curl against her warm round backside and get a few minutes of sleep himself.

In seven day's time Ixtac would be dead, and his wife, and half of the village, and the disease would have a foothold in Mexico.

Chapter 37

Akumal, November 14, present day

Robert prepared for the invasion. They needed a building, near the highway but away from the Cancún population. It would have to be an isolated place with no guests or staff to move out. He made a dozen phone calls and located a medium-sized hotel under construction north of Akumal with no neighbors, then spoke to the developer and general contractor, Pedro Lalos from the firm of Lalos and Talan.

"*Sí*, we have such a property; I am standing in it now. Eighty rooms, all nice. Completion in three months." Circular saws screamed in the background.

"Can we rent the entire hotel for a few weeks?"

"The hotel, she is not ready. She has no carpets. No lampshades. No plates on the electrical fixtures. No paint."

"Sounds perfect. How's the telephones, water, and electricity?"

"They are working, but there are no towel bars. Mattresses, in storage, but no beds. No fire alarms. Floors and walls unfinished. The occupancy would not be approved."

"Who signs the occupancy permits?"

"Colonel Muñoz from the local *Federales*. Tough. Even everything perfect, two thousand pesos to the Colonel."

Robert thought to himself: Two thousand dollars to Muñoz for bending the regulations. He was getting the hang of Mexican business.

"We'll take care of the occupancy permits. If the property is acceptable, we'll pay your firm four thousand dollars a day. We don't need towels or continental breakfast buffet."

"What is continental breakfast buffet?"

"You don't want to know. Do we have a deal?"

"Enjoy your new hotel. Stay as long as you wish."

"Wait there for me; I need to make sure it is acceptable. Does it have a name?"

"Not yet; you can name it whatever you want."

"Hotel Austin, I think."

The hotel was big enough, five stories high in a long rectangle, parallel to the ocean view. The cleared land on the inland side would presumably turn into a parking lot. The lobby entrance, perhaps twenty feet high by thirty wide, was open to the unobtrusive elements. The atrium lobby showcased a huge semi-abstract sculpture in marble, maybe Neptune rising from the sea. Or maybe not. The lobby merged seamlessly into the bar/lounge area that opened to the ocean side, featuring a roughed-in bar and quarry tile floors mostly covered with heavy gray paper. The walls were blue plasterboard, and the light fixtures, for the moment, were bare hundred-fifty watt bulbs dangling from loose wires.

The place smelled like new construction: a mix of fresh concrete, plaster, and newly sawn lumber. Robert checked the other ground floor rooms. Restaurant on the southeast corner: immense crystal chandelier, rough plywood floors, big commercial kitchen, no gas pressure yet, coffee shop on the southwest corner. The two rooms on the north side looked like good lab space.

Towards the ocean the landscaping was finished. Hibiscus, oleander, casuarinas, and banana trees were scattered beneath graceful coconut palms.

"What do you think?" asked Lalos. "Perfect, no?"

"Turn on the gas in the kitchen, store your equipment in the basement, clean it up a little and we'll take it."

Robert signed a check for forty thousand dollars on their new Mérida bank account for ten days of occupancy. The newly wealthy contractor, in a spirit of generosity, offered the services of his wife and his partner's wife to help with the kitchen and the laundry and linens for an additional twenty-five dollars a day.

Robert heard a voice behind him. "Papa, I brought the books."
He turned to see a young and pretty woman with dark hair and
skin and a big white-toothed smile, carrying an armful of cata-
logs. He had met her before, where was it? Yes, Conchita, from
Phil Schwartz' place.

"Hi, Conchita," he said.

"Oh, Mister Robert!" she squealed in delight. "From the *hacienda*!
Buenos Dias!"

Pedro Lalos smiled. "I see you have met my stepdaughter. This is
Doctor Robert Asher, Shirley, you should show great respect." He
turned to Robert, "Shirley to me and to her mother, Schwartz has
everyone else calling her Conchita." Looking back at his daughter, he
asked, "And also Doctor Teresa Welles, you have met her?"

"*Sí*," said Conchita. She did not look at Teresa. "At the *hacienda*
with Señor Schwartz." She smiled at Robert. "You see me now at my
morning job."

"She's helping with the decor," said Lalos. "Paint chips. Art
prints." He took the books from Conchita. "We will not be doing the
prints for a few weeks, but I will go through these with you now."

Robert turned to Teresa. "I'll pick up our luggage from *Bolero*. And
swing by Playa del Carmen for bed sheets and soap and stuff."

"I've reached translation burnout. My brain is all mush. I'll help
with the supplies, I need the fresh air."

Conchita joined in from across the room, "Oh, Playa del Carmen, perfect, I came on the bus, I need a ride back, can I come? And I will show
you the store where you can buy the best sheets. I will do the prints
some other time with papa, *sí*, papa?" She ran with them to the battered
rental van and jumped into the passenger seat as Robert took the wheel.
"Here, I will show you the best way to drive to Playa del Carmen."

"There's a choice?" said Teresa from the back seat. "And what
about *Bolero*?"

"What is this *Bolero*?" asked Conchita. "It is a dance, no?"

"It is a place where I keep my important things right now," said
Teresa. "You will find it in Puerto Aventuras."

"We'll stop on the way back," said Robert.

• • •

The van was filled with sheets and pillows, further blocking visibility through the cracked rear window. Robert negotiated the bumpy dirt streets, avoiding the stray dogs and street vendors, and the pleasant aroma of grilled sausage reminded him that they had missed lunch.

"Anybody else interested in dinner? Conchita, you live here, where's a quick restaurant?"

"You want a tourist place or a good place?"

"The good place, please."

"Turn right here. Just at the end of the block, no sign."

"You will be our guest," said Robert. "With thanks for your help."

She led them through a small door in a building that looked more like a rambling home than a restaurant, into a dimly lit rustic space with dark wood walls hung with colorful serapes. They were greeted by the smell of tortillas and *cerveza* and a large friendly older woman who embraced Conchita and smiled over her shoulder at Robert and Teresa. "Sit, sit, there under the fan is the best place." She produced a match and lit the candle stuck into an empty tequila bottle, and the darkness receded somewhat.

Conchita sat down and turned to Teresa, arching her supple back like a big cat as she pushed her abundant black hair back from her face. "You like Mexican food, Dr. Welles? Spicy hot *caliente, sí?*"

"I can handle anything, with enough *cerveza*," said Teresa.

"And you, Robert Asher," she asked him, turning to him and placing a hand on his chest. "Oh, you are all muscles! Is amazing, no? *Caramba*. How do you like eet?"

Robert thought for a minute before he got her meaning. "I like it hot, too."

She slowly removed her hand, looking up at Robert through the corners of her large eyes. "You want me to do the order? *Muy caliente*, you will not catch a cold for two weeks?"

"*Por favor*," said Robert.

Conchita rattled off a string of rapid Spanish to the proprietor. Soon a variety of chicken and tomatoes and refried beans and tortillas and tacos was delivered to the table, accompanied by cool beer in large clear bottles with no labels and some green liquid that tasted to Robert like rocket fuel.

After dinner they drove to the small home where Conchita lived with her parents on the edge of town.

"Robert Asher," she said through the window. "Let me know next time you need to buy sheets." She giggled and blew him a kiss and ran to the house.

Robert headed back south to Akumal, with the van further burdened with their luggage, looking at the impressive sunset. The large dinner still pleasantly filled his stomach and the glow from the *cerveza* had not quite disappeared. Teresa, now sitting beside him, was unusually quiet, probably also enjoying the evening. As he turned from the bright sunset back to the road, he looked ahead in disbelief as an approaching car was being passed by a large truck, now the two were side by side and taking up the full width of the road and too close, moving too fast.

The car sounded his horn, the truck sounded his, but neither seemed to slow down. Robert's options dwindled quickly, and at the last millisecond he jerked the wheel to avoid a head-on collision. The van bumped violently off the road, throwing up a cloud of dust with the brakes locked, and slid down a steep slope before coming to a sudden stop against a small tree. Pillows cascaded into the front seat.

The sound of the collision and the fading blasts of the horns subsided into silence as Robert tossed the pillows back and looked over at Teresa. "Are you all right?" he asked. She glared at him. She was probably all right. He got the door open and checked for damage. The front bumper looked about the same, badly dented. The van had crossed a narrow drainage ditch that now made getting back on the road a little problematic. The ditch was right behind the van and deep enough to be impassable. They had no room to maneuver. Should he see if a tow truck was available? It would be a long walk, maybe there was another way.

He opened the rear hatch of the van and burrowed through the sheets to find the jack. Good, it was one of the old style bumper jacks with the ratchet handle, obsolete now because of plastic bumpers but useful for this sort of situation. He opened the passenger door and invited Teresa to watch from a safer spot, then set the jack up under the center of the rear bumper, racked it up to the top notch, and gave the van—teetering on a precarious balance point—a shove back to the road.

The van tilted sideways and fell off the jack, moving its rear end a foot up the slope, and after Robert repeated the exercise a few times the van's rear end was firmly back on the asphalt. Robert engaged reverse, backed the van up the slope, and opened the door for the still silent Teresa.

"Nice, hey?" he said, happily. "Another trick from my misspent youth."

"What else did you do with your misspent youth?" she snapped. "Seduce junior high school girls?"

"Hey, wait, what? What's this all about?"

"That slut practically had your clothes off in the restaurant. She could be your daughter."

"Conchita? I thought she was just, you know, outgoing. I liked her. I think she's probably like that with everybody."

"Sure you liked her. I think she's only like that with men. She didn't put her hands all over me. Stay away from her."

"So now you're my den mother? Why don't we keep our relationship professional, not social? How old is your boyfriend, what's his name, Armand? Twice your age, I bet."

"Armand is three," she said primly, hands clasped in her lap, looking ahead through the dirty windshield. "I am older."

Robert thought this over for a while. "Three? I don't understand," he admitted, finally.

"Of course you don't understand. You men have a piece of your brain missing. Armand is a French poodle. He is at the dog kennel now, probably faithfully pining away for me. Underline faithful. Watch the road. Close your mouth."

His eyes snapped back to the road. "But why did you tell me a dog was your boyfriend?"

"Warning sign. This territory posted no trespassing."

"Well, then, why did you tell me your boyfriend was a dog?"

"You tricked me. Watch the road. I'll watch the stupid sunset."

They finished the trip in silence, with Robert sneaking peeks at her attractive but stern face from time to time.

They checked two mattresses out of storage and took adjacent second-floor rooms on the ocean side. Robert walked out on the large balcony, surveying his new place. The rooms were arranged in a saw-tooth pattern for privacy. The railing was an eight-inch log, complete with bark, and the floor was diagonal hardwood. The effect was like a deck on a private oceanside home, with a sweeping view past the nearly-completed pool area and the row of coconut palms to the sea. Plenty good enough, and a bargain at only four thousand a night. Now, if he could just figure out what was bothering Teresa.

The slider next door scraped open and he heard quiet footsteps on the far side of the partition. After a minute Robert felt a subtle pressure as if Teresa had now realized that he was also on the terrace, also looking out at the dark sea.

"Hey!" she spoke softly. "That you?"

"Who did you expect?" he answered.

"Don't try to deny it. That's you."

A half a minute passed. "Robert?"

"Yes, Teresa?"

"I'm sorry."

"It's been a little crazy. There's nothing to be sorry about."

"You still like me?"

"I still like you," he said.

"Do you have anything to drink over there?" she asked.

"Sure."

"OK, wait right there."

Robert answered the quiet knock on his door and she entered the room, wearing a long white beach dress with big sleeves, white bandages replacing the cast on her fingers, smelling of soap and flowers, hair undone, smiling up at him. She flowed into the room, her body moving invitingly under the thin cloth. Robert was spellbound by the vision.

"So?" she said.

"What?"

"You said you had something to drink."

"Oh, yeah, here." He dug into his luggage and found the bottled water and the plastic glasses. They moved onto the terrace, touched the glasses and sipped.

"See," she said, looking at him with the disturbing direct gaze from the compelling eyes, "I like you a whole lot. I'm a little confused. I haven't been handling it well."

"But why..."

"I thought you were pretty strange, before. I was coming off a destructive relationship. I told myself I couldn't invest in another emotional trap without screwing up my work again."

"What changed?"

"I don't think you're looney tunes any more. You're sort of serious, but you're nice."

"If we're doing confessions, I lied, too, when I told you that you weren't my type."

"I thought so," she said, comfortably, moving closer. She kissed him softly on his mouth and his emotions clanged between awe and disbelief. She stepped back and looked at him carefully, then held him tightly and kissed him again.

"Robert Asher," she murmured into his neck, pressing her body closely to him. "What would you like to do now?"

My God, do I want to do this? What has it been, two years? "Are you OK? Your hand isn't healed yet."

"Oh, relax and enjoy it," she said. "You scientist types, you intel-lectualize everything. You're all shot up. Move slow."

OK, he told himself, ride with it. She pulled the caftan over her head and draped it over her shoulder, revealing, concealing, right there on the terrace. Robert got a double hit of adrenaline, her body was hard to believe. What fascinating curved places she had. Her skin looked lit from within, a lamp shining through the blood vessels and the smooth skin, all sunset colors. Could anyone else see this? He didn't want to share. He grabbed her hand and led her back into the room.

Quickly naked on the bed with her, Robert was broken into two separate parts as he experienced the act of love. One part remained the scientist, analytical, observing his performance from afar, capturing the images of her beautiful body for later replay, trying to find and fill her needs, desperately trying to do a good job at making love so she would want to do it again. The other part of him was fuzzy and unthinking, still bathed in sunset glow, the glow growing in his abdomen, spreading to his whole lower body and carrying so much heat and sensation that he was unable to determine if he was handling the mechanics correctly. His analytical part was trying to tell his unthinking part not to have so much fun or he'd ejaculate prematurely when his unthinking part ejaculated prematurely anyway, in a swirl of pain and pleasure.

Teresa smiled up at him and turned him onto his back.

"Now look here, we're just going to have to keep doing it until you get it right."

She moved over him and kissed his lips, her soft hair brushing his cheek. She touched his body with soft hands until he reacted again, and she kept touching him softly until the hydraulic pressure seemed unbearable, then she softly lowered herself onto him and moved slowly, softly, and the analytical part of him went away and the unthinking part grew enormous, filling the room, filling the world, until her cries merged with his own.

. . .

Robert awoke to the sound of the surf outside the open window. He checked his watch: 9:00. Overslept. He remembered the extraordinary events of the previous evening and moved his hand behind him to see if he had been dreaming. The bed, except for him, was empty.

Teresa stepped out of the shower, naked, lovely, toweling her hair. Robert felt a surge of relief closely followed by a surge of lust.

"Oh, no, none of that," she said, looking at the bedclothes. "Work day today and you are late, late, late."

"Tonight for sure?"

"Wouldn't miss it." She laughed gaily at his sad face. "Or, gosh, I suppose it would be all right if you promise to work late." She threw the towel back into the bathroom and pulled the sheet down.

Chapter 38

The bus unloaded twenty people and their luggage in the cleared area behind the hotel. Robert got everybody into the unfinished dining room and logged the skill set of the arrivals on a whiteboard. They had six medical researchers, four general-purpose Spanish-speaking management types, two undergraduates, a geneticist, three industrial process chemists, three Maya scholars, and an accountant.

Robert knew several from B.U. The others were revealed by their introductions as volunteers from industry or other Boston-area colleges. He was glad to see Dr. Margo Sanford, her familiar face reminding him of a bull terrier. Her bull terrier personality went with it; she would not give up on a project once she had her teeth set in it. She was followed closely by Leo Halpirin, the little bald process chemist, who always seemed to follow closely behind Margo.

He updated the group on the events of the last few weeks and on the search for the antiviral in the cave writing. Then he ticked off names and assignments. "Curtis, arrange food with a local restaurant. Margo, good to have you here. Can you run production?"

"Sure, Dr. Asher, just get me something to produce."

"Great. Pick a staff of five and set up a production line for the antiviral. We don't know if it will be injection, oral, or what, stay loose. We're not even totally sure if we're getting a vaccine or drug therapy or both. Maya scholars report to Teresa, you'll be helping with the translation. Halpirin, pick a staff of four and work on medical and isolation facilities. Art Baker, hi, good to see you again. Hook up with the researchers in Austin and the Mexican authorities, give us a report daily."

"What's our schedule?" asked Sanford.

"We'll meet here at 8:00 A.M. every morning for breakfast. Baker can start the day off with the reports. Giovanni, handle the rest of the communications with the States, feed the interesting data to Baker, set up a Web page, coordinate with Dr. Teppin in Boston. Accounting, do your thing. Don't get in the way too much. Or, better still, don't worry too much about accounting. You can help with purchasing."

"What's the Web page for?"

"Post the glyphs and the translations we're sure about. We'll update it as we make progress. Publicize it through ProMED and the CDC. Call the media. We'll get free help."

"Aren't there a lot of other teams working on cures?" asked Sanford. "What's the chances somebody else comes up with a fix?"

"There is one new possibility for a cure; they're working on it back home," said Robert. "We now have reports of fifteen cases among the Maya and we have had five complete recoveries: thirty-three percent survival compared to less than one percent for the non-Maya cases. The survivors are on their way to Atlanta with blood from the Maya victims. There's a possibility that the specific antigen can be isolated and we may get some chance at immunization. That will require several months at a minimum, even with multiple teams working around the clock."

A researcher asked, "The Maya are immune? Do we know why?"

"Our early guess was that the Maya civilization's decline was caused by the virus. Even if one percent of the population survived at that time, they could have bred the antibody back into the general population. This is substantiated by the writing we've been translating in the cave."

"Is antigen isolation going to happen here?"

"No, that's being handled in Atlanta. Our job is still to dig out the cure that the Maya apparently found twelve centuries ago. Remember, the Maya did not lose ninety-nine percent of their population, maybe only twenty or thirty percent, and the difference may be that cure, as if it came too late to prevent some loss of life."

"Yeah, but what's the status here?" asked a truculent process chemist. He stood up. "We're doing all this thrashing around and you still don't have a cure? You're looking at cave drawings or something? I don't believe this. I was pulled off an important product development for this, and my product works."

Teresa spoke, "We think we're quite close to a translation. The evidence seems to say that the Maya had the antiviral."

"But there's no guarantee—even if you find a translation—that it will work. This is a billion to one shot. Madness."

Robert felt his blood pressure rising rapidly and tried to keep it under control. "We are definitely a long way from a sure thing. But I'd say we're about a thousand to one shot. At those odds, we are a long way from madness. This virus could make the Black Plague look like a hangnail, a million people might be saved from a horrible death if this long shot pays off, and that's worth damn near any effort we can give it. There's a thousand different groups working their butts off on thousand to one long shots, you do the math. I expect I'll be working sixteen-hour days, and I expect most of you will be working sixteen-hour days. Not because I say so, but because you realize the importance of what we're doing here. If we find an antiviral we go on twenty-four hour days until we ship it. If you're not ready for this, go home. We cannot afford to have anybody here who is not signed up for the program."

The chemist glared. Five seconds passed. "All right, I'll give it one week."

Chapter 39

Playa del Carmen, November 15, present day Midnight

Ernesto Porfirio Raul Diaz with his sergeant Hector and his troops filed off the sixty-foot sport fishing boat onto the creaking town dock and into an old school bus. They were dressed like locals, not an invading army, and nobody paid any particular attention as they drove off down the coast. They pulled off the road south of Xel-Ha, dismissed the bus and waited there for a few minutes until an old stake-back truck drove south. Ernesto signaled with his flashlight, and the truck pulled off into the small clearing. They pulled the canvas cover off the truck bed and handed each soldier a backpack, a large flashlight, and a rifle. The truck rattled off to the north.

Ernesto led the soldiers single file five miles into the brush to a flat area, screened from above by a tangle of branches and protected on the north side by an irregular limestone cliff face ten feet high. A shallow cenote at the base of the cliff held fresh water. Hector deployed the troops and assigned sentry duty in a small four-hundred-yard perimeter, with the sentries communicating by radio and staying in place rather than attracting attention by patrolling.

This was perfect, peaceful, almost, this camp in the jungle. It must be in his *Revolutionista* blood. So much more honest than the fancy hotel. He broke off a few branches of springy brush to help out his mattress and settled in comfortably.

At dawn, Ernesto arose early and checked his force. They were scattered haphazardly around the jungle site. It was near a huge ragged pothole in the earth where a cavern roof had fallen, and the cliff face and large erratic boulders made convenient backstops for the tarpaulins the soldiers had set up in case of rain. Well, good enough, he didn't need boy scouts, he needed fighters. These men looked like fighters, desperate to prove their worth so that they could move up the organization's food chain from five pesos day to, who knows, ten a day?

Ernesto located four of the city boys he had asked for, three of whom had been in the Yucatán before, and sent two teams of two off to Playa del Carmen and Tulum to scout the terrain. What else? Nothing more until the scouts reported back. He could smell tortillas browning in corn oil, and Hector brought him a tin cup full of good dark Columbian coffee, better even than the fancy restaurant in the fancy hotel. But a light misty rain started falling, unusual in this season. He growled to himself and tightened his coat.

Chapter 40

Akumal, November 16, present day

Robert Asher was pleased to find that Hotel Austin's food committee had managed a continental breakfast, perhaps from the week-old bakery shelf. But the coffee was good and plentiful. Art Baker cleared his throat self-consciously and began his report.

"Good morning. Dr. Asher asked me to collect and report on the progress of the virus. I talked yesterday afternoon with Gary Spender, he's running the Austin operation. There is also a web site that C.D.C. started, it includes postings from other researchers and it front-ends a large international database. We will add our status reports to this web site unless anybody has an objection?" He looked at Robert who confirmed the idea with a nod. "I have also drawn a graph of mortality count vs. time in Texas, posted on the far wall, which I will be keeping up to date."

"Bad news," continued Baker, his brow furrowing. "As we had feared, we have more evidence that the original outbreak of the virus was in fact here in the Yucatán. The hospital in Mérida admitted a young Maya patient yesterday afternoon at 1:30 with a black tongue and high fever. They had been on alert and they quickly moved him into a biosafety level three isolation room, but they don't have good decon or Racal equipment and they are worried about contamination."

"Where was he from?" asked Robert.

"A jungle settlement not all that far from here, near Cobá. The settlement had only a dozen people. They're being isolated and watched. There are also reports of another settlement farther into the jungle with many deaths."

"How are you coming with setting up communications?"

"Giorgio is handling it. E-mail is through ProMED. He has also made contact with PAHO, the Pan American Health Organization, and with officials in Mérida as well as Austin and Washington and Boston, so our phone number and e-mail address is in circulation. The Mexican government through our Mérida consul has let us know that they are standing by with whatever support we need. I think that with the Mérida case and the nearness of Austin to the border, they are more concerned now. That concludes my report. Dr. Asher, should I also prepare an update for the lunch or the dinner meal?"

Robert nodded. "Yes, please. If you get interesting data, share it. Teresa, anything on the translation?"

She looked sad. "Sorry, no. With the additional staff the cave was getting a little crowded, so we made same-size Cibachrome photos of the cave wall glyphs and pasted them up in the function room. Most of us are working there now. We have no guess when or if a full translation will be available, but we're making slow progress and we're hopeful."

"Anything else?" asked Robert.

"Some of the Bolero crew are helping. They're anchored just offshore. You should all meet Todd Goldstein and Gabor; they helped us break into the cave. Todd scanned the Cibachromes piece by piece into the computer and posted them on the web site. This will extend our reach to other Maya experts."

"Great idea," said Robert.

"We translated an interesting sub-plot in the glyphs, describing the setup of the laboratory and the university. Seems as though the big guy was a scientist called Peloc. He invented the microscope, assembled the staff, and cataloged the elements. He must have been a genius."

A loud exhaust noise from a broken or missing muffler announced the arrival of a large van. Robert cranked open a window as the truck pulled into the clearing. The truck driver yelled, "Delivery." They off-loaded several hundred masks that fitted over the nose and mouth, directing the breath through an activated charcoal membrane. "Ugly," said Teresa.

"Keep it with you," said Robert. "Wear it if the humidity rises." They had installed big relative humidity gauges in the main rooms and everyone glanced at them nervously from time to time, but the air stayed dry—less than twenty percent humidity.

Two trailers full of lab and biological process equipment arrived.

No progress was made on the translation.

Later in the day more bad news: more Mexicans from inland had come down with the first symptoms. Federal authorities asked Robert if his installation could provide an isolation ward and Robert readily agreed—as he might need test cases if he ever got to an antiviral—but he said he could not handle more than a dozen. He dispatched three staff members to prepare a trailer with filtered air conditioning, dehumidifiers, and a dozen beds.

Chapter 41

"**P**edro, report!" barked Ernesto, gesturing with his nine mm pistol.

The small man smiled nervously.

"It is not so easy, Señor Ernesto. I wait for dark as you say and go into the cave from the land side. There is one guard, a *Federale*, and I talk to him and give him five hundred *pesos,* and he says I can look around but I am not to disturb anything. So I look and our Remoras are there, and the hatches are in place, but there is a big hole in the side of one and the product is gone."

"Shit," said Ernesto.

"*Sí*," said Pedro, nodding, "but only on one, there is the hole. The others—no holes—still good, I think."

"Someone has a loose mouth," said Ernesto, looking at the circle of his men. "There is no other way they could have known about the explosives. That person will die slowly."

"In the cave, I find a new hole in the wall near the storeroom," said Pedro. Everyone turned to look at him again.

"I go through. Two other rooms are there, one has many small statues, maybe good ones. Some are heavy like metal."

"And you left them in place?" asked Ernesto.

"No, Señor Ernesto, I put one little one in my shirt in the back for you, but the guard find it anyway when I leave and he take it for himself."

"What about the second room?"

"Nothing. Very small doorway. Shiny black stone with writing. Walls tip in. Pieces of wood and metal, like old workbench. Long wood benches. Metal junk. Maybe old lamps, hung up on walls, all black. Smells old. People work in there, bright lights, maybe cameras, I just peek in."

"How many people? What kind of work?"

"Maybe ten people, with the cameras and little television things and notebooks. All talking."

"That is all?"

"*Sí*, Señor Ernesto."

"Where are the college boys?"

"I do not know, Señor Ernesto. I came back quickly to tell you this. Maybe I go back and look now? Maybe Sanchez has found them?"

"Stay here. Sanchez should return soon."

An hour later, Sanchez reported on the frantic activity, with more than twenty-five people working at the converted hotel in Akumal. The hotel was not difficult to discover, as most of the population on the coast knew of the *gringos* and the bad disease in America. Ernesto listened to all of this and heard of the *Federales* and the Army stationed in the hotel and thought for a while.

This would be a bigger operation than he thought. Grab everybody except security? Maybe twenty, twenty-five people? The float plane would hold six people—not big enough. OK, what did they need for a minimum? The formula—probably written on the black rocks; hit the cave and grab the rocks. Along with the product. We can leave the Remora, they are not so useful now as the D.E.A. pigs know about them.

So as soon as we make our move, we'll be hip deep in Federales. Gotta move 'em out before anybody finds out. The timing is critical. Start by grabbing two of 'em, coming out of the cave, find out if they're making any progress on the translation. Probably we can set up with the black rocks and maybe a dozen of the college people in Columbia, even if they're not quite finished.

He spoke to the group again, "Hector, get over to the cave, or maybe to the place where they will park their cars. Grab one or two people when they go to their car. Bring them here. Wait, have somebody take their car south and wreck it first, like they drove off the road."

He thought for a minute longer, then said, "OK, listen to this. One, two days, we'll move into the cave, take our product, take the black rocks, take a few of the college boys. Then the boat sends in the dingy, we take the dingy to the float planes. I will call on the radio to arrange a second float plane. Are there questions?" He pointed the pistol at them as if it were a microphone.

"Señor Ernesto," asked Pedro, almost shaking with the difficulty of the question. "In town they said that the people at the hotel are looking for a way to cure a bad disease. The disease makes the tongue turn black and swell up, and then you die. Can we not just take the product without killing the people?"

Ernesto hit him in the mouth with his pistol. "Are there any questions that are not so stupid?"

Pedro sopped up the blood with his shirt, thinking he would not tell Ernesto that the black rocks were stuck to the walls.

Chapter 42

Ernesto's camp, November 18, present day

Hector appeared at sundown carrying two people, one over each wide shoulder. They were bound and gagged with duct tape. He shrugged his shoulders and they dropped to the dirt in front of Ernesto, then he ripped the duct tape from their mouths. One male, one female.

"Rojas!" called Ernesto, smiling happily. "Get over here. We gotta talk to these nice people."

Rojas joined him as Ernesto was dragging out four of the big plastic pails for chairs. "Sit down here, please." He gestured as if the pails were upholstered lounge chairs. "We are honored to have you as our guests. Excuse Hector, sometimes he is not so polite. If there is anything we can do to make you comfortable, please let me know. I am Ernesto."

The man, a small thin man with a bald head and a myopic stare, looked at him with an expression of profound mistrust. The woman said, "Margo Sanford. Leo Halpirin. You can now take us back to the hotel." She had about the shape and the face of a Saint Bernard.

"Of course, but please accept our hospitality for just a few more hours. There are a few items we wish to know about. We have no secrets, yes? I am a simple Columbian businessman, I wish only to have my business run smoothly."

"I know what your business is," said the woman. "And I wish it did not run smoothly."

"Margo, please, can't we be friends?" Ernesto slapped her backhand, his ring tearing a small gash in her cheek. Leo jumped from his chair, but Hector's hand closed around his neck painfully and forced him back.

"Fuck you," said the woman, wiping the blood with the back of her hand.

"Oh, Margo, this is so disappointing. Rojas, she does not want our hospitality. Leo, is it?" Ernesto asked the man. "Can we talk? Or would you like to watch Hector kill this woman by tearing the skin off her face?"

Hector smiled happily. The man seemed to crumble into himself. "What do you want?"

"Ah, there now, so much more civilized." Margo started to speak, but Ernesto slapped her again in the same spot but with a little more force and she subsided. "Margo, my dear, what are you looking for, in our little cave?"

"We need to find a cure for the Austin virus. The one in Texas," said the man. "We think the Maya may have contracted the virus twelve centuries ago; here in the Yucatan. And they may have figured out a cure, probably something from the jungle."

"And how would you know that? Reading the medical records from 800? Did I say what would happen if you did not tell the truth?" He slapped the woman again. She exploded in an ear-splitting stream of verbiage and lurched upwards against a restraining hand from Hector. Ernesto listened in admiration for a minute, and then thumbed off the safety and pointed the Glock at the man. He was almost disappointed when her screams subsided.

"They left clues in glyphs, chiseled in Uxmal and Tulum. The clues pointed to caves under Tulum. We found glyphs in the caves, it looks like if we can translate them we can find out how the Maya were able to cure the disease."

"And when will the translation be complete?"

"I don't know, a day, two, maybe three."

Ernesto thought a minute. So we wait. Get a man in the hotel, cleaner, cook, something. We'll know when they get it, then we run off with the key people. "Suppose we give you the translation? Can you make the medicine?"

Margo screamed, "Hell, no." But Leo answered, "Yes, Margo can, no problem."

"What's that worth, US dollars? A cure for the disease?"

The man seemed shocked, "You don't want to sell it."

"Oh yes, I do. Answer the question." He bounced the Glock's barrel off the man's forehead.

"God, who knows, the goddamn gross national product of the world. More. Anything you want. But you can't sell it."

Ernesto turned to Rojas. "Son of a bitch. I was thinking, first, millions. Then maybe billions. But this makes more sense, we'll only need one percent of the gross national product of the whole fucking world. We will be the most hated men in history. But the richest. What do you think? Can we make it work? This would make the drug business look like a dime store operation."

Chapter 43

Hotel Austin, November 21, present day

Robert walked into the cafeteria just after 7:00 A.M. The room was illuminated by the red and purple light of a spectacular sunrise. Several of the troops were sipping the local coffee from the styrofoam cups, and the usual continental breakfast was arrayed on the large center table. Robert grabbed a corn muffin and coffee and sat down.

A few days ago Baker had set up a television receiver with CNN broadcasts, and one of the evening's diversions was catching up on the news from the States. This morning, Baker arrived with a videodisk.

"Two things," he said as he waved the disk in the air for attention. "We saw a couple of things on CNN last night. Didn't catch the first one on video, thank God. The first mass grave in the U.S. in more than two hundred years, bulldozers, trenches, a long line of people in body bags. Then the president was on the news, we did catch that."

He plugged in the video and text crawled up the screen.

"While the human race battles itself, fighting over ever more crowded turf and scarcer resources, the advantage moves to the microbes' court. They are our predators and they will be victorious if we, *Homo sapiens*, do not learn how to live in a rational global village that affords the microbes few opportunities. It's either that or we brace ourselves for the coming plague." —Laurie Garret, *The Coming Plague*, 1994. Engraved on the ProMED building.

Robert identified the background music, Mahler's Resurrection Symphony.

The president's pale blue eyes stared out of a lined and haggard face.

"Fellow Americans," he began, his voice ragged. "No. Fellow human beings. I will not minimize the danger we all face. You have heard that there is an epidemic in Texas of a deadly virus. You have heard that over fifteen thousand people have died and that many more fatalities are expected. You have seen the faces of the victims and the terrible agony of their death. And you are afraid. As I am afraid."

"You look to the massive resources of the finest medical establishment in history for help. You look at the accelerating curve of the virus' progress and pray for a miracle. And you consider the incredible chance that the virus may win a final victory."

Robert heard the room quiet down as people put down their silverware and listened to the broadcast.

The president continued. "But we can help the odds, you and I, if we can control the fear. We must understand that we are in a battle where a single human life has become unimportant. We may be in a battle for survival as a species."

He closed his eyes and tilted his head back a moment, the strain showing in the lines around his mouth. Then he leaned forward again.

"Survival as a species. Believe it. Accept it. If we take this conflict lightly, we may not survive. We must find the strength to put the good of the species over the good of the individual.

"This is not a new concept. Several times in history, a sudden event has eradicated up to ninety percent of the species of life on our planet. The last time this happened was 65 million years ago. In a sense, we are overdue.

"Over the next hour you will hear from experts in epidemic control. They will present to you the best advice we can assemble, and they will ask you to put the good of the species ahead of the good of the individual. They will ask you to try to control your fear, and to realize that each of you may hold a piece of the solution in your hand.

"We will be asking you to evacuate your homes and perhaps to suffer the loss of your possessions. And we cannot guarantee that you will ever be repaid, but we can guarantee that we will be doing the best job we can to be fair.

"Here's what is being done right now," the president said, turning to point to a graphic behind him. "A dozen major efforts, all under the supervision of the Centers for Disease Control and Prevention, the CDC.

"We have expanded the quarantine zone in Texas. We've drawn a two hundred mile circle around Austin, and a four hundred mile circle around that. Inside the smaller circle, nothing moves but technicians in fully sealed suits. Inside the larger circle, we're decontaminating everything suspicious, attending to the dead and dying, and controlling even bird and animal movements as best we can. As you know, the virus can travel long distances in humid air. A light windblown rain could pick up a virus particle and drop it many miles away, so we anticipate that it will be only a matter of time and weather before our cordon is breached.

"We're working on an antiviral with a total of fifty thousand researchers in over a hundred countries, reporting to a CDC central staff which has now grown thirty-fold to fourteen thousand people in Georgia, Colorado, and Switzerland. The international cooperation is unprecedented. We are sure that we will eventually come up with a solution, but it could take a week, a month or more than a year.

"We have a doomsday team working on dry and sterile subterranean bunkers, and another looking at massive population migration to desert areas such as the Sahara and Mojave.

"A small percent of the population seems to be immune, and several research groups are tracking this effect, attempting to map to racial characteristics and beginning to do DNA studies.

"Several clues point to a previously unknown breakout of the virus among the ancient Maya of the Yucatán peninsula in Mexico. One clue is the significantly greater resistance of the native Maya. Another is that the apparent source of the current outbreak is an archaeological dig near Uxmal. And another is an unexplained connection between the structure of the virus molecule and some carvings on stone columns in the Yucatán that were done almost twelve centuries ago. This may sound like a wild fantasy, but some of our best scientists now think that there is a chance that these connections may lead to a cure."

Robert shook his head slowly. If he only knew. These connections were leading only to frustration. The president and his experts droned on but Robert disengaged, his field of view pulling back to the table in front of him, his focus narrowing to the corn muffin in the center of a yellow handmade plate with a chip in the side. Tiny little muffin, they didn't seem to subscribe to the bigger was better philosophy like back home.

Not quite in the center of the plate, he thought, looking at the pattern in the plate. He adjusted the position microscopically. There, handled that problem nicely.

Robert took a bite of the muffin, furrowed his brow at the taste, and spat out a piece of the pleated paper the big-time bakeries used so they didn't have to oil their pans. Where'd they find a big-time bakery down here? He pulled the remaining paper off the muffin with half the muffin stuck to it. He couldn't save humanity, he couldn't even peel the paper off a damn muffin.

As Robert drank his second cup of coffee, the report from Baker was more of the same. Baker noted that Margo and Leo Halpirin had not returned to the hotel and that a car was missing. People nodded, smiling. Then Baker went into more details about the progress of the virus in Austin and the unsuccessful efforts of other researchers to find a cure. The production crew reported that the production line was ready and standing by, fully equipped for centrifuging and purifying and buffering and bottling and filling disposable syringes. But they still had nothing to produce. Teresa, her face showing tension and unhappiness, again had to report no progress. She said that just about all of the world's Maya language experts were working via the Internet without success.

"Do you think we're in danger of becoming infected here?" asked one of the researchers who did not wear a mask.

"The relative humidity today is ten percent," said a lab technician. "I'd say the effective range of the virus is less than a foot."

"Keep a mask with you," said Robert. "Wear it if the humidity goes over thirty-five percent. Be careful of contact with the native Maya, they may be immune carriers. There will be more chance of infection every day now."

• • •

During a morning coffee break, Robert was a little surprised to see Kiraly alone at a table in the corner, styrofoam cup in hand. Kiraly caught his eye and gestured minimally with an inclination of his head to an empty chair. Kiraly was wearing black cotton trousers and a black T-shirt and with his dark tan, he would have been almost invisible in a shadow. His face was impassive but his pale eyes were alert, scanning each new face, glancing at the nearby window with its view of the parking lot. His body looked, as always, like a bent steel spring waiting for the right signal to uncoil.

"Kiraly. What's happening?"

"Those two missing people show up?"

"Not yet. Found their car, wrecked, five miles down the coast. We've notified Munoz, for what it's worth."

"I've been thinking. These guys we tossed out of the caves. Somewhere down in Columbia, there's some angry dudes."

"Yes."

"The way their business works, they need respect. If somebody in their distribution chain is skimming, they get killed in a way that sends a message. The whole thing is held together by fear. Without the fear, they go out of business in a hurry. And what we did was a hell of a lot more disrespectful than skimming. They will need to land on us with everything they got."

"Maybe they don't think we'll tell anybody what happened," said Robert.

"They know. The cops know. The story will go through their organization like wildfire. Anyway, I figure that they could probably mobilize easily fifty troops, some of their own people, maybe some mercenaries. And the timetable would be about now, figuring a few days for logistics. Back on the boat you thought you'd be out of here in two or three days. It's been a week and a half. You're on borrowed time. We could set up heavy artillery here, but there would be more fatalities."

"Makes sense. How do we find out for sure if they're here?"

"I asked around in town. There's a rumor from Playa del Carmen that a large group of men, not in uniform, was walking down the pier early yesterday morning, around midnight. Another guy said that his friend saw a truckload of weapons getting loaded up in Cancún City and watched it head south."

"So, Columbians. What's your best guess, what will they do next?"

"There was a runner in Tijuana last month with sticky fingers. They found his body in a car trunk with his hands sticking out. They had beaten his hands with something heavy, flattened them, broke every bone, and then put a slug through his head. For maybe five hundred American. What do you think they'll do to you?"

"Mmmmm. Rather not guess."

"This guy got off easy. I've heard they have a new game in Columbia if anybody's skimming. They strip him, tie him to a tree, and set off a pound or two of Semtex in front of him. Rips off all the smaller pieces, rips off most of the skin, doesn't kill him if they're careful with the charge. Then he's dropped off in the village to die."

"Holy Christ."

"They'd have no problem locating the operation here, you didn't put up a sign, but the news coverage has been pretty good. Their next move is probably to move into the cave, reclaim what's left of their coke, grab whatever's loose, and shoot us up."

"Do you think they grabbed Margo and Leo?" asked Robert.

"I'd bet on it. Interrogation. They'd need to find out what to expect before walking in there again, we might have a battalion of Marines."

"So they wait for somebody to come out," said Robert, "follow the car, grab them, interrogate them."

"And make it seem like they're wandering around lost somewhere by wrecking the car."

The room was at the southwest corner, and Robert shifted his chair to get a view out the window that looked out on the clearing. "The local police commander is Colonel Muñoz. We talk with him from time to time. He seems to be trying to avoid offending the Colombians."

"Payoff."

"At least. But he also seems to be aware of his government's interest in our mission, he's getting pulled two ways. We might get him to send some cops, but there's an even chance they'd be looking the other way if the drug guys showed up in force."

"Makes sense. Maybe the best option is to locate their camp, hang out until they make their move, and then have you and the staff disappear for a few days. That would confuse them."

"What would their response be?"

Kiraly walked over to the buffet table and came back with a fresh cup of coffee and a muffin. "They'd probably station a couple guys here and send scouts around to find you. If they're still plugged in with the cops, they'd get help. How long can you hide, what, twenty or twenty-five people?"

"*Bolero?*"

"We could sail around until the situation was secure. That boat could hold off a light cruiser until July."

"I don't like the delay," said Robert. "It would set us back days. That could cause the death of thousands of people. Maybe we should relocate to the U.S., we've got everything we need from the caves."

"That's a couple of days, too. Tell you what. I'll go see if I can find these guys—talk to them—see if I can explain the virus thing. Show them some humility and respect. Offer to compensate them for their unfortunate losses—at wholesale, of course, not street price. Get 'em thinking. Buy some time. If I find the two missing people, I'll see if I can get 'em out."

"I'll join you."

Kiraly stared at him for a long moment. "Could be dangerous."

"That's OK. I'm not getting anywhere here. One other idea, I bet we could track them with satellite images. There's a group in D.C., I think it's called N.R.O., that handles imaging and interpretation."

"Makes sense," said Kiraly.

Robert pulled out his satellite phone and dialed up Teppin.

"Teppin."

"Robert again. Dr. Teppin, do you know anybody in the N.R.O.?"

"The National Reconnaissance Office? Yes, I have a contact there. What do you need?"

"A group of Columbians, maybe twenty-five people, got off a boat in Playa del Carmen yesterday around midnight. They got into a bus and drove south. They may have met a truck with firearms and supplies. They probably did not check into a hotel, so we think they could be located inland, maybe camping."

"If they did go inland, and if the right bird was in place, we can easily track them with infrared. I'll make a call."

"We'll be moving," said Robert. "If you can find anything, call us back on this channel." He signed off and turned to Kiraly. "So, we could see if we can track them on land before the trail gets too cold?"

Kiraly nodded. "Do you have any glasses?"

"Glasses? No, why?"

"Deception. We need to look like nerdy scientist types. Get that Hawaiian shirt you were wearing, and a notebook, and a pocketful of pens. And when we talk to them, don't excite their macho streak. It'll be a mile wide."

Teresa walked up to their table carrying a cup of coffee and sat down. "Hi, fellows. Makes me nervous, seeing you guys together. Probably gonna get in trouble again."

"Us?" Kiraly's face was open-eyed innocence and surprise. "Just planning a little field trip, olive branch, white flag, apology, peace at any price. You should be proud of us."

"Where are you going?"

"We're going to see if we can locate any nearby representatives of the unfriendly forces, negotiate, compromise. We don't know exactly where they are, though. Do you know any locals we can borrow? We need a guide."

"Miguel?" asked Teresa. "He has a car, or he can get one, and he's lived here all his life."

"Sounds good. Where do we find him?"

"He'll be fishing, I bet, on the reef, with his son. He has a small boat with a black motor in the back, I think the boat is blue."

"Get changed, Robert," said Kiraly. "I'll meet you on the beach with the Zodiac in ten minutes." He uncoiled from the chair and glided through the gathering lunch crowd like a brown trout through eelgrass.

Teresa pressed his cheek with a hand, looked at him sternly, and said, "You be careful, now. Stay behind Kiraly. Don't get hurt."

Robert felt the warmth linger when she removed her hand. He smelled her scent, a light floral scent and a heavier but infinitely subtle musk, which seemed to work on him like the attractant of the female animal in heat. He looked at her and nodded and saw the color of her eyes seem to darken. He pulled away through the magnetic force. No other woman had touched him like this, ever.

• • •

Robert was startled at the transformation. Kiraly stumbled up to him, shoulders hunched forward and head downcast, wearing professorial rimless glasses, a linen shirt and baggy khaki pants tucked into tall cowboy boots. Kiraly squinted at him and coughed nervously. "Uh, perfect, uh, Doctor, get into the boat, please, sir, if you would."

Over the noise of the outboard, Kiraly asked about the chances that the Colombians would be able to recognize them.

"There's only one of them that's not in custody—I think his name is Lopez. He was in the cave the first time, and he would certainly recognize me. And somebody may have snuck out the back door the second time, but I'd guess not."

"Let's hope Lopez is on siesta. Or back home being disciplined. This could be the boat," as the Zodiac approached a blue fishing boat and cut the motor.

Pépé spotted him and said, happily, "Señor Drowned Man! *Hola!*"

Kiraly caught the gunwale, held the boats together, and asked, "Are you Miguel?"

Miguel said, "*Buenos Dias. Hola*, Dr. Asher, you are much more alive-looking than the last time."

"Miguel, I owe you my life. If there is anything you want, please, just ask."

"*Graciàs*, señor doctor, but it was nothing. Can we help you again? You do not look like you need a hospital this time."

"We wonder if we could borrow your eyes and your car for a few hours," said Kiraly. "We need somebody that knows the area. We'll pay for your time."

"Papa knows every blade of grass within twenty miles," said Pépé.

"And I will use Ricardo's car," said Miguel. "But there is no need to pay for our time. Time is all we have. As you see, the fish here today are somewhere else."

• • •

Robert opened the telephone after the first ring. "Dr. Teppin?"

"Yes. I spoke to my contact in the N.R.O. They did have a bird in the right orbit, or close enough, and there are not too many large groups of people traveling together at midnight, so the infrared satellite scan could track them easily. They followed the group south from Playa del Carmen on route 307 to a spot just south of Tulum. We lost them there, but picked them up an orbit later inland a few miles. There was no bird in position until four A.M., at which time we recorded infrared signatures of twenty-eight people in prone position, scattered over a hundred-yard area. I'll give you the GPS coordinates if you are ready to write them down."

Robert recorded the coordinates and checked them with his handheld GPS. "Great, we're heading in the right direction. Ten miles south. Thanks, Dr. T., we'll call tomorrow and let you know how it worked out."

"What's the N.R.O.?" asked Kiraly. "They sound useful."

"They run imaging satellites for the U.S.," said Robert. "I did a job for them a couple of years ago when they were ultra secret. Now they're just fairly secret. Three thousand people work there, burning six billion a year; it's nice to get some use out of them. They can read your license plate from space, or get an infrared image right through your roof if they want to see what's happening in your bedroom."

"Sinister."

"Not the N.R.O., Washington thinks they're pretty amusing. Their first launch went a little off course and killed a cow in Cuba. Lately their success rate has been about the same as the Boston Red Sox. But they do sometimes get an imaging satellite into orbit."

"So where are they camped?"

"Just a few miles inland from 307."

• • •

"There!" said Miguel.

It was unmistakable, a recent bruising of vegetation in a clearing near the west side of the road.

"They did not take the straight line," said Miguel. "The jungle there is very thick, it would take a day with machetes. They would leave the road here and follow the path."

"They must have some locals with them," said Kiraly.

"Miguel, is there a place to camp, a few miles inland?" asked Kiraly. "Some protected area without much underbrush?"

"Good place, five kilometers west, big trees, good shade, a small cliff and a cenote."

"Thanks for everything, Miguel. Don't wait for us, we'll catch the bus back to town."

"I go with you?"

"Half way," said Kiraly. "Then it could get a little dangerous."

• • •

As Kiraly and Robert followed the trail through the bush, Robert asked, "Why the high boots? Expecting snakes?"

"No, not snakes. The boots were custom made by a Belgian guy, they've got more firepower than most heavy weapons platoons."

Robert looked at the boots. Well-worn dark leather, Western style, nothing unusual. "Pretty well hidden firepower. A knife?"

"Yeah, several, and Semtex boot heels with one-second fuses, and a nice little no-handle airport-safe carbon composite and ceramic .30 cal automatic, and a telescoping blowgun with tranq darts. And a few other things. See, my feet are size eight, but the boots are size thirteen. Lots of storage space for the playthings. The boot heels? If I say 'down,' you have half a second to hit the dirt."

"I see. Any other words of advice?"

"Just be unthreatening. We're mild-mannered archaeologists."

Ten minutes later, Kiraly motioned Robert to stop, then he grabbed Robert's arm, motioning for quiet, and pointed ahead. Robert looked through the thick vegetation for a minute and finally spotted a man in camouflage—face smeared with black and green paint—lounging ten feet up in the crook of a big tree, smoking a cigarette and scanning the area.

Kiraly waited motionless for maybe ten minutes until the man's radio whispered. The man unclipped the radio and said, "Number three. Code nineteen," in a rough smoker's rasp.

Kiraly pulled up on the leather loop at one boot heel to reveal a telescoping tube, half an inch in diameter. He extended the tube from six inches to two feet, removed the boot and felt inside the toe. His hand emerged with a small flat leather case that revealed half a dozen color-coded darts. He selected one, inserted it in the tube, motioned Robert to stay in place and slid noiselessly closer to the sentry.

In a few feet he had disappeared into the low vegetation. The blowgun reappeared ten feet from the sentry, emerging from a broad-leafed plant, and made a whuff sound. The bright yellow dart appeared on the sentry's cheek. He looked annoyed, reached out a hand to brush off the dart, pulled it out instead and studied it carefully for a moment. Then he pulled the radio off his belt, brought it to his mouth, and fell out of the tree into a relaxed, quiet slumber in the ferns.

Kiraly motioned Robert forward, checked the sentry's pockets, and clipped the radio to his own belt. Then he stowed his equipment back in his boot and moved forward again.

In a few paces he stopped again, studying the vegetation carefully. He pointed to a bush with a broken twig and to a tree with a horizontal scrape in its bark. Then he picked a blade of grass, bent it in its center and gently released it in midair. It settled a few inches and remained suspended, a foot up, as if by magic. Robert looked more closely and saw the fine black wire.

Kiraly and Robert stepped carefully over the wire and moved forward again.

A voice came from the radio, 'Number one, check in," followed by "*Si*, number one, code twenty-eight."

"Number two, check in," was followed by "*Si*, number two, code four."

Robert and Kiraly looked at each other and shrugged.

"Number three, check in."

A few seconds passed.

"Number three, Sanchez, put it back in your pants and pick up the damn radio."

Kiraly grabbed the radio, covered the mouthpiece with the tail of his shirt and spoke in a decent imitation of the sentry's rasp. "*Si*, number three, sorry, I heard a noise. I thought I had something, here. But it is just a wild pig. It is headed your way, if you can shoot it we will have a pork dinner."

The man laughed. "Good, very good. Number four, check in. And keep your eyes open for a pig."

Kiraly and Robert moved again, following the wide trail left by many booted feet, feeling exposed with the sun now high overhead. They skirted a group of canvas shelters near a small clearing, then backtracked when they heard Margo Sanford's voice coming from one: "Goddamn assholes, the whole pile of you creeps, gimme a goddamn break, go back to jail or wherever the hell else you came from. Warm goddamn water, just what we needed."

A small man in dark clothing emerged from the tent and disappeared into the thick vegetation on the other side of the clearing. Kiraly waited a minute, then moved under the shelter with Robert close behind. Margo looked up in anger, then in relief. She opened her mouth, thought better of it, and closed it again. Leo lay nearby, looking a little dazed. Both had their hands tied around a small tree, but in front of them where they had a chance to drink from the plastic water bottles the man had left.

Kiraly produced a knife and sliced through the ropes. Leo fell to the side, eyes open, and apparently conscious but unable to balance. Margo whispered, "They hit him pretty hard. We may have to carry him."

Kiraly took one arm and Robert the other, and they half-carried Leo from the shelter. Emerging into the sunlight, they faced ten men carrying assault rifles, well spaced around the clearing. One stepped forward, a tall man who carried himself with the unmistakable confidence of authority.

"Ah, we have more visitors," he said in passable English. "Good to see you. I am Ernesto Diaz."

Diaz shifted his feet, leaning forward, his face a few inches from Robert's. "Why are you here?"

"We're with the medical people looking for a cure for the virus," answered Robert. "We needed to gain access to the cave that you were using. You lost some inventory in the process, and we will pay you for this loss. We're not with the police, and we do not want to interfere with you or your business. The epidemic has killed thousands of people. You can help us stop it."

Robert thought that Diaz was considering him seriously when Lopez entered the clearing carrying an automatic weapon. Robert's confidence dropped like a rock.

"You fuck!" screamed Lopez. "Ernesto, that's the guy from the cave, the guy with the broad! He led 'em back! They killed our people!"

Ernesto drew a pistol, his expression darkening. Robert didn't like the odds. They were grouped in a loose circle in front of the limestone cliff rising behind Diaz, near a camouflage canvas shelter. They had infiltrated through at least twenty troops to reach this command post, and half a dozen of the well-armed troops were now watching the conversation. Suddenly this seemed like a bad idea.

Kiraly stood on the other side of the circle, shoulders slumped, apparently defeated, but Robert noticed his pale eyes missed nothing. But Kiraly was shadowed by a man with a body like a front end loader, as tall as Kiraly but twice as wide.

Ernesto Diaz slammed the pistol barrel into the side of Robert's face, drawing blood. Damn, this again. So much for peace at any price.

"Tie him up," screamed Ernesto. "Tie those two up again." A man tied Robert's hands together, swung the loose end of the rope over a tree branch, pulled it so tight that Robert was standing on his tiptoes and tied it off. No topological tricks possible here. Maybe those Semtex boot heels.

"Diaz, damn it, you're really making a bad mistake. We're not your problem, the virus is your problem. Believe me. There's cases in the Yucatan. Haven't you seen it on television?"

"Where's your girl friend? How many more with you?"

"Just us," said Robert.

"Just you creeps? Right. Ten men, safeties off, get out past the perimeter and see who you can flush. Three men, check the road, do not engage. Report back quickly. Me and Hector can handle these assholes. Hector, kill that one."

Hector nodded and smiled happily and with no warning brought his left hand around into Kiraly's face. Kiraly appeared startled, gave a little scream and stumbled forwards, bending his head down into the blow and catching the force on the top of his shaved head. There was a crack like a breaking twig and Hector stepped back in surprise, puzzled, looking at his hand. Kiraly held his hands up apologetically, stepping back to the cliff face.

Hector charged like an angry rhino and Kiraly put his hands in front of his face and stumbled back a step, tripped and fell heavily onto his back. Hector drew back a leg and swung it like a placekicker directly towards Kiraly's testicles. Kiraly seemed to draw back into a fetal position and somehow the kick was intercepted as his shin landed on Kiraly's outthrust boots. Robert could almost feel the pain himself as Hector drew back, grunting and rubbing his shin as Kiraly lurched back to his feet.

Hector made a noise like a big truck in low gear and closed quickly on Kiraly, wrapped both big arms around his midsection, and squeezed.

Kiraly looked at Robert over Hector's head and flicked a glance at Ernesto. What was he trying to say? Maybe his pistol. Robert tore his eyes away from the execution and saw Ernesto, grinning in anticipation, pistol dangling from his hand, but a little too far away for Robert to reach. The other troops had fanned out into the brush. Kiraly's expression changed from his look of fear into a happy smile as he slid both hands onto Hector's neck and worked his thumbs through the sheets of muscle. Robert understood; the carotid artery, Kiraly could go without breath for maybe two or three minutes but Hector's brain would not function without blood for more than a minute.

Robert watched for what seemed an hour as Kiraly's expression again registered convincing distress, and he caught the first slackening of the huge man's muscles. But Ernesto was out of his range. Macho streak a mile wide, Kiraly had said. "Hey, big man," Robert said. "Do you always hide behind a gun and a gorilla?"

Ernesto spun towards him, his face darkening, reversed the gun in his hand and took two steps closer. As he pulled back the gun to swing, Robert jackknifed back, then kicked forward to hook his right foot around Ernesto's neck. He pulled Ernesto towards him and slammed his left foot into his throat. Ernesto dropped the gun and spun down on hands and knees, out of range, shaking his head back and forth.

Kiraly caught Hector's bulk as Hector lost consciousness. With Hector under an arm like a sack of potatoes, he ran towards Ernesto, now frantically searching the ground for the gun, and, using Hector as a battering ram, drove Ernesto into the rock wall. The men fell in a tangle. Kiraly stepped from the pile holding a knife and the gun, his jungle-cat fluidity regained. Again slipping off a boot, he dug out more of the yellow darts and inserted one into each exposed neck. Then he cut Robert's rope and freed Leo and Margo again and they retreated into the brush.

Kiraly stopped them, listened for a minute, then picked up a few small stones and launched them well into the jungle on the other side of the clearing, and they heard a satisfying hue and cry converge on that spot.

"Hey, Kiraly," said Robert, when they'd finally cleared the area. "Good job. Are we back to Plan B? Hope they can't find us?"

"Yeah, and I'll hang out here and keep an eye on them."

"Another thing. Why didn't you use the Semtex boot heels?"

"Screws up walking. Didn't need 'em."

• • •

A television news truck from Mexico City was now parked in the back of the hotel near the equipment trailers and a newswoman and her cameraman were underfoot, either snooping for a catastrophe or eager to share in the breakthrough. In the next few hours, more news trucks arrived from CBS and ABC and a satellite antenna farm appeared in the brush. They were continually underfoot, but at least they took over cafeteria duty, with a significant improvement in quality. Robert, after initially answering requests for interviews, finally had to politely refuse, or he would get no work done.

In the evening the stress of the situation carried over to the sleeping arrangements. Teresa kissed him softly on the lips after dinner and told him not to worry, but she could not bear to think of all those people dying. She worked until two or three o'clock in the morning, slept fitfully, and arose at six or seven. The translation effort had hit a wall. Some tree, some plant held the answer. But which one?

Chapter 44

Austin, Texas, November 23, present day

A cold misty rain was falling on the red mud and the remnants of last year's corn crop. The big round humidity gage was in the high nineties and the wind was twenty mph from the south, a lethal combination. The rain had been falling off and on for days, the humidity had been well into the danger zone, but the wind had been at zero until a few hours ago, giving the medics at least a chance of survival with the new masks.

A hundred miscellaneous vehicles were moving in the field— a slice of farmland that had escaped the urban sprawl, another failing link in the latest chain of quarantine and isolation which had broken under the relentless assault of the outbreak. The virus had overrun the isolation barrier somehow, maybe through the air, maybe through a human or animal carrier, and a dozen cases had been reported behind them.

Dr. Gary Spender spoke into a bullhorn. The tension in his voice survived the distortion of the small speaker. "Leave it! Forget the equipment! Get out now, we'll pull back to Bull Creek. We're going to set up a new barrier zone. Don't forget to leave your radios on!"

The biochemists who had been struggling with a portable generator let it go and walked quickly to the trucks. Dr. Mort Scheinfeld sat with the driver of the BL-3 trailer, in a truck cab intended for tandem eighteen-wheelers, complete with a microscopic bedroom in the back. The trailer carried their losses, as they called them. Twenty five of them in this vehicle alone, crowded in bunk beds but floating uncomplainingly on heavy doses of morphine. They were not dead yet, but most would be dead within a day or two. Scheinfeld's friend of twenty years, Al Giovanni, was among them, victimized by a second of inattention while mopping perspiration off his face. Giovanni was well into the disease's final days. Scheinfeld had finished with his grieving; the disease was heartless, it did not permit even a slender thread of hope.

Dr. Spender moved towards their vehicle and Scheinfeld slid over to give him room. Spender hauled himself slowly onto the step, let out a long breath and sprawled, loose-limbed, on the seat. "Thanks, Mort. Helluva thing. Sorry about Al, I know you were friends. Did you talk to his family?"

"Last week, yes. Not the easiest thing I've done in my life. I think they were numb, Al and Joyce were close. And his kids, God, how he loved his kids. I suppose I shouldn't talk about him in the past tense."

"It's all right."

"I guess. Where are we going?"

"Up route three sixty, past Bull Creek. We're giving up on thirty square miles of pretty crowded real estate, but I think the residents should all be cleared out. It should be all right. We'll park there for a day to make sure the evacuation is under control, then we move again, back another twenty miles. Bastrop, Thorndale, Spicewood, Wimberly. Live around here?"

"Waukegan, Illinois," said Scheinfeld.

"Jeez, I used to live in Waukegan," said the driver, grinding his way into sixth gear. "Sorry, I haven't driven one of these rigs since Jimmy Carter was shelling peanuts in the White House. No synchro. We're all amateurs, National Guard. My day job is plumbing. Well, you guys are pros, I guess."

"Speaking of the National Guard, where's George Hapwell Theslie? I haven't seen him lately," said Scheinfeld. "I kind of miss his inspirational speeches, in a way."

Spender answered, "He had a family emergency, he said. The rumor is that he got a flight up to British Columbia right after the night we lost six people."

"Our George? I can't believe it."

They passed a group of motorcyclists heading into the city, wearing respirators, baseball caps, and rubber gloves. Looters. The young gang members thought they'd be safe with the gloves and masks. As Spender turned to watch, the group headed off the road single file and into the tree line, hoping to avoid the guard.

Spender keyed his radio. "This is Spender. I'm in the last vehicle, we're heading up the ramp to three sixty now. You drivers should all have the new site map. Make sure you keep separation as you park, the grid is on fifty yard spacing. Drive slowly and carefully near the site, the ground is a little rough and we don't want to dump any isolation trailers."

He put down the radio as if it weighed ten pounds. "Geez, I'm beat. I can hardly talk."

"Gary?" said Scheinfeld, his voice suddenly hoarse. "That's what Al said..."

"Oh, Christ," said Spender. "My tongue feels thick. Look at it for me." He turned to Scheinfeld and stuck out his tongue.

"Gary, I'm sorry. It's black."

"Stop the truck," said Spender. He stepped down to the asphalt. His shoulders sagged; his arms seemed to be too heavy to hold up. He lifted his head with an effort. "I'm sorry, guys. You need to check into isolation at Bull Creek. Until then, keep the windows closed and the blower fan off. I'll be in the back. Tell Carla for me. Keep up the fight."

They heard the door open and close, and they looked at each other. The heavy despair showed in their eyes.

Chapter 45

Hotel Austin, November 23, present day

At breakfast, several Maya came quietly into the hotel and listened with the news people and the staff to the report. Baker announced an explosion of cases in the Yucatán and a major setback in Austin, Texas where the isolation zone was moved back again. He also said that a new case was reported in El Paso and thirty-five city blocks had been evacuated and burned.

Robert felt his heart tearing inside him. They were losing. The Government of the United States was losing. His species was losing. He wandered aimlessly from the production and lab spaces, where he felt competent to help but where nothing was happening, to the translation room where he did not feel competent to help but where everyone was busy. Bela and Bartok were talking together, comparing glyphs.

The researchers were interrupted by the lobby door slamming closed with a noise like a pistol shot. Robert spun to find five security guards filing in, shamefaced, holsters empty. They were followed by Hector, the big man from the camp, with a bandage on his forehead, and two other Hispanic men with ragged beards, bush hats, dirt-stained clothing and semiautomatic rifles. Hector was carrying another big man.

Robert felt a flash of anger at himself, he had screwed up. Not enough security, just Kiraly, probably dead, now. The facility should have been guarded, fenced off. The Colombians had found them so easily, disarmed them so easily.

What were they waiting for? When would they shoot? He had wrecked their drug warehouse, caused the deaths of two of their men, and caused them to lose millions of dollars worth of cocaine and heroin. He looked in their faces for the anger and saw, instead, fear. But how could they be afraid? And why just the four of them? They had brought twenty-five troops for this raid. And who was the big man, unconscious—one of their security people? But he was dressed like the other Columbians.

He glanced at a disturbance from the breakfast room. The news people were catching it all on video. What a profession, they behaved as if they were bulletproof. He almost expected Makeup to rush in and apply a little lipstick to the visitors.

One of the men spoke. "So, Dr. Robert Asher?"

"Yes."

"You are really a doctor?"

"Yes." Robert got suddenly angry at the cat and mouse game. "Why can't you believe that? Want my résumé? Don't play games." He braced for a shot. Hector looked capable of any act, it would come from there. But the big man looked afraid, and he carried his rifle by the stock, finger nowhere near the trigger, as if it was an embarrassment to him.

The man spoke again. "Hector, drop him." The big man dropped to the floor and rolled over on his back, muscle tone like a rag doll, mouth gaping open to reveal a black tongue. He was breathing noisily, with effort. It was Ernesto Diaz.

"You have met Ernesto Raoul Porfirio Diaz, I think. I am Rojas. You are working on a way to cure the disease of the black tongue?"

"Yes."

"When will you have a cure?"

Margo Sanford, still wearing a bandage on her cheek, took a step forward. "Dr. Asher, don't give these jerks the time of day."

Robert felt the synapses uncurl, felt his muscles loosen, felt the tightness in his chest smooth out. "Within a few days we may have something to try, but it is still far from certain. It is maybe a thousand to one long shot. What do you want?" But he thought he already knew.

"We are just here to wish you luck, Dr. Asher. We understand you found the cure in the Tulum cave?"

"Yes, in a room that the Maya used as a laboratory."

"Amazing."

No one spoke for a moment and Robert could feel the tension of the twenty medical researchers watching the drama. What was going on? But the visitors still did not seem aggressive, and their red-rimmed eyes were still afraid. It did seem like a cry for help.

The tension was dissolved by Hector, who suddenly looked stricken and asked, "Toilet?"

Robert gestured and the man shambled quickly out of the room.

"Could you put the guns down, please?" Robert asked the remaining three Colombians. "Is there something you want from us?"

"Many of my men have the black tongue," said Rojas. "One is dead. I am afraid we too will be sick. You may keep Ernesto Raoul Porfirio Diaz for us. Tell us when you have the cure, we will be in contact twice a day. Good luck."

Hector returned, the Columbians left the room, and conversation started instantly. "Robert, were those the guys you beat up in the cave?"

"Masks, everyone," he said. "Clear the room. Two men, get biosuits and a gurney, take him to isolation. Wash everything down. These people are from the same organization that we found in the cave."

Robert called Kiraly on the cell phone.

"Yes, I let a few of them through, they didn't look too dangerous. I was just about to pull back, the rest of these people are hurting badly. What's happening there?"

Robert filled him in. Kiraly said the troops seemed to be packing up to break camp and the ammo had been packed up and shifted to a van heading south. But the effort had slowed, the remaining people were mostly lying down. He would keep an eye on them for a few minutes longer and then come back in.

• • •

Robert resumed his random walk through the useless production lab and the impotent translation facility. The graph of virus mortality, updated daily, continued its exponential increase. In the analytic laboratory, a new arrival was assembling a familiar piece of equipment. Robert recognized his charge microscope, but slimmed down and motorized. His Van de Graaf generator had been replaced with a miniaturized high voltage supply, and the talcum powder seemed to have been replaced with a toner-paper handling stage borrowed from an office copier. Very nice.

"Hi, I'm Robert Asher."

The technician turned around and smiled. "Of course, Dr. Asher, it's an honor to meet you. I'm Ed Reines; Dr. Teppin sent me down with the latest version of your microscope. It's working great. How did you figure it out, anyway?"

"Nothing to it," said Robert. "The Maya didn't bother to file a US patent, so the whole field was clear. How's it working?"

"About the same as your prototype, but we've automated it so anybody can use it, and we get a plain paper output. We built twenty of this version, they're all being used to help in the Austin virus effort. I guess you're stalled, down here, on trying to find the ancient Maya solution?"

"We're real close, but we're definitely stalled right now."

"How can I help?"

Robert looked at the charge microscope and thought for a minute. "The Uxmal glyph showed the charge microscope image of the virus molecule, next to another column of glyphs which we haven't translated. One possibility is that the second column shows the charge microscope image of the antiviral."

"So, can we work backwards from the charge image to the molecular structure of the antiviral?" asked Reines.

"That's going to be tough. But if we did stumble on something that had the same image, we could test it as an antiviral. Worth a shot, anyway. A long shot. Can you stick around and maybe get lucky?"

"Happy to help. Get me samples of anything you want tested."

Teresa appeared in the door. "Robert, there you are," she said. "Got a minute?"

"Of course."

"I need somebody to talk this over with. Somebody who isn't too close to the problem. Wanna do lunch?"

"Sure. The usual place?"

They sat down at one of the long tables in what would become the hotel coffee shop. A large alabaster chandelier seemed out of place in the unpainted wallboard room with the raw plywood flooring. Looking through the double doors to the translation room, Palladian windows gave a view through the palms to the Caribbean Sea, white-capped today as the trade winds had returned. Big puffy clouds sailed the horizon. As he watched, a gull landed on the railing, looking for a free lunch.

Robert studied the drawn look on Teresa's face and wondered about their relationship. He had felt guilty at not being attentive to her, but he was overloaded with the details of managing their task force and at the same time trying to contribute to the solution. And she seemed to be equally preoccupied, or worse, as she had the responsibility of untangling the glyphs.

The lunch committee had provided a buffet today: stacks of tortillas, refried beans, onions, tomatoes, spiced ground beef, green peppers and two different types of salsa—too hot and much too hot. The buffet bar served bottled water, juice, and coffee. They built their tortilla roll-ups and moved to a table where they were alone at this early forenoon hour.

"How do you feel, Robert?" she asked, looking at him closely.

"Oh, you know, depressed, worried—the usual. And I care a lot about you and we don't have time for each other. How about yourself? You look burned out. Your eyes are all blurry."

"Right after this, I'll sleep for a week. I feel a little afraid, but the pressure drives everything else down so it doesn't really register. I have friends in El Paso, they don't answer the phone but they're not on anybody's list yet. I don't know if we can continue at this pace. Everything seems sort of hollow and ringing. And now I'm catching some stupid cold." She cleared her throat.

"And we thought it was going to be a few days at the beach."

"Those days at Cancún seem like a year ago. Damn you, I love you a whole lot. I am still strongly attracted to you. But I'm all twisted up inside. I don't think I'll get unsnarled until this situation resolves." She smiled with one side of her mouth. "I have to solve this damn puzzle. Then I'd like us to get back together. Soon."

"Second the motion. Second both motions."

"Bela and Bartok are really getting into the language, they're picking it up faster than I can believe. Would you like to learn Maya? Give us a hand?"

"Hey, I'm well into my fourth decade. Those boys are mere children, their brain cells haven't been filled up yet. Mine are all loaded with useless information. Would you like to know Pee Wee Reese's lifetime batting average?"

"Robert, help us now, we need it. You have a way of coming up with the answer, of seeing things differently. Like in the cave, when you untangled yourself from the pipes. Or the welding helmet you used as a, what, disguise?"

"I was thinking of the old pirates, they dressed up in strange things before a battle to upset the opposition. But that was sort of a blunder, the little window closed and I couldn't see too well."

"See, even your blunders work out OK. We need you.

"I'd like to help if I can."

"We're stuck on a group of glyphs with a different pattern than either date glyphs or normal syllabic glyphs, and I think it's because we're too close to the problem...trying to make the answer come out like something we're familiar with."

"If you want somebody who isn't familiar with anything, I'd be as good as you can get. What's my job?"

She led him back to the room with the walls covered with the glyph photographs, still busy with nearly a dozen people and a computer operator who was coordinating the international effort on the Net.

"Here, this is the group we're having trouble with. Look around and let your mind free associate. The ones we don't have translations for are circled, we call them dot glyphs. They look something like the date symbols, the long count, but much more complicated. They seem to be nouns, describing something, maybe a chemical. Maybe something to do with the antiviral."

Robert pulled up a chair and stared fixedly at the glyphs for half an hour. They bent and twisted like Rorschach patterns, flipped back and forth like optical illusions, snapped in and out like 3D simulations. The repeated shape, a complex array of little dots, was hauntingly familiar. He almost had it, and then it slipped further away. He looked away for many minutes and then looked back. There! No, gone again—like a dream, like snow, foggy, melting in a warm rain. No rain since that drizzle last week, if it just stays dry we should be in good shape here. But not so dry in the mountains, or in Texas, they had rain in Texas. Poor people.

He closed his eyes. He used to play blindfold chess, after a while it hadn't seemed to matter much whether he looked at the real chessboard or the image in his brain. He called up the starting position, the chessboard with its array of thirty-two chess pieces, looking like different size dots from the top view. Maybe the glyphs were a Maya chess game. Count the dots in your head: seven wide, eighteen high, but an incomplete array. He tried playing chess with the seven by eighteen array and got nowhere. He tried checkers and Go. Nothing. Abacus? No. Binary numbers? No. Hadamard transform? No. He opened his eyes and looked at the glyph again. Escher. Figure. Ground. Bird. Fish. Stairway up. Stairway down.

Size, try size. It represented something a mile across. Troop formation? No. Fifty feet across? Football formation? No. Small, try small. A diagram of a molecule? Too rectangular.

The answer was there somewhere, around some twisted corner. That shape. Two complete columns of eighteen dots, with two incomplete columns of fourteen and four dots on its left side, and three incomplete columns raggedly arrayed on its right side. Sure, he knew the shape. No problem. It was...was...

Don't think of the glyph. Clear the mind, let the unconscious work. Blank screen. Think of something else, like a New York City taxicab. The noise in the room faded. He brought in the image from way back in his memory and turned it around, a yellow Checker, or maybe, sure, a '57 DeSoto with the enormous tail fins that started somewhere near the front door. Dented, big chrome bumper, "XYZ Cab Co $0.50 First Mile $0.15 Each Additional Mile" clumsily screen-printed on the door. Rusty coathanger for a radio antenna. Big, powerful image—it drove out the glyph with its tenuous explanation hovering at the edge of his conscious; playful glyph, coltishly skittering away if he got close; maybe he could sneak up under cover of a big noisy New York taxi.

He pretended that the taxi was all he would ever be interested in all day, that the taxi was his only priority until dinner; taxi, hum de de hum, la la la, taxi, and then he blinked and burst the taxi like a soap bubble in a fraction of a millisecond, his visual field stripped clean, bare, except for...the glyph. Exposed. Embarrassed to be seen in public without clothes, but having nowhere to hide. Robert got a good, clear look. Gotcha. Nailed you, you sneak.

So obvious, now. The periodic table, but mirrored and rotated from the version every high school chemistry class had on the wall, with dots representing chemical elements the same way that dots represented Maya numbers. Missing a few elements, like the lanthanides and the actinides, and what was the element down at the lower left? Radon, something like that. Those old guys weren't all that clever, couldn't come up with radon.

Clearly, each of the untranslated glyphs represented a chemical compound. All the known elements were posted but only a few were highlighted by their size; those were the elements that made up the compound. It was a complicated, verbose, awkward way to represent chemical compounds, but their calendars were worse, a date took practically an entire *stela*. They probably loved chiseling obsidian.

"Periodic table," he said quietly. He thought about the implications. The technical background for that discovery took the Europeans another five centuries.

Teresa saw his smile and sat down. "What?" she whispered. There was something in the tone of their quiet words that stilled conversation in the room and drew the others closer to listen.

"It's simple. It's a periodic table—a table of all known elements—rows are valance, atomic weight increases top to bottom, left to right. Mendeléev invented it in 1870 or something. Re-invented it, I guess you would have to say. I'm not the only one that re-invents Maya stuff. You had one of these charts on the wall in your high school chemistry class. Elements in the same column—or in this case, row—behave similarly. Top row is hydrogen, then helium, etc. On the bottom are the heavy elements. The Maya hadn't discovered the rare earths or the radioactives, so theirs is more like a partial version of Mendeléev's original than our modern tables. But the shape is unmistakable, except theirs is rotated and mirrored so it didn't exactly snap in."

"What does it mean?" asked a linguist.

"Each of the dot glyphs represents a different chemical. The big dots show which elements are represented in that chemical. It shows the chemical composition of the antiviral. It will help find the cure. There's still work to do, it looks like there's lots of carbon and hydrogen, and they go together in a lot of different ways. But with this, and the charge microscope pictures, we're getting close."

Teresa looked at the glyph with her head turned sideways. "That fits perfectly. Sonavagun. You did it again. The periodic table. Sonavagun. What a complicated way to represent a chemical compound, though."

"What else would you expect from a civilization that used fifty-seven symbols for a date?"

The room was silent for a minute as people gathered around and looked at the symbols and found that the periodic table fit seamlessly into the translation.

"Yes! That's it! Periodic table!" somebody announced.

"Hey, hey, everybody!" somebody else yelled. "Hey, get in here, it's a periodic table!"

People came running in from three different directions and news crews turned on their cameras. Reporters got quick refresher courses on high school chemistry from the researchers. Robert left through the back as Teresa was explaining to the room what had happened.

Teresa found him in the lab, helping to set up the bottling equipment. "Robert, bad news."

"What is it?"

"More cases. One is Miguel's son, Pépé. He's in isolation." She coughed spasmodically, her whole body shaking.

"Teresa, you should check into sick bay, your cough is getting worse."

"Oh, I'm fine, I always get a cold in the winter."

Robert felt a chill. "Come with me, I mean it. This will take ten minutes."

He led Teresa into the lab. A technician drew a cc of blood from her arm, decanted it into a test tube, added a staining agent, and placed the test tube into the centrifuge. For the next few minutes, the three people listened to the slow rising and falling audio tone, like a far off siren, as the centrifuge spun up to fifty thousand rpm and back down, separating the blood into its mass density fractions. Then the room was quiet; the loudest sound was from outside, small waves running up on the sandy shore. The technician removed the tube and with a small pipette carefully drew a sample from the center. She brushed a strand of blond hair from her face, deposited the sample on a glass slide and inserted the slide into the optical microscope.

The technician, her eye to the display and her fingers moving the micromanipulator controls, shook her head slightly. Then she turned, her young face drawn and sad, and shook her head again.

Robert asked, "What? What is it?"

The technician shook her head again, her eyes liquid. "The Austin virus. Early phase, but there's no mistake. I'm sorry. I'm so sorry."

Robert felt as if a knife had been thrust into his stomach and twisted. He choked back a scream of anger.

He turned to Teresa and saw shock and confusion. She closed her eyes and her muscles contracted and she twisted her head from one side to the other, quickly, frantically, as if she could fling the virus out of her body. Then she opened her eyes and they showed quiet acceptance. She smiled at him and gave her shoulders a little shrug.

Robert could feel the blood rushing through his veins as if the flow had just increased. He felt like he was walking underwater as he went over to her and picked her up in his arms. Her arms closed around his neck and she said, softly, "It's all right. You'll fix it."

He pulled her close and watched his own tears slide down her face as she tucked her head into his neck and reached up and ruffled his hair and said even more softly, "You'll fix it. You always fix it."

Chapter 46

Hotel Austin, November 26, present day

Robert strode into the translation room, still shaking. Three researchers were making notes on laptop computers and two more were working the Internet, their faces illuminated with the blue glow of the monitors.

"Doctor Welles has the virus," he said to the shocked workers. "We have just a few days to save her life. Where do we stand?"

"If there's a quick cure, it's here," said one. "We've just about finished the translation in the last few hours."

A man added, "We're getting to understand the man who wrote these records, Peloc, his name was. He's like Leonardo da Vinci, so incredibly brilliant. Every century there's a mind like da Vinci's, but a mind like Peloc's must come along once every thousand years."

The knife twisting in Robert's stomach eased off a bit. He asked, "Does it really look as if they figured out the cure?"

"Look here. This one panel, forty-two glyphs, is the core. Here's the story, with conventional notation, of the runner from Uxmal who arrives with a description of the disease in his backpack and the disease itself in his blood. He also brings the record of the progress of the disease in Uxmal, where thirty-five percent of the population is dead or dying and the remainder is abandoning the city for the safety of the jungle. The runner dies two days later and Peloc takes a sample of his blood. Here's the charge microscope image of the virus. This section shows the symptoms, look at the pictogram of a dead man with a protruding black tongue."

"Then the glyphs become non-conventional," said Robert.

"Yes." The researcher dragged over a large whiteboard covered with tiny lettering, which he stood near the glyphs. "Here's the translation so far. Peloc shows that the virus is different from any he has cataloged. Then he injects the blood of the dead runner into a dozen captives to have a test population."

"Jesus Christ," said Robert.

"It's all right, they're from another city. Then he looks for the antidote. He shows the composition of a hundred chemicals that have a reasonably good charge pattern. He tries these chemicals on the infected captives and sends his warriors out to round up more captives from Cobá. He goes through a hundred captives and a thousand chemicals in the next four months, but here he finds the answer."

"What? What is it?"

"That's the question. Whatever it is, it seems that it can't be depicted in the dot glyphs, it's probably not a simple chemical or compound, or at least Peloc had no way of knowing what its chemical composition was. Probably a long hydrocarbon chain, like you thought. It seems to be described in this group of a dozen new glyphs. Some we know, a tree, a leaf, a flower, a color, a unit of length."

"The length, how long?" asked Robert.

"It describes something about two hundred feet high."

"Not two hundred feet long?"

"No, high, we're pretty sure. Maybe a pyramid."

"What tree?"

"Don't know, but the leaf may be from the tree, the leaf drawn in this pictogram."

"Botanist," said Robert. "We got a botanist?"

"No," said a woman, catching the sense of excitement from Robert. "But I met a woman who teaches botany, she's down here at Playacar."

"Got her phone number?"

"No, but she's at the Reefs, I can find her."

"Do it now, please. Tell her we need her. Now. Tell her why. If she needs money, give it to her."

"Doctor Asher, it's past midnight!"

"Please."

She grabbed a phone and started dialing.

"You guys working the Net?" asked Robert of the two men in front of computer monitors.

"Yessir, we scanned these glyphs into our website a day ago and we've been coordinating the translation from here. There are two hundred people on line right now. We're getting swamped."

"What've you got on the leaf?"

"We just figured it was a leaf an hour ago. Nothing's in yet."

Half an hour later, a security guard escorted a dark-haired, middle-aged woman into the room. She was wearing a black evening gown and a pearl necklace and looked a little out of place among the unwashed, bearded scientists.

"Did you need a botanist?" she said. "I'm Joyce Lord."

"Thanks for coming," said Robert. "Sorry if we dragged you away from anything."

"Nothing interesting. Terry said come as you are, it's important. I understand you're the group working on a cure for the Austin virus. I'd be happy to help any way I can."

"We're trying to find a bioactive substance that's described in these ancient Maya glyphs. Tell us about this leaf, this tree, this flower. We have a few clues, the leaf may come from the tree, the tree may be two hundred feet high, the flower may be somehow associated with the tree, and the color of the flower may be—what was it?"

"Blue, maybe violet," said a Net operator. "The color of the sky it says, but low in the sky, and opposite the sun. They seem to have many words for blue."

Joyce Lord stared at the glyphs and the whiteboard for a few minutes.

"There are no two hundred foot trees on this coast, of course. On the west coast you get bigger trees. I'd say in that habitat it would have to be eucalyptus, and eucalyptus can reach two hundred fifty feet."

The room grew quiet. "Go on," said Robert.

"Well, I don't think there are any flowering big trees in the Yucatán, or at least any with blue or purple flowers."

A few seconds passed. "But I think there's a flower which grows on a vine which prefers eucalyptus. Eucalyptus is not native, of course, but the flower prefers to live near the top of the canopy, hence it would now live on eucalyptus." She dug into her bag and consulted a well-thumbed field guide. "The flower is a bromeliad, probably *Nidularium innocenti*." She smiled. "Is that what you wanted?"

"God, I hope so," said Robert. "Could you stay on for a while?"

"Of course. I've been following your work on television, everybody has."

"One more thing. What are the chances that the flower could be an antiviral?"

"Flowers are one of the best chemical factories in nature, and the Maya would have the biologic effects pretty well cataloged, I would think."

"Get all that?" asked Robert.

The Net operators nodded. "The audio clip went out real time. Three people just checked in with a verification of the habitat, apparently the flower is quite common, at least on eucalyptus."

"OK, we'll go get 'em," said Robert, but he saw the impossibility of organizing the collection at night. "First light." He set his alarm watch for six A.M., sat in an upholstered chair and was instantly asleep.

Chapter 47

Hotel Austin, November 27, present day

"Quiet!" roared Asher. "Sit down!"

The team, stunned into silence, looked at their normally-relaxed leader and sank into chairs. Robert's face was pinched, the eyes dark and red and sad.

"Are you online, Dr. Teppin?" Teppin's face moved into the monitor picture. "Right here," he said. "I couldn't conference in Dr. Spender, however. He has contracted the disease. I am sorry. Please go on with your briefing, and I'll record it here and forward it to CDC."

Robert faced the room. "Bad news, if you haven't heard. Dr. Welles is infected."

"Oh, my God, no!" said a scientist.

"We detected the disease last night. She is in isolation now, it is still in early prodrome phase. She has six or seven days of life, unless a cure is found. Unless we find a cure."

"How was she infected?"

"We have a dozen new cases, apparently seeded inland somehow, fifteen miles from Akumal in a Maya village. We can expect more new cases." Robert stopped talking and hung his head in defeat, his lips compressing, his eyes losing focus.

He raised his head again. "We have made excellent progress. The translation of the cave drawing is complete and accurate as of yesterday evening, according to our eight local experts and over two hundred translators helping on the Internet. The cave writing shows the chemicals in the antiviral. And it seems to say that a flower is the cure. The exact interpretation is not too clear, but we have to go full speed on this one. There's no other chance for Teresa."

"A flower? Any flower?" asked Gabor from his usual back row seat, speaking in an almost normal voice.

"Plants are sophisticated chemical factories," said Robert. We expected to find an antiviral in the form of an RNA strand, but complex proteins or amino acids can have a charge pattern which bonds preferentially to the Austin virus, deactivating it. We hired a new team member last night, a botanist, Joyce Lord. Joyce?"

Joyce Lord spoke. "Plants create a huge variety of proteins and amino acids, and the highest concentration is generally in the flower and near the outside layers of the root. In rhubarb, for example, the stems are edible but the blossoms are full of oxalic acid, quite toxic. Scientists have used viruses recently to alter the genetic code of flowers, perhaps the Maya have used flowers to alter the genetic code of the Austin virus."

A researcher raised a hand. "How would the flower control a virus? I thought the idea was usually to develop a vaccine, using killed virus cells to wake up our immune system."

"Not my field," said Lord. "Can anybody help?"

"That's true," said Margo Sanford. "As you know, the virus is shaped to bond with a receptor site on a host cell, in this case a human smooth muscle cell. In human blood, it wanders around until it is very close to the muscle cell. Then a combination of its shape and the distribution of its electric charges match with the host cell, like a key and a lock, and the virus is sucked in the last few microns and latches on. Then it shoots some nucleic acid into the muscle cell and the muscle cell is reprogrammed to build virus particles."

"That's what the charge microscope is good for," said Ed Reines. "It can show us the exact shape of the receptor site, like a cryoelectron microscope, but it can also show its charge distribution. You look for a receptor site with exactly opposite charges."

Sanford resumed, "Normally, the body's white blood cells surround a virus cell and digest it. But some viruses aren't recognized, and here the vaccine is used. The vaccine gets the white blood cells, or the T-cells, to attack the killed or weakened virus vaccine. The white cells win easily and generate antibodies that hang around in the blood for decades."

"Why doesn't that work for us?"

"The Austin virus's binding sites are hidden by its nailhead structure and the white cells can't find them. Very clever adaptation. We think the Maya must have cataloged most of the rain forest flowers and bark and root chemicals by charge microscope image, and just randomly found a molecule with the right shape and charge pattern to attract the Austin virus preferentially to the smooth muscle cell."

"Maybe not random," said Robert. "Perhaps the flower was attacked by a version of the virus and developed its own antibody. But go on with the botany, please, Joyce."

She resumed, "The Maya and most other native populations knew probably more than we do about the medicinal uses of plants; they used the rain forest as their pharmacy. The cave writing shows a flower and a chemical composition. The chemical is a fairly simple protein compound, found in concentrated form in a flower represented in this glyph from the cave. The flower is clearly a bromeliad, probably *Nidularium innocenti*. It has pink leaves, graceful slender stems, grows on a tree-climbing vine. The bloom is about nine inches across. We'll need to harvest the bloom. The habitat is the tropical rain forest, and it prefers large big-leaved trees as a host, particularly the eucalyptus. It likes a little sun. It blooms near the top of the tree. It is not common, but where it has taken hold, it will be in high concentration."

"How do we find a few thousand of them in a hurry?" asked Robert.

"Hah. We find the vine?" asked Gabor, gaining volume and enthusiasm, "Climb the tree? Get the flower?"

"It looks like lots of other vines," said Joyce Lord. "We'll need to find the bloom, it's unique. But it will be way up near the top of the canopy and difficult to spot from ground level. It could be more than two hundred feet up."

"Visible from the air? We'll use a helicopter!" announced Gabor in a loud voice.

"The air currents would shred the blooms," Joyce Lord answered. "They'll be rather fragile."

"Helicopters, go ahead and shred them," bellowed Gabor. "Pick up the flowers from the ground."

"The ground will be covered with eight to ten feet of heavy vegetation," said Joyce.

"We could mobilize a big group of Maya in a hurry, I think," offered a Mexican official, "But it will be a day or two to set it up."

"Get it started. Joyce, get him pictures of the bloom. Manuelo, warm up the helicopter and airlift him to the nearest village. Recruit some Maya. Lower them on a winch if there's no clearing. Take radios, we'll all tune to 840 MHz. Joyce, return here after you get him the pictures. Move," said Robert, and they left with several of the Maya, walking quickly.

"More ideas?" asked Robert.

The room was silent except for Bela and Bartok in the back, whispering together and gesturing with their hands. Several people turned to look as they both stood up, big smiles on their young, tanned faces. Bela spoke first. "We have these ultralight airplanes, you see. Slow, twenty-five mph. You can fly just ten feet above the trees."

"I am glad your mother is not with us," said Gabor. "I think she would not like this."

"We don't even know if the flower's extract will work yet," said Robert. "Don't do anything dangerous."

"Absolutely not, sir," said Bartok, smiling broadly. "Caution is our middle name."

"I'll keep an eye on him, sir," said Bela. "He's just a kid. Sometimes he tends to get carried away. I will be a moderating influence. Mature. Responsible."

Gabor looked at the ceiling for guidance and found none.

Chapter 48

Yucatán Peninsula, November 27, present day

Bela and Bartok flew over the jungle canopy in the ultralight aircraft at twenty-five mph—wingtip to wingtip—clearing the treetops by a dozen feet. Bela's plane was equipped with a wireless video camera and a GPS satellite navigation receiver to log position. Robert and Kiraly had fixed Bartok up with some hastily improvised flower harvesting gear. In the hotel, the botanist, Joyce Lord, watched a television monitor showing the camera's view and listened to Bela's spirited rendition of "Up in the Air, Junior Birdmen! Up in the Air, Upside Down!" The picture rotated through three-sixty degrees and stabilized again.

"Hold it!" she said. "Over to your right!"

"Aye, Captain." The view tilted sharply and swung obediently to the right and the sound track changed to the theme from Jaws.

"There! Just under you now. The tallest tree, there. Move in closer." As the camera swung low over the treetop, she said, "That looks good, I think I see dozens of blooms."

Bartok circled once and throttled down, unbuckling his seat belt and checking his helmet. "Incoming! Heavy flak! Losing number three! Abandon ship! Curse you, Red Baron!" Then he killed the engine, dived from his seat and fell twenty feet into the thick canopy of interlocking tree branches. He wore a harness and a backpack, and the mesh of nylon line attached to his harness soon entangled in the branches, bringing him up short. A hundred feet away the plane landed like a feather in the thick interlocking treetops.

Bartok looped a line around a large branch and cut away from the mesh, dropping through the green canopy, and hung suspended on twenty feet of line. "Roger, Akumal, contact!" he said into the microphone. "We have entry!"

The botanist's voice in his ear asked, "Can you point your camera at the flowers?"

"10-4, Akumal, commencing point camera on my mark. Mark." He swung the camera around in a full circle. He was surrounded by hundreds of blooms, a hundred fifty feet in the air.

"Yes!" said the botanist's excited voice. "There they are! All around you!"

"Roger that, confirm all around. Commencing extravehicular activity on my count. One." Bartok took a nylon line with a grapnel from his pack and slung it over a tree branch, swung to a new position, and repeated the process with a second grapnel. Then, pulling a empty pointed plastic two-gallon bottle from the pack, he grabbed the flowers and filled the bottle, jockeying himself around by pulling on the nylon lines, humming "Hooray for Hollywood" to himself.

"Hey, Joyce Lord," Bartok asked in a more normal tone.

"Yes?" asked the botanist.

"Can I smush the flowers, or should I keep 'em separate?"

"Smush is OK."

"Roger that, Akumal, confirm smush OK," he repeated. Then he reached a little too far for a bloom and lost a grapnel, swinging momentarily in a huge arc through the air. His Tarzan yell reverberated through the jungle.

"I didn't get that," asked Lord. "Are you still there?"

He began climbing the remaining rope to regain the treetops.

"Dropped the vine. But I'm still here, Jane."

"Joyce."

"Joyce. I've got about a gallon of flower mush, if that'll get you started."

A cheer from the distant room filled his ears.

"Send it on up," said Bela, circling in the other plane.

"Roger roger, 10-4, flowers coming on up." Bartok pulled a tiny gas cylinder and a deflated weather balloon from his pack and filled the balloon to a diameter of three feet. He played out the eighth-inch nylon line spliced to the balloon. The balloon disappeared through the leaves.

Bela's voice, again: "I see it. Tie off the bottle."

Bartok tied the line to the pointed end of his plastic flower bottle so it couldn't get hung up on a limb and added a piece of duct tape to make sure. He held the bottle upraised as Bela flew his plane's under-carriage into the balloon, deflating the balloon but picking up the looped end of the line in the metal hook that Kiraly had fitted to the plane. The bottle crashed through the leaves, and Bela hauled it in, flying with his knees.

"We have lift-off, Houston," advised Bartok. Then he pulled out another bottle and began filling it.

"Comin' on in," said Bela. "I got a gallon of flower mush, and Bartok's working on another two gallons. I hope this stuff works. I hope the chopper gets here before his plane disappears into the trees."

Chapter 49

Akumal, November 28, present day

Bela circled the compound in the float-equipped ultralight, touched down in the ocean, and ran the airplane up on the beach. The bottle containing the flowers was carried on the run up to the lab, to the waiting technicians. Ed Reines, the operator of the charge microscope, grabbed a sample and ran off to his lab.

In the hotel and in the equipment trailers in the parking lot, the production line was ready. They were going to try three preparations: a simple whole-flower purée for oral administration, a liquids-only oral preparation and a filter-sterilized fraction for oral and hypodermic injection. They had no idea what the active ingredients would be or what the appropriate dosage would be, so they prepared various dilutions down to one part in a thousand in saline solution in the hope that the needed dosage would be low.

Each preparation had a hastily assembled production line, the whole-flower preparation in a trailer and the two others in two of the large ground-floor hotel rooms. In each venue long tables were arrayed with equipment, with cardboard cartons of bottles and disposable hypodermics racked underneath. On the tables label stock was waiting in the paper trays of the computer printer to receive the final description of the contents. White-coated technicians worked the machines, spun the centrifuges, doled out the precious flowers carefully to each new process, cultured centrifuge fractions in agar, and brought samples to the second trailer to get an analysis with the gas chromatograph.

Robert ran from one lab to the next, following the progress. He was interrupted by Ed Reines, the charge microscope operator, wearing a wide grin and holding a piece of paper. "Look, sir!" he said, happily. "It's an exact match!"

Robert compared the images, the Tulum glyph and the flower's charge pattern. Identical. The flower was the one that Peloc had discovered and used as an antidote. He grabbed a surprised Ed Reines and hugged him, and ran back to try to speed up the already frantic activity in the labs.

Robert helped out on the production line as the flowers were diluted, strained, bottled in the rubber-cap hypodermic bottle and the fifty cc liquid bottle, pipetted into the disposable syringes, and labeled "BROMELIAD EXTRACT 1% *EXPERIMENTAL not FDA approved.*"

Robert waited by the first table for the first syringes. He grabbed twelve and jogged over to the isolation trailer. Outside, the Mexican government had dispatched a hundred medical professionals and another hundred *Guardia Nacional* troops to the area. The hotel looked like a military base.

The paramedics working in the isolation trailer stopped Robert. "Sorry, Dr. Asher, you need a Racal suit."

"The respirator should work, if I'm careful. I'm in a hurry, I have the flower extract, the Maya cure."

"We'll help. Are the disposables set up with the correct dose?"

"We have no idea. They're set up with half a cc each, we hope that's overkill. There's a range of dilutions, also, marked on the syringes. Full dose to everybody, more dilute to the recent victims. Mark the dilution on their card."

They moved through the airlock. A nurse looked up in alarm, safe in her orange Racal suit, her brown eyes showing worry about his lack of correct precautions. Robert reassured her in his improving Spanish as he snapped on rubber gloves. They fanned out to administer the extract.

A dozen people—men, women and children—were on makeshift cots. Some had IV drips, all had EKG electrodes bandaged to their skin and blood pressure cuffs connected to a full rack of equipment with bright green oscilloscope displays showing cardiac activity profiles. Two patients had oxygen tubes taped to their nostrils.

Robert saw Pépé's card. His eyes were closed, forehead beaded with sweat, and he was breathing with great difficulty, mouth wide open and filled with a huge swollen tongue covered with pustules and with a color halfway between blood red and black. Robert swabbed the brown arm and administered the preparation.

Teresa lay in the next bed. She stirred restlessly in the soggy heat of the aluminum isolation trailer, fanned by the warm breeze from an ineffective air conditioner. She was not as involved as Pépé. Her eyes were tight shut and she was trying ineffectively to clear her throat. Her body was spasming with each exhalation.

Robert stood by her bed wearing gown, gloves, and respirator. Her eyes opened, unfocused, and he put a hand on her forehead. His own throat suddenly felt constricted in sympathy. This had to work—make this work, please make this work. If there is a God, we need him now. Please, I will never ask for anything else. Please. He swabbed her arm.

"I'm still here?" she asked.

"You're still here. Hang on for a few minutes, we've harvested the flower. Here's one for you."

He injected the preparation.

"Atta boy," she said, smiling, her eyes more alive. "Gonna fix us up, huh? Did you test it yet?"

"This is the test. This is the Maya cure."

"It'll work. Did you get enough for everybody?"

"Teresa, you are the loveliest woman in Mexico. And the most exciting. The most intelligent. The most caring. And when we get through this, I will personally get you anything in the world."

"Recording contract with Julio Iglesias?"

"Almost anything in the world. Are you comfortable, is there anything you need now?"

"OK," she coughed. "I'll trade the recording gig for dry sheets."

He worked the sheet replacement with the help of the nurse, touched her forehead again, and watched for a minute as she fell asleep, her breathing labored and noisy and her face beaded with perspiration.

In the isolation trailer, Robert and the technicians finished their ministrations and delegated a technician and the Mexican nurse to monitor vital signs. If the extract was going to work, they would expect some indication in two or three hours for the injections, maybe an hour longer for the oral doses.

On the way back to the hotel he found Miguel and embraced him.

"Is there hope?" Miguel asked.

"He is in the hands of God, and the hands of the Maya scientist who worked here twelve centuries ago. I have no right to say this, but I will. Officially, it is a thousand to one against, especially as the disease has progressed quite far with your son. I am not sure if he will fully recover, and we have no experience with anyone who recovered from the virus at this stage, so we cannot say what shape his organs will be in. But I think that he will live, he was fighting hard. I trust this Maya, this Peloc who showed us the cure."

"How long?"

"Hours, now, one way or the other. Stay here, we'll keep you informed."

"*Graciàs a Dios*," said Miguel, and sank to his knees in prayer.

• • •

They faced a phalanx of reporters in the hotel, their ranks increased to more than two dozen. "I say!" said a man with "Reuters" on his tape recorder. "Dr. Asher! Did we understand correctly? Have you indeed found the cure?"

"We translated the Maya writing," he said. "It said that the Maya cured a black-tongue disease in the year 850 with a tropical flower extract and it named the flower, a bromeliad. We harvested the flower and prepared a dilute extract that we have administered to twelve people in the Mexican medical trailer. There are literally a hundred things that could go wrong, the flower may have evolved in twelve centuries, it may not have been the flower itself but a particular local mold colony, we may have misinterpreted the cave writing, and the virus may have the same symptoms but not be the same virus at all."

CBS asked, "When will you know for sure?"

"Eight hours minimum, if the progress is equivalent to the course of similar viral infections. Two or three hours until we see the first upturn in the vital signs. Blood pressure, white blood cell count, and pulse will show changes if we're on the right track. Then a day or two for most symptoms to disappear. Then we do a final check for side effects. Don't forget, we're still long odds against. There are a lot of things that can go wrong."

NBC spoke next. "Suppose it works? There's almost twenty thousand people with the disease, and a thousand a day are dying. Do you have enough of these flowers?"

"We have a limited supply of flowers. We sent a helicopter into the forest a few hours ago, and fifty volunteers are being airlifted into the jungle canopy to do the harvesting. We have a way using helium balloons to pick up the flower extract—that's working well. But we have no idea if we have enough flowers until we find out how much we can dilute the extract and still have it medically active. If it is medically active."

"How do you find out what dilution works?"

"We try it. We prepared a thousand to one span of dilutions for the first victims in the truck."

A woman from *Star* magazine was horrified. "You mean some of those poor people might not get enough to cure them?"

"We gave dilute doses only to people in the early stages of the disease. If they show no improvement, we'll give them a larger dose. But this is all conjecture, most likely the flower extract will do nothing. It's much too soon to predict victory."

Star magazine spoke again. "Your associate, Doctor Welles, we understand she has the virus. Can you confirm that?"

"She is sick, yes, early stages. She has received the preparation."

"Can you handle production and distribution?" asked *RadioGrafica de Mexico*.

"We can have dosage for fifty thousand people bottled in two to four hours, if the dilute doses work, and a military jet is standing by in Cancún," said Robert.

Art Baker spoke in Robert's ear. "There is a *Federale*, a Colonel Muñoz, in a fast car waiting outside to make the run to Cancún. He says he used to race in the Daytona 500 before he became a policeman. His men are stationed between here and Cancún ready to stop other traffic. He will be accompanied by a man in mechanic's coveralls who says he can change a tire on a Lamborghini in less than a minute. He estimates fifteen minutes for the trip."

"Lord save us all," said Robert. "You couldn't get a helicopter?"

"There were none in Cancún, and ours is two hours out," responded Baker.

"This mechanic," asked Robert, "is he a short bald guy? Smoking a cigar?"

"That's him."

"Lord save us all," said Robert, again.

The next two hours dragged by. The translators, for form's sake, were finishing up the details and dotting the i's. Robert talked with Dr. Teppin on the big videoconference screen in the corner, updating him on the progress, and Dr. Teppin gave him the latest statistics from Texas. They were not good—same story again—a rainstorm had left the air with high humidity and the virus had jumped the latest isolation barrier. The medical team had retreated with more losses. With the collapsing bureaucracy, Teppin's contact in Houston had not been able to locate Robert's daughter.

Finally Robert couldn't stand the charged atmosphere and retreated to the isolation truck with a clipboard and a pencil. He stood by Teresa's bed, watching her sleep. Her vital signs were unchanged but her breath was becoming labored.

He entered her numbers, plotting blood pressure, pulse rate, arterial blood gases, and core temperature, and repeated the exercise with the other victims. The plot lines were all a little jagged but showed no clear trend. He took the portable videoconference camera with him and called up the display screen in the hotel's large ballroom so the reporters and technicians could also follow the progress of the graphs. As each new measurement was made, he would add a pencil tick and connect the line. The reporters learned about acidosis, carbon dioxide partial pressure, and the significance of rising blood pressure.

For the next hour, a tense silence settled on the little community as more and more people gathered in the ballroom and watched the screen, including Miguel and the other Maya who were invited from the parking lot. The dots marched relentlessly horizontal, with perhaps a slight downward trend—the disease was still winning the fight. Robert thought of all the preparation—the hope, the condemned victims in Texas, Teresa with her trust and courage—and a numbness overtook him.

Then an up tick happened. Blood Ph edged upwards from seven point two to seven point two five. PO_2, the concentration of oxygen in the blood, improved a fraction. Or was it just a random occurrence? Everyone edged forward and the silence deepened. Another slight improvement. And then another.

In the ballroom, it felt as if everyone was holding his breath. Robert, in the trailer, could not dare hope yet. The respiration and cardiac data was interesting, but the white blood cell counts would tell the story and these were being taken only every fifteen minutes. Another up tick, but then a down tick. Nobody spoke. Ten minutes passed. Another up tick. And then a white blood cell count: better. And fifteen minutes later, another: much better. Then PO_2 and Ph moved in the good direction. Robert felt the huge vise that had clamped his chest for the last four hours slowly releasing. He closed his eyes and said softly, "Thank you, thank you."

In the ballroom, researchers and reporters and technicians and accountants looked away from the upward lines on the screen to each other's tense faces: Was this it? Was this good enough? When would anyone break the silence? Now? Now? Robert added one more dot and drew a steep upward curve through it with a slash of his pencil.

"Yes!" screamed a doctor. "All Right!" yelled a technician. Everyone let out the compressed emotion of the last weeks in a celebration that rocked the hotel and was seen and heard through the live network satellite feeds on every television channel and on every radio band. The reporters felt no need to comment, the upward curve of the graph and the hoarse voices of the researchers told the story.

"Hold it! Hold it! Quiet down!" Robert's voice through the speaker caught them off guard and they settled down, guilty, what had they forgotten? It was all right, wasn't it?

"We have a little more work to do before we break out the champagne. We don't have a cure yet, just an improvement in vital signs. But we'll assume it's a complete cure. Another thing, look at the graphs. Even the most dilute dose worked. Contact the *Federales* and get another medical truck here. Hell, get 'em all here, and give 'em one thousand dilute extract for everybody, the Yucatán only has a few hundred cases. When those drug guys check in give them the antidote. Or, better, have the *Federales* take it to them with handcuffs."

"But we don't have enough stock even at one part in a thousand for Texas, do we?" asked a technician.

"No, we don't. But maybe we can use a more dilute preparation. Make up more serum in one two-thousandth, one five-thousandth, one ten-thousandth, we'll try it on early cases in the second isolation trailer. Get some more help harvesting the flower."

The next few hours showed that the 1/5000 dilution was more than acceptable, and the hotel turned into a bottling plant. As each bottle could treat a hundred patients, a manageable thousand small bottles were quickly produced and boxed. Robert walked to the parking lot where Colonel Muñoz sat in the Lamborghini, gunning the engine and adjusting his goggles. Phil Schwartz sat in the driver's seat in Penske coveralls and a Bell crash helmet, grinning at them. Robert put the big box in Phil's lap, as the car did not seem to have a back seat, and they screamed out of the parking lot in a searing parabola of acceleration, spraying gravel from the enormous wide tires and startling pelicans into flight with the loud exhaust.

Robert walked back to the lab and suggested that they start another thousand bottles in case the first shipment met with an accident. Then he hurried back to the trailer without protective equipment to check on Teresa. Her vital signs were improving almost by the minute, and even heavily drugged and in sleep her face was beautiful despite the swollen tongue.

He asked the nurse to make sure that anybody who may have come in contact with the virus got an injection and administered half a cc to himself. Then he dragged the only empty gurney next to Teresa's, lay down in his clothes, reached under the restraining bar to put a hand on hers, and closed his eyes, trying to remember how long it had been since he had slept.

• • •

He awoke, feeling drugged and still dead tired, with the sunrise streaming in the window. Teresa. He looked over at her. One eye opened and looked at him, then the other eye. She closed her mouth on her tongue—now appreciably smaller—and seemed to judge its size. Robert read the details on the bank of monitors. All the vital signs had returned to nearly normal. He said a silent thanks.

"Did it again, hey, ace?" she said in a thick, awkward voice. The effort seemed to tire her, and she lay back with her eyes closed.

"Teresa, we both did it. And the *Bolero* crew. And all those troops Dr. Teppin airmailed us. How are you feeling?"

"Like reprocessed buffalo dung, but much better than I was, thanks. How's everyone else?"

"It looks like we nailed it. Or the Maya nailed it, and we borrowed it. Anyway, we're twenty for twenty so far. The people we caught early on are already fully recovered."

"What day is it?"

"Thursday. You've been out for about twenty-four hours, we got to you pretty early, you should be up in another day or so."

"Wow, that works fast."

Robert pulled himself out of the gurney, kissed Teresa on her cheek, and checked on Pépé. His vital signs were almost normal, also. Ah, youth. His tongue was still distended and dark, but much smaller than just six hours ago, and he was awake and alert. Robert ruffled his hair. "So, kid, we'll have you back in school tomorrow."

"Thank you, Señor drowned man, I think."

He found Miguel, administered an injection and brought him to his son's bedside.

• • •

The hotel looked like a stock market trading floor. Robert walked through the busy scene, with quantities of bromeliad blossoms arriving by ultralight, helicopter, and automobile. Margo and her crew were working three shifts, cranking out caseloads of the antiviral. He had chatted with Teppin earlier that morning, and the professor confirmed that the success rate was one hundred percent if the treatment began during the prodrome cycle. Teppin also announced that the dilute solutions of the antiviral seemed to work as an inoculation, giving the CDC team a way to check the spread of the disease as well as curing its victims.

Teresa rolled through the big front door on a wheelchair and gave him a big smile. "They sprung me early, Robert Asher, old buddy. I feel relatively great. Thanks again. I can even talk good now, you'll be happy to know, just a little weak in the leg parts. I'll be out of this before dark. Did I say thanks? Thanks. My mouth works great, by the way. Thanks. You can run me down the beach in the chair later if you want your aerobic exercise. You should try the cure yourself. Helluva trip, those guys give great drugs, you know. Have you ever tried morphine? Awesome stuff. Floats you away on a little pink cloud."

Robert whirled and snapped his fingers at a nurse. "Two morphines, please."

"No, no, not yet, you have to tell me what I missed. What did I miss?"

• • •

Robert and Teresa, holding hands, wandered to the terrace after sunset. They sat facing the ocean on a comfortable wooden bench, its orange and black striped cushions still in their original plastic wrapping. The bright moon made patchy shadows of the casuarinas, the big leaves moving and clicking together in the breeze, and the waves added their slow rhythmic sound from the beach a few dozen feet away.

Robert closed his eyes and saw the image of the Maya scientist, Peloc, twelve centuries and a few miles from here, going through the same experience, sharing the same exultation, and he tried to project his thanks back in time. What an amazing man he must have been. Too bad they couldn't work together. But they had, sort of.

"So, *Jéfé*," Teresa whispered, cuddled up against his left side, her hair bringing the scent of bath soap to his nose, "Now what do you want to do?"

"You mean before or after I sleep for a month?"

"After."

"I think I would like to go back to the beach at Cancún, and stay in the most absurdly expensive hotel we can find. One room, this time, none of that down the hall stuff. We still have that account in Mérida?"

"Right. We're down to a hundred twenty thousand, though."

"*Pesos?*"

"Dollars."

"That'll do. And then I want to have dinner in the most incredibly luxurious restaurant on the strip. Maybe a three hour job, starting off with a cold martini and a bit of the Beluga caviar, then moving on to the Maryland soft shell crabs. With the crabs, I will order the Chassagne-Montrachet, we will drink half the bottle only and then change to the red, probably the excellent Lafitte-Rothschild '71. We will give the remaining white to the chef to cook with."

"We?"

"Sure, you're coming with me. Then perhaps the pompano *en pap-iotte*, if they can do the white wine reduction sauce I've always been partial to, or, failing that, the *filet au poivre flambée*. It is a French restaurant, right?"

"Feel free."

"OK, French restaurant. Then I will order us the cherries jubilee and ask the maitre d' to turn out the room lights so we can admire the little flickering blue flames. Other diners may complain about the dark, but we will buy them all a liqueur of their choice to shut them up. Or perhaps we will retain Kiraly as our enforcer. After dessert, we will go back to that lounge with the wicker walls and I'll let you sing to me again."

"I like it. Sign me up. After, we can go back to the hotel room, just you and me. And snuggle."

"Sure." He pulled her closer. The little waves struck small rocks together at the surf line, and in the increasing darkness he could see a little explosion of phosphorescence triggered by each tiny collision.

They fell asleep in that position a minute later, awakened after a few hours, and shuffled back to his room where they cuddled in the spoon position and slept another ten hours, barely moving. The next morning they woke, groggy and still tired, got dressed, and checked the time: half past ten, too late for breakfast. They walked into the big room. It had the look of a New Year's party, the morning after. There were distinct signs of late-night revelry, which Robert and Teresa had been too unconscious to hear. And the breakfast schedule seemed to have been pushed back by popular demand, the buffet was not only still open but they seemed to even be early. They got plates of pancakes and coffee and found a table, although every one in the room seemed to want to shake their hands and grin. It was sort of catching, Robert found himself grinning too.

• • •

Art Baker pulled up a chair. His hair was mussed and he had a lipstick smear on his forehead. He filled them in on progress. "God damn, this is great. You guys did it. It's just going so great. The antiviral got to Texas two hours and thirty minutes after the car left the lot. They had a fleet of helicopters and medics standing by, and the last of the victims were inoculated in the next hour. We got a report this morning; seventeen thousand doses administered so far, nearly ninety-seven percent remission, with the three percent failure rate explained by the fact that those people were just caught too late. Congratulations, sir, ma'am. I can't tell you how proud I am to have been a part of this. I'll leave you to your breakfast now."

• • •

Later in the day as they were packing the equipment and closing the books on the operation, *Bolero* drifted in and anchored off the reef. The Zodiac bumped through the chop and pulled up on the beach, and the crew stepped out. The medical staff knocked off work to meet them.

Kiraly pulled the rubber inflatable farther up on the beach, reached back and brought up a case of champagne. Gabor and Goldstein and Sarah produced a few dozen thin-stemmed crystal glasses. Bela and Bartok started to work on the corks at five paces, launching them at each other like western gunfighters.

The glasses were filled and passed around. "*Moet et Chandon*," shouted Gabor. "Best I could do in Mexico. Enjoy."

"Bela, did you get your ultralight back before the birds ate it?" asked Robert.

"Sure, no problemo, one of the choppers let me down on a line, right into the seat, and then hauled us both into the air. I cut loose and did a chopper takeoff, my first."

"Where are you going next?" asked Teresa.

"Costa Rica," yelled Gabor.

"Rio de Janeiro," said Sarah.

"Patagonia," said Bartok.

"Mutiny. Total communications breakdown. Lack of respect. Inattention to duty," screamed Gabor. Sarah chuckled and put an arm around him.

"Goldstein," said Robert, "give me *Bolero's* e-mail address, if you would. We may need you again, sometime."

An hour later nearly everything was packed, but the videoconference system in the corner was still on line. It lit up with the image of a young man dressed in a pinstripe charcoal suit with a patterned red tie and retro horn-rimmed glasses. "Is this Akumal?" the man asked.

"Who wants to know?" asked Robert, a little loopy from the champagne.

"The President of the United States."

The technicians and Teresa looked over, startled. "OK, then, it's Akumal," said Teresa.

The President appeared in the screen. "Are Robert Asher and Teresa Welles there?"

Robert sobered up. "Yessir, I'm Robert Asher, this is Teresa Welles."

"Dr. Asher, Dr. Welles, the nation is in your debt. Your actions may have saved millions of lives, maybe more. The first lady and I would like to have the great honor of your presence at dinner, at your convenience."

"Of course, sir. Anytime. Teresa?"

She appeared to think for a minute. "Saturday is still free, for me. Anything but enchiladas." She lifted her glass to the screen and took another sip.

"Excellent, my aide will set it up. Meanwhile, is there anything we can do for you?"

"No, sir, thank you," said Robert.

Teresa elbowed him in the side. "One thing, maybe, sir," she said. "We couldn't have done it without Phil Schwartz. And he was involved in some confusion with the IRS, and now he is sort of insecure about returning to the U.S."

The President laughed. "Schwartz!" he gasped out. "Phil goddamn Schwartz!" Finally getting himself under control, he managed to go on, "I like 'confusion with the IRS,' would you be interested in writing speeches for me after this?"

"Do you think you could help?" she went on, unperturbed. "He just wants to be able to come back into the country."

"And I just want a third term. Tell you what, bring him along with a check for a million dollars. He can write that from petty cash. He can sign it over to the U.S. charity of his choice, I'll put in a good word with the IRS. He can join us for dinner if he doesn't drink too much wine."

"Thank you, sir, I'm sure he will be happy to do that."

Epilogue

A week later

Teppin chuckled, spearing a piece of smoked salmon. "While you folks were vacationing in Mexico, the TV news up here did not cover much else besides the virus, and a lot of it was from your operation. I brought a typical newspaper for your memoirs." He was sitting with Robert and Teresa at a corner table in a Cambridge restaurant at noon.

He pulled a folded front page from his pocket. The Boston Globe headline screamed, in hundred point bold type, "College Profs Stop Virus." The story reported on the Yucatán operation and said that the amazing charge microscope showed Dr. Robert Asher, B.U., and Dr. Teresa Welles, Harvard, where to look for the cure for the Austin virus.

"We're not professors," complained Teresa, "and they missed the Maya connection. To whom do I complain?"

"Nicely phrased," said Teppin. "You will get a chance to tell your side of the story. And you will have to catch up on the details from Texas sometime. Gary Spender became something of a hero, too. He recovered completely from the virus. He contacted me, he wants to buy you dinner sometime."

"I'd like to meet him. He's the catalyst for the whole thing."

"You may have to wait a bit, there is a risk that the virus could be reverse zoonotic, that it could have jumped from a person to a bird or animal before we eradicated it. Spender is now leading a major effort to trap and test. But they have found nothing so far. Robert, did you locate your daughter successfully?"

"Your man got in touch with me, he traced them to Quebec City. They decided that discretion was the better part of valor. I just talked to them last night, they are fine and they will be swinging through Boston to visit. Thanks for your help."

"I get to meet Katie?" said Teresa.

"Tomorrow. You'll love her," said Robert.

Teppin studied their faces. "You two are special friends now?"

Robert smiled, reached out and held Teresa's hand. Teresa kissed him and lowered her eyes demurely, lashes fluttering. "Yes, you are special friends," said Teppin. "How did you like the White House thing yesterday, by the way?"

"Good party," she said. "My first White House dinner. We didn't get to stay the night, though, the Lincoln bedroom was full of Asian lobbyists."

"Yep, it was pretty nice," said Robert. "I thought the President would crack up when Phil told that story about the FBI agent in Mexico."

"I thought the FBI agents at the table would crack up Phil," said Teresa. "Speaking of FBI, what do you hear from the Columbians?"

"I called Muñoz yesterday to see what was happening," said Robert.

"He's not in jail?" asked Teresa.

"Not yet," said Robert. "He says that Ernesto unfortunately died by suffocation before they could get him to the hospital. The others were temporary guests of the Mexican government—something about drug smuggling, assault, and attempted murder. But the Mexican government was a little nervous about security, and is handing them over to the D.E.A."

"Dr. Teppin," said Robert, "The key to this whole thing is the level of Maya science. It was a huge factor beyond what anybody could have guessed. Teresa and I have been debating the odds—aliens from outer space, or ten or twenty generations of Maya scientists, or one phenomenal superbrain, this Peloc?"

"Civilization's advance has always been lumpy," said Teppin. "Starting maybe 2500 years B.C., there has been a history of dramatic scientific advance which has been subsequently lost, and then rediscovered centuries later. With books, and even more strongly with electronic communication and storage, we are losing the lumps. But back in the ninth century, it is easy to imagine profound advances in a civilization like the Maya. We know they had hot and cold running water, expert mathematicians and astronomers, and an advanced language and calendar. I have no problem with the Maya achieving that level of chemistry and medicine without invoking aliens."

"I can see the knowledge of plant chemistry," said Teresa. "But what about the complete periodic table? Well, complete except for a few rare earth elements. How could they have collected that kind of data? If it's not aliens, is it Peloc or a bunch of people?"

"Both, I would guess," said Teppin, anchoring some capers on his toast points with a little Dijon mustard. "Statistically, you get an IQ of two hundred every billion people. In the last millennium, there have been, what, sixty or seventy billion people? In that big a pile, you'd probably find an IQ of three hundred or more once."

"And for Peloc to have made that kind of discovery, he would need to have started from some baseline of knowledge," said Robert. "He would need to have been born in a civilization which honored scientific knowledge, and which had already created some knowledge base that he could build on."

"Why the underground caves?" asked Teresa. "Do you suppose Peloc believed in the Lords of the Dark?"

Teppin answered. "More likely he used the people's respect for the underworld to protect his laboratory. Or possibly he feared some kind of upheaval and wanted to make sure that his contribution did not get lost."

"And he got Spanish conquistadors," said Teresa. "They probably destroyed all the tree bark codices he would have written and all the aboveground records. So, anyway, we saved the world and had our fifteen minutes of fame. But we missed out on the fancy dinner at the most expensive restaurant in Cancún. And we didn't get to sleep for a month yet."

"Are you going back to work, after your nap?" asked Teppin. "The school has been contacted by people from CNN, ABC, CBS, NBC, and *Letterman*."

"Oprah Winfry?" asked Teresa, brightening noticeably.

"Yes. They'll be all over you two as soon as you surface. In fact, I am surprised that they didn't find you in Washington."

"We snuck out the back," said Teresa.

"You are coming back to work? Or do you wish to bask in your new notoriety?"

"Bask." said Teresa. "Then maybe see where *Bolero* is going."

"Work," said Robert.

"Oh, all right, work—except for Oprah."

"What's happened with the charge microscope?" asked Robert. "You'd mentioned that you had several other groups improving the technology."

"That effort is going well. There are maybe three hundred in operation now. CDC is convinced that it will become an important tool in disease diagnostics and control. We essentially got a blank check for rapid production and further refinement, and a consortium including Foxboro and Bectin-Dickinson will be releasing a large-quantity production version in about a month."

"Fast work," said Robert.

"Highly motivated teams. CDC thought that the charge microscope would be our best chance at a quick fix for the Austin virus. Now they're looking at AIDS research."

"You know," said Robert. "Peloc had one big advantage over our civilization."

"What was that?"

"No wheels. The fastest anybody could commute was maybe six miles per hour. The virus just sat there while he figured out the cure. Piece of cake. By the way, have they made any progress at crystallizing different molecules?"

"Yes, quite a lot," said Teppin. "One group in Geneva has a new process that crystallizes almost anything out of solution. In fact, we're now managing about four hundred million dollars in grants, and the field is attracting new researchers."

"Four hundred *million*?" said Teresa.

"I believe the amounts may decrease with the emergency under control, but perhaps not. Crystalline precipitation from solution is becoming a hot field again, after lying dormant for twenty years. There is a lot of activity. A group in Japan is trying to precipitate carbon as diamond."

"I heard from Lalos, he sent an email," said Robert.

"Who's that? Oh, the contractor from Hotel Austin? How's he doing?" asked Teresa.

"He's using the Cibachromes of the glyphs as decor. He says the hotel is fully booked for its opening in two months, I guess people want to stay at the place where it all happened. Oh, yeah, he says Conchita sends her love." He waggled his eyebrows at Teresa. She squinted at him with a frown.

They turned to look at a commotion across the room. A small crowd of people was standing in the doorway, pointing at them.

"That's them."

"That's the same guys."

They moved closer. "Hey, Dr. Asher, could I just get an autograph for my kids?"

"Teresa? It's you, isn't it? Could I just shake your hand? Sorry to interrupt your lunch, but could I just shake your hand?"

They exchanged wry smiles and stood to receive the accolades, augmented now by other diners who had joined the autograph seekers. Ten minutes later they returned to their cold lunch.

Teresa sighed. "Maybe I'll skip Oprah."